House of Johann

by

Kathi Gosz

YESTERDAY'S RHINELAND, Book I

House of Johann
Copyright © 2016 Kathi Gosz
Based on the source records of a real family from the village of Oberzerf, Germany, 1827 to 1845
All rights reserved.
ISBN: 1535012471
ISBN-13: 978-1535012478

All Rights Reserved

House of Johann is a work of historical fiction. Apart from the actual people, events, and locales that figure in the narrative, all names, characters, places, and incidents are the products of the author's imagination or are used fictitiously. Any resemblance to current events or locales, or to living persons, is entirely coincidental.

For Marilyn,
Who brightened every writing step I took!

"If there's a book you want to read but it hasn't been written yet, then you must write it."

Toni Morrison

My Ancestors' Story

This novel about peasant farmer Johann Rauls, his wife Maria, and their seven children takes place between 1827 and 1845 in the small Rhineland village of Oberzerf.

The men and women who labored in German provinces and who tilled the soil that Prussia ruled in the 1800s are unusual subjects for a historical novel. In fact, there seems to be no English language novel about a group of people so invisible. That is what pushed me toward writing a novel about my own ancestors, hard-working peasant farmers with almost no rights although they lived in a mighty and powerful *Reich*. It is not surprising that such an empire would soon lose countless numbers of its ordinary, tax paying inhabitants to a far-away continent known to the emigrants as "Amerika."

As with any historical novel, real citizens and undeniable historic events form the framework for my story of the Rauls family in nineteenth century Oberzerf. My imagination filled in the unrecorded parts of their lives that may or may not have happened as I surmised. All of the birth, marriage and death dates for the Rauls family and other residents of the village of Oberzerf introduced in this novel have been carefully authenticated, but family conversations and unrecorded incidents cannot be unearthed by the most skilled historians.

The village of Oberzerf, where the Rauls family lived, still exists in 2016. In 1981 its citizens celebrated one thousand years of staying power. Some of my distant Rauls relatives live in Oberzerf, others in the United States.

There are a great many German words used throughout the novel, a number of which are difficult to put into English. I have provided, to the best of my ability, a glossary of German words and expressions at the end of the story.

THE CHILDREN OF JOHANN AND MARIA RAULS

Magda (Magdalena) – born 1811, married Hanni (Johannes) Rauls

Anna Maria – born 1815, married Claus (Nikolaus) Marx

Pitt (Peter) – born 1816, unmarried

Mathes (Mathias) – born 1818, husband of Betta (Elizabeth) Meyer-Elsen

Lis (Elizabeth) – born 1820, second wife of Nicholas Birk

Theiss (Mathias) – born 1822, unmarried

Leni (Magdalena) – born 1827, unmarried

Additional Relatives and Villagers

Nikolaus Birk – husband of Lis (Elizabeth) Rauls

Dunicha – Gypsy woman (fictional)

Eva Kautenberger – cousin of Maria Kautenberger Rauls (fictional)

Tante Susanna Kautenberger – relative of Maria Rauls (fictional)

Claus (Nikolaus) Marx – husband of Anna Maria Rauls

Hannes (Johann) Meyer – oldest son of farmer Mathias Meyer

Mathias Meyer – farmer in the village of Irsch

Michel Meyer – younger son of Mathias Meyer

Betta (Elizabetha) Meyer-Elsen - wife of Mathes Rauls

Tante Mari (Maria) Rauls – wife of Nikolaus Rauls

Onkel Nikolaus Rauls – brother of Johann Rauls, husband of *Tante* Mari

Hanni (Johann) Rauls – son of Peter Rauls, husband of Magdalena Rauls

Mathias Rauls – Youngest brother of Johann, Nikolaus and Peter Rauls

Nikla (Nikolaus) Meyer-Elsen – Brother of Betta (Elizabeth) Meyer Rauls

Peter Rauls – Oldest brother of Nikolaus, Johann, and Mathias Rauls

CHAPTER 1
Joyful Expectation – December 24, 1827

*On Christmas Eve of December 24, 1827, the village of Oberzerf was home to: Johann Rauls, farmer, age 44; Maria Kautenberger Rauls, his wife, age 41; Children: Magdalena age 16, Anna Maria age 12, Peter age 11, Mathias age 9; Elisabeth age 7, and Mathias age 5. Children first saw the Christmas tree and received treats on the evening of December 24 when the **Christkind**, an angelic figure with golden wings and long blond hair, brought them. He lit the candles on the Christmas tree, decorated it with apples, nuts, or straw ornaments and put a treat on a waiting table for each child. In many parts of Germany, it was also a custom for farmers to put fresh straw in their animals' stalls on Christmas Eve.*

To look into the future is a gift given only to a few. Maria Rauls, wife of village farmer Johann, was not one of them. She anticipated nothing more than the celebration of Christmas when she awoke on the day before her youngest daughter was born. She opened her eyes to the thick darkness of early morning, her breath forming a white vapor that as yet she could not see because of the heavy wooden shutters that kept out the cold. It was Christmas Eve day. Maria always felt a special energy when it arrived, an energy that reached into soul and body, an especially welcome thing this year since the child in her womb had begun to draw nourishment out of her flesh and bones eight months ago.

Her husband Johann lay on his back beside her with an arm across the mound of her stomach. He was snoring, still asleep on the straw-filled sack that was their mattress. The two thick quilts stuffed tight with goose feathers and the heat of their bodies kept out the worst part of the cold that chilled nose and cheeks. She rolled to the edge of the bed, trying to keep warm as she pulled off her night bonnet and smoothed her fair hair, heavily streaked with gray, into a hasty braid.

Maria Rauls was a pale, lean woman, with breasts that hung heavy after 41 years of life and the birth of nine children. Her hips were wide, and Johann said she was made for carrying babies as she did now.

She pushed aside the quilts and brought first one leg, then the other to the floor, sitting up with difficulty because of her expanding belly. When she stood, the unease low in her womb, which she had noticed yesterday for the first time, was still there. It worried her that this child might come too early.

Maria moved quietly to the far wall, shivering as the cold air took her into its embrace. Her outer clothes hung on pegs and she reached for them. Her shift, woolen stockings, and the undergarments that were never removed on cold winter nights did little to stop her shivering. Eagerly she pulled her coarse woolen overdress over her shift and covered her thick braid with her heavy linen bonnet, which she tied into a neat bow.

Feeling her way to the door she opened it, making almost no sound as she stepped into the hall. The house was silent. The windowless hall that stretched from the front of the house to the rear did not allow light from the outside to compromise its blackness. Maria had wondered many times if the child in her womb lived in such darkness, never knowing the dawn.

She had placed her shoes just outside the sleeping room door the evening before. Sliding her feet along the slate floor of the hall, she found them; they were almost as cold as the floor itself. The banked fire in the kitchen fireplace had not lasted until morning. She blew on her fingers to warm them and then groped for the three-legged table that stood nearby. Instinctively she found the punk stick and tinderbox. She picked both up and opened the cover of the tinderbox so that she could strike the small flint inside against the iron plate. Sparks flew, dropping into the char, and she fanned them until they smoldered. She did it all with almost no conscious thought. It was an act as familiar as breathing; she had performed it countless times in the 25 years since her marriage to Johann.

Waiting for the dry tinder underneath the char to glow hot and red, she thought about the first time she had tried to light the fire in the fireplace. She was a bride of just one day then, eager to impress her new husband with her housewifely competence. She had taken the tinderbox in her hand as if she was skilled with it. The truth was that she had never lit the fire in her parents' house. Her mother was the keeper of the flame; it was a thing of pride for her. But Maria had watched her mother perform the act countless times and it seemed easy enough. She struck flint to metal, and when the spark came she began to fan. Nothing happened. Her new husband stood near the fireplace watching her. She struck the flint again and fanned the sparks harder. The tinder remained cold, but her cheeks had grown hot with embarrassment and frustration. Another strike of the flint. Now she was fanning furiously, and her hand hit the tinderbox. She lost her grip on it, and it crashed to the floor.

Maria turned her flushed face to Johann, and watched him double over in laughter. He laughed until he had to sit down on the stone floor of the kitchen. It made her so angry that she walked toward him; fists clenched. With all her strength, she punched his shoulder. He laughed even harder, grabbing her wrists and pulling her down into his lap. He kissed her until he fanned another kind of flame while they both forgot all about the tinderbox.

Maria reached up to get the lantern that hung on its black iron hook on the wall. Setting it on the table, she lighted the punk stick and set the thick, tallow candle inside the lantern aflame. When she was sure that the candle would keep burning, she closed the lantern door and replaced the top of the tinderbox. Grasping the lantern by its rounded wire handle, she made her way to the door leading to the outdoor bake oven.

Her heavy wool cloak hung from a large peg. She pulled it down and flung it around her shoulders. Shadows danced merrily on the walls as the lantern swayed while she worked at closing the clasp.

A sharp, icy December wind whipped at her skirt and tugged at her bonnet the moment that the door opened. She moved toward the bake oven, its squat form a black outline against the dark sky where a few stars still glittered, waiting for the dawn. The cold was working its way through her clothes, and she quickly built the fire inside the oven, using twig bundles that filled the wheelbarrow next to it. The inside of the oven had to be glowing bright red by noon if they were to have their special Christmas meal.

As she labored, the little one in her belly again kicked hard, as if it wanted to come out to join the family for its *Heiligabend* celebration. "Patience, little one," she said aloud. The chill air frosted her words as soon as they left her lips. "Next month you will be out here with us." The kicking stopped as if the child listened and was satisfied.

When she was sure the fire in the bake oven had caught hold and would burn properly, Maria hurried back inside, placing the lantern on the long narrow table in the kitchen. She took off her cloak, exchanged it for her wool shawl and prepared to light the fire in the fireplace, her teeth still chattering with cold. It warmed her to take up her twig broom and sweep up yesterday's ashes until the inner floor of the fireplace and the raised slate of the hearth were clean and the cinders saved in a bucket.

A wooden box under the kitchen's worktable held bundles of the scrawny branches of scrub trees and bush branches that she and the children had gathered from the forestland during the autumn. She brought two of the bundles to the fireplace, took them apart, and mounded them to start the fire.

Johann's footsteps echoed on the slate floor as he walked down the hall from their sleeping room. The livestock stable lay across the hall from the kitchen, and he used the kitchen's glow to guide him to the stable door and the unlit lantern that hung beside it. When he came into the kitchen, Maria, on her knees, still coaxed the fire in the fireplace.

When she had first met him, Maria had mistaken his shy seriousness for arrogance and had not wanted to be courted by the short, olive skinned young man with curling coal-black hair. He had looked like a solemn hawk, watching his prey.

"He comes from good stock; his father is one of the richest farmers in the *Kreis*," her mother said when he declared himself and asked Maria to wed him. "You must learn to love him."

Maria smiled, remembering those words. Over the years of their marriage, as Johann's hair had gone from black to grizzled gray, she had discovered the depth of his love for her and delighted in returning it.

Johann carried the lantern to the hearth, knelt beside Maria, and pulled a twig that was beginning to catch fire from the pile in the fireplace. He held it to the lantern's candle. When there was a steady flame, he tossed the twig back into the fireplace and closed the lantern's door.

He put his arm around Maria's shoulders and drew her near him, his hand caressing her breast. "*Du bist eine schöne Frau,*" he said. They smiled at each other. Maria thought how odd and how wonderful it was that after all these years and so many children, his touch never failed to move her, and that he still desired her too.

She took his hand in both of hers and held it a moment, feeling the well-known terrain of calluses and sinewy cords. "You are a beautiful man," she said, laughing at the surprised look that came to his face, "and I am a lucky wife."

"Don't you be telling any of the villagers that I am beautiful," he said, making his face stern. I could never go to the *Gasthaus* again!" He chuckled as he stood up; then turned his head to listen.

"I hear the *Kinder* moving around upstairs."

"They wake without being called on *Heiligabend* day and think about nothing else," Maria said. "Even Magda and Anna Maria can't hide their excitement." She struggled to get up, and Johann held out his hands to pull her to her feet. He grinned at her, picked up the lantern and went back across the hall. The stable door opened and a draft of air blew the familiar smell of damp straw and fresh animal dung into the kitchen.

The footsteps coming from the two upper bedrooms grew louder and there was a clatter of wooden shoes on the stairs. Pitt, Mathes and Theiss slept together in one room; Magda, Anna Maria and Lis in the other. The first one to arrive in the kitchen was Anna Maria who was tying the strings of her linen bonnet under her chin, her eyes still clouded with sleep. Her older sister, Magda, followed her, taking an almost identical bonnet from the pegs of the board outside the kitchen.

"*Hast du gut geschlafen?*" Maria asked, kissing each of her daughters good morning.

"*Ja*, Mamm," Magda said, rubbing her hands in front of the fire to warm them. She picked up the wooden bucket that stood just inside the kitchen door and went to get water from the well outside.

Their oldest daughter was petite and so slender that she looked much younger than her 17 years. She had lately begun to wear her long dark braids mounded in a smooth circle at the very top of her head, trying to add an extra inch to her stature and grownup dignity to her appearance. Magda was such a help to her. She was a willing worker and serious of temperament. She had been quick to learn how to cook, bake, knit and spin. In the last three years she had lightened Maria's burdens by taking on many of the household chores and caring for her younger brothers and sisters.

Anna Maria yawned and stretched, raising her arms and clasping her hands behind her head, bringing her shoulder blades together and her firm young breast forward. Maria saw the beginning of a rip in the seam of the bodice of the overdress Anna Maria wore. Her daughter's body was rounding in new places. Magda's outgrown clothes were becoming too small for Anna Maria, especially in the bosom.

Anna Maria bent to get the milk pail. When she stood up, her eyes were bright. "Mamm, I think that dreams sometimes tell about the future, don't you?"

"Some say they do. What did you dream about, then?"

"That it was tonight, Christmas Eve. All us *Kinder* stood in the shadows outside the door of the *Stube*, waiting for you and Papp to open it up. But the door stayed closed. We got so impatient, and Mathes grabbed the door's handle and pulled it wide open. Nikolaus Hendrichs was inside. There was an altar, just like in the church; and I walked to it. But then Magda and Lis shook me awake."

Maria sighed. It seemed the girl was always thinking about young men and marriage. "You see it as a sign that young Hendrichs will be your husband?"

Anna Maria dimpled, swinging the empty milking bucket. "It could be, Mamm. He likes me; he always looks at me when he thinks I don't see it. He turns away when I catch him at it, and his face gets red as one of the field beets."

"Many *Buben* look at you like that, Anna Maria, and you cannot be marrying all of them. A dream about the Hendrichs boy does not mean that you should be getting a husband. When you can cook and not let the pot boil over or wash every part of the floor without missing parts of it, that is a sign that you are ready for some young man to come court you. Now you go get started with the milking."

The corners of Anna Maria's pretty mouth turned down. Without another word she left the kitchen and went into the stable, banging the door behind her. Maria watched her go, sorry that she had to say hard things that the girl needed to hear, not the words that she wanted.

There were more footsteps on the stairs. Two of the boys, Pitt and Mathes, came into the kitchen with Lis. As usual, Lis was on the heels of Mathes. Two years younger than her brother, 7-year-old Lis adored him, fought with him, and made him furious by copying everything he did. Whether it was a race or skipping stones or balancing on a narrow stone wall, Lis was there, Mathes' ever-present shadow. She begged for a boy's tunic and breeches and had no patience with the shift, blouse and overdress of homespun linen she was constrained to wear.

Physically, Mathes and Lis were opposites. Lis favored Maria, with fine, light-brown hair, light skin and blue eyes. Her narrow face and sharp chin gave her a faintly skeptical look that went away only when she laughed. She would not be as pretty as Anna Maria, and she would make a marriage choice only when the time was right.

Mathes was a little-boy copy of his father. His hair was black as Johann's had once been and just as curly and thick as the pelt of a lamb. His skin stayed brown all through the winter, and his eyes were large and dark. He noticed everything but kept his thoughts to himself.

"After you finish your stable chores, bring in enough wood for a warm fire tonight when the *Christkind* comes," their mother reminded her young ones. For them the hours of this day could not go fast enough.

Mathes ran across the hall to the stable door, Lis and Pitt right behind him.

"Elisabetha, come back here," Maria commanded.

Lis stopped and turned her head toward her mother with a frustrated sigh. When her mother called her by her hated baptismal name, Lis knew it was time to beware. Pitt stood still too, as if he was the one who had been summoned. Their oldest son lived to please, but his thoughts came slowly, and he needed to be taught even simple tasks over and over again.

"Pitt, you can go with Mathes," Maria said and smiled at him. Pitt grinned now that he knew what was expected of him. He pushed open the stable door and lumbered through it. He was a sturdy boy with brown curly hair, a ruddy face and he was already strong and broad shouldered at the age of 11. Maybe his body is so healthy and strong to make up for the slowness of his mind, Maria told herself once again. She and Johann worried about what would happen to him when they were both gone.

She turned to Lis, "Now Elisabetha, where is Theiss? Why did you not bring him with you this morning? Did you make sure he was dressed?"

"He was dressed - almost."

"Go find him and bring him down here. If he is not in the boys' room, look in the little storage room. Whenever no one is watching, he tries to climb the shelves or open the bags that are tied shut."

Mice and spiders inhabited the storage space that shared a wall with the hayloft. Maria knew that Lis, in spite of her boyish ways, did not like the smell of mouse droppings or walking through the webs that brushed the face and the interrupted spiders that crawled to meet her. She had hoped to get away before anyone noticed Theiss was missing this morning.

Lis gave her mother a narrow-eyed frown that said she knew how to look for her brother without special instructions. She turned unwillingly and mounted the stairs, taking heavy, deliberate steps, each foot pounding down on the worn wooden treads beneath her feet.

The church bell rang the sixth hour of the morning, and Maria bowed her head and prayed the three Hail Mary prayers of the Angelus as she always did, asking the mother of God to keep her husband and children safe and healthy. The baby in Maria's womb was kicking as if she wanted to emphasize the prayer. Maria was convinced she would deliver a girl and that this would be her last child. She wondered if she and Johann would live long enough to see her grown.

Magda came back into the kitchen. "It feels like the snow is coming," she said. She carried the heavy wooden bucket full of water that she had drawn from the well at the front of the house. She put it down on the hearth next to the iron pot that sat on the three-legged iron trivet.

"I hope so, Maria said. "Christmas Eve is best when some flakes of snow dance around us on our way to Midnight Mass," She went to fetch the cloth bag full of ground buckwheat from the cupboard. She brought it and a scoop of salt from the wooden saltbox on the wall and mixed both in the black iron pot.

Magda added water from the bucket and stirred, nodding to herself when she judged everything was as it should be, then pushed the hook and pot into position over the flame in the fireplace.

Maria pulled wooden bowls and tin mugs from the shelves and put them, along with the honey pot and an empty jug awaiting today's milk, on the long wooden board that served as a tray as well as the cover for the bread mixing trough.

There was still that unease in her womb. Was it a warning that the baby might come early? She didn't want to think it could be so, but it would be wise to tell Magda to do most of the heavy work this morning.

She glanced at Magda, who was still stirring the porridge with a long handled wooden spoon, her cheeks red and her face flushed from the heat of the fire.

"The man you marry one day surely will be a lucky one," Maria told her oldest daughter.

Magda smiled at these words but said nothing. Her expression was a mixture of embarrassment and pleasure, and her cheeks grew even redder.

I wonder if Magda thinks of her cousin Hanni as the young man who will walk to the church with her, Maria thought. When those two look at each other, it is like the first spark that flies from the flint; the one that is not quite strong enough to set the char in the tinderbox on fire, but a signal that soon the flame will be lit.

Her mind went back to Anna Maria. She laughed to herself. Anna Maria's husband might not be as fortunate as Magda's. Her second daughter would probably lead her man a merry chase. While she chattered and charmed him, he would hardly realize that he was the one who stirred the porridge.

The loaves of the coarse, dark bread made of buckwheat, barley, and a little of their precious rye flour lay inside a tightly covered tin box on the counter of the cupboard. Maria pulled a loaf from it. She used the tip of her knife to scratch three crosses into the top of the loaf, saying aloud the traditional prayer: "Lord, our God, bless this bread. Let all who eat it not forget You." Then she cut the loaf into thick slices and placed them in the waiting breadbasket. Their *Heiligeabend* breakfast was ready.

When breakfast was over, Johann Rauls went to the stable. Everyone, including Maria, thought that he was splitting wood for the winter fires. Instead he was finishing a gift that he had started to make soon after Saint Nikolaus Day.

Mathes sat on the other side of the stable door, never suspecting he was a sentry. There was a sack of red ice apples next to the stool on which he sat, and to the stem of each he tied a piece of yarn to prepare the fruit for hanging on the Christmas tree. Johann knew that should Maria come to the stable, she would take a moment to admire Mathes' work and give him encouragement or help, should he need it. That would stop her unexpected entry before he could hide a project that absorbed him.

This Christmas would be special, a celebration of a good harvest year, of receiving part of his inheritance from his aging father, and most of all, the way Maria's latest pregnancy seemed to have brought back her smile after the death of baby Anna who had breathed her last 20 days after her birth.

Instead of a pyramid shaped tree built from cast-aside oak wood that was nailed together and polished, this year the *Christkind* would bring a fresh tree that could be decorated with apples, hazelnuts, and a straw garland that Maria had braided. Those decorations would be set off by the small wax candles in tin holders snapped on to the tree branches, an extravagance. The live tree also had cost him a fat fee in the form of a bribe to the Prussian-appointed forester who protected the *Kaiser's* forestlands, but who would look the other way for the right price. He felt the pride of his position as one of the wealthiest farmers in Zerf and Oberzerf, and he was grateful to God for allowing him and his family to prosper.

The task before him now was to complete an overlooked gift for Maria. Johann smiled to himself as he remembered the night of December 6, just three weeks ago, when St. Nikolaus and the ugly demon known as the *Pelzebock* burst into the *Stube*. He huffed and growled, threatening them all.

The little *Mäuse* shrieked and giggled, as the horned demon, dressed in black and wearing heavy chains, lurched around the *Stube*, trying to catch them. When the *Pelzebock* grabbed Theiss and put the bag he carried over the struggling child, Saint Nikolaus rebuked the ugly monster, raising his hand and declaring that these were good children. The *Pelzebock* released his frightened prey and slouched away, his body hunched and his head low.

After Saint Nikolaus listened intently as each child recited a prayer or Christmas song, he reached into his sack. All of them received baskets of nuts, sweet sugar lumps to be sucked, and something extra, which their father had carved. Lis and Mathes each had a miniature wagon with high rails and moving wheels. Pitt and Theiss had tops to spin. Two plump round doves with furled wings were Magda and Anna Maria's gifts. Johann couldn't help feeling very proud of his carving skill.

Theiss, recovered from his frightening encounter with the *Pelzebock*, innocent eyes wide, asked Saint Nikolaus, "Isn't there something for Mamm and Papp? Were they bad?"

As the Saint explained that his duty was only to reward good *Kinder* and to punish bad ones, it struck Johann like a blow. Why had he never thought to also make a gift for Maria, the wife who was the center of his life. His labor today was his attempt to make up for his error and show her the appreciation she deserved.

As he worked Johann frowned in concentration, deepening the lines across his forehead and between his eyes. After a long time, he smiled as his work-hardened hands brushed fine wood shavings from his dark blue tunic. He had almost finished all the carving. Tonight the *Christkind*, helped along by Johann, would bring this special gift for Maria.

Maria was always impatient for their *Heckenrose* to bloom, picking the first rose and putting her nose to the delicate pink, curved petals as she carried the blossom into the house. When their first child, a boy who now lay buried in the cemetery, was born, Johann had just planted this wild rose near the house wall to please his young wife. Although it was the custom for the husband and midwife to bury the afterbirth under a fruit-bearing tree, Maria had begged Johann to plant it deep in the ground beneath her *Heckenrose* bush to nourish it.

Every birth that followed had provided another special feeding for the bush. The *Heckenrose,* which most called the dog rose, spurned it as a weed. However by the time Theiss was born, Maria's "dog rose" bush flowered with magnificence. Usually very generous, Maria always refused requests for a small piece of the beautiful bush. She believed that this rose bush held a part of each of her children's souls. During June and July she picked bloom after bloom of the pale pink blossoms and put them in her prettiest pottery jar to decorate the Virgin Mary's altar in the *Stube*. When the bush gave up its last few blooms to her knife, she kept them until they were shriveling and brown with age.

Johann wanted this *Heckenrose* carving to give Maria joy until the real rose bloomed again in summer. Completely absorbed in his work, he bent over the bench again. His knife was sure as he finished the intricate shaping that would imitate the fluted edges of the rose petals.

Some time later, the finished rose lay before him on the table, tinted to a soft pink hue. Johann relaxed. It had turned out well. Only then did he notice how tight the muscles in his shoulders had become and how thirsty he was. He left the stable to get a dipper of water from the bucket in the kitchen.

As he entered the room, he was met by a pleasing confusion of sounds and smells. Maria and Magda sang together as they mixed batter for the honey and spice *Spitzkuchen*. The fire in the fireplace made the kitchen cozy, and both of them had pushed the full sleeves of their linen blouses up to their elbows. Their forearms and hands were dusted with flour. Anna Maria, sitting on a stool near the fire, stirred the batter for apple and plum *Torte*. She hummed along with her mother and sister; off key as usual, the bowl in her lap. Her foot tapped in time with the song. Brown braids escaped from the linen cap Lis wore as she worked over the chopping board in the dry sink. Her nimble little fingers used a paring knife to peel, core, and cut the apples that would soon be in the batter. With the enthusiasm only a five year old can sustain, Theis ran here and there, picking up the nutshells that fell to the floor as Pitt cracked *Haselnüsse* for the baking. The smell of the yeasty dough, spices and honey blended with the crackling of the wood in the fireplace. For a long moment Johann savored the pleasure of the scent of Christmas before he turned and went back to the stable.

The oven was hot enough to begin the baking. Shawl tightly wrapped around her shoulders, Maria watched as Magda cleared the glowing slag from the oven's interior with the rusty iron poker, careful not to let any of it fall on her skirt or her shoes and start her on fire. Next she brushed the floor of the oven until it was clean.

Anna Maria brought the board with the *Kurbeln* baskets full of bread dough that had been rising overnight. One by one, Magda removed each loaf from its resting place, positioning it carefully on the long handled *Brotschiess*. She used it to push each round loaf well back inside the oven, as near as possible to the iron plate at its rear.

"Are they right, Mamm?" Magda asked when she had put in the last loaf.

Maria stepped to the oven and peered inside, the intense heat radiating out to hit her face like a gust of summer wind. "You did it just as good as I do, child. You learn fast." She closed the door of the oven, and they hurried back into the house as the first small snowflakes started to fall.

Sitting around the big table in the *Stube*, they ate their noon meal. Buckwheat noodles and the bread from last week's baking, spread with pear marmalade, disappeared into hungry mouths. Snowflakes were racing past the window, pursued by the wind. Already there was a fresh white coating of snow on the outstretched limbs of the leafless trees outside the window.

After the table was cleared, everyone left the *Stube*. Johann brought in the fir tree that the *Christkind* would trim tonight and the door to the room was closed.

"Theiss, Lis," Maria reminded her two youngest "I must work in the *Stube* now so that the Christkind finds it clean when he comes tonight. You stay in the kitchen with Anna Maria and Magda and help with the *Spitzkuchen*. You do not come out here into the hall unless I call you. The *Christkind* will not leave gifts on the table in the *Stube* if you don't obey me and your Papp today.

Theiss lingered in the hall. "Can we hear when He comes, Mamm?" he asked. "Does He come to the door and knock?" A flicker of fear crossed the little boy's face. Theiss wasn't sure he wanted to see the holy visitor who knew everything and might punish as well as reward, and he remembered his narrow escape from Krampus.

"Your Papp and I will go into the *Stube* after the evening chores to wait for Him," she said. He comes without a sound, so quiet nobody hears him. We open the door and let you in only after He goes."

Theiss started toward the kitchen, stopped and came back to her. He shifted from one foot to the other and asked, "What does the *Christkind* look like? Is He like the baby Jesus in the church? Will He bring angels?"

With his innocent blue eyes wide and his blond hair curling around his face, Theiss could almost be mistaken for an angel himself, Maria thought; a wiggling angel with a curious mind and no end of questions to come tumbling from his mouth.

"Your father and I don't know what He looks like or if there are angels," Maria told him, putting her hands on his shoulders to quiet him.

"But you are right there when He comes. Why don't know what He looks like? You must know." Theiss' cheeks were flushed and red with what Maria and Johann called "the Christmas fever." The Christmas fever painted bright red gashes on children's cheeks and made them shiver with anticipation. On any other day of the year such a thing would have sent Theiss to bed to be treated with healing herbs, but today Maria knew what ailed him.

"When the *Christkind* hangs the red apples on the tree, your Papp and I see a golden glow, and it grows so bright that we just close our eyes and cover them with our hands. Like when you stare up at the sun too long. It hurts and almost makes you blind. There might be angels with Him." These were answers she had given often over the years as her children asked such questions.

Lis had been listening at the door to the kitchen. "The *Christkind* don't have anything for you, Theiss," she said, coming out into the hall. "You've been bad too many times." She raised her voice to be sure that Maria heard her. "I saw what you did. You pushed cousin Hans into the mud. You did it on purpose too."

"Did not," Theiss said. "He just can't walk good. I only bumped him a little and then he went *platsch* into the puddle."

Maria hid a smile as she remembered the astonished look on little Hans' face.

"And remember, Mamm?" He took my bird's nest that had the blue egg in it and he lost it." This was an old, deep wound for Lis. "The *Christkind* sees everything. He won't bring anything for Theiss."

Theiss stood looking from his mother to Lis. His eyes filled with tears, his chin wobbled, and he started to cry.

"Hush, Lis," Maria said. "To make your little brother cry on Christmas Eve day is also a bad thing. Theiss, don't cry. If the Holy Child knows that you tried to be good all the year and especially today, I think some candies for you will be on the table."

Theiss stopped crying, snuffled a few times, wiped his nose with the back of his hand, and ran to the kitchen.

"Lis," Maria said in her sternest voice, "You go to the kitchen too."

"Mamm, do I have to help with the *Nussmakronen*? I hate spooning sticky egg white, and I'll make a mess. Let me go with Mathes and Pitt instead. They're cutting lots of straw so that our animals will have fresh bedding this Christmas Eve. I know how to cut straw."

"I've told you what I want you to do, Lis. The *Christkind* won't be leaving a present for a stubborn girl who will not obey her mother."

"Yes, Mamm." Lis turned away. She was sure that Mamm and Papp were the ones who gave the Christmas gifts and put the apples on the Christmas tree. Unlike the *Christkind*, they didn't know that she pulled her little brother's hair and pinched him whenever he made her mad; that she threatened to lock him out of the house for the gypsies to kidnap if he told.

A tiny seed of fear took root in her brain, sprouted and began to grow like a kernel of rye seed after a warm spring rain. In a few seconds, the possibility of an angry *Christkind* was all she could think about.

Instead of going into the kitchen as she had been told, Lis tiptoed up the stairs to the storeroom, went inside and quietly closed the door behind her. She dropped to her knees in front of one of the big baskets of hackled flax strands and brought her hands together, fingertips touching and thumbs crossed as she had been taught. She raised her eyes to the rafters where a spider had begun a new web. She hoped that the heavenly throne was somewhere in that general direction.

Taking a deep breath she whispered, "Forgive me, *Christkind*; I believe." She decided to bargain. "And if you forgive me for the things I did to Theiss; I promise to always obey Mamm the first time she tells me, and not pinch Theiss." She thought again and added, "Unless he really deserves it." Satisfied that she had erased any black mark on her heavenly report card, she got up, dusted off her skirt, and went down to the kitchen to chop the nuts and help spread the egg on the *Nussmakronen* to be baked in the still hot oven after the bread came out.

Maria spent most of the afternoon in the *Stube*. She was almost finished tying the last of the shiny red apples to the little fir tree, making a bow at the top of each branch. The white yarn of the bow, the red of the apples, and the deep green of the tree made a pleasing picture, but she was glad when the last apple was fastened securely to a branch. Her back ached again, and it was proving difficult to get close to the tree with her rounded belly. "I hope this *Kind* of ours likes the smell of your sap," she said to the fir tree as her apron-covered stomach rubbed against it, releasing more of its pungent fresh scent into the room.

Johann carried a large basket used for hauling potatoes from field to wagon. Now though it was filled with the things that were the magic of the holiday. He moved quietly through the hall in stocking feet and tapped lightly at the door of the *Stube* so that Lis and Theiss would not hear him.

When Maria opened the door, he hurried inside and put his burden down on one of the table's long benches. Maria exclaimed in delight. "Hanse, this will be a truly wonderful Christmas for the *Kinder*." She picked up the bags that she made for each child on their first Christmas, embroidering them with their names. Husband and wife began filling each one with nuts, colorful pieces of hard sugar candy, and an orange.

Johann smiled to himself, picturing his wife's face when she received the carved rose he had made for her. Her eyes would shine and the dimple he loved would appear in her cheek. He was as excited as the children and just as anxious as they for the Christmas Eve celebration to begin.

Maria had gone back to the tree. "Will you put the manger under the tree for me, Hanse?" Maria said, anticipating his willingness and handing him the little stable with the carved figures of Mary, Joseph, and the baby Jesus. "If I get down there, perhaps I cannot get up again."

Johann bent and put the *Krippe* under the tree's low branches, arranging the wooden figures of the Holy Family, the shepherds and sheep. From her marriage chest that stood near the door, Maria took the good linen cloth and put it on the table. Together she and Johann arranged the well-filled sacks among the fragrant boughs at its center. Next the small wax candles were pulled from their hiding place and slipped into tin holders that were clipped to the tree's outer branches. Johann brought two buckets filled with water and put them in the corner, just in case any errant sparks should set the tree on fire.

Maria stood appraising everything. It would be beautiful in the dark room when the candles' flickering flames lighted the tree and left all else in shadow. She was so happy that she held out her skirt and curtsied to Johann, forgetting her ungainly body might not keep its balance. She wobbled, dropping awkwardly to her hands and knees to stop herself from a bad fall.

Immediately Johann was at her side. "Are you all right, Maria?"

She put her hand to her distended stomach and left it there a moment. Breathing deeply, she answered, "You married a stupid woman, husband; one who thinks she can dance like a girl of 18 when she is carrying her tenth child. Help me get up." She held out her hands, laughing as he gently pulled her to her feet but he did not laugh with her. She saw he was worried, the two furrows at the bridge of his nose deeper than ever. She took his face between her hands, caressing the stubble of beard on his cheeks. "I have no pains, Hanse," she assured him before she turned back to look at the tree one final time.

Johann put his hands on her shoulders, kneading the muscles beneath his fingers. She closed her eyes and leaned back against him, breathing deeply, wanting to stretch out this moment of tenderness and get drunk on the tangy scent of the fir tree and boughs.

As they closed the door of the *Stube* behind them, the stable door burst open and Pitt came into the hall. "Papp," he said, taking Johann's hand, "come and see how much straw we cut. Such a big pile!" His eyes were shining. Johann's answering smile was tinged with the sadness both he and Maria felt. So many gifts of a normal life were denied to Pitt and his innocence only led to ridicule by other children who called him *Dummkopf* or shouted "stupid ass" when he made a mistake.

"*Ja* Pitt, our animals will have the freshest straw of any in the village when the *Christkind* visits them tonight. You and Mathes make me proud." Pitt threw his arms around Johann's waist and hugged him in delight. Then they both went into the stable to start the evening chores.

As she walked down the hall to the kitchen, Maria's nose told her that the golden-brown loaves of rye bread and the apple cakes, *Nussmakronen* and *Spitzkuchen* had come in from the bake oven. The hall was filled with an aroma that would surely tantalize even one so well fed as the Prussian *Kaiser*. Tonight, the family of Johann Rauls would eat as well as the emperor's court.

Then the first pain came.

CHAPTER 2
A Child is Born – December 25, 1827

At the first labor pains, the midwife was called. Doctors were only called in case of disaster, and probably they were not available at all in the small villages. Upon arriving the midwife started the heating of a generous quantity of water at the fireplace. She pushed the men, young children, and even the husband out of the room. Pious figures were hung where they could be seen from the laboring woman's bed. The mother did not usually give birth in bed but on a table, which was covered with hemp sacking cloth and was placed near the fireplace. Or the woman might sit at the foot of the bed for the delivery. Immediately after the birth and the announcement of the sex, the midwife separated the infant from the mother and cut the umbilical cord. When the placenta was expelled, the cord and placenta were buried, often at the foot of a fruit-bearing tree.

Maria told Johann of the childbirth pains just as he, Mathes, and Pitt were finishing up in the stable. Mathes was sent to fetch his uncle Nikolaus and *Tante* Mari.

Johann built up the fire in both fireplaces so that the Stube, soon to be the birthing room, would warm. All thought of Christmas disappeared. There was no more time for the *Christkind*. Lis and Theiss, the two youngest, eyed the *Stube's* closed door anxiously, their eyes wide with anxiety as their mother cried out; but their expressions still held a glimmer of hope that the *Christkind* would come in spite of their mother's moans that sounded through the door.

When his brother and sister-in-law arrived, Johann was holding Maria's hand as she squeezed it with the strength of a man each time a pain came. His dread eased a little. *Tante* Mari, the wife of his brother Nikolaus, was not officially a midwife; but she had taken on many of those responsibilities since the former midwife died.

Hardly taller than Lis, *Tante* Mari immediately took charge. "Anna Maria, help Lis and Theiss bundle up for the walk to our farm; Pitt, put on your coat too. Mathes is there already; I told him not to come back with us."

Theiss tried to ask about the *Christkind's* visit, but getting little attention, obediently joined Pitt and Lis. Anna Maria supervised her brothers and sister as they wrapped themselves in their heavy coats and shawls. All the children except for Magda were to walk the short distance to the warm *Stube* that was *Tante* Mari's domain in the *Einhaus* of Uncle Nikolaus. It was just down the road, an easy walk.

Johann and Nikolaus Rauls were put to work drawing water and then filling the large cauldron. Johann raised the heavy pot by its handle, placing it on the tripod on the hearth, turning the hook inward toward the blazing fire. His brother Nikolaus was going in and out to the shed where the bundles of dry twigs and branches were piled. Soon he had deposited enough of them in the kitchen's woodbox to keep the fire in the fireplace blazing from tonight into Christmas morning.

"You can't do anything for Maria but pray that all goes good and that the new baby lives," *Tante* Mari whispered to Johann, "and the place to pray for that is at the church altar this holy night. Magda and I will be taking care of the birthing." Seeing his inclination to argue, the little woman took his arm and walked him to the outside door, releasing him only as he made the first step over the threshold and followed his brother Nikolaus to wait at the latter's farm.

Maria sat on the bench before the cast iron *Takenplatte*. It was one of her favorite things in this house. The iron plate in the wall, its shiny black surface decorated with a tall and slender crane, was now absorbing the heat from the kitchen fireplace and spreading it into the *Stube*. Her pains were coming closer together. When they came she could think of nothing else. But when they passed she prayed for the safety of the child coming into the world too early. Her heart ached also for her little Theiss and Lis who would not know the joyful surprises that the *Christkind* should have brought for them. She hoped they would not blame this little one.

Magda came through the door of the *Stube*, closing it quickly so as not to let any warmth escape. "I'm helping *Tante* Mari," she had told her father before he left. This would be her first time to see a birth. Maria was glad she would be helping. It was also good that she should see the duty of a woman in the agonizing stage that followed lovemaking. It might break the strong bond between Magda and her cousin Hanni before it became an overwhelming desire.

Tante Mari came in. Magda was taking the evergreen boughs and bags of candies from the *Stube* table and layering them in a pile on the floor. When the surface of the table was clear, *Tante* Mari covered it with a blanket and rough, unbleached linen sheets.

"Come, Magda," she directed. "Help me move the table next to the warmth of the *Takenplatte* to keep your Mamm comfortable while she gives birth. We must be ready when it is time."

Father Mathias Guckeisen chanted "*Dominus vobiscum,*" his baritone voice ringing through the little village church. He wore a white vestment with fine gold embroidery, the mark of a Church celebration of the greatest magnitude - the birth of the Savior of the world.

As the response, "*Et cum spiritu tuo,*" came from the lips of the two altar boys dressed in their black cassocks and white linen surplices, he turned from the baroque altar and walked toward the pulpit. Tonight, in the glow of the candles, the high altar gleamed as if it were really made of the marble it had been crafted to imitate. At the pinnacle of the carved wooden altar, a sunburst with the eye of God at its center served as a constant reminder that God was watching over this little village at the foot of the Hunsrück mountain range. The tall candles stood in their brass holders on the main and side altars and in each of the wall niches. Newly cut fir boughs on the windowsills gave off their rich fragrance, and Father Guckeisen liked to imagine that the statue of the holy Hubertus, patron of foresters and hunters, had gathered and blessed them and then gone back to his place at the side altar.

The young priest climbed the winding steps to the eight-sided wooden pulpit, anchored his feet firmly, and opened the large leather-bound missal. It was his first midnight Mass in the chapel in Oberzerf. This year, his older brother Michel, a Benedictine priest, had been allowed to travel from his abbey in Traben to Niederzerf to spend Christmas. They were both offering the Holy Sacrifice, Michel in the lower village church and Mathias at the Oberzerf chapel. This year the villagers of Oberzerf had not made a cold, long walk over rough, snow-covered roads to attend the Midnight Mass in the mother church, as was the usual custom.

The priest cleared his throat and began to read the first words from the second chapter of St. Luke's gospel: "At that time, a decree went forth from Caesar Augustus that a census of the whole world should be taken." While the familiar words came reverently from his lips, he looked down at his flock through his small round glasses and took his own census. Almost every villager was there; men on one side, women on the other. They were wrapped in dark wool coats and cloaks on this winter night, their breath visible in the cold air inside the church. He saw that some familiar faces were missing. Maria Rauls and her oldest daughter Magdalena were not on the bench near the front of the church where they usually sat; only the younger daughters, Elizabeth and Anna Maria were there. Johann Rauls and his sons sat across the aisle. Johann seemed preoccupied; his head bowed. And where was Johann's sister-in-law? She was not with her husband Nikolaus. Could she be acting the midwife for an impending birth at the Rauls' *Einhaus*?

"And she brought forth her firstborn son and wrapped him in swaddling clothes and laid him in a manger," he read, while his mind was considering another child, the one Maria Rauls was likely giving birth to on this Christmas day. Frau Rauls had told him the baby would be coming during the cold days of late January. A birth today would be early. That had also been the case with the last child. The little girl, who gave her first cry three year ago, had been born at eight months and had not lived even sixty days. Church law said that a woman must honor her husband's desire whatever the circumstances, whenever he wanted. Sometimes the priest wondered if that was what Jesus would have commanded as he ministered to women in their forties, worn out from birth after birth.

"And this shall be a sign onto you: you will find an infant wrapped in swaddling clothes and lying in a manger." It was a blessing for a child to be born on the Savior's birthday. Perhaps it would be a very special child, destined, like the Savior, for an extraordinary life.

Father Guckeisen's mind was not the only one that contemplated the impending birth. Johann Rauls heard not a word of the Christmas gospel or the sermon, which followed. His right thumb traced thoughtless patterns on the leg of his long black wool trousers, back and forth, then side-to-side concentric circles. His other hand lay clenched in his lap, holding the rosary that Maria had given him on their wedding day. Once again Maria was beginning her labor too early, and there was no way for him to help her. All he could do was sit here and worry about the danger to the person he treasured most in the world.

Now, with the story of the first Christmas barely brushing his consciousness, Johann raised his head and tried to concentrate on the words being spoken from the pulpit. Then he frowned. Anna Maria was obviously as distracted as he was - but for another reason. She was exchanging furtive smiles with young Nikolaus Hendrichs who sat across the aisle on the men's side of the church. Some days it seemed that the girl's head was filled with nothing other than attracting the attention of all the young males in the village. Most of them openly admired her pretty face and developing bosom. He wondered how best to keep her safe from those who would take advantage of her youth and her vanity and bring disgrace on her.

His daughter's cheeks, flushed and rosy, reminded him of a day when he had sat on these same benches and looked across the aisle at Maria Kautenberger. Like Anna Maria, she had been fair and slender, her golden hair braided neatly under her lace-covered bonnet, her eyes a blue-green that reminded him of the Saar River when it sparkled with sunshine. There was a dimple in the right cheek of her heart-shaped face, and she blushed becomingly whenever she saw him looking her way. Johann had lost his heart to her in this very place when she was just a little older than Anna Maria.

Father Guckeisen had finished the Christmas sermon. His simple, heartfelt words about God's love for man, especially the poor and humble, moved many a villager who heard them, but they were as incomprehensible to Johann Rauls as the Latin that now flowed out over the congregation once again. In his distraction, Johann sat, stood, and knelt when everyone else did. Like many others, his hands held his rosary beads, but they were not prayed. The altar boys rang their brass bells as Father Guckeisen said the words of consecration, "*Hoc est enim Corpus meum.*" He elevated the Sacred Host high above his head. Johann woke from his troubled thoughts and raised his eyes to the round wafer of wheat that was now Christ the Lord. He bowed his head and prayed what was in his heart, "Have mercy on Maria and the child. But if I must lose one of them, let it be the child. Please let it be the child!"

After the final blessing, the Mass ended. The time for Latin hymns was over and the men's choir, along with the rest of the congregation, stood for the singing of a German carol as Father Guckeisen left the altar. The organist began to play *"Es ist ein Ros' entsprungen"*, with words that compared the birth of Jesus at Bethlehem to the springing up of a delicate and perfect rose, Christ the Lord. It reminded Johann of the rose he had made for Maria. His plan to place it in her hands tonight while the candles on the tree cast flickers of light on the walls of the *Stube* was not to be. There was such tightness in his throat that he could not sing. This carol was an omen but whether it was good or bad he did not know.

Theiss tugged at his hand. "Why don't you sing, Papp?" he asked. How could he explain to a child that without Maria on the other side of the aisle he was mute? Johann had grown up in a stern family where songs were not sung. After their marriage, Maria had begun to coax him to join her in singing as they worked in the fields. Her voice was sweet as the sound of the nightingale. Soon he looked forward to hearing her say, "Hanse, sing with me please to make the work go faster." Their hands had formed many bundles of flax into shocks while they sang the folk songs she had taught him. Tonight there was no Maria to start him singing. The Christmas hymn had no joy in it. The notes were dull as lumps of lead falling into a wooden bowl.

As they left the little church, the people of Oberzerf wished each other a happy Christmas. Many of them inquired after Maria and assured Johann of their prayers and that all would go well for her on such a special and holy day.

Laughing and talking, neighbors walked with neighbors along the road to their houses where later today they would sit down to their Christmas meal. In a few hours, the smell of roast goose and roast pig would be in the air, a rare treat that most of the families tasted only at Easter to celebrate the Savior's resurrection and at Christmas to celebrate His birth.

Lis and Anna Maria held tight to Theiss' hands as they trudged up the little hill toward home. Pitt and Mathes came along behind their father who walked with their uncle Nikolaus. No one spoke on the short trip. Johann's mouth felt too dry to make sounds as he wondered what would await them when they reached their destination.

Theiss looked back at his father as they neared their door, "Papp, will Mamm still be sick when we go inside?"

"I don't know, boy." Johann said. He struggled to keep a calm voice. "Maybe she will be well and the *Christkind* will have left a *Heiligabend* present.

They had reached the house. Anna Maria and Lis, still holding on to Theiss' hands, hesitated, looking askance of their father. Johann grasped the latch, pushed open the heavy wooden door, and stepped over the doorsill. Silence was not what he had expected. The door to the *Stube* was still closed and so was the door to their sleeping room. He heard only the loud pounding of his heart and the crackle of the fire in the kitchen fireplace. He had been sure that Maria would have given birth by now but why was the bedroom door closed when it should be open wide so that the heat from the fireplace could keep it warm.

The last four children had been born within two or three hours of Maria's first pains. The silence must mean that the child was very sickly or even dead. Or that Maria herself died with the infant and Magda and his sister-in-law Mari prayed at the bedside. Dear God, had he lost her? He marveled that, with legs so weak, he could still stand.

Unsure what to do, he stayed in the darkened hall with the children and his brother Nikolaus. They all stood looking at him, still wearing coats and cloaks, no one sure what should be done next and waiting for him to decide.

A cry like the frantic mewling of a newborn kitten came through the closed door of the *Stube*; a sound so welcome that he thought his face might crack with the width of the smile that came to it. Their new child had safely made the entry from the warm womb into the chill world outside and protested.

Their Magda threw the door open wide and came out into the hallway, her hands full of soiled cloth pieces. Seven heads turned to look at her and seven faces silently asked the same question. She told them, "Mamm is doing well, Aunt Maria says. Papp, you have another daughter, and her cries, as you can hear, are strong.

"Papp," Theiss said, "Did the *Christkind* bring a baby tonight? I thought the stork brought babies."

Johann patted his son's blond curls. "Only very lucky people get such a gift as this delivered by the Christ Child himself."

"Papp, is that what we got? I wanted a Christmas tree with nuts and candies," groaned Lis, her face dismayed.

Nikolaus Rauls smothered his laugh with a fit of coughing. Johann's shoulders started to shake, and his laughter came. He laughed and laughed until his stomach hurt, and he had to sit down on the bench behind him. Nikolaus, Magda and Anna Maria joined in, while Mathes, Pitt, Lis, and Theiss stood looking at them, not understanding the joke.

When he could speak again, Johann said, "There might be a tree in the *Stube*, Lis, and some oranges and candies for each of you. We'll look after Mamm shows us the other Christmas surprise, your little sister." He wiped the tears of laughter from his eyes and went into the *Stube*. A lantern lit the bed fashioned of two straw-filled mattresses which lay on the frame that had been made especially for the birth of their children when the first one, Magda, was due to be born.

The baby's cries had stopped. Maria lay still, their little daughter cradled in her arm. She looked exhausted; her hair tangled and still damp with sweat, but she wore a clean smock and had her shawl wrapped about her shoulders. In the dim light he could see that she also wore a tender smile.

"Bring the children here, Papp, so they can meet their little sister." Fatigue sounded in her voice; Johann, relieved the moment before was now worried. She had always been able to bounce back from a birth. She said it was a special energy known only to mothers of the newly born.

As the children came to the bedside, Nikolaus Rauls beckoned to his Mari to join him in the dark corner where the little Christmas tree now stood on the table.

Lis, the last through the door, smelled the fresh fir sap that had been heated by the warmth of the room. Hope rose in her, even though the room was too dark to see if they had had a visit from the *Christkind*. From time to time she glanced over her shoulder to where she guessed the pine tree would stand. Turning back toward her new sister she said, "She's little. I thought she would be bigger."

Theiss looked from his mother to the infant she held. "She's funny looking," he said. "Her face is all red and shriveled and she's grunts like a little pig."

Anna Maria laughed, "She looks just like you did, Theiss, except that you didn't have any hair at all the first time we saw you."

Theiss opened his mouth to protest but no one was paying any attention to him so he closed it again.

Pitt reached out and touched the baby's tiny fist that was moving aimlessly. "She's so soft, Mamm," he said. "Can I hold her?"

"Maybe in a few days, Pitt," Maria answered. "Now let your Papp come and see her."

Johann moved forward until he stood next to the bed. He reached out and ran the backs of his fingers along one of Maria's flushed checks, hoping that the heat he felt there did not mean a fever.

"She is beautiful, like all our children," he said and bent down to take the little bundle wrapped in a soft woolen blanket. "Little Magdalena, our Leni," he whispered as the child moved her tiny fists. Supporting her head in the crook of his arm, he kissed the top of her head, its matted hair as dark as his own. Baby Leni opened her eyes, made a gurgling sound and blew a tiny bubble that lingered on the delicate lips. The children, who were crowded around him, laughed in pleasure, and the baby was startled. She waved her fists and kicked at her blanket, then made a sound that now reminded him again of the cry of a kitten searching for its mother. The love he felt was as overpowering as it had been when he had held his first child and every one thereafter. He was ashamed of the bargain that he had tried to make with God. This little one's life was precious too. With tender care, he put Leni back into her mother's arms.

"I think it is time for our Leni to have her Christmas dinner," Maria said, rubbing her daughter's cheek. Leni's lips made sucking sounds as she nuzzled the clean linen smock Maria wore.

"Come, *Kinder*," Johann said, "Let us see what the *Christkind* brought in addition to your little sister."

Onkel Nikolaus brought a lantern to cast a light on the *Stube*'s table. Lis was the first to notice two pinpoints of light on the Christmas tree. More and more of them appeared as *Tante* Mari lit the small candles with the punk stick. "Oh, this is much better than the new baby," she said. "The candles on the tree are like stars and the cookies and apples are wonderful." She was too absorbed in the beauty to notice the laughter of the grownups.

As her baby girl sucked greedily at her breast, Maria heard her children's laughter coming from the other end of the *Stube*. She had thought she would be there with them, watching their faces as they discovered the Christmas tree and when they all said an Our Father and Hail Mary in front of the nativity stable; but God had another plan for her this Christmas. To have a child that shared the Lord's birthday could only be a special blessing.

As the excited voices of her other children began to sound further and further away, she murmured "my little Christmas gift" softly to the baby, as she fought the sleep that was overtaking her tired body.

Johann came to her, one hand behind his back. "A blessed Christmas to you, *mein Schatz*," he said. She opened her eyes and saw that he held a *Heckenrose* so beautifully carved that it seemed to be alive.

The lump in her throat made her speechless. She wanted to get up from the straw bed, hold his dear face between her palms and kiss away the worry she could see in his eyes. But she had used up all of her energy birthing the small bundle that her arm held to her breast. She just reached out and took the rose from him, cradling it in her hand a moment before bringing it to her nose as if to smell it.

Johann leaned down and kissed her cheek, a little smile curving his lips. "Afraid it smells only of the wood I used," he said. "You have to wait for the summer to smell our roses by the house wall."

Maria laid the rose at her side. She took the baby from her breast, and put her over her shoulder, patting her back. "Husband, see, tonight I have got myself two roses."

As Maria closed her eyes again, Johann whispered "*Ja*, my dear wife, *Es ist ein Ros' ensprungen*." When she wasn't so tired, he would tell her of the joyful hymn that had ended midnight Mass and that it was an omen from the Savior who had shared His birthday with this beautiful child he and Maria made together.

CHAPTER 3
The Ferkel – November 1832

St. Martin's Day, November 11, is the traditional day for animal slaughter in the Rhine villages. The pig to be slaughtered is brought into the farmyard and his two hind legs are tied together; then he is thrown into a heap of straw and stabbed in the neck and heart with a long, sharp knife. The farmwife catches the spurting blood in a big pan. Even though there is sympathy for the pig, the family is very glad for the fresh meat, the bacon, and the sausage. Morette, Jean, <u>Landleben im Jahreslauf.</u>

An ear-splitting shriek cut through the crisp autumn air as the frightened pig sensed the doom that lay waiting in the heap of straw outside the big rounded stable door. Ferkel, Leni's best friend, was in a death struggle with his captors.

It was a few days past the feast of St. Martin, the mid-November time when most of the geese and pigs that had roamed and foraged in the pastures or barnyards would themselves become food. Her brothers and sisters looked forward to the smoked bacon and ham that their large pig would put on the table; but little Leni Rauls had fed garden and table scraps to Ferkel since he was a pink and black spotted baby. Ferkel was a good listener, a confidant. Leni talked with him, telling him the many ideas in her four-year-old head, while he snuffled and rooted in his pen. Day by day the little piglet grew into a fine porker and that sealed his fate.

Leni was not supposed to be anywhere near the barnyard. Her mother had told Anna Maria to take her little sister to the scrub brush in their far-away pasture land section that lay close to the border with Zerf. There the two could cut and gather brush branches for winter fires, far away from the shrieks of the terrified pig and the smell of his straw-coated bristles being burned away once the kill had been made. But Anna Maria had put off leaving so she could talk to the young man, wearing a leather apron and pants and a rough linen tunic dotted with brown stains, who came to the front of the farmhouse to get water from the well. He was the son of the traveling butcher and was learning his father's trade. This good-to-look-at young stranger had an easy laugh, and he flirted with Anna Maria.

There were amusing stories about people in the surrounding villages. That was the reason Leni was still sitting on the bench near the shuttered window listening to Anna Maria's giggles when the pig gave his first anguished squeal. "That is the Ferkel," she shouted. She jumped up and started to run toward the sound.

It took only a split second for Anna Maria to realize that Leni was on her way to the very spot she had been told to keep her from. Papp will strap me for this, she thought. She ran after her sister, grabbing her by the waist and held her tight as Leni struggled to get away. But Leni had enough time to round the corner of the farmhouse and see what was happening. Ferkel was being dragged from his pen, his hind legs tied together, to meet his fate at the hands of the butcher from Greimerath. The big man, who like his son, wore a leather apron and stained tunic, was bending over a long wooden box on the ground, taking out something that flashed in the sun. Maria Rauls stood nearby, holding an empty tin basin to catch the pig's blood when it spurted from his throat and heart.

Leni kicked as Anna Maria almost dragged her to the road that led through the village and out toward the stubble of the flax field that must be crossed to get to the scrub brush on the edge of the pasture land.

"What are they doing to Ferkel? Let me go, let me go," she screamed, but luckily for Anna Maria, Leni's cries were covered by the terrified squeals of the pig and carried away from the farm by the wind. She held her little sister's hand tight, and they hustled along the road until they had lost sight of their farm. They heard the pig's high-pitched shrieks for a time before there was silence.

Leni stopped trying to pull her hand free and began to walk more willingly, but her large brown eyes were full of tears. She turned her head back to see behind her, as if she hoped that Ferkel would come trotting up the rutted road behind them. But the road was quiet and empty. Tears stained her face and she brushed them and her dripping nose on the sleeve of her dress, leaving a damp streak on its brown wool.

Anna Maria hadn't meant to cause her little sister pain. Because she had loitered with the butcher's son, Leni guessed that Ferkel was in danger. It would be even worse if she found out about the pig's bloody end. Anna Maria put down the willow basket that carried their lunch, knelt, and gave Leni a comforting hug while she tried to think of a way to put a smile back on the sad little face.

"What were they doing to Ferkel?" Leni asked again.

Anna Maria loved inventing stories, especially if they held a bit of romance and suddenly a stream of ideas popped into her mind and came out of her mouth. "They had to tie him up like that because the man who came today was going to give him a bath. That way he won't be dirty and stink when he meets his new wife. He's going away to get married."

"Ferkel is getting married?"

"He sure is."

"But I didn't get a chance to say goodbye to him. Why didn't you let me stay so I could say goodbye?" Leni's tears had stopped but her expression was full of doubt.

Anna Maria searched her mind for a good answer that would keep her out of trouble and comfort Leni too. She dropped her voice to a loud whisper. "You weren't supposed to be there when they came to get Ferkel. See, Mamm and Papp didn't want you to know that Ferkel would go off and leave you without a second thought. They knew that would make you sad. So they told me to take you to cut some bundles of brush for making winter fires. When we get back to the farm, Mamm and Papp will say that the stranger that came this morning scared off Ferkel, and he ran away for a while. So don't go telling them what you saw or that I told you the truth. Please Leni, not a word or I'll be in trouble."

Leni nodded solemnly. She was trying to take in all this new information. She had not known that pigs got married. She wondered how they got them to stand quiet in the church, or even how they got them into the church. Her Ferkel could be so stubborn about going into new places. And he tried to eat everything. He'd probably try to eat his new wife's wedding bonnet, nibbling away at it even if it was tied to her head with a big ribbon that formed a bow under her neck.

"Where will he live after he gets married?"

"At a pig sty near Trier." Anna Maria knew this was a safe location. Leni would be a lot older before she ever got a chance to go to a big place like Trier.

Leni was quiet, seemingly happy, and as they walked along Anna Maria's thoughts drifted back to the butcher's son. Maybe he would want to court her. Papp would probably like him as a son-in-law. A table with meat on it and the feet of a handsome man under it was a pleasant prospect. But was her stomach strong enough to ignore the sight of the dried blood that would always stain his tunic and that would lay under his fingernails even when his hands were clean. The smell of blood would linger in the air wherever he was, an unmistakable reminder of the animals that died under his knife.

"What's her name?" Leni asked Anna Maria as they turned away from the road and started across the fields on the way to the scrub brush hill.

"Whose name?"

"Ferkel's wife."

"Darling," said Anna Maria without thinking twice. "They call her Darling because she is so pretty. She was born pure white with bright red eyes." Anna Maria had heard about such a pig once and began having fun making up this story as they walked along.

"Pigs have brown eyes," Leni said.

"Not this one, she's very special, just like Ferkel. They will have pink and white spotted piglets with one eye brown and the other one red. People will come from all over to look at them. Or maybe Ferkel and his wife and those piglets will live their lives traveling from town to town with the carnival people, in a fancy cart with scrolled iron railings. They'll wear ruffles around their necks and eat only the best of scraps, like the cores and peeling from bright red apples."

Leni giggled. "Ferkel won't wear a ruffle."

"Bet he will," her sister said.

"Will not," said Leni but there was no answering reply. She had lost her sister's attention.

"Oh no." Anna Maria wailed. "I'm a *Dummkopf.* I am empty-headed and thoughtless, just like Mamm and Papp say. I forgot to bring the sickle so I could cut the brush. Leni, it will take us forever to break the pieces by hand."

"It is not too far to run back," Leni was excited. "Let's just go back, Anna Maria. Then I can say goodbye to Ferkel before he goes away to get married. I promise not to cry. I promise." Leni turned and started running back the way they had come, all smiles at the thought of seeing Ferkel scrubbed clean and smelling like soap.

Anna Maria had gotten herself into a bad predicament. She could not let Leni go back. The Ferkel was well on his way to becoming ham and bacon. But Anna Maria did need a sickle, and even more she needed a story that Leni would believe and that would keep her away from the farm.

"Stop, Leni," she called. "That will take too long, and Papp will get mad at me. I'm just going to run back to the Zimmer's. Their *Einhaus* is the closest to where we are now. They will let me borrow a sickle. You stay here and wait. Don't move. I'll be back right away. Just stay right here and mind the lunch basket." Anna Maria's feet almost flew as she ran back the way they had come.

Leni meant to stay put, just like Anna Maria said. Leaves were falling from a couple of small oak trees that stood as markers between neighboring fields, and they fluttered down near her feet. She ran to catch each new one as it fell. When it was beneath her wooden clog, she stamped on it, delighting in the sound it made as she crushed it. After awhile, she watched a ladybug slowly crawl up to the very top of the slender stem of a wild shepherd's purse that had grown tall in the time since the flax had been harvested. Mamm said those bright red bugs with the black spots were lucky. Leni caught the bug in her hand and gently cupped it there while she wished hard that she would sometime get to visit Ferkel and his pretty white-colored wife with the bright red eyes. She released the ladybug and scanned the road. No sign yet of Anna Maria. She was bored with chasing leaves and watching bugs. The wind was blowing harder, tugging at the skirt of her dress and penetrating her shawl even though it was made of heavy boiled wool. She decided to walk to keep herself warm. Anna Maria would see her. She must be coming soon now. She picked up the basket and started moving.

A slight rustling sound startled her. A little field rabbit was sitting behind a patch of yellow ragwort, its gray brown fur blending with the drying leaves of the weed. It regarded her with fright, its nose and ears twitching. She ran toward it holding out her hand, wanting to pet its soft fur. "Come little *Kaninchen*," she called but the frightened creature jumped up and darted away.

Leni put down the willow basket and ran after it. Theiss said that a mother rabbit made a soft nest, lining it with downy hair torn from her own skin; fur softer than thistle down. He had found a nest of baby rabbits in the field in summer, but he wouldn't tell Leni where it was. It would be wonderful to follow this rabbit to its nest, put her hand down inside and feel the wiggling babies resting on the softness of silken fur. That would show Theiss he wasn't so smart.

The rabbit raced to the top of the hill through the short grass growing among the stubble of the flax field and stopped far ahead of Leni to hide behind a rosette of dried chicory leaves. Leni was almost upon it before the little animal knew it was discovered and ran again. It leapt through a hay meadow, then changed course and ran in almost the opposite direction. Leni was breathless with excitement and exertion; she kept going. Her heart was pounding so hard that it felt like it might jump right out of her chest. Her legs began to tremble as she ran through one field and then another. She still had the rabbit in sight. It made for the thicket of dry broom, gorse and basket willow that surrounded the forest of oak trees. Leni dived after it, but one of her clogs caught on a piece of root and she fell, hitting her knee against a jagged stone and scratching one of her hands on the low, dry underbrush. By the time she stood up, the rabbit had disappeared, and she was left with only a tear in her woolen stocking, a stinging bloody scrape on her knee, and a track of rapidly reddening scratches on the back of her hand. She cried in vexation and disappointment while she rubbed at her knee and stained her fingers red.

No one came to comfort her. She stopped crying and looked around, a little frightened. Where was she? She didn't see the village anymore. Anna Maria was going to be so mad. Leni listened but no one was calling for her. She wasn't sure how far she and the rabbit had run from the spot where they had first met each other. She decided to walk along the edge of the thicket, trying to remember the path by which she had come. After a few minutes of turning first left and then right she came to a strip of hay meadow and beyond it a stubble field. This must be the right way, she thought. She walked on, through more harvested fields and hay meadows and still nothing looked familiar. She was very frightened now.

When she came over the top of a hill, she saw their village in the distance. She wasn't lost any more. She began to hurry toward it, hoping to find the willow basket and wait for Anna Maria. Or maybe she should just go home. Even if they punished her, she might get to see Ferkel one last time, and she would be able to get away from the cold wind that blew down her neck, making her shiver.

Leni's legs were very tired by the time she got to the edge of the village, but that didn't stop her from running when she got near to the first farm. Only her village it didn't look quite the same as before. The road through it turned in a different way than she remembered. Nothing was the same. The houses, though they seemed like the ones at the edge of Oberzerf, were slightly changed, having windows where she remembered doors, or stables where entrances to houses used to be.

She stopped at a stone building near the edge of town. How had it sprung up here on the farm of Herr Zimmer? Smoke poured from the chimney and the door was propped open with a large stone. She slowed her pace and stared inside as she walked by. She caught a glimpse of a glowing hot fire in a very large and strange-looking fireplace. Her stomach growled and she wished she still had the willow basket with the lunch Magda had packed in them. She hurried on down the road, looking for her own house until she came to the end of the village but nothing was familiar. Where was their house with the wide, round stable door and the garden at the back where dry and withered vines still clung to the stone wall? This wasn't like their village at all. She had no idea where she was, and the road was empty; there was no one to ask for help. She shivered and her stomach growled. She ran back the way she had come.

Anna Maria stood next to the willow basket, calling Leni's name. Then she listened but there was no answer. "Where could that girl have gotten?" she muttered to herself. And why had the silly little thing left their lunch behind.

It had taken Anna Maria a very long time to get the sickle. She had lied to Leni. Instead of going to the Zimmer farm where embarrassing questions would be asked and tales told to her parents, she had decided to get a sickle from their own farm. She counted on the busy activity in the back of the farmyard to protect her from being caught. She approached the farm from the side opposite, planning to slip into the stable like a wily thief. It was rather exciting. But as she looked around the corner of the *Einhaus*, she saw that her father stood near to the stable door she had planned to enter. He was laughing with the pig butcher and his son who had loaded their cart and stood beside it. It seemed they would go on talking forever but finally the butcher climbed up to the wagon seat and his son slapped the reins. The two-wheeled cart began to rumble off down the road.

When Johann Rauls had gone back to the rear barnyard, Anna Maria dashed to the stable door, opened it quietly and went inside to where the sickles and scythes hung. Everything will be all right, she thought as she hurried outside again. I'll work so hard that Papp won't know I wasted lots of time today and acted so foolish.

But now everything had gone wrong again. There was no little sister at the side of the road. As she hurried in the direction of the hill where they were to cut brush, Anna Marie tried to convince herself that Leni must have gone there and was waiting. Even so, she went on calling "Leni, Leni." The chill wind tugging at her cape and bonnet

In a few minutes she was on the high land that held the wild thickets of scrub brush. There was no sign of Leni.

Where should she look next? Leni could be anywhere. "Or nowhere," a small voice in her head loudly hinted. "Maybe she was taken away by gypsies."

Anna Maria shivered as she pushed that thought aside. Surely she would find Leni if she just kept calling and looking. She scanned the landscape below her. She saw an old man who leaned heavily on his walking stick as he made his way along the road toward Zerf. Perhaps he had seen her sister. She ran down the hill and in the direction that the hunched grandfather was taking.

When the old man heard her footsteps behind him, he stopped and turned around to see who was approaching.

"Please, sir, have you seen a little girl? Not quite five years old? She's small for her age. She has black curly hair and is wearing a brown wool cloak."

"No, *Mädchen*, I have not. Why do you look for her?" His blue eyes, narrowed by the drooping folds of his eyelids, were faded like the last petals of the cornflowers that lay dead and drying at the edge of the road.

"Because I told her to wait near the road while I went back to our farm, but she disobeyed and I can't find her. She's my little sister. Her name is Leni."

"I knew a little one who went missing once. She wandered into the deep forest way up there. They didn't find her for three days. Nearly died, she did. Never was the same afterward." A little smile came to the thin lips of the old man as if that pleased him. "You'd best go get help to look for her, girl. Tell your folks to start searching." He abruptly turned away from her, pulling his raveling stocking cap down lower on his forehead, and walked on. In spite of the biting wind, Anna Maria's cheeks were so hot that she reached up to cool them with her cold hands as she started back toward the Rauls farm. The lump in her throat was as big as a cuckoo's egg.

The nail maker Schreiner was busy at his trade. Now that his crops were harvested, it was nail-making season at his farm. He would work here at his anvil through the winter, pounding out nails that would keep his customers supplied during the summer months when he needed time for his own farm fields.

He called "Fritz, *zurück*" to his dog to start him running inside the wheel, rotating it so that it inflated the huge bellows and sent air to the fire in the forge. The flame in his forge grew red again. He was gathering up a handful of the short iron rods from the bucket next to the forge when a movement at the edge of the open doorway caught his eye. He saw a little girl sidle through the door and stand staring at the fire. He knew all the children in Zerf. This one was a stranger. Her skin was almost as brown as a gypsy's and her hair as black. But she wore the dress, cloak and wooden clogs that proclaimed her a farm child. Her bonnet had slipped backward and the dark curly hair framed a little face full of intelligence. Her eyes were bright with curiosity. When she saw the dog inside the wheel, a little sound, half gasp, half soft cry, came from her.

He smiled at her. "Who are you then, little one? I don't know you, do I?"

"I'm Leni," she said. "Who are you?"

"I'm Herr Schreiner. Glad to know you, little Leni." The nail maker kept working, pushing one of the thin four-sided iron rods onto the hottest coals with his tongs until it began to glow. He was not surprised to see a child. His forge was like a magnet to curious children. This one must have wandered off from folks who were from another village. Probably they were a family helping relatives with the pig slaughter. Someone would be here looking for her soon. Everyone in the village knew to look here if a child was missing.

"Why are you burning up those black sticks?" the child asked, her head tilted sideways as she stared at the glowing red rod that he held in his tongs.

"I make them into nails."

"How can burning them up make them into nails?"

"They won't burn up if I can help it," the nail maker laughed as he pulled the hot red piece of iron from the fire and placed it on his anvil. He took up his heavy hammer and began to pound the softened metal to a point. Sparks flew, glimmering like the eyes of the child who watched him so intently.

"Where are your parents, young one?"

"They're with Ferkel. He's going away to get married."

I was right, thought the nail maker. Her brother is here with his mother and father, maybe to show the relatives his wedding suit before he leaves. But what an odd nickname he has; not many folks call a son Piglet. Must make his friends laugh at him.

"Where is the wedding," he asked as he dropped the pointed piece of iron back into the red, hot coals, heating it again.

"In the big city, Trier," the little one said. "Ferkel had a bath this morning, and he's smelling clean and sweet now. I think his new wife will be pleased when she nuzzles him, don't you?"

"I suppose so." The nail maker was surprised that this innocent looking child would say such a thing about her brother and the marriage night. Her parents must have very loose morals. Perhaps she did have gypsy blood. Still, it was none of his business if the child's family talked among themselves of intimate things.

The fire was glowing red. "Halt," Schreiner called to the dog who immediately dropped to his haunches to rest, his long tongue slipping out from between his teeth as he panted.

"What's his name?" The little girl was moving closer to the dog

"Fritz. He likes people. You don't have to be afraid of him."

The child put out her hand and patted the dog, running it along the white strip of hair that went from the back of Fritz's head to his muzzle, dividing his brown face the way a road separates two fields of soft brown earth. His long pink tongue darted out of his mouth to wash her cheeks and nose in an enthusiastic kiss. She giggled and threw her arms around his neck.

Herr Schreiner smiled to himself. He didn't mind having children in his smithy. His sons and daughters were grown now and had children of their own. His grandchildren were often with him as he worked; he was comfortable with them and liked showing them how he made the nails.

He pulled the reheated rod out of the fire, deftly inserting the flat end into an indentation in his anvil and, with a few blows of his hammer, formed its head.

"Come over here, *Mädchen*, and I will show you how a nail is made from the very beginning. Do you know what nails are used for?" He pushed a new iron rod toward the hot coals.

"To keep the boards together when Papp builds something." She walked toward the forge and Fritz's soft brown eyes followed her, imploring her to come back.

"So you see how important one little nail is and how many I must make to hold a table or a stable together."

"Why do you keep Fritz in that cage?"

"That's his work. He's my helper. I trained him myself, and I feed him good so he has the strength to move the wheel. When I say '*zuruck*' he starts to run so that the wheel turns and moves this big thing here. What do you think this is?"

The little girl regarded the big leather bag with wooden sides. "It's big as me," she said.

"Almost as big as you, *ja*," Herr Schreiner said. "It is called a bellows. It makes a wind to fan the flame in my fireplace. It is like your mama does when she lights the tinderbox. My bellows, well it is like a big hand that brings air to the fire and makes it burn bright." He snapped his fingers and shouted *"zurück"* to the brown and white dog who got to his feet and began to walk. The wheel started to turn, moving the rope attached to the lever at the bottom chamber of the bellows.

"It sounds like the wind," the child said as she looked from the big leather bag to the dog that walked inside his round cage, then back to the bellows again. After a few minutes the coals were glowing red once more and the nail maker shouted, *"halt"* to Fritz.

"Now, little Leni, I must make this iron rod so hot that it can be shaped by my hammer. Do you want to see how heavy it is?"

He put his hammer on the packed lime floor and the child tugged at it, managing to lift it a few centimeters before she let it go and it dropped to the ground. "Heavy," she said, as solemnly as a judge pronouncing sentence.

He brought the iron rod out of the fire, lifting it carefully with the tongs, and placed it on his anvil. Picking up the hammer, he pounded the glowing end of the rod, five swift strokes. "The rod is soft like butter when I take it from the fire," he said to the child, 'but it will be hard as a stone in just a few minutes so I must work very fast. When I am finished, I put the rod back in the fire."

"Why," the child asked. "Didn't you get it right?"

"It's finished on one end but what is still missing?"

She thought. "The hat," she said.

The nail head did look a little like a hat. He smiled at her. "That is it truly. See this hole in my anvil. That is where I make the nail's hat." He grasped the reheated rod, shoved it into the nail header with his tongs and hammered again. "There it is, all done – point and hat. He tossed the nail into a bucket of cold water.

It was then that old Heinrich came into the smithy. The little girl did not notice him as she watched another nail start to take shape under the big hammer. But the old man stared at her, as if he had seen her before and was considering where it might have been.

Herr Schreiner glanced at him and frowned. Stringy old vulture he is and just as mean, Schneider thought. Why don't he go and sit in the corner like he usually does? Why stand there like he is growing roots?

"Do you know this girl then?" *Alter* Heinrich asked in his raspy voice. "Is she kin to you?"

Nosy old bird, Schreiner thought. "How come you don't know?" he said. "I thought you had the second sight. You tell womenfolk what they carry in their belly, boy or girl, if they bring you some eggs or a pot of honey. You take a coin from a man to tell him where to look for a tool or money he lost. The young girls bring you bread they baked to find out about the man they are going to marry. You already know the answer to your question."

The *Alter* Heinrich scowled at the nail maker's sarcasm.

The little girl said, "I can tell you who I am. I'm Leni."

"You are who I thought, then." The *Alter* Heinrich rubbed his thin hands together, warming them. They were covered with splotches as big and brown as hazelnuts. "Your sister hunts for you." He gave a scornful look to the nail maker who scowled back.

"You saw Anna Maria? Where is she?" The child ran out of the door, calling, "Anna Maria, Anna Maria, here I am." She was back inside in a moment. "Where is she; I can't see her," she said.

"I did not say she was here," the *Alter* Heinrich growled. "I seen her on the road about an hour ago. I think she went to look for you in the forest."

Tears formed in the dark brown eyes of the child. "How will she find me here?" She looked at the nail maker and pleaded, "Will you come and help me find her so I can go back home to Mamm and Papp?"

Herr Schreiner got down on one knee so he could look directly at Leni and spoke softly and slowly. "Where are your Mamm and Papp? Are they visiting here in Zerf?"

"No. They are at our farm, waiting for Anna Maria and me to come home."

"But I thought you came here to visit because your brother Ferkel is getting married."

There was an explosion of giggles. "Ferkel ain't my brother; he's our pig. Pitt, Mathes and Theiss are my brothers."

The nail maker saw his mistake and laughed with the child. Someone had been teasing her. Then he sobered. He asked her, "Well Leni, can you tell me how you come to be in Zerf?

Leni explained about Ferkel and the rabbit and the many fields and how she found a village that didn't have her Papp's farm in it.

She must be from Oberzerf, he realized. Her family was probably searching the fields right now, frightened that some disaster had befallen her. He got to his feet and pulled the rest of the iron rods from the forge to be worked on another time. "We'll go find your Papp," he said as he took off his leather apron. "We will go find him right away."

As they walked past the *Alter* Heinrich, the wizened oldster said, "Mark my words, it ain't the last time this little one roams like the gypsies do."

Johann Rauls was on his way north on the high meadow path that ran along the edge of the forestland and led toward Zerf. As he strode along his eyes scanned left, then right, then back again, hoping for a glimpse of a brown woolen cape. He called his daughter's name over and over again until his throat was dry and raw. Mathes and Pitt were taking the same direction but along the low path. His brothers Nikolaus and Mathias were headed west across the fields that stretched toward Irsch. If there were no sign of Leni in any of those places, they would come back to Oberzerf and call out the village guard and all of their neighbors to search the high forest. It was past noon, and Leni had to be found before darkness fell.

He gave his anger free rein because it helped to hold his fear at bay. He would take the leather strap to Anna Maria as soon as Leni was found. To have forsaken a child not yet five years old just to come home to get a sickle. He was going to strap her good. He would not let her tears stop him. Just as soon as they found Leni, Anna Maria had to be punished. If they found her. He pushed the thought away and prayed, "Oh God, please let us find her. Let me hear that familiar little voice the next time I call her name."

Leni was his favorite child, fair or unfair as it might be. Was it God's chastisement for trying to trade Leni's life for her mother's? Was it to be a punishment, to lose this child before she was grown? Leni brought him laughter and joy almost every day. He loved her even though her birth had surely weakened his other love, his Maria.

Without warning the memory of baby Leni crawling into his lap as he sat mending a harness came to him. She had arranged herself with one of his arms on each side of her wiry little body and babbled happily, telling him baby stories with sounds he wished he could understand. But it was a pleasant background noise for his work as he cut and patched, and he almost forgot he was holding her. After awhile she twisted round and knelt in his lap, her face close to his. Her tiny fingers pushed at his nose as if she wanted to move it to a new place on his face. *"Vash,"* she demanded, her fine eyebrows drawn together. Each time he pulled her fingers away from his nose, they came right back. *"Vash?"* she said again, the note of impatient inquiry again in her voice. Did she want to know the word for nose? He pointed to his nose, then hers, and said *"Nase."* *"Na"*, she said. He repeated *"Nase."* After five tries she said the word almost as well as he did. She touched his eyelid and waited. *"Auge"* he told her. *"Owg,"* she repeated and touched her eyelid, *"Owg, Owg, Owg."* She jumped down from his lap and sat on the floor near his feet, rolling her new words around in her mouth as if she liked their taste on her tongue.

He was walking faster and faster, almost running. His eyes burned with the strain of looking and not finding. He had heard that the events that shaped a man's life flashed before his eyes in the few moments before he died. But he had not known that the special times in life with his child could run wild through his head when he feared that her safety was threatened.

As Johann tramped through a field of oat stubble, calling and watching, a brown little finch flew away in fright when he came too near to the tree where it had been chirping. It reminded him of *Kuckuck*, the brown bird who had stepped out of one of the songs that Maria taught Leni and who sang *koo, koo, koo* with her. *Kuckuck* was just one of her imaginary friends. There was Jagermann the hunter who aimed his arrows at the apples on the trees and *Bi-Ba Butzemann di-del-dum* who danced and tried to take hold of Leni while she skipped back and forth to avoid being caught. And of course there was Ferkel, the pig they had killed this morning. He and Maria had thought the worst part of their evening would be the consolation of Leni over the loss of her animal friend. Now they both prayed such an event would take place.

A shout attracted his attention. He listened and hope took hold. It was Mathes' voice calling him. He couldn't make out the words but he took off at a run, down the hilly fields toward the low road.

The call was clearer now, "Papp, Papp, we got Leni. We found Leni." He could make out figures on the road, his two sons, a stranger and a small child in a brown cloak. Leni.

As soon as he was close enough, he bent down and scooped her up in his arms. "Leni, where have you been?"

"With him." She pointed at the man Johann recognized as the nail maker from Zerf. "Papp, he showed me how to make a nail's hat and how his bellows makes a big wind when Fritz runs in his wheel. I told him about Ferkel. Will I see Ferkel when we go home or is he gone to his wedding already?"

"What are you saying, Leni?" Johann asked. This was his Leni but her words weren't making any sense. He shook his head to clear it.

The short, barrel-chested nailmaker stepped forward. He smiled. "Your Leni has been keeping me company while I worked. You have a little wanderer here, Herr Rauls. When she is older, she will travel very far, I think." He reached out and squeezed Leni's hand. "Come back and see me again sometime, little one, but next time you must tell your Papp where you are going."

"*Vielen Dank*, Herr Schreiner," Johann said. I am most grateful to you." The two men shook hands, and Herr Schreiner turned to go back to his shop. But almost immediately he turned back to them. He spoke very slowly and with great emphasis. "Herr Rauls, I wish also to send my congratulations to your pig, Ferkel, upon this, his wedding day. I hope he will be very happy with his bride and with his new sty in Trier."

Pitt opened his mouth to protest, "But Papp, Ferkel is..."

Johann turned on him, thick, black eyebrows drawn together into a scowling V shape. "Be still, Pitt, while I answer this gentleman. Save your talk until we get back home."

Pitt looked confused and a little hurt, but he stopped talking. Johann nodded his comprehension to the nail maker. "You are a kind man, Herr Schreiner. It is good of you to remember about Ferkel. He's gone already, but I'll tell him what you said if I see him again."

As Herr Schreiner turned and left them, Leni called after him. "*Wiedersehen*. Say me a goodbye to Fritz." She wiggled in her father's grasp. "Ferkel's gone already, Papp? At her father's nod, she said, "I wish I could see Ferkel one time more. And smell him all cleaned up. Was he sad to leave me?"

He hugged Leni before he let her down to walk beside him on the road. "You must ask Anna Maria. I think she can answer your questions much better than me."

Mathes was whispering to Pitt, on whose face the dawning light of understanding had just appeared.

The sun was slanting toward the west, already beginning to slide into late afternoon. "Come *Kinder*, " Johann said. Let's go home to Mamm and have our supper."

With Leni's hand in his, Johann gave thanks to God. The wind had died down, the afternoon sun now warmed the November day, and he felt enveloped in the protection of the Almighty.

When they were once again in Oberzerf, falling leaves crunching beneath their shoes, Johann called out, "Our little gypsy girl is back home." Theiss and Lis, too young to go searching for their sister, had stayed at home with Maria. As Maria rushed toward Leni, an oddly shaped ball caught her little girl's attention as Lis and Theiss threw it back and forth to each other. His bladder filled with water was all that was left of Ferkel.

"Lis, Theiss where did you get that funny looking ball?" Leni shouted as she ran toward them.

Maria stopped Leni before she reached her brother and sister, hugged her and scowled at the ball players who were more interested in their game than in their little sister's return.

"Mamm, I'm sorry I got lost." But Leni's eyes were sparkling in anticipation of joining the pig bladder ball game.

Maria gave a questioning look at Johann who nodded his head, smiled, and mouthed. "I'll hide the bladder after our supper!"

CHAPTER 4
A Mother's Song – September 1833

"Fuchs du hast die Gans gestohlen," or "Fox, you have stolen the goose," is a German language children's song consisting of three verses. The song lyrics were composed by Ernst Anschuetz set to the melody of an old folk song and published in 1824 under the title "Warnung." It is still considered one of the most well known children's songs in German speaking regions.

Purple storm clouds were gathering in the west but the scalding sun would not yield to them. It still seared the grass in the meadows, turning it yellow. It baked the flesh of the ripening purple plums that hung heavy on slender tree branches, intensifying their sugar. It penetrated even the shady woodlots where pigs rooted for acorns among fallen leaves where the crowns of the trees touched and kept the worst of the heat at bay.

Leni was on her hands and knees in the garden, her loose smock pushed away from knees that were covered with a mixture of brown soil and her own sweat. Now that she was five, regular chores were expected of her. Her strong little fingers tore at the stems of the yellow bean pods, stripping them from the bean plants along with some of the heart-shaped leaves that had the bad luck to be in her way. The willow basket beside her was half full, but she was not even close to finishing her chore.

Leni looked around her. No one was in sight. Mamm, Papp and all of her brothers and sisters were in the fields working to harvest the hay crop. She got to her feet, hitching up her smock and brushing off her knees. The air on her legs felt so good that she held the garment above her thighs, making a breeze as she fanned her skirt back and forth. Skirt still lifted, she started to walk in the direction of her uncle's farm leaving basket and bean plants behind. There were newborn kittens in the stable of the *Onkel* Nikolaus, and he had said she should come to see them sometime. She decided to take a walk to see them now.

The village road was quiet. Almost everyone was in the fields today except for the very young and the very old who were not strong enough to carry large armloads of hay to the waiting wagons.

One of those too old for work in the hay meadows sat at an open window, watching for any activity along the dusty stretch of road that would break the monotony of the clicking of the needles as she knit. It was the *Oma* Ailer. Even in the heat of the day, she wore a wool shawl over her shoulders. As Leni walked by, her skirt hiked up almost to her waist, the old woman called out in a voice that cracked with age, "Little *Mädchen*, shame, shame. Cover thy legs and remember that thou art a child of God who sees all."

Feeling both guilty and rebellious, Leni let her smock drop, but she narrowed her eyes and when she was a few steps down the road she looked back over her shoulder and stuck out her tongue in defiance. Her equanimity restored, her pleasure in her excursion came back, and she forgot all about the old woman as she continued contemplating the mysteries of her tongue. I wish I could make my tongue curl up at the edges the way Mathes does, she thought. She squeezed her eyes into small slits and commanded her tongue to obey her will, struggling with the stubborn little organ until she thought she felt its edges begin to curve. Trying to see, she focused her eyes downward and two deep frown lines formed on either side of her puckered nose. The floor of her mouth and underside of her tongue were tensed with the strain of it, but she still couldn't see even its tip.

Her mind being elsewhere, the warning honk of a large white goose that was waddling across the road directly into her path went unheeded. The goose gave a second honk, spread it wings wide, flapped them, and sped toward her at the same moment Leni realized her danger. She turned her back on the bird and walked hurriedly in the direction from which she had come, but the goose followed her and nipped at her ankle with its beak, breaking the skin and drawing blood. Leni gave a scream and ran, the squawking bird still in pursuit.

The angry honks and a child's cries reverberated down the road for the old Grandmother Ailer to hear. She stuck her head out of the window and saw that the same child who had passed by a few minutes earlier was in trouble. She dropped her knitting, reached out for her twig broom, which she often used for support, and left her seat. She hobbled to her door and then out into the road as fast as her rheumatic limbs would permit. Garnering all of her strength, she used the flat side of her broom to hit hard at the goose as soon as the child ran past her. She croaked, "*Whusch whusch,* goose go away." and hit again and again until the goose squawked in protest and flapped to the far side of the road. Leni ran on without looking back while her savior painfully returned to her window and her knitting.

Maria Rauls had just come home from the hay field, her energy depleted, her forearms reddened by the hot sun. She was standing at the stone sink, peeling potatoes for the supper meal when Leni burst through the kitchen door, sobbing in gulping breaths.

"*Die Gans,*" Leni wailed, "The goose, it bit me. My leg, Mamm, see the blood. It hurts Mamm, it hurts; it hurts."

"Come here and let me see." Her mother knelt down on the stone floor, the slice of a potato she had been cutting still in her hand. Her fingers gently probed at the wound where the marks of the goose bite clearly showed. "It is not so bad, *mein Kindlein*; it is not at all deep, this bite."

At her mother's soothing words, Leni's sobs trailed away into whimpers, but she cried out when the piece of potato in her mother's hand was pressed against the wound. After the first sting of it went away, the potato seemed to draw the hurt into itself, and the juice from it began to soothe and cool away the pain. After a few moments, the potato slice turned a pale brown from its encounter with the air of the room, little drops of blood and the mud on Leni's leg.

After a few minutes, Maria removed the simple home remedy from Leni's leg and stood up. "Lenchen," she questioned, "our geese are too tame to bite any of us. Did you leave the garden to go wandering?"

This was a question Leni did not want to answer, but she never lied to her Mamm. She confessed about her walk down the road, and the meeting with *Oma* Ailer who had saved her by beating the angry goose with her broom. She left out the part about how she had stuck out her tongue at the old woman.

Maria listened with a deepening frown, her eyebrows drawn together. It was the same expression that she wore when a penitent Anna Maria or Lis stood before her. "You are a very selfish girl, Leni, thinking about nobody but yourself. It was only good luck that you had the kind *Oma* Ailer to aid you or you would be hurt much worse. You put that good-hearted old lady who helped you in a bad way. What if the goose bit her too? She is not young like you and quick to heal."

Leni's lower lip trembled and her eyes flooded with tears as she thought about what her mother had just said. Filled with shame, she looked down at the floor, thinking how the *Oma* Ailer had helped her even after she had been nasty and stuck out her tongue.

Her mother was still scolding. "Tomorrow you will go to the Ailer house to thank the Grandmother Ailer and to say you are sorry for the terrible way you behaved. I will send a pot of currant jam with you."

"Yes, Mamm," Leni said, her voice just a whisper. "I'm sorry I was bad. Her mother was silent for a moment. Then she went to the stool next to the fireplace and sat down. It was the stool she used for spanking Lis, Theiss and Leni. She said, "Come over here, Leni."

Mamm looked blurry through Leni's tear-filled eyes, as if she was a reflection in the water of the creek. She balled her fists and wiped at the wetness, but that only sent tears racing down her cheeks. She walked to her mother and stifled a sob as she bent her body over her mother's knees. She could not see the tenderness that played across her mother's face as she waited for the first slap to fall. Much to her surprise, she was pulled into a sitting position. Mamm rocked her gently as she wiped Leni's tears away with her rough linen apron that smelled of potato, onion and flour.

"Maybe the goose bite is punishment enough," her mother said. She touched the wound with lightly moving fingers, making sure that the bleeding had really stopped.

Now that the danger of punishment was past, Leni remembered her anger at what the goose had done. "I wish Papp would cut the head off of that goose," she muttered, burrowing her face into her mother's shoulder.

"Do you know the song about the fox and the goose, Lenchen?" her mother asked.

Leni shook her head and her mother started to sing, gently rocking her from side to side, her arm wrapped tight around Leni's waist.

"Fox, our goose you have just stolen!
Give her back again.

>Give her back or soon a hunter's
>Gun will make your end."

>"Dear little fox let me remind you,
>You thieving little beast.
>Leave us to roast our fat old goose;
>A mouse should be your feast!"

Her mother's voice was a shimmering thing, as splendid as the sound of the nightingales serenading the night. Leni lifted her hand and touched her mother's lips, just for an instant, because she wanted to feel those beautiful sounds before they disappeared into the air.

Mamm smiled and stopped singing. "So you understand what happens to the goose, my little Leni? She has to be fierce because a fox is always around the corner, wanting to carry her off and eat her. And if he fails, someone in the village will roast her brown and feast on her someday. So the goose has a hard life, and she tries to defend herself. She didn't know you wouldn't hurt her. She thought you might put her in the brick baking oven."

"Mamm, will you learn me that song about the fox and goose?" Leni begged, her eyes sparkling.

"Oh Leni, I have so much more to get done. I must get the supper ready."

Just then they saw a flash of lightening and heard thunder in the distance. Her mother gently pushed Leni off of her lap and stood up.

"Get back to your work in the garden and pick the rest of those beans before the rain comes. I'll help you. We can sing the song I about the fox and goose while we finish the job you didn't do."

Leni turned her head away so that Mamm would not know how happy she was to have walked away from her work. Now it was just Leni and her Mamm, singing together. For the first time in her young life she had all her mother's attention.

The storm was almost on them by the time all of the beans were picked.

"You go sit in the hall, Leni," Mamm directed when they heard the horn of the pig herder, telling the villagers that he was bringing each farmer's pigs back from the woodlot pasture where he guarded them as they fed. "I'll open the stable door and get our pigs inside."

Leni pushed through the hall door and sat on the bench outside the *Stube*, fingering the scab that was already starting to form over the goose bite. She hummed the fox and goose song while her mother, on the other side of the wall, shouted at the pigs as they jostled each other and pushed through the stable door.

In just a few moments, there was the rasp of the iron hinges, as the big barn doors at the side of the *Einhaus* swung wide open. Leni looked out of the hall door to see Papp and Pitt guiding the oxen hitched to the wagon full of hay. Her sisters ran along the road toward the house while the raindrops fell. Her mother came around the side of the *Einhaus*, running too.

Leni moved further back in the hall as the deluge began, and a moment later the wind seemed to blow Mamm into the house. She clutched a bunch of wildflowers, her cap as wet as her blouse and overdress, strands of loose hair clinging to her neck, but she was smiling.

"*Majusepeta,* what a storm has come," she said, as she untied and pulled off her cap, taking a towel from the pile on the table in the hall to dry her hair, face, and neck. She had placed the bouquet of small daisies on the table next to the towels. They still held large drops of rain.

"Here are some little *Ganseblumchen*, Lenchen," she said. "These little goose flowers won't bite you. We'll take them into the *Stube* where we can all see them tonight when we say the rosary together."

Anna Maria, Magda, Lis, Mathes, and Theiss all seemed to burst through the door at once, pushing each other out of the way, soaked to the skin and laughing. Papp came in behind them, smiling at the pandemonium.

Mathes swung Leni into his arms and danced down the hall with her, his wet clothes making damp splotches on her smock. "Poor little Leni, you were left behind to pluck the beans from the garden," he teased. "Maybe tomorrow you won't have to stay home. Maybe I'll take you with me."

Leni shook her head and, when she was back on the ground, she ran to take Mamm's hand. She had forgotten all about the bite of the goose. It had been a special thing to have Mamm all to herself. The best of adventures. She hoped it would happen many more times before she started school next year.

CHAPTER 5
A Death in the Village – October, 1833

In the third decade of the century, there were high rates of scarlet and typhoid fever all over Europe and in 1833, a virulent strain of cholera. The death rate was high, especially for the women and younger children. The Parish Priest recorded one name after another in the Zerf Parish Death Register during the summer of 1833. In October of that year, the name "Rauls" appears for the first time. <u>Zerf, Hentern, and Greimerath Catholic Parish Death Register.</u>

On this cool, sunny mid-October day, Leni was headed for the bed where her Mamm lay bundled in a quilt, face pale except for the red gashes of color at her cheekbones. But Leni was no match for the strong woman with the heavy eyebrows and frowning face who stood guard at the bedside of Maria Rauls. Leni was pushed unceremoniously through the door of the sleeping room and into the hall, her protests and tears to no avail.

Leni had only wanted to give Mamm a kiss because her mother always said that Leni's kisses made her feel better. Cousin Eva had grabbed the little girl before she got near the sickbed; and as Leni struggled to pull free, her captor had hissed, "Your Mamm is sleeping. She don't need a big lump of a girl waking her up. She's too sick for your chatter." Another woman might have softened those words, given a hug, or promised to let Leni come in when her mother was better. The *Fräulein* Eva's mind was set on doing her nursing job and making her cousin Maria comfortable. She had no children of her own; didn't know much about them. It had not seemed important to her that this child also receive some comfort. She had left a frightened Leni in the hall and gone back into the sickroom without a second thought, closing the door behind her.

"I hate you," Leni said to the closed door. She was angry but there was fear too, a raw feeling in her chest that made her breath come in short little gulps. She wished someone would make a potion that would stop this feeling, like the one Mamm used to soothe the welts on her legs after she had run through the stinging nettle.

Anna Maria came into the hall as Leni spoke. She carried the big mattress sack from her mother's bed that had been drying on the grassy banks of the *Grossbach*, the stream in which it had been washed this morning. She held it loosely in her arms, so that one corner trailed on the floor. There was no Mamm to scold her for not folding it neatly. She dropped her bundle on the hall bench, knelt down, and hugged her little sister.

"I hate cousin Eva too, Lenchen," she said. "She's as mean as an old tough goose. She struts around like she owns the world, all bad temper, sharp bite and she nips at people." Anna Maria started to laugh, caught up in the comparison of her second cousin to the waddling birds that scratched in the dirt outside the door. "Why she even looks like a goose. She's got that peaked nose and those little beady eyes, and her bottom is bigger than her top. Is she not just like that goose that chased you in summer? Just like it?" She tickled Leni until she too began to giggle.

Cousin Eva came into the hall just then, a tin bucket's rope handle over her arm. She glared at Anna Maria, "That how you help, miss? You toss the clean washing on a bench to wrinkle and drag on the floor while you laugh with your sister when your mother's got her hand on death's door and when there is so much to be done? Get yourself back to work." Anna Maria stood up, her face flushed with anger. She picked up the mattress sack and folded it with exaggerated care, handing it to Eva and then turned on her heel to go into the stable. She did not look back as cousin Eva walked to the front door that led to the street.

Leni was thinking about what Eva had said and what she knew about death. There was old Josef who used to sit on a bench outside of the Ostermann farmhouse making willow baskets. He always called "God's blessing on you, *Schönes Mädchen*, when he saw her. One day his bench was empty, and he never came back again to call her a pretty little girl. Magda told her he had died and gone away to heaven to meet the Lord Jesus. Leni now knew what must have happened. When no one was watching, he had walked through the death door. She shivered as she made the connection. If Mamm got through the death door, then she would never come back to them either. That must be what Cousin Eva did in there, kept watch so Mamm would stay with them and not go to meet the Lord Jesus and old Josef. But why would Eva come out to scold them just when Mamm had her hand at the death door, the worst possible time? There was no satisfactory explanation so Leni pushed open the door to try to hold on to Mamm until Eva got back.

She had been afraid she would find an empty room or see her mother just closing the death door behind her. But her mother lay there in the bed, breathing noisily. Eva must have lied to scare them. Leni studied each wall of the room seeking the source of danger, but the rough plaster did not reveal any door-like lines or cracks. The death door had to be in the floor then, a door hidden away under the big rag rug. Before she could grab the rug and look underneath, Eva was back in the room. Leni turned her head to look at her and demanded, "Why do you leave Mamm alone? There was no one but me, Leni, to stop her going. What if I couldn't keep her here?"

"What are you babbling about now, girl?" Eva didn't understand what Leni meant and didn't care. Her dark eyes narrowed and a vein at the side of her temple pulsed with her anger. "You always disobey me. Maybe this makes you remember next time." She dragged Leni into the hall, sat on the wooden bench next to the little table with the uneven legs, and pulled Leni over her knees.

Leni didn't resist. She hardly felt the slaps on her bottom. Through the open door of the sleeping room, she could see the rug. Mamm did not go near it. When Eva set her on her feet again and went back to the sickroom, Leni relaxed. She sat down on the hall floor, its cold stone cooling her stinging buttocks. The afternoon sun was lowering and the hall was filled with long shadows. She brought her knees to her chin, her hands clasped around them. She knew one important thing. Mamm was safe as long as Eva was guarding her. She would keep watch too, in case she was needed.

The next morning, Leni woke alone. Papp or Magda must have carried her up to the bed. The sky was bright. But the house was so silent. She was alone in the bed. Lis, Magda and Anna Maria were gone. There were no sounds of breakfast being readied or scuffles from her brothers' sleeping room. For the first time she could remember, no one had shaken her awake. She rubbed the sleep from her eyes and listened again. There it was, the muffled sound of coughing. Mamm was still sick, but she had not gone through the death door last night. Cousin Eva or Papp must have kept her safe.

The October mornings had a chill to them even though by midday the sun would be warm. Leni's feet met the cold of the wooden floor as she climbed out from under the feather quilt and started toward the wall hooks to get her dress. The old floor creaked a little at each step. Reaching up, she pulled her coarse dark blue linen overdress and buff-colored, long-sleeved blouse from the peg and put them on over her undershift. Then she pushed aside the curtain in the doorway and crept downstairs. Now she could hear a ragged rattle in her mother's breathing. It was a frightening sound, as if her Mamm's chest was full of gravel pieces that rubbed together.

The door to the room where her mother lay was not shut tight so Leni pushed it open and tiptoed inside. She looked around uncertainly. *Tante* Mari held a wet cloth to her mother's head, regularly rewinding it in cool water from the bucket next to the bed. Her father, cousin Eva, and her sisters, Magda and Anna Maria, were kneeling near the bed where her mother seemed to struggle for breath. Lis, Theiss and Pitt knelt at the far corner of the room. They were praying the Hail Mary's of the rosary over and over in a desperate chant, a frightened look on each of their faces. Mamm's hands clutched at the quilt that covered her. Her coughing seemed to come from someplace deep in her belly. When the spasm stopped, she tried to sit up; her eyes fixed on the window. She begged for buckets of water to put out the fire in her bed. Leni didn't see flames, only the morning sun that brightened the room and emphasized the dark circles around Mamm's unfocused, sunken eyes.

Johann Rauls stood and beckoned Magda to come with him. He took Leni's hand and brought her back out into the hall. "Take her to *Onkel* Nikolaus, Magda. She must not stay in here," he said.

"But Papp, I want to be here with Mamm if…" Her voice trailed off as Leni's father hurried back into the sleeping room.

Magda took Leni's small warm hand in her cold one. "Mamm is very sick today, Lenchen. *Onkel* Nikolaus will take care of you for awhile." She led Leni down the hall, closing the sickroom door behind her as they went. In another minute, they were out of the house and walking on the gravel-covered road.

Leni's short legs could hardly keep up as Magda pulled her along toward the farm of Nikolaus Rauls. All of Leni's aunts and uncles were farmers in Oberzerf but the house of *Onkel* Nikolaus and *Tante* Mari was closest. It stood alone at the crossroads where the Chapel Road met the *Hauptstrasse*.

Nikolaus Rauls was sitting on the bench at the front of the wide arched door that was the wagon entrance to the *Einhaus*. He was surrounded by dry branches, busy making a twig broom for the fireplace hearth. As they approached, he glanced up from his work and gave Magda a questioning look. She shook her head.

"Stay here until I come for you," Magda said to Leni. She turned and ran back up the road, leaving Leni in her uncle's care.

Father Mathias Guckeisen was hurrying after young Mathes Rauls. They were on the way to the house of Johann Rauls where Maria Rauls lay dying of the terrible fever that had taken so many people this autumn. He was carrying with him, in a well-worn leather pouch, the precious oils for the holy sacrament that Catholic theology called Extreme Unction. To the villagers it was "the last sacrament," the rite that could help to save them from an eternity of hellfire and bring them to heaven.

As he and the boy came out from the narrow alley beside the church and on to the Chapel road, a small figure darted toward them. It was the youngest child of the Rauls family, the one named Magdalena but called Leni. The child reached out, trying to slip her hand into her brother's; but the boy pushed her hand away and kept walking, wiping at his eyes with his clenched fist. She stood looking after him, her mouth slightly open as if a question she had wanted to ask had stopped at her lips and turned to stone.

Father Guckeisen paused and placed his free hand on the girl's head with its mop of shiny black curls. The little one wore no cap. In a house where death was hovering, the child must have dressed herself. He paused until Nikolaus Rauls, coming toward them with a half-finished broom, took the child by the hand. So young to be without a mother, the priest thought, as he silently said a prayer for the little girl. He wished he could change what was happening; and push this death into the far future when the child before him was grown and had a family of her own. But God, it seemed, willed it otherwise. In a few minutes he would take the holy oils from the case he carried and anoint the forehead, hands and feet of Maria Kautenberger Rauls while the good woman slipped away from husband and children forever.

Nikolaus Rauls stood in the street with Leni until Father Guckeisen had gone inside the house of Johann Rauls and the door closed behind him. Then he coaxed Leni back to the bench where he had been sitting. He pushed the half-finished broom out of the way so she could sit beside him and waited for her to ask the fearful questions that darkened her eyes.

"Mamm will get better, won't she *Onkel?*" she said. He held out his arms and she crawled into his lap, crying a little as he rocked her back and forth. "Don't cry, don't cry, my sweet girl," he whispered in her ear. "Your Mamm will get better." He knew that wasn't true, but he said it anyway. Pain and sadness were all too common in life, waiting around every bend in the road. He saw no reason why the child should face this tragedy even one moment before it occurred. There would be time enough for that. As he rocked her, he felt Leni relax a little. It had been almost 15 years since he had cradled the last of his own children in his arms. As always, it soothed him too.

"Shall I make a broom for you, little Leni," he whispered into her ear. She turned her head to look at him. "A broom of your own, just like your Mamm's?" Eyes wide, her head bobbed up and down in assent. "So good then. You bring me those beech twigs over there, and I will work with them."

An hour later, Leni's broom and two others were almost finished. The twigs had been tightly pressed together in the metal broom press. Pliant hazelnut tree switches bound each short twig bundle to a broom handle of peeled beech wood. Nikolaus was working with the twig knife; doing the final trimming of the twigs of Leni's small broom, making the ends even. Leni sang a little song to herself as she picked up the scraps of bark and twigs that were scattered around the bench and put them in a neat pile.

They both looked up when they heard the footsteps. Father Guckeisen and Magda were walking back along the *Hauptstrasse*. When they reached the Chapel road, the parish priest went on toward the church but Magda came and stood before them. Her eyes and nose were red, and her voice trembled as she said, "*Onkel*, it is over. *Tante* Mari has closed the door and is with Mamm now. Papp asks if you will bring your carpenter tools and help him with what must be done." Nikolaus glanced at Leni. The child clutched the little broom he had made for her as though, if she held it tight enough, the familiar things in her life would never change.

Midwife Maria Rauls gently washed the pale, cold skin of the body in the bed. It was not usually her duty to bathe the dead. That was left to the grieving relatives when, after she had done her best to save a family member, it had not been enough. She was the one who cleansed the soft, living flesh of villagers struggling with illness or of mothers at the end of childbirth. As she wrung her cloth again, she remembered the Christmas night almost six years ago when she had bathed her sister-in-law, anticipating the happiness that would flow into the room when she had finished and opened the door wide so that Johann and the children could come in and see Maria and the little Leni lying together in the bed. Today she would hesitate before opening the door and stepping into the hallway to encounter the grieving faces of the family as they moved quietly through the house. She would close the door behind her, leaving Maria's remains inside to await the visits from comforting relatives and friends, a trip to the church, and then to her final resting place in the cemetery.

After finishing the washing of the body, *Tante* Mari dressed her sister-in-law in her best clothing, the white stockings made of soft wool, the blouse with lace at collar and cuff, the embroidered overdress and the linen shift that went under it. Reaching up to the bedpost, she untied the chastity arrow with its oblong bezel. Johann had removed the little symbol of virginity from his new wife's hair on their wedding night. She used the thin cord of faded ribbon that had held it in its place on the bedpost these 25 years to fasten the lace collar at Maria Rauls' throat. With the passage of time, the collar, the silk cord and Maria's flesh would rot away, leaving only this little ornament and dry bones in the ground of the cemetery.

She sat on the bed and lifted the lifeless head into her lap so she could braid the hair. When she was finished, she reached for the linen bonnet, put it over the braids, and tied the ends in a perfect bow, just the way Maria always had. Now that all was in place, she bent down and kissed her sister-in-law's cold cheek, wiping away the tears that were filling her eyes and escaping one by one. "Goodbye, dear Maria," she whispered and caressed the cold hand that had so lately washed the linens on which she now lay. "Nikolaus and I will do our best to look out for Johann and the children, especially the little Leni, until we come join you."

The table, holding a candle and a bowl filled with holy water blessed on Easter Saturday, stood at the foot of the bed, and she dipped her fingers in the bowl to bless herself and to make a blessing over Maria's body. The room lay in shadow. *Fräulein* Eva had closed the shutters on all of the windows, both house and stable, and covered the mirrors in the customary manner. This was now a house of mourning, where even the beehives in the pasture were draped with black cloth. Maria knelt at the side of the bed and prayed the prayer for the dead, "Eternal rest grant to her, Oh Lord, and let your perpetual light shine upon her. May she rest in peace."

When the bells of the Oberzerf chapel stopped ringing the Angelus at noon, the single tolling bell began to sound, one toll for each of Maria Rauls' 46 years of life. Mathes, Theiss, and Pitt were digging the potato crop in the house garden down the road near the edge of the village. From force of habit they counted, even though they knew only too well how many years their mother had lived. Anna Maria and Lis were scrubbing the floor and the furniture in the darkened *Stube* in anticipation of the mourners who would come to sit with the family. Cousin Eva and Magda did the same in the room where their mother's body lay. The sisters were glad they could not see each other's faces; the tears in each other's eyes.

Leni lay on her stomach on the floor of the hay wagon, chin in hands, and watched her father and *Onkel* Nikolaus make a large wooden box and a cover for it. She was not sure what it was meant to hold. The sound of the cutting of boards and the pounding of nails filled the stable.

There was no talking, no laughter, only a grunt of effort now and then, as the two men worked in the midday light coming in the small window. Her father's face was set in hard lines like it was the time that Anna Maria had disobeyed him and run to the woods to meet Nikolaus Henrichs. Leni was frightened of that face.

Moving carefully so that they would not hear her, Leni crawled down from the wagon and slipped through the door of the stable into the darkened house. The door to her parent's sleeping room was closed. When she grasped its latch, it did not move. She had to get in. She kicked at the door and called out to her mother. Magda came out of the room and talked gently to Leni while she carried her to her bed upstairs; then stayed until Leni pretended she was asleep.

After Magda went back downstairs, Leni followed her. She crouched in a forlorn little heap near the cooking fire, waiting for the sleeping room door to open so she could run to it before it was closed again. Anna Maria found her, tried to comfort her and struggled to take her up the stairs and to the bed they both shared with Lis now that Cousin Eva slept in the other bed with Magda.

"Let me go to Mama," Leni begged.

"Leni, we told you already. You have to be a brave girl. Mama has walked the road to heaven."

Leni shouted, "She went through the death door and now you won't let me try to go after her and bring her back? Why doesn't anyone run after her?"

"You can't go after somebody when they take the road to heaven." Anna Maria's eyes filled with tears. "Their body stays behind but their soul is gone like a raindrop on dry ground. Remember when the mother cat died? It is like that. The life inside the cat was gone in an instant, and we had to bury her body. Mama's life was in her soul and that has gone; her body will go into the ground after all our aunts and uncles and our neighbors come and pray her into heaven."

Leni shook the tangle of her black curls. "No," she said.

"Yes," Anna Maria said and her mouth quivered. "Mama is gone, Leni. She can't ever come back to us." She buried her face in her hands and her shoulders shook as she cried softly. Leni's face puckered, and she began to sniffle, wiping her nose on her arm. Anna Maria heard the sound and raised her tear stained face to look at Leni. She held out her arms and Leni hurled herself into them. They sat together, Anna Maria crying harder and harder while Leni sobbed, until they both fell asleep.

When she woke up it was dark. Her sister, Lis, was asleep next to her. Leni heard the soft murmur of the prayers being said by her father, brothers, sisters, and the relatives who had come to watch with the family while the body of Maria Rauls lay in the sleeping room downstairs. She pinched her eyes shut tight, covered her ears with her fists and finally drifted off to sleep again.

Two days later, dressed in their wool overdresses, capes and bonnets, their usual attire for church, Leni sat on the hard church bench with her sisters and aunts, across from her father, brothers and uncles. A cold rain pattered on the roof of the church with much the same sound as the holy water that fell on the homemade coffin that still smelled of the freshly hewn beech wood. The wood box rested in the center aisle and held what was left of the woman who had kissed away the pain of bee stings and cut fingers; the woman who had always filled her home with laughter and singing.

The Latin words being chanted by Father Guckeisen meant nothing to Leni; but they made her shiver all the same, even before the church bell began to toll. At that sound, six of her uncles and cousins rose and walked to the coffin, lifting it from the floor to their shoulders, carrying it to the church's door. Father Guckeisen walked ahead of it, leading the funeral procession on the long walk to the cemetery at Zerf. The mourners and villagers followed behind.

The rain had almost stopped, but the wind blew hard. The pewter sky was filled with black-edged clouds, which dulled the golden autumn color of the beech and oak trees' leaves. Leni's uncles and cousins exchanged places now and then, to allow first one group, then the other to rest for a time from the weight of their burden.

Several old women walked in the funeral procession, clutching their rosary beads under their black shawls, wool bonnets tied tight over coarse gray hair. They looked and sounded like black crows as they talked in their raspy voices. One of them said, "I knew the minute she got the influenza that she was *kaputt*. She is wore out," I said to my

Susanna, "not strong enough to have one babe after another like she done."

Her friend agreed and added, "She never looked good after her last one. A child that comes that late in life can suck the life right out of a woman."

Leni heard those words. Were they saying it was her fault that Mamm died? She turned around and stared at them. Anna Maria glared at the old women who had spoken too loud, and she held Leni's hand very tight as they walked. There were teardrops on the ends of her eyelashes and, as Leni watched, they dropped, one by one, to her sister's cheeks where they kept their shape for just a moment before they turned into wet streaks. Lis and Mathes walked side-by-side, heads down, fists clenched. Mathes was only as tall as Lis, even though he was two years older, and they were a team taking on trouble together. Theiss tagged after them, the younger brother they always excluded.

Magda walked with her cousin Johann. They would be married soon if the Bishop would grant a dispensation for the two first cousins to marry. During the requiem Mass, Magda's Johann sat with the men on the left side of the aisle, but as the procession to the cemetery walked along, he moved close to Magda and defying the custom of unmarried men and women keeping separate, had taken her hand and walked with her.

The walk along the rough road from Oberzerf to the *Niederzerf* cemetery, which lay behind the main church in lower Zerf, took a long time. Finally the procession of family and villagers came to a stop at the freshly dug grave. The coffin was gently placed on ropes and lowered down into the hole in the earth. There were dull thudding noises when it reached bottom, and the ropes that had supported the coffin on its descent were slipped off and removed.

The mourners arranged themselves around three sides of the open grave. Father Guckeisen stood alone at the head of the gaping hole. He held his biretta in place at the top of his head whenever a strong gust of wind tore at the black cope and the cassock that he wore.

Johann Rauls had not joined the rest of the mourners; he stood apart. He had taken Pitt's hand as they walked to the cemetery, and he continued to grasp it, holding it so tightly that Pitt shifted uneasily and tried now and then to tug it away. The long lines that creased Johann's cheeks from eye to chin were deeper than ever before. As the priest prayed to God to grant this daughter eternal rest, Johann turned his head away and began looking out over the hillside, away from the hole in the earth and the people around it. Leni watched her father watching the hillside.

"What does Papp see over there?" she whispered to Anna Maria and received a stern look and a "psssht, be still," as her only answer.

Cousin Eva moved toward Johann Rauls and touched his arm. She seemed to be urging him to join the rest of the mourners; but he stayed where he was, not looking at her. Leni was glad. Eva had known about the door of death, but she didn't stop Mamm from walking through it. Her eyes narrowed: she asked God to change his mind, take cousin Eva to heaven, and let Mamm come back to them. But God's only answer was a clap of thunder. The rain began again and the wind blew while Father Guckeisen said one last prayer over the grave.

CHAPTER 6
Life Goes On – October 1833

"It was the duty of the married woman to take care of the house, to look after the children, to help with work in the field, to milk the cow and feed the small animals each day. In addition she was responsible for putting three meals a day on the table for the hungry mouths of her family." <u>Essens-Zeiten; Eifeler Tisch-Szenen aus 100 Jahren</u>, *Arbeitskreises Eiferer Museen, 2002.*

As the clods of earth fell on Maria Rauls' coffin, her family and the other mourners left the cemetery and began the walk back to Oberzerf. The dark clouds, chased by a strong wind, had lost their hold on each other so that the sun could break through and tease with moments of golden warmth.

Johann and his children were silent, but relatives and neighbors talked. Now and then a burst of laughter rang out briefly and was quickly smothered in deference to the sorrow that hung heavily around the newly bereaved Rauls family.

Eva Kautenberger walked alone, not quite a part of any of the groups on the road. When they were close to the Rauls' farm, she lengthened her stride until she was able to fall into step with Johann. He started as she touched his arm and said, "My brother and sister-in-law do not have much need for me until St. Martin's Day when they will do the slaughtering. If you wish, cousin Johann, I could stay for awhile to bring the household back to order."

Johann had made no plans for a future that did not include Maria. He did not want to think about it now. "Yes, all right," he said.

Eva had hoped for gratitude or at least a kind word. She bit her lip in frustration. The sharp words she wanted to say tasted bitter as she held them on her tongue but she kept them back. She reminded herself that this man was grieving. Sooner or later he would see that she was generous and thoughtful. She could wait for the thanks that would surely come. A little smile flickered to her lips; then disappeared so quickly that only heaven saw it.

The women of Oberzerf watched Eva and Johann. Most had no book learning, but they were experts in reading motives and hidden desires. They smiled and exchanged sly glances while their mouths talked of other things.

Johann's hand reached out to touch Maria but there was only emptiness beside him in the bed. Trying not to think, he pulled on his outer clothes, left the lonely sleeping room and walked to the stable door. That was when he heard it; Maria was singing softly in the kitchen. He stood motionless in the hall with his hand on the door latch, experiencing a moment of intense, uplifting joy that was immediately replaced by anguish so deep that he thought he would drown in its depths. His knees went weak. The woman singing in the kitchen was not his wife. It was Magda, his oldest daughter. Never again would he see Maria when he came into a room or sing with her in the hay meadow. He stumbled through the stable door to pound his fists against the stones on the barn wall until the skin on his work-hardened hands broke and bled.

When he had finally exhausted himself, his despair was replaced by a numbness that he welcomed as a friend. If he was to go on living, working, and caring for his children, he must stop any repetition of the kind of pain that had just overwhelmed him. It is the singing, he thought. The ghost of Maria will always be in the singing.

That afternoon, he called his children and his wife's cousin Eva into the *Stube*. He sat in the chair near the window as they stood facing him. He was about to do the most selfish thing he had ever done or would ever do again.

"Your mother was a good person," he began, "But no man or woman is free of sin, and it is important for us to offer prayer and sacrifice so that she is soon out of the fires of purgatory and into heaven."

Leni interrupted him before he could go on. "Anna Maria said that Mamm walked the road to heaven already. Why is she in a fire somewhere? If she's not in heaven, why can't she be here with us, away from the fire?" Her fists clenched, she walked toward the wall where Eva stood.

She shouted, "It's your fault. You could have stopped Mamm before she went through that death door and got lost in a fire. Go and find her and bring her back." Her balled fists flailed at Eva's apron clad stomach as Eva pushed her away.

Johann stopped speaking. He had carefully prepared the words that would achieve what he wanted. At Leni's interruption, his mind stumbled. For a moment he was unable to think.

Eva, her face red with anger, grabbed Leni by the shoulders and was trying to push her toward the door. Leni kicked at her and then sat down on the floor and curled into a ball.

Eva knelt and pried at Leni's hands that were locked around her knees in a surprisingly strong grip. "Get up Leni," she commanded, "and show some respect to your father and to me."

Leni yelled, "Go away. I hate you." She started to cry.

Johann stood up. As quick as a cat pouncing on a mouse, he scooped Leni into his arms and strode to the door with her. They heard his footsteps on the stairs as Leni's sobs faded away and then stopped. For the first time since she had been with them, Eva seemed uncertain about what to do. Her cheeks aflame, she stayed on her knees for a few moments, looking at the open door, her mouth not quite closed. Then she recovered and got to her feet, brushing off her skirt.

"This floor needs another scrubbing," she said, knowing very well that Magda and Anna Maria had washed it that morning. "You must get at it first thing tomorrow." The *Stube* grew so quiet that it seemed they could hear the tiny dust motes that moved in the warm October breeze coming in the open window.

When Johann finally made his way back into the room, Eva was seated at the table. His children still stood, their faces so sad that he wanted to close his eyes. He made no mention of Leni or what he had done to stop her cries. He sat and began to speak again as if he had not been interrupted.

"Your mother will spend time in the fires of purgatory until all stain of sin is cleansed from her soul. She waits there now, and we must find ways to shorten her time of atonement."

Magda and Anna Maria, Mathes and Lis, exchanged glances, uncertain of what their father wished them to do. Pitt fidgeted. Theiss, eyes round with innocence, asked, "Do you want us to kneel and pray for her right now, Papp?"

"Not now. Of course, you must say prayers for the repose of her soul each morning and evening for the rest of your lives, and I will do the same. But sacrifice is also needed, some penance that will be difficult for all of us and therefore pleasing to God. I have decided what it will be. From this time on we will no longer sing, not together or by ourselves, not in the house or in the fields. We will give up this pleasure forever to help your mother's soul make its way into God's arms."

He reached for the wooden crucifix that hung on the wall and lifted it from its hook. "I ask each of you to put your hand on this crucifix and swear in the name of our Lord and His Blessed Mother that you will do what I have asked."

Johann's children stared at him, not wanting to believe what they had just heard. They had always sung together. It was their mother's way. Their father was commanding them to give up their most precious memory of her. Anna Maria was about to protest but changed her mind. Her father's expression was uncompromising; his narrowed eyes dared them to disobey.

They filed past him, each placing a hand on the rough wood of the cross, taking the oath he required of them.

Johann did not believe that Maria's soul suffered in purgatory. He had lost his faith as his wife took her last, agonized breath. He did not believe in anything but the lonely bed he would go to every night for the rest of his life and the freshly dug grave in the cemetery. There was no sin, no kind and loving God who answered prayers. His belief in heaven, hell, and purgatory was gone; but the useless teachings of the church could stop the singing that mocked him with its reminders of all that he had lost.

Magda sat down on the straw-stuffed mattress where Leni lay on her side, left arm curled under her head, eyelids puffy and closed so tight that little wrinkles had formed at the corners of her eyes. She reached out and stroked the flushed cheek of her little sister. "What is the matter, *Kleine*? Why didn't you come when I called you? Are you sick?"

Leni shook her head and a solitary tear worked its way out from under her eyelid and hung on her long dark lashes.

"Then why won't you look at me? Tell me what's wrong." Magda waited for a response but none came.

"Did Papp strap you? Are you mad at him? Is that why you will not come downstairs?"

Leni shook her head again and another tear slid out from under her lashes.

"Are you afraid of Papp? What did he say to you when he brought you up here?"

Leni's eyes opened; they glistened with the tears she had been holding back.

"Tell me, Leni. What did Papp say?" Leni shivered and Magda pulled the quilt up to cover her.

"He said I can't sing ever again or he will walk through the death door too. He was crying, Mag. How can I stop him from walking after Mamm?"

Eva Kautenberger sat on the wagon bench waiting for Johann Rauls to come around to its other side, climb up to take the reins and start the horse moving down the road to Greimerath. She clutched her brown wool shawl tighter around her shoulders but not because of the November wind. It was the coldness of the man on whom she had pinned her marriage hopes that chilled her. Her dream of becoming Johann's wife and the mistress of this farm had disappeared as quickly as the dusting of morning snow that melted when the sun rose high in the sky. She kept her head turned away from Johann, looking at the plastered-stone *Einhaus* where she had lived for more than a month. So much had happened since she had come to its door with no thought other than nursing Maria and doing the work that Maria could not do until she recovered.

During the week of Maria's fever, while Eva had wrung countless cool clothes to put on her cousin's feverish forehead and tried to make her swallow just a few spoonfuls of nourishing broth each hour, she had barely noticed Johann Rauls. He was useless and in the way; she had no time for him. But when Maria died, all was changed. She was an unmarried woman living in the house of a still-handsome man who was suddenly without a wife. If she could remain with him until his grieving was over, making herself indispensable, there was every chance that he might see her as a mate who would ease his burdens and also his physical needs.

With that in mind, she had offered her help to him and stayed on at the farm. She willingly shouldered the housekeeping and farm chores that Maria had once done, even though Johann didn't seem to notice. He had sunk so deep into his sorrow that he rarely spoke to her, except to say *"Gute Nacht"* when he went to his bed at night. He did not join in the talk at the supper table and afterward sat silent in his chair in the *Stube* smoking his pipe. She knew it was too soon for him to do otherwise, but she longed for a kind word from him all the same.

The boys, Mathes and Theiss gave her little trouble. Pitt, the slow one, liked her and often sought her out, hoping to be praised for some task he had completed. She found it easy to be patient with all three of them.

The girls, Magda, Anna Maria, Lis, and young Leni, were quite another story. Their mother had been much too lenient with them, but Eva had not reckoned with the resistance she encountered when she tried to establish better order within the house itself. She scolded them and told them that the way their mother had taught them was not always the best way. She showed them the proper way to do each chore. She took them to task when a piece of work was not up to her standards. How else could they learn? She would not compromise, and she could feel their resentment whenever she was with them. After just a few days, all four of Johann's daughters rebelled in some way. Leni had temper tantrums and ran off without permission. Anna Maria was disrespectful, defying Eva and making fun of her when she thought Eva could not hear. Magda was coolly polite but resisted any efforts Eva made to befriend her. Lis ignored her, pretending not to hear her when she spoke to her.

Still, she had been surprised when, just two days ago, Johann had looked up from his supper, gazed at her thoughtfully, and said, "Your brother will need your help on his own farm now that we are approaching St. Martin's day. I am grateful for all the work you do for us, Cousin Eva, but you must be lonesome for home. Lis, Magda and Anna Maria are ready to take on your work, so I will hitch the horses to the wagon and drive you over to Greimerath after the Mass on Sunday."

"Certainly. It's high time," she said. Disappointment made her voice harsh.

Anna Maria made no attempt to hide how she felt about her father's words. She smiled widely as she saw the expression on Eva's face. Magda, Leni, and Lis kept their heads down but Eva knew that they too anticipated her departure with pleasure. Eva suspected that Magda had gone to her father and asked him to let her take over the household, but the instigator was Anna Maria. Without that girl's bad influence, the younger ones might have accepted her, even have come to like her. Her stomach knotted each time she thought about Anna Maria, so pretty and disdainful. She had everything that Eva longed for – youth, beauty, charm, and a way with men. When Eva had been Anna Maria's age, the lads of the village had treated her as if she was invisible. They had looked right through her at other girls, the ones like Anna Maria, who laughed and tossed their pretty heads, aware that they were desirable. Her soul cried out at the unfairness and longed to have some revenge.

Today she had packed her scant belongings in her willow basket and readied herself to return to Greimerath for the rest of her life. She had no illusions. Her hope of staying here with Johann was gone. Magda, Anna Maria, Lis and Leni would be happy to see the last of her, and their brothers wouldn't miss her for long. Johann would take as little notice of her absence as he had of her presence. Her chance at marriage had slipped through her rough, reddened fingers as she toiled.

Only Pitt stood waving goodbye as the wagon started to move. Eva blinked away the wetness of her eyes and set her lips in a tight, narrow line.

CHAPTER 7
Marriage and Disappointment – Spring/Summer 1834

On April 21, 1834, Magdalena (Magda) Rauls married Johann (Hannes) Rauls, the son of Peter Rauls and Catharine Muller. The two were first cousins and their marriage required a special dispensation. On Oct. 16, 1834, Magda's first child was born, 5 months and 25 days after the wedding. Information taken from: <u>*The Marriage and Baptismal Records of the Catholic Parish of Zerf, Greimerath, and Hentern.*</u>

There was talk and laughter at the Rauls' long wooden table on this Sunday in March, a rare occurrence in the months since Maria Rauls' death. The Archbishop in Trier had granted Magda and her first cousin Hanni an ecclesiastical dispensation from the Church law forbidding marriage of first cousins. They could marry next month as planned. The betrothal dinner, with Hanni, his father Peter, and his soon-to-be-married sister Katharina, was nearly at an end.

In preparation for this very special midday meal, Magda, Lis, and Anna Maria had baked the whole of Saturday and been up in the very early morning hours today. The smell of a pork stew simmering in the kettle hung over the fireplace had begun by the time the family left for Sunday Mass and by dinner time the aroma of the pork, cabbage, onions, potatoes and tart apples filled the house. The smell still lingered in the *Stube* after the last crumbs of the plum *Kuchen* disappeared.

The wine pitcher was passed from hand to hand, and everyone was smiling, even Johann Rauls. He slapped the wooden table as a signal that he wanted attention, and picked up the rounded, opaque wine mug. He made a toast. "To Magda and Hanni – long life, few sorrows, many healthy children," he said; and they all drank, even Leni who raised her mug of milk to her lips, then put it down and wiped the white mustache from her upper lip with her hand.

Johann's brother Peter, not to be outdone, raised his own mug high and toasted too. "To my son, Hannes who has chosen the finest *Mädchen* in Oberzerf as his bride-to-be." There was laughter and clapping as they all drank again. Magda's cheeks were red with her pleasure and embarrassment.

Uncle Peter was usually taciturn but now the wine had loosened his tongue. "Then, brother," he said, "when the Magda comes to cook and mind the house and help out in the fields for Hanni and me, you will miss her, for sure. Especially her *Kuchen*. Lucky there are three more daughters to take her place. You make *Kuchen* good too, Anna Maria?"

Mathes said, "Our *Kuchen* will be hard as an old leather strap when Anna Maria is in charge."

Anna Maria shook her finger at her brother. "Then I can use it to strap you when I'm the boss around here," she retorted.

"Magda, why do you have to leave us when you marry Hannes?" Leni asked as she sat beside her sister. They were in the kitchen with baskets of potatoes around them, removing the sprouts to keep them from shriveling before new potatoes grew and replaced the old crop.

Magda stripped the sprouts off of the potato she held and tossed it into the basket where its fellows lay, smooth save for tiny white spots that showed where each sprout had been removed. "That's the way it is when you marry a man, Lenchen. You go with him to the place where he lives. You will do the same when you marry."

The six-year old Leni shook her head violently, her dark eyes flashing. "When I get married, I won't leave the people who love me."

She took a large potato from the basket beside her, twisting off its sprouts as fast as the words came out of her mouth. "My husband will have to come and live here or I won't love him anymore."

Magda laughed. "Oh little sister, if only it was that easy. You can't just stop loving someone once you've started. It's not like stopping the wheel when you get tired of spinning."

"Why?" Leni asked.

Magda didn't answer the question. Instead she said, "Will you stop loving me if I go away?"

"*Ja.*" Leni tossed her potato into the basket. She turned her head away so that Magda could not see her face.

"That makes me very sad but it won't change my going. Truly, you won't love me anymore when I go to be with Hanni?"

Leni lowered her head and stared at her clogs. She was on the verge of tears when she looked back up at her sister. She whispered, "Don't leave us Mag. Mamm left us already. Please don't you go too."

"Come and sit in my lap, Lenchen," Magda said and circled her arms around her little sister, holding her very tight. "These arms that are holding on to you are my circle of love for you, my Leni,' she whispered. "This circle will never go away, no matter where we live, no matter how far apart. This I promise. Whenever you need me, my circle of love will find you somehow."

Leni turned her head to look back at Magda. "Can I come live with you and Hanni until Papp is happy again?"

Magda kissed the brown little cheek where a tear had made a streak. "No Leni. You must stay here with Papp. He needs you to help him to smile."

Three days before Magda's wedding, Johann Rauls walked to the stable with his oldest daughter, who was ready to take her marriage trousseau to her new home. On the farm wagon was his wedding gift to her, the hand carved wooden chest he had made. It was packed with her clothes, quilts, and linens and would go the short distance to her new home after the wedding.

Magda reached up, stroking the smooth surface of the trunk's flat lid and running her fingers across the carvings there. She could smell the rich odor of the oak wood. "Thank you again, Papp. My wedding trunk is the most beautiful anyone ever had."

"You have always made me proud," Johann's voice was husky with emotion as he drew a small pouch from his pocket and placed it in Magda's hand. "This belongs to you now."

Magda cheeks were flaming as she pulled the little cloth sack open. Inside was the thin golden cross that Maria Rauls had worn every Sunday that Magda could remember. She gave a startled gasp. "Why?" was all she could say."

"Your mother and I always said that this would be her gift to the first daughter to marry. I gave it to your mother on our wedding day. I thought she would give it to you; but since she cannot, I do it now."

Wiping the tears from her eyes, Magda kissed her father's hands. She wanted to throw herself into his arms and cry, but she knew she must not. She loved him too much to ask him to carry both his mourning and her secret. Carefully, she returned the cross to its pouch and slipped it into her dress pocket. "I will treasure this as long as I live," she said. Father and daughter shared the same thought; that the woman who had last worn it would not be with them to tie the cross with its slender black velvet ribbon around Magda's neck on her wedding day.

On Monday, the 21st of April, six months after the family had gathered in mourning at Maria Rauls funeral, her daughter Magda stood before the altar of the same church and took the hand of her cousin Hanni, promising God, Father Guckeisen, and the assembled congregation that she would love, honor, and obey her husband for the rest of her life.

Magda wore the dark blue linen overdress that Aunt Maria Bernardi had worked at lovingly through the late winter months, embroidering delicate white flowers on its fitted, low-necked bodice. Today they stood out against the deep blue of the dress like white apple blossoms against a twilight summer sky. The white blouse beneath it, shirred at neckline and wrists, was partly covered by her mother's silk-fringed red shawl, and she carried a small bouquet of blue violets tied with a white ribbon. Her new husband Hanni stood tall and uncomfortable in his starched collar and brown double-breasted jacket with its silver buttons, his dark hair newly trimmed, leaving a narrow white band of untanned skin where neck met hair.

When the wedding Mass ended, and the marriage documents had been witnessed in the sacristy, Magda and Hanni walked hand in hand down the aisle into the welcoming sun outside. A warm playful breeze tugged at jackets, skirts, caps, and bonnets as relatives and friends clustered around, waiting their turn to wish the couple well. Magda's face glowed with her happiness, and her dimpled cheeks grew more and more rosy as men and women, young and old, kissed her there. Her chestnut braids began to escape from under her ruffled white bonnet. It was a day of joy, softening the memory of that other day when this same family had emerged from this church and followed Maria Rauls' coffin through the churchyard toward the cemetery.

Anna Maria realized soon enough that being the woman of the house had many drawbacks. Her work never ended, and she lacked a lot of the skills she needed. She had not learned as much from her mother and her sister as she had thought. Chores that had looked simple when Mamm or Magda did them were maddeningly complex. Sometime she burned the bread; sometimes it still tasted of dough. Her brothers groaned when she brought sticky dumplings in watery broth to the table. Her thread on the spinning wheel was usually too thick or too thin. While she was tending to the chickens, she forgot the pot on the hearth and it boiled over. She went to her bed exhausted each night, wishing she had paid more attention when Mamm had tried to teach her.

Leni was Anna Maria's faithful shadow. Already she had a knack for sewing and loved sitting next to her far-less talented older sister and mending while Anna Maria told ghostly tales or made up funny stories. The ugly stepmother always resembled cousin Eva.

Even though Leni tried to help, in the two months since Magda's wedding, the flax yarn that had been turned into linen cloth on Herr Koltes' weavering loom and which was meant to be made into new tunics and overdresses lay unstitched. Many pairs of pants that needed patches still had holes. The yarn for knitting socks was undisturbed in its basket, and a tiny spider had already made a home there. In the beginning, she waited with apprehension for her father to call her to him and reprimand her for a household that grew more untidy each day. May came and went; then June and July. Her father uttered no harsh words. He barely seemed to notice.

By the time the hot days of August arrived, Anna Maria had stopped worrying about the many things left undone. On nice days when they were not working in the fields, she took Leni to the cool woods to look for berries that they squeezed into juice or to find the mushrooms that could be dried and then added to their winter stores. With trial and error, she learned how to bake almost-golden loaves of bread, and her brothers stopped complaining about the food she fed them. She tackled the mending with Leni's help, and her stitches, though not perfect, were neater. Next year at this time, she said to herself, Papp will be just as proud of me as he was of Magda.

It was an unseasonably cool night in late August when Magda came to make her confession to her father. Instead of sitting on the wooden bench outside the window, Johann sat smoking his pipe in the *Stube* because the winds were from the west and had a chill about them. He had not seen his daughter these last two weeks. They had all been busy in the flax fields and Hanni's fields went east from the village while Johann's lay south and west.

Johann looked up as he heard the sound of the door latch turning. Magda walked into the room. The light was already dim but as she came toward him he knew what she would say to him. Her overdress and apron did not hide her swollen stomach any longer. She stood before him, her cheeks as red as if she had a raging fever.

"I'm going to have a baby in October, Papp," she said.

He looked at her as if she were a stranger. Magda was his virtuous daughter, always honest and modest in her actions. When Magda and Hannes had been so insistent on marrying right before Hanni's sister wed and left their father's house, he had never suspected there might be another reason to marry Magda quickly.

"We only did it once, Papp; please do believe me. It was in January after we all missed Mamm during the Christmas days. Hannes was comforting me one night and we sinned." Her voice trailed off.

Hannes should be here with you, he thought. You did this thing together. He had taken such pride in her virtue, his Magda. It was Anna Maria he had watched closely and distrusted, never Magda. His anger rose up from under the sad darkness in him. It tasted bitter in his mouth, like poison. He feared it might come out in terrible words so he set his lips together to keep them back. Nearby, a wagon's wooden wheels rattled along the gravel road. In the distance he could hear a meadowlark. They were such ordinary sounds, hardly a fitting background for his anger or Magda's fear.

Leni walked into the hallway on her way to fill her empty bucket with water and she was happily swinging it at her side. She stopped when Magda's next words drifted into the hallway through the open door of the *Stube*.

"Papp, we never meant it to happen. Hannes and I beg your forgiveness for sinning before marriage."

Without speaking a word, either of condemnation or pardon, Johann stood up and walked to the window, turning his back on his daughter. He stood motionless while she cried and pleaded for him to speak to her, to tell her that he forgave her. Finally she stopped and the room was silent except for the sound of a fly that buzzed and bumped against the windowpane. Then there were footsteps and Magda found herself face to face with little Leni who was hurrying to the door, a look of shock on her face. Magda followed Leni outside but said nothing as she left her father's house.

From his place at the window Johann watched Magda walk away down the rutted road in that evening's soft purple twilight. So many eyes are out there, he thought, and so many clucking tongues. The village women will stare at Magda and ignore her greeting as they meet her in the road. Or they will watch her at a distance from a nearby field or through an open window and blame me for being lax with her. There will be whispers and snickers from the men. "Have you seen the Magda, the wife of Hannes Rauls? Big already she is. I think that girl had a little Hannes in the cellar when she walked up the aisle on her wedding morning." Magda, even though married now, was stained forever in their eyes – and in his.

The next day he did not work in the flax fields with everyone else. He hitched his horse to the wagon and made a trip to Greimerath to visit Maria's cousin Eva. His Maria had been the invisible cord that had held his family together, and it had begun to unravel, separating into fibers that were frayed and weak. He must do something to repair it.

By church decree, Magda, like every other woman who had given birth, was unclean for nine days afterward. Hanni, his father, and his sister Katharina did the "woman's work" of the farm because Magda could not take the milk from the cow nor pour it in the pitcher lest it sour, could not bake or cut the bread lest it mold and harden after only a day. She was not even allowed to draw the water from the well for it might be filled with bugs thereafter and no longer fit to drink. A few men said that these were only superstition made up by old women but none of them were willing to put it to the test when their own wives gave birth.

On the tenth day Magda left the house for the churching ceremony. This was a ritual of purification, blessing, and re-entry into the life of the village. *Tante* Mari, who had been her midwife, walked with her to the little chapel church. They arrived to the sound of the bells signaling the start of the "low Mass," where the prayers would be spoken in Latin and not sung. As was the custom, the midwife Rauls had baked a special loaf of bread for the ceremony. She carried it in a cloth-lined basket that hung from her arm.

When they entered the church, Magda, hair neatly braided and almost concealed by her white bonnet, took the very last place in the church. She knelt on the hard wood of the floor. There she would stay throughout the rest of the service. Her father, brothers and sisters occupied benches at the front of the church along with Hannes and his father, *Tante* Mari, and the other aunts. Some of the old women of the village were there too. They came to every Mass celebration, aware of the short time left to them to prepare for the day when God would call them to him for an accounting of their deeds, both good and evil.

After the Mass ended, Father Guckeisen returned to the sacristy and came back to the sanctuary wearing only his surplice and stole over his cassock. Flanked by two altar boys, one of who carried the large, leather-bound book that contained the liturgical prayers of the Church and one who held a small glass container filled with the water that had been blessed on Easter Saturday. He opened the gate of the communion railing and walked down the aisle. When he reached Magda, the priest took the leather book, grasped the long white ribbon that trailed from it and opened it to the page which he had marked. He prayed "Enter into the temple of God, adore the Son of the Blessed Virgin Mary, who gave you fruitfulness of offspring." He dipped his fingers into the holy water and made the sign of the cross over her.

Magda stood up and Father Guckeisen held out the tip of the delicately embroidered silk stole to her. Magda took it and the small procession came back to the front of the church. As they reached the communion railing, Magda knelt and Father Guckeisen turned to her and prayed, "Almighty, everlasting God, through the delivery of the Blessed Virgin Mary, You turned into joy the pains of the faithful in childbirth; look mercifully upon Your handmaid, coming in gladness to Your temple to offer up her thanks; and grant that after this life, by the merits and intercession of the same blessed Mary, she may merit to arrive, together with her offspring, at the joys of everlasting happiness. Through Christ our Lord. Amen."

He dipped his hand into the blessed water, and made the sign of the cross over Magda once more. Tante Mari brought the basket that held the loaf of bread. She placed it on the wide communion railing, removing the cloth that covered the loaf. The priest blessed the loaf and using the knife that lay in the basket, cut a small slice and ate it. Mari cut the rest of the bread into thin slices, offering it to family and friends. The old women smiled as they took it; it would taste of long gone memories when they chewed it.

More fresh baked rye and apple bread next to pots of honey and preserves lay on the family table at the big house where Magda and Hanni lived with Uncle Peter. No one sat to eat. They carried their food with them as they clustered around the chair where Magda sat with baby Helena's cradle next to her. The aunts admired the perfection of the new baby, passing her from one to another while they gave Magda advice about her care. They congratulated Hanni and predicted the next child would be a boy. Their talk and laughter was a little too exuberant, too loud, as they pretended that they did not notice the shadow of shame that hovered at the edges of the room, an uninvited guest.

When Johann took his first grandchild in his arms, her perfection brought him little joy. The girl child was as pretty a babe as he had ever seen, but she was also undeniably one that had been carried in her mother's womb for a full term. Such a child could not have been made in the marriage bed less than six months ago. She had been conceived in sin, and everyone in the room and in the village of Oberzerf knew it.

After only a few moments, he handed baby Helena back to Magda. Both had been irrevocably changed on the August night when she had held out her arms to seek forgiveness and had received cold silence instead. They had made a fragile peace, but they no longer trusted one another.

The young ones, Theiss and Leni, laughed with excitement as each one took a turn holding the baby girl.

Pitt gave his father his wide innocent smile. "I'm so happy for the Magda. She didn't have to wait hardly any time at all to get a baby." The room grew quiet but Pitt didn't notice. His brow furrowed a little as he thought. "Do we still call her Magda, now that she's got a baby and is a Mamm?"

Johann's anger emerged as a venom-covered dart of a reply. "Call her hasty just like everyone in the village does." He was sorry as soon as he said the words but there was no way to call them back.

"Did I ask something foolish, Papp?" Pitt asked as he heard those around him draw in breath." Lis and Mathes had heard the gossip, knew how babies were made. They exchanged glances, and then studied their shoes. Hannes clenched and unclenched his fists as he saw Magda's eyes fill with tears.

Hanni's father, *Onkel* Peter, broke the shocked silence. "Pitt, it is a wise boy who asks a question when he is not sure. You must still call your sister Magda, just like you always done."

Anna Maria tossed her hair and gave her father a defiant look. "Mag was a mother to all of us after Mamm died. We'll always call her our little stand-in Mamm." She took baby Helena from Leni and put her in Pitt's arms. "Give her your thumb, Pitt, and see what she does."

The baby's little fingers curled around his thumb and Pitt let out a whoop of laughter. Everyone else laughed too. The bad moment had passed. The room grew noisy again.

The other grandfather, Hanni's father Peter, sat in his chair next to the cast iron *Takenplatte* which conducted waves of heat into the *Stube* from the fire he had made in the kitchen fireplace to fight the chill of this foggy October day. He did not see why Johann was so angry about a little tumble in the hay before the wedding day. Hanni and Magda were not the first young ones to do it and would not be the last. People forget after awhile. He tried to steer his brother's thoughts away from the baby. "Johann," he said in a voice that carried to all the corners of the room, "I hear that the Anna Maria is pretty near as good a housewife as Magda is. One of these days some young guy will come to you and ask to marry her, just like my Hanni did after he and the Magda fell for each other. It was an unfortunate choice of words. Magda's face reddened and Johann glared at Peter, his jaw clenched.

"That's just what I fear, brother," he said in a low, tense voice. "To have another fallen daughter. That is why I have thought to have a good and moral woman keep the house for us in the future. I want everyone here to know that I have invited Maria's cousin Eva to live with us again. She will come to us soon."

Every person in the room stared at him, startled both by the harshness of his treatment of his oldest daughter and by the idea of Eva Kautenberger returning to the village. It was unheard of for a man with a daughter almost twenty to have a housekeeper, especially a woman that was still of childbearing age. Was Johann considering a new wife? In the quiet room, the aunts pretended they had not heard, or if they had heard, not understood the significance of what Johann had just said.

Anna Maria's chin came up and she held her head high, daring anyone to think that she was hurt. Lis and Leni looked up at their father, eyes dark with disbelief. For them the pleasure of the day and the new baby had drained away as quickly as wine pours out of a pitcher.

Peter Rauls hesitated before making his reply to Johann. He was a gentle man, many years older than his brother, and those years had taught him much. Although he wanted to defend Magda and Anna Maria, he knew it would only make matters worse. He said the only thing he could, "So—the *Fräulein* Eva will be back. When does she come?"

"The middle of November."

Pitt looked from his father to Anna Maria where tight-lipped anger was slowly replacing her pretended indifference. He asked, "What's the matter? Don't you want Cousin Eva to come back, Anna Maria? I like her. She cooks good."

"I think so too," Theiss said. "She makes dumplings much better than Anna Maria." He saw the expression on Anna Maria's face and added apologetically, "But Anna Maria makes good bread now." There was nervous laughter as Mathes applied his knuckles to the top of Theiss' head and said, "Do you have a brain in there. It sounds hollow."

Johann Rauls slowly chewed a piece of crusty rye bread, but it could have been made of straw for all the pleasure he could find in it. He had vented his anger twice today and insulted both of his daughters. It would have been better, he knew, if he had awakened on this morning with the throat pain that took away the voice and made one so hoarse as to be mute.

That evening Johann had a hard time going to sleep. Magda's pale, sad face was there whenever he closed his eyes. He loved her; why did he have this deep, angry urge to punish her? He wished that he still believed in God. He wanted forgiveness but could not bring himself to ask it from his daughter. God's forgiveness was distant and impersonal, a confession made to and forgiveness given by a priest whose face was hidden behind a curtain.

He let his mind stray to Eva Kautenberger. He knew that when she moved in, the village women's tongues would wag until there was enough wind to dry the hay. Let them blow. While the *Fräulein* Kautenberger was keeping watch on his daughters' virtue, her own was safe from him.

It pained him, though, that Anna Maria was so angry with him. It would be a good thing to have tasty food and mended clothing again, but his sole purpose in bringing Eva here was to protect Anna Maria from the dangerous road her sister had chosen. And trouble always seemed to follow Anna Maria, even when she meant well. She had a loving heart, but was too impulsive, too passionate. She would also influence Lis and Leni. In time Anna Maria would get used to Eva. She had no choice.

As he felt sleep coming, his mind drifted further. Eva had never married. It was said that she had never been courted. Maybe most men, like he himself, did not find her face or her outspoken ways attractive. But she would be a good helpmate. And making love was done in the dark mostly. A sharp tongue might become gentler when it was used for kissing.

On that same evening, Eva Kautenberger sat up late sewing by lantern light. She worked in the cramped little room that held her bed, her storage chest, and the ancient four-legged stool on which she sat.

She was picturing the day when she would leave the wretched little farmhouse she shared with her brother and his wife and travel to Oberzerf. She hardly noticed the cold draft that came in through the room's small window. God had answered her prayers after all. In January she would go to the Rauls' farm, this time for good. Everyone knew that when a widower invited an unmarried woman to take up housekeeping for him, an eventual marriage had to be the outcome. "Frau Rauls," she whispered to herself.

CHAPTER 8
The Big Wash – October 1834 to April 1835

In the spring, along with cleaning the house from top to bottom, the housewife had to do the "big wash." During the long winter, a mountain of wash had accumulated and all had to be made fresh and clean by the time Easter came…Morette, Jean, <u>Landleben im Jahreslauf.</u>

On the last Sunday of October, Eva Kautenberger arrived at the Rauls' farm, bringing her storage chest in a two-wheeled cart that she and her brother Gerhard had pushed all the way from Greimerath. Gerhard would be described as a square of a man, squat and solid with a bull-neck. His farm was so poor that when it was time to plow, he did not have enough money to rent a horse from a wealthier farmer unless he earned it by breaking stone at the Greimerath quarry.

Johann Rauls and Eva had agreed that he would come to Greimerath after *Martini* to collect Eva and her possessions and bring them to Zerf. He was as bewildered as his children when Eva and Gerhard arrived much sooner than expected. For Anna Maria, Lis, and Leni it was a disappointment of major import: to lose a dozen or more days when they would still be free from the scoldings that were sure to begin with Eva's arrival was a calamity. Johann, although puzzled by this change of plan, was glad that the many unfinished household chores that his daughters had happily ignored under Anna Maria's supervision would be dealt with much sooner than he had expected.

As if the weather was an indication of things to come, the sky was dark with murky clouds, which as yet merely rolled with the winds, their purple edges predicting a storm that was building force and surely would break soon on this unexpectedly mild November day. The smell of rain, which had already started to the west, was in the air.

Leni watched with wide eyes as Gerhard pulled the heavy wooden chest from the cart and hoisted it to his shoulders as if it weighed no more than a featherbed. Anna Maria glared and Lis' mouth tightened noticeably when Eva opened the door to their house and then showed Gerhard the way up the stairs, already taking charge.

"Are you girls going to stand about staring all day?" she called back over her shoulder as she followed Gerhard, her voice sharp. "Your chores are waiting, are they not? I will be down to work with you in a little while." A look, easy to read, passed among the three sisters before they separated company. Their father turned his back and started off to the threshing floor to clean as much grain seed as possible before a storm hit.

Eva opened the door to the big square room that the Rauls sisters shared, and Gerhard put the chest where she pointed, at the foot of the bed that had been Magda's. Eva and Leni were to share it; Anna Maria and Lis would sleep in the other.

"Thank you, brother," Eva said.

"Welcome," Gerhard answered. They looked at each other for a moment. It seemed there was nothing else to say. He turned and left the room, shuffling down the wooden stairs to the door. Outside, he shouldered the poles of the cart. The sound of its wheels bumping along the road quickly faded into the distance.

Eva knelt before the wooden chest that held her under linens, her summer shawl, her church bonnet, aprons, and rough linen work blouses. One blouse was new and made with a finer weave. It had a low neckline, embroidered with red berries and shirred with a red ribbon that would hint at the ample bosom just below it. She smoothed its fabric, thinking of the coming summer when she would wear it on festival days and how Johann might undo the bow at night and place his strong hands where no man had ever touched her. Johann must still have needs, just as I do, she thought. She felt no guilt as she daydreamed. Within the marriage she imagined, caresses and kisses were pure and holy things.

She closed the lid of the chest, got up and looked around her. She was the lieutenant making the first inspection of the new barracks under her command, moving with determination and an eye to the future. It was high time, she thought, that someone took this house in hand. Her gaze fell on the room's only window and then on the little mirror that hung beside it. The film of dust on the mirror's surface was disgraceful. As she ran her apron across the mirror to clean it, her image stared back at her. She saw a strong, large-boned woman, well into her childbearing years. The face in the mirror was plain and angular with a prominent chin and long nose. Thick brown eyebrows that matched the color of her tightly braided hair overshadowed dark eyes that were small and short lashed. Two vertical frown lines, seldom smoothed by a smile, lay on each side of the bridge of the pointed nose. Eva Kautenberger was no beauty, and she knew it. No matter, she thought. Johann Rauls will discover that a woman can please her husband in other ways.

She surveyed the bedroom once more before she turned toward the door. It would do quite nicely for the time being though it hadn't been well cleaned for her arrival. She would set that right, along with many other things around this house that needed doing. She planned to be in charge for a long time.

The storm that had threatened broke, and the day turned to darkness almost as black as night.

Standing side by side with the brims of their linen bonnets almost hiding their faces, Frau Wagner and Frau Thielen cast surreptitious glances at Eva Kautenberger as she strode along the road as if she owned it. In the months since she had come to Oberzerf, Eva had offended first this one, then that one with a sharp retort or with a frown when a smile was required. She made no friends among the women of the village. Soon she was greeted only with stiff politeness. Once she was out of hearing, there was gossip and discussion about her status in the Rauls' household.

"I seen the *Fräulein* Kautenberger when she and her brother brought her chest to the Rauls' house," Margaretha Wagner was saying to her neighbor, Katharina. "She acted like a bride-to-be. I wonder what she had inside. Maybe her trousseau?"

"My Pitt saw that too," Katharina answered. "Her head was held so high and proud, he said, that she must have strained her neck muscles."

Margaretha whispered, "I asked Father Guckeisen if there were any church announcements of new marriages coming up this Sunday?"

Katharina shook her head at her neighbor's audacity. "The nerve you have, asking our priest such a thing. He knew that you were asking about the living arrangement at the Rauls' place." Then she added, with a wicked smile, "What did he say? Did you get him to tell you?"

"He asked if there was some couple I had in mind. What could I answer? I told him what I wanted to know."

"*Ach du lieber Gott!* You didn't! What did he say to that?

"He said that when I come to the Holy Mass this Sunday, I will know as much as he knows. My face was red then, I tell you."

Katharina Theilen laughed, "Johann Rauls told my Pittchen that he brought the *Fräulein* Kautenberger here so she can teach his Anna Maria and Lis what they need to know about keeping a house, cooking, baking, and such like. Do you think she is just a servant, working for bed and board and a few coins to spend?"

"Depends on where the bed is."

The two women went back into their houses laughing.

Almost everyone in the village gossiped about Eva and Johann. The men drinking and playing a hand of cards at the Gasthaus nudged each other and made jokes when Eva passed by the door. The women raised their eyebrows in speculation when Eva came into the church followed by Johann and his children. Those with relatives in Greimerath told stories about the time years back when another man, newly widowed, had courted her; then spurned her for an Oberzerf girl. They said that it had turned her sour as a green apple.

Johann paid as little attention to the village gossip as he did to the woman who was its subject. Eva had reintroduced good order to his home. The food she prepared was wholesome, the house was kept clean, clothes were mended, chores completed. He sat in his chair each evening, satisfied that his children were being watched over and cared for and that the woman in charge seemed capable and reliable. The undercurrents of suspicion in the village and the unease around him at home did not often penetrate the gray, sad world in which he continued to live. He did not notice that Leni had stopped making up poems, or that Anna Maria and Lis neither fought nor laughed together as they had once done. He rose before the dawn, worked until after dark, and went early to bed day after day, grateful for a body so tired that his brain could hardly think.

Each week, he paid Eva the small salary he had promised her. At the end of March when he laid the coins in her hand, he said. "I am grateful for your good care of my children and my house, Cousin Eva. I hope you know that. We are fortunate to have you here."

That night as she lay in bed beside Leni, Eva lay sleepless, thinking of those words, savoring them as a nobleman might roll the first mouthful of fine wine around his mouth to relish it before enjoying the remainder. Surely it would not be long now before Johann asked her to share his bed. She imagined his body touching hers and went to sleep before the smile left her face.

The early days of spring took the entire Rauls family as well as Eva into the fields to plant potatoes and grain. The long narrow fields of winter-packed ground were covered with dead vegetation and sprouting weeds, a gray green crust that turned brown as the plow made furrows in it. Johann forced the plow's handles into the ground and trod behind the oxen. He first broke the earth with Pitt holding the yoke of the larger of the two animals to keep the team moving evenly. The air began to smell of mud and new beginnings.

When the plowing had loosened the earth, everyone worked. Johann and Pitt dug deep rows for planting the potatoes. Leni, Lis and Anna Maria carefully placed cut seed potatoes in the furrows, or they moved along the shallow rows holding an ox horn with its tip cut away, trickling flax or barley or rapeseed into newly made trenches. Eva, Mathes and Theiss closed the furrows, using shovel or hoe. They all labored from early morning to late evening during the planting season, stopping only to take the lunches that Eva prepared for them at the beginning of each day and placed in a large willow basket they had carried to the fields with them. When stable and household chores called the women home, the planting went on but with fewer hands and more rests for the remaining workers.

Lis, Leni and Anna Maria envied their brothers who could stay in the fields until dark, far away from the demanding Eva. It seemed that, no matter how hard they tried, they mostly fell short of Eva's expectations. There was nothing they could complain to their father about. There was no physical punishment given. Eva punished them in other ways--with a few stinging words or a scornful smile that said her worst expectations had been met. After awhile, Lis just set her jaw, and tried not to pay attention when Eva scolded. Anna Maria glared at Eva or gave her a defiant little smile and worked on. Leni watched for the deep frown lines that appeared between Eva's eyebrows. That meant that something unpleasant was about to happen and she moved closer to the outside door.

One autumn morning when Eva's brow furrowed as she drew in breath to scold them, Leni turned and ran through the door to the road. She heard Eva shouting for her to come back but ignored the command. She didn't know where she was going but she had to be away. In the meadow she stopped, turned her face up to the spring sun, and saw a flock of storks flying south. Here she might be left in peace. She sat on the meadow grass that looked dry but wasn't. As the damp grass stained her skirt, her fingers teased a fuzzy caterpillar and she listened to the song thrushes. When she came back to the house, Eva ignored her until bedtime; then she was made to say prayers of contrition until Eva and Eva's God were satisfied.

Once the planting season was over, Eva turned her attention back to the household chores and the big spring wash. Leni, Lis and Anna Maria had forebodings of a wretched week ahead, but no one in the family could have foreseen the dangerous changes that were coming.

True spring arrived in Oberzerf in late April. On a day when there were signs everywhere of the earth waking up and stretching to push new green shoots ever higher, a day when the air that came in through open windows held the smell of furled blossoms trying to escape from cozy buds, the crisis that had been slowly building since Cousin Eva's arrival was about to emerge too.

Eva sent Anna Maria and Lis to the kitchen to begin the preparations for the big wash, which was done only once a year. While Lis went to the well and drew buckets of water to fill the large pot that was mostly used to mix the pig slops, Anna Maria piled extra wood on the fire in the fireplace, tending it until it burned hot. When the hog kettle was filled with water, both girls lifted it and hung it on the moveable hook that protruded from the back wall of the fireplace. While they waited for the water to heat, they brought in the big wooden tub from the stable and set it on the stone floor to await all the soiled things that needed their soaking from their winter accumulation of soil.

Eva and Leni went from room to room, gathering together bed linens, undergarments, work clothes, curtains, bed and pillow covers – all the things that were either deeply soiled or dingy from the effects of the smoke of wood fires and infrequent winter washing. They layered armload after armload into the big wooden tub, until it was nearly filled to the top.

"Can I trust the two of you to finish up with the water and ashes?" Eva stood with hands on hips, implying that she questioned Anna Maria's and Lis' ability to handle the rest of the procedure for the daylong lye soaking of the tub's contents.

Anna Maria narrowed her eyes and gave a curt nod of her head.

Lis, her back turned, watched the pot of water that was nearly boiling. She didn't bother to reply. Her temper boiled too.

Eva waited a moment, her face reflecting her conflicting thoughts – should she say the bitter words that came to her lips or refuse to show that she was angered by the two girls' near defiance. She turned abruptly and left the kitchen.

Anna Maria made a face at Eva's departing back. "Can I trust you, you idiot girls who never do anything right? Can you pour water in a tub? Can you find the ashes? Do you have any brains inside those empty heads?" she mocked in a quiet scornful voice as she walked to the tub and chose a large linen sheet from the pile inside. Leni giggled, pressing her hand to her lips.

"Help me with this sheet, Leni, please." The kitchen was warm and steamy; Anna Maria's hair under her cap was damp and escaping into curling strands. She tossed her head to clear the hair away. Her cheeks were hot and a headache throbbed at her temples.

Leni took up two of the ends of the rough linen sheet and together she and Anna Maria positioned it over the top of the oblong tub, one end trailing and ready to be folded back up to cover the ashes when they were distributed on the bottom half.

"Thank you, Lenchen; that was a big help," Anna Maria said. Leni's eyes glowed. Praise was in short supply these days.

Anna Maria went to the hearth where the big ash bucket filled with the gray-black remnants of winter fires stood waiting. "Wait; I'll help you lift that," Lis said and started toward Anna Maria as she bent to pick up the heavy bucket.

As Lis came quickly across the hearth, she stepped on the long handled fireplace shovel that had dropped there and her ankle turned. Anna Maria saw the danger and lunged forward to stop Lis from falling into the fireplace, but she couldn't hold on to the heavy bucket of ashes as well. The bucket went clattering to the stone floor as Anna Maria grabbed Lis, pulling her backward. Both girls tumbled to the ground. There were ashes everywhere.

Eva ran through the doorway. She saw two stunned girls whose arms, hands, and clothes were ash-covered. She asked no questions, assuming the worst. "When will you be able to do something right, Anna Maria?" she said. "I give you a simple job and still you make a mess of it. A twenty-year-old maiden who still gets more ashes on herself than in the washtub. What a wife you will make for someone. Clean up that *Schweinerei* before there are dirty footmarks everywhere." She strode out of the room.

Anna Maria got to her feet and looked at the bucket where only a few ashes remained. She bit her lip but said nothing. Lis, the shock of what had almost happened keeping her sprawled on the floor, was completely speechless. Anna Maria helped Lis up and wiped ashes from the younger girl's skirt, apron, and knees, then from her own dress. "Is your ankle all right?" she asked Lis.

Lis took a few tentative steps. "I'm not hurt."

"She got it all wrong," said Leni. She took a broom and tried to sweep the ashes into a pile. "You saved Lis from falling into the fire, Anna Maria. Why didn't you tell her?"

"Would it make her treat me any better?" mumbled Anna Maria. "She hates me; whatever I do is wrong." She busied herself with a brush to clean the floor of the ashes that the brooms left behind, attacking them with its stiff bristles. Her vision was blurred with the angry tears that she vowed she would not shed.

When the ashes were back in the bucket, Lis and Anna Maria sprinkled them over the section of the sheet that covered the washtub and brought its other half up, making folds to keep the ashes in place. Together they lifted the pig pot from its hook and carried the boiling water to the tub, pouring the water on the ash-filled sheet. While their wash sticks swirled the acidic solution through everything in the tub, even the pieces at the very bottom, Lis brooded as she worked. She and

Anna Maria were like the water and Eva like the ash. When they mixed together, they turned into lye.

An uneasy truce reigned in the Rauls house the next morning. Lis and Anna Maria's anger smoldered and their self-control was like a strained seam about to split apart. Eva was armed with the self-righteousness of one who, through no fault of her own, has been insulted. No one spoke. Trying not to look at each other, they scooped the dripping articles from the lye water, bundled them into large baskets, and dumped them into the wheelbarrows that stood outside the door. When they finished, both wheelbarrows were piled high. Anna Maria pushed one, Eva the other as they headed for the banks of the *Grossbach* stream. Lis and Leni were left behind to empty the washtub and clean away the water that had been spilled on the floor.

Two years before, Anna Maria had gone to the stream with her mother. The other village women there had laughed and chatted with Maria Rauls who scrubbed away at stains or dirt not removed during the soaking. She handed pieces to Magda and Anna Maria who beat them with the wooden wash paddles. And that night Maria had kissed them both and called them "My strong girls who work so hard to help their Mamm."

Some of the village women were already at the stream when Eva and Anna Maria arrived. They laughed and called to each other, sharing tidbits of gossip. Frau Müller, on her hands and knees, looked up from the bed ticking she was beating, "You get prettier every day, Anna Maria. I bet the young men are lining up at the church door, wanting to walk home with you."

Anna Maria smiled in spite of herself. Eva thrust the wash paddle at her and moved far away to beat and wring the smocks and sheets that were piled in her own basket. Some of the women exchanged glances. Then they went back to their washing and their gossiping.

Eva and Anna Maria said nothing to each other on the walk home with their baskets of clean, wet laundry. When they reached their house, Eva said, "Start hanging the wash to dry. At least there you can't spend half of your time admiring your face in the water." It was a cruel remark and Eva knew it but could not stop her tongue before the words were out of her mouth.

"Do it yourself," Anna Maria shouted, flinging the wet clothing she held in her arms at Eva. "You're an ugly, horse faced bitch - did you see that in YOUR water." She turned and ran into the house and up the stairs to the sleeping room as Lis and Leni stared after her and Eva shouted, "Your father will punish you for that."

Johann Rauls did punish Anna Maria, but not in the way that Eva had wanted. After he heard Eva's version of the story, he called Anna Maria to him. He told her that after their supper and the evening chores, she was to kneel with her face to the *Stube* wall where the crucifix hung and pray the rosary aloud until she could say she was sorry and beg forgiveness of Cousin Eva. At midnight, Anna Maria still knelt, voice hoarse, repeating one "Hail Mary" after another. Johann told her to go to bed.

For the next three nights the punishment was repeated but Anna Maria would not yield. She prayed aloud, her face as hard as the stones of the floor on which she knelt. No words of apology were spoken. Anna Maria still showed no signs of remorse or of yielding. Johann wanted to end the punishment but without diminishing his authority. Would he have to whip her with his belt? She looked so much like the young woman he had courted, loved, and married. The whipping would punish him more than Anna Maria. So the praying continued until he sent her to bed each night, ignoring Eva's disapproving eyes.

"I'm going to get away from here; you see if I don't," Anna Maria said to Lis and Leni as she pulled weeds in the garden and then used her spade to turn the soil which soon would be planted with cabbage, potatoes and beets. It pleased her to see Eva's face in each clump of ground when she attacked it with her hoe and ground it into fine soil.

"Why don't Papp send her away," asked Leni. "Don't he know how mean she is?"

"She's not as mean when he is near us. It's when he's working in the fields and cannot hear - then she shows what she is." Anna Maria rested on her hoe for a minute. "He will not believe me if I say she is cruel, not you either. Without Mamm, he is not the father we once knew." He thinks if our clothes are clean and the work gets done, there is nothing else we need."

The afternoon of the fourth day, a stranger driving a wagon pulled by two brown oxen hailed Johann and his sons as they walked along the road to one of their most distant fields. The wagon carried a ladder, hayforks, shovels, two geese in a cage, and a basket well filled with straw used as packing around some breakable dishware. Obviously he had been to a farm auction. Probably some poor, misguided farmer and his family had decided to leave their homeland and go to the new country called Amerika. Johann did not believe the stories about cheap land and no taxes to pay; sold at a cost so low that anyone could afford to buy more *Morgen* than the *Gut* owned by the Count who lived in that palace-like house on the hill overlooking Saarburg.

The young man called to them, "Do you know of any family around here named Rauls? I think the wife was a Kautenberger." Johann walked to the side of the road and studied the man in the wagon. He had never seen him before. "My name is Rauls," he said, "and my wife, Maria, was a Kautenberger.

"Was?" the man questioned.

"She died a year ago last autumn." Johann's face did not show the deep, unrelenting pain he still felt.

"So sorry, Herr Rauls," the stranger said, "I did not know that. I am very sorry for your loss. May God give her eternal rest."

"Why are you looking for us?" Johann asked, wanting to turn his mind away from Maria's death.

"My name is Michel Annen, and I live in Paschel. I'm a neighbor to an old woman who is your wife's third cousin. She, Frau Susanna Theilen, sent me to ask a favor of your late wife."

"A favor," Johann repeated. "You've come too late, as you see." He gave a bitter half laugh and turned to walk away.

"Let me finish, Herr Rauls," the young man called after him. "Frau Susanna too has suffered loss."

Johann paused and turned around, unable to show rudeness to anyone who suffered the same pain he himself carried. "I send my condolence to Frau Thielen."

"I will tell her. All of us in the village wish we could change the bad way life has treated her; it does not seem fair that such a good lady should have to bear so much."

Johann didn't want to hear it; how could anyone pity an old one so close to death. Why not her in the grave, not Maria!

The man went on with his telling. "It was her only son who just died. He married but never had children. Lost his wife to the influenza just a year ago. Now he is gone too. Frau Susanna is our good neighbor, always generous to all of us *Kinder* when we were growing up. She was a strong woman once. Used to work all day long in the fields. But these last few years she has been taken with a strange illness. It makes her hands and head shake all the time and her legs are getting so weak she can hardly walk. Nothing seems to help her. Some of the old women think she is possessed, but thanks be to God the priest says no. That is why I was coming - to ask your wife if she could send one of her daughters to help Frau Susanna if she could spare her. But you have too much hardship, what with your own wife gone so early."

Puzzled, Johann asked, "How could one of my daughters help? They know nothing of nursing and certainly not of hexing."

"It isn't nursing or hexing that's needed. What she surely needs is an extra pair of hands to keep up the house, cook some meals, and tend the garden. We've been trying to help Frau Susanna, my wife and I, but Margaretha will have our first child soon. We are stretched too thin to keep up all the extra farm work and the house chores besides. Susanna thought that maybe one of your daughters could come and stay for a while."

Johann pondered. He had begun to see a way out of the impasse that he had created in his home.

The sun had set and the room was in deep shadows. The sounds of the village children playing came through the open windows. Anna Maria was on her knees in the corner of the *Stube*, beginning a new decade of the rosary, "Our Father, who art in heaven," she prayed, her words sounding not like worship but like angry darts aimed at the woman sitting on the bench by the table.

Eva laid aside her knitting, got up from her stool, and called through the open window, "Leni, Theiss, Pitt, come in right now and be off to bed." Theiss and Pitt stopped their game and approached the house. Leni still crouched by the bush at the front of the door, watching a ladybug crawl up her arm. Eva strode to the door and called again, then came outside and tugged Leni to her feet. Leni's ladybug flew away as she was pulled into the house, her head still turned in a vain attempt to see where the insect that brought luck had gone.

Johann had made up his mind. When he heard Eva's steps on the stairs, he spoke quietly. "Anna Maria, come here." His daughter stood up slowly and came to stand before him, eyes defiant. He studied her for a moment before speaking. Except for the light brown hair, a lock of which escaped her bonnet and fell along the side of her face, she was the picture of her mother. The oval face with its blue-green eyes, delicately slanted brows, and the sprinkling of freckles across her cheeks and nose, were all her mother's. It was a copy of the face that had looked up at him, sweet and mischievous, after their first night together in their wedding bed.

He hardened his heart because it was the only way. "You have been disobedient, disrespectful and rude to the woman I have chosen to run this house. You still refuse to apologize and make amends for your bad behavior. This cannot go on. It is clear to me that you are unhappy that *Fräulein* Eva is living here in my house. Therefore I have told your mother's cousin that you will come to help her for a time. It will be necessary for you to live with her. She lives in Paschel and the walk there and back each day would be completely impractical."

"Walk to Paschel? Papp, what do you mean? Anna Maria took her father's hand. This had to be a bad dream. She shook her head hard, trying to awaken.

Johann was still speaking. "On Sunday after Mass I will take you there. Please go to bed now and begin to think about what you wish to take with you."

For a few minutes more, Anna Maria stared at him in disbelief. Then she nodded and, moving like a sleepwalker, left the room.

On Sunday, Anna Maria put her few clothes in a basket that she carried over her arm. She tearfully kissed her brothers and sisters goodbye. Lis and Leni did not cry until the wagon disappeared up the road. Mathes patted their shoulders awkwardly as both girls gave in to their unhappiness and sobbed. Theiss swallowed hard and wiped his nose on the back of his hand. Pitt looked from one to another, not able to understand that Anna Maria was really gone. Leni wondered who was going to keep the family from becoming as despondent as Papp now that there was no Anna Maria to make them laugh sometimes.

Eva watched from the window of the *Stube* and thought that her troubles were over.

CHAPTER 9
Klöpfelnacht and Memories – November 1835

November 30 is dedicated in the evangelical, catholic and orthodox church to Saint Andreas the Apostle, the brother of Saint Peter. The eve of the Saint's feast, Nov. 29 for a long while was one of the few ways by which the poor could earn a meal during the winter season. The feast of St. Andreas was also a traditional time of "oracles" for girls who pray to the saint for a husband. A girl would peel a whole apple without breaking the peel and throw the peel over her shoulder. If the peel formed a letter of the alphabet, then this suggested the name of her future groom."

Leni sat on the bench in the hall and waited for another "*Klöpfel,*" a light knock on the door. It was the night of November 29, the "*Klöpfelnacht*" when, in honor of the feast of St. Andreas, the landed farmers and prospering townspeople gave a warm meal to families of the landless day workers and craftsmen who had much less than the well-landed farmers did.

How different it had all been last year. Anna Maria and Lis had been in the kitchen that night, making batches of onion cake and the sauerkraut soup that they would hand to anyone who asked; struggling families who had so many mouths to feed and perhaps not even one small piece of rented land for their own use.

When the last bowl of the soup had been served and their own suppers eaten, both Anna Maria and Lis had stood in the kitchen, the long apple peel that had no break in the skin from top to bottom in hand, ready to be tossed over their shoulders. Lis had protested that this old custom made no sense. How could the peel of an apple tell you the first letter of the name of the man you would marry? But when Anna Maria tossed the long curling peel over her shoulder, Lis did the same. Then they both stood studying the peels.

"It looks like an 'N', do you see it, Lis, Leni?" Anna Maria said. "It's an 'N'; I'm sure of it."

Lis, always hard to convince about anything, stared at the peel, deep frown lines on her face. "It looks like a 'B' to me," she said.

"You can't see a 'B' there," Anna Maria protested. "Leni, come look. Is this a 'B' or an 'N'?" Leni thought it looked like neither. But she knew what answer Anna Maria wanted and she loved Anna Maria. "It is an 'N' for sure," she said confidently with a defiant look at Lis who was scowling at her.

"You haven't learned to write the alphabet yet. How would you know?" Lis sneered.

Leni's chin jutted forward, "I watch when Theiss makes his letters, and I know all of them. I practice drawing them in the dust sometimes."

"Lis, yours looks like a 'P'. I bet it's for Peter Müller." Anna Maria was examining the peel that Lis had tossed. "I've seen him looking at you at Mass on Sunday. He watches you the whole time we are in church."

"Maybe he looks at you. He wonders why you are always looking over at the aisle where the men and boys sit and how come you are not praying like everyone else,' Lis retorted. No one ever got the last word with Lis.

A timid knock at the door brought Leni back to the present, and she jumped up to answer it. She was the doorkeeper on this St. Andreas night, and the *Fräulein* Eva and Lis were stirring the soup in the kitchen while they fried potato pancakes. No one would be peeling any apples.

She opened the door to Maria Kramp who stood waiting with a large empty kettle over her arm. Maria was two or three years older than Leni and no longer in the school, needed by her family to work in the fields. At times the Kramps helped in the Rauls' fields to earn money or to be given a small part of the harvest. They knew they could expect generosity at Johann Rauls' door on *Klöpfelnacht*.

Leni took the kettle from Maria and went to the kitchen. When she came back, the pungent smell of the sauerkraut mixed with heavy cream, bread, and onions steamed in the cold hallway.

"St. Andreas blessings on you and your family." Leni said the formula prayer as she handed the steaming kettle of thick soup along with potato pancakes wrapped in a square of rough linen cloth to the girl who stood like a statue in the flickering light of the one candle of the hallway.

"*Danke*. And yours as well," Maria Kramp answered and turned away quickly, to hurry home while the soup was still warm.

Leni returned to the bench and wondered, for the hundredth time, about the subtle alteration in the relationship between her father, the *Fräulein* Eva and Lis, which had started in the autumn after Anna Maria left. The harvest days had been filled with the usual hard work in the fields along with the house and stable chores, but ever since the day of the church festival, Eva's focus had shifted away from Leni, away from everyone except for Papp. Eva's head turned to watch whenever Papp was about, her eyes following his progress around farmyard or field the way a flower inclines its stem to seek the light. Lis too had become watchful, stopping her work to cock her head and listen whenever Papp and Eva were nearby. At all times, Lis and Eva kept a wary eye on each other. Had they been dogs, a low growl would have come from deep inside them as they moved into range of one another.

Leni hoped that Anna Maria had been able to toss her apple peeling again this year.

Anna Maria was also in a kitchen, helping *Tante* Susanna make onion cakes for anyone who might come knocking at her door. She, too, was thinking about the previous year's Saint Andreas *Klöpfelnacht*. She missed her brothers and sisters, especially Leni and Pitt; but she could not go back to her father's house very often because the *Fräulein* Eva still expected an apology, and Anna Maria's body stiffened whenever she saw Eva. When she looked at her father, it was with a longing for love so interwoven with anger that it kept her at arms length from him. While she wanted with all her heart to rush to him and ask him to forgive her, she wanted the same forgiveness from him. So both father and daughter waited and the distance was not crossed. Anna Maria went back to Oberzerf only for the holidays, pleading *Tante* Susanna's need to have someone always nearby. It was a half-truth, for in fact, the neighborhood women were friendly and more than willing to look out for the widow Theilen for a day or two if Anna Maria wanted to visit her family. She could have gone each month, but she didn't. She had gone back at Easter and again for the mid-summer celebration, staying with Magda where there was an empty bed. She and Magda had not been great friends until Mamm had died. The one good thing that had come from all of the agony of Mamm's death and Eva's coming was the love that she and Magda now felt for each other. Magda, the good sister, had made the same kinds of mistakes that Anna Maria did. They began to trust each other with the feelings that both had kept so hidden before. The result was a sisterly bond that was healing and protective for them both.

Anna Maria once again lost concentration and the apple strip she had been peeling for her St. Andreas eve foretelling broke. Even at the best of times, Anna Maria had little skill with a paring knife. Last year Lis had teased her about her attempts, saying that Anna Maria would remain an old maid and the family would have to go without apples all winter long.

As if she had been listening in on Anna Maria's thoughts, the *Tante* Susanna called from her chair, "Anna Maria, when will you have an apple peel long enough to find the name of your true love?"

"Soon, *Tante*, soon," Anna Maria said. "*Majusapeta*" under her breath as another peeling fell apart at mid section when her knife went out of control again and the strip became too narrow.

"Perhaps we must ask the neighbor Michel for a little nail to keep a peel in one piece for you." The *Tante* laughed in such a good-hearted way that Anna Maria laughed too.

"If this apple that I am starting does not give me one long peel from top to bottom, I shall go and get the hammer and nails myself."

"It is good for me to have you here, girl. You always make me feel good," *Tante* Susanna said, and Anna Maria thought, "If just one time I could hear my Papp say that, everything would be all right with me."

Then she smiled, for she had an unbroken piece of peel at last.

Magda too had made the Sauerkraut soup and potato pancakes for the St. Andreas feast, but unlike Leni, she was glad that a full year had gone by since the really bad days that began a short time after the Andreas night last year. Two weeks after St. Andrea's day, their little Helena had developed the diarrhea that killed at least a dozen infants every year.

By the time the tiny corpse lay motionless in the wooden cradle, shock mixed with lack of sleep had robbed Magda of emotion. She might have been made of wood. She could only stare at the body while Hanni stood beside her, silent sobs shaking his shoulders. She turned away and went to their bed, crawling beneath the quilt to try to warm herself as her body shivered. It was sleep that she wanted. She closed her eyes and let the emptiness claim her. Within minutes she was asleep.

When she awoke, Hanni was not beside her in their bed, and she called out to him, groggy from her deep sleep. As she said his name, memory came back and so did her husband, back from the *Gasthaus* where he had gone to ease his own suffering, drinking one strong *Schnapps* after another until he too could not feel.

It was so dark in the room that Magda could hardly see him, but she heard his lurching steps as he stumbled into their sleeping room and the low gurgle that came with the spewing of the contents of his stomach onto the treasured little rug, made by her mother, that lay next to their bed. As Hanni fell into the bed beside her and began to snore, she got up and washed the rug, then sat up for the rest of the night holding her dead baby in her arms, as she rocked back and forth and cried.

The next day, while *Tante* Mari prepared the baby's body for burial, Hanni had begged Magda for forgiveness. She had turned away without a word. When he tried to hold her in his arms, she slapped his face and screamed, "Damn you to hell; do not ever touch me again." She despised him for his weakness; she wanted to hurt him. Hanni stepped back from her, his hand to his face. This was a Magda he had never seen before.

That afternoon Magda went to the Oberzerf chapel to pray. She knelt in front of the statue of St. Anne and the Virgin Mary. Both were mothers. She begged them to bring Helena back to her. She started when there was a soft touch to her shoulder. It was Father Guckeisen's sympathetic face that looked down at her. He blessed her with the sign of the cross and asked, "Is there anything I can do to help you in this time of sorrow, Magdalena?"

"I have just asked Mother Mary and St. Anne to bring back my little one, Father," she whispered, "I asked them for a miracle. Will you pray with me?"

Father Guckeisen's eyes, magnified by the thick round little glasses he wore, were full of sympathy. He was silent, asking for the grace to say the right words, listening for the voice that came to him at times, telling him what to say. He heard it now. "I think you must make your confession to me, my daughter," he said and sat in the pew beside her.

When she heard those words, Magda felt the rightness of them. It would be a great relief if she could let go of the anger inside her, an anger she would have to give up in order to be forgiven. She gave no thought to walking to the confessional. No one else was in the little chapel. She bowed her head, eyes on the stones of the floor, and spoke to the priest of the suffering she and Hanni had inflicted on each other so soon after the death of their child. She confessed how much she had wanted to hurt her husband for his betrayal of her trust in him and the terrible words she had said to him. She kept her head bowed as she ended this unconventional confession with the traditional words, "I am sorry for these and for all my sins."

Father Guckeisen sat in silence, again listening to a voice that only he could hear. Finally he said, "All of us, Magdalena, have at some time disappointed or betrayed a trust and when we asked for forgiveness, it was refused or given grudgingly. But our Savior Jesus Christ always forgives us, always opens his arms wide to us and gives us another chance. He will do that for you when I say the words of absolution. All of your sins will be erased, forgotten by the God who says, 'I love you still.' But in order to be forgiven, you must not only be sorry for what you have done, you must forgive and make amends. Before you leave the church, you must say one rosary for each of the three months of the little Helena's life. Then you must go to your husband and forgive him fully as the Lord is about to absolve you. In addition, if there is anyone else in your life you have not forgiven, you must do so. Now, make an act of contrition."

It sounded possible when she was there in the church with the gentle words of the priest's absolution calming her and strengthening her resolution. But the doing of it, saying the words of forgiveness to Hanni, was quite another thing. For when she saw him on her return from the church, the memory of his drunken head spewing vomit as their child lay dead in the next room turned her tongue to a leaden chunk too heavy to move. She remained silent. They spent the day before Helena's burial as strangers, keeping distant from each other in physical space and in emotion.

As she lay in bed beside her husband on that evening after the day of hurt and silence between them, Magda dreamed of her father, who stood unforgiving as she held Helena in her arms, a Helena who had become so heavy that Magda could no longer hold her up. Hanni stood beside her, trying to help her but she pushed him away. "Papp, Papp," she shouted, but her father did not reach out to her. He stood unmoving while she cried and struggled and began to fall into a bottomless void. "Help me Papp," she screamed. "Give me your hand and save me." Her father, moving in slow motion, began to bend to her but it was too late and the void claimed her.

She woke with a start, her eyes streaming tears. The dream was so clear in her mind. Why had she rejected Hanni like that and turned instead to her father? She supposed it was because he had always been there to help her, strong and loving, at least until the time she had disappointed him. And then in a burst of understanding so strong that she gave a little cry, the meaning of the dream was clear. She had been the one person Papp had counted on the help him through the pain of Mamm's death and instead she had given him more anguish. And as she herself had just done with Hanni, he had lashed out at her because he felt abandoned by the one who should have brought him nothing but comfort. He had pushed her away before she could hurt him again.

Magda did not sleep for the rest of the night and in the early hours of the dawn when Hanni came awake, she took her husband in her arms. Silently they held one another for a long time in silent contrition.

"I'm sorry, Mag," Hanni finally whispered, his head buried in her shoulder. "I didn't know what to do to comfort you so I ran away. I'm a coward."

"Hanni," she sobbed, "our Helena is dead. I couldn't save her and then I failed you too. Just hold me." Her tears made long tracks down her pale face and Hanni wiped at them with his hand as he rocked her in his arms until long after her crying stopped.

Later in the morning, they held on to each other again while the small box that held the baby Helena was buried in the cemetery beside the church.

Johann Rauls had come to the burial. No words passed between father and daughter as he took her hand in his and held it for a moment, but Magda felt his sorrow in the gentleness of his hand on her shoulder and silently forgave him as she wept at her child's freshly dug grave.

Her reverie was interrupted by a knock at the door. It brought her back to the kitchen, the stove, and the *Klöpfelnacht* soup she was still stirring. She heard her father-in-law's halting steps and the sound of the door, which creaked a little as it opened. She filled the soup ladle, ready to give good measure to the kettle of whoever stood outside. She did not permit herself to look at the empty place near the fire where the baby's cradle had stood, but she said a prayer to St. Andreas, asking his intercession to bring her another child by his next feast.

CHAPTER 10
Moment of Truth – Summer/Fall 1837

The Saar River, so fascinating to Leni, flows for about 78 miles through the French Region of Alsace-Champagne-Ardenne-Lorraine and marks the border between France and Germany for about 7 miles until it flows into Germany, widens enough for larger boat travel and joins the Mosel River at Konz between Trier and the Luxembourg border.

By the time Leni was almost ten, life had regained a facade of cohesion that substituted for the mortar of love and trust that had once bound the Rauls family together. The *Fräulein* Eva had established an unquestioned authority in household matters; and although she sometimes showed a gentler side, especially with the boys, Lis and Leni kept their distance.

Leni learned that she could avoid Cousin Eva's sharp tongue by staying as close as possible to her father. The *Fräulein* Eva was always nicer to her when Papp was nearby. Her memories of her mother faded, and it seemed a long time ago that Anna Maria had been the woman of the house, turning the drudgery of work into fun by inventing madcap adventures for *Herr* Broom, *Frau* Water Bucket and *Fräulein* Scrubbing Brush. Once she was gone, solemnity ruled and boredom was Leni's usual companion as she did her daily chores. She accepted her life for what it was and dreamed about what it might become.

Lis did her work and made no effort to avoid the *Fräulein* Eva. She was stoic when Eva criticized or punished her, keeping her feelings to herself. It seemed to Leni that there was a tenuous truce between Lis and Eva, based on Eva's grudging admiration of Lis' self-control. Mathes was Lis' confidant while Leni was just a nuisance Lis accepted, like weeds in the garden or flies around the honey jar.

Leni saw little of Magda and Hanni. After baby Helena died of the infant diarrhea and Hanni's father, the *Onkel* Peter, was partially crippled by the apoplexy that had struck him down during the hay harvest of the early summer, Magda's eyes were often sad as Papp's. She and Hanni worked for long hours in the fields. They went to Mass each Sunday but they kept to themselves most of the time.

Leni had only Theiss to confide in. At first he had seemed to resent having two shadows, his own and the talkative one which was likely to bump into him if he turned too fast or stopped too short. But lately he had seemed glad to have Leni with him on his trips into the meadows and woods. Sometimes they would stretch out on their backs in the long grass of a meadow where patches of poppies and cornflowers swayed in the wind, finding names for the clouds that changed shape while they watched. Or, as they were doing on this warm summer evening, they would finish their chores and go barefoot through the fields to the *Grossbach* stream to dangle their feet in it and look for frogs and snakes until the light faded away.

"What do you think it would be like to fly, Theiss?" Leni asked as she watched a blackbird take wing from the branch of a larch tree. "What would it look like down here from way up there?"

"I bet we'd look like crawly bugs," he said. "Lucky for us we ain't. How'd you like it to be a spotted bug and have a bird snap you up in one bite?" He opened and closed his mouth; teeth making a loud click, to illustrate how fast Leni would disappear.

Leni ignored that. She wanted to talk more about the birds. "If I could fly, I would go right over those hills there so that I could see all the towns along the river," she told Theiss. I'd drop down to look into the houses in Saarburg and then I'd fly up again and watch the barges on the Saar go by. Or I could fly away to Trier and sit on the top of the tallest chimney there. I'd watch the people come and go to the market, and I'd sing my special birdsong for them. They'd look up to see what bird had such a beautiful voice. I would be the Lenibird, with rust feathers, a sky blue breast, and a white crown on my head."

"You'd probably croak like one of the frogs here in the creek," Theiss said. He wanted a water fight. But as he was bending down for a handful of water to splash Leni, a black fly that had been crawling along the collar of his tunic shirt moved to the back of his neck and bit him. Theiss jumped and swatted, splashing himself instead. "*Verdammt Fliege,*" he cursed.

Leni giggled. "You said 'damn.'" Good that Papp didn't hear that."

"You just said it too," he shot back at her.

Leni covered her mouth with her hands.

Theiss gave a wicked grin. "I'll tell *Fräulein* Eva. You'll be praying for an hour before she lets you go to bed tonight."

"Why does she like you and Mathes and Pitt so much more than me and Lis?"

Theiss considered the question. "Cause we're boys, I guess. She don't seem to like any women very much. She's got no friends to gossip with in the village; the women keep away from her. But more than us boys, the one she really likes is Papp. You've seen that, *ja*?"

"*Ja*. I think she'd do anything Papp asked her, no matter what it was. She might even have been nice to Anna Maria if he had asked her to be." Leni wanted to stop talking about this. It made her feel strange inside; like when she picked up a rock and found gray grub worms under it. She stared into the water, listening to the frog songs from the creek. They sounded of joy and their innate need to procreate and to increase their numbers.

Theiss ended the silence between them by throwing a handful of water at Leni.

Leni gave a little squeal and brushed the wetness from her cheeks. A nightingale hidden somewhere in the scrub growth of the woods began its melodious song.

"Theiss" Leni said, "don't you sometimes want to sing?"

"*Ja*, all the time. But we can never do that, Leni. Papp made us swear."

"I know," she said. How could she forget the day when Papp had talked about the death door? If she sang he would go away forever, just like Mamm. But sometimes a melody she remembered went around and around in her head, wanting to burst out of her; and she had to clench her jaw to keep it inside.

Theiss scowled at her "If you know it, then don't say anything about it anymore. It just makes it worse"

"But, if I was Lenibird flying along the Saar, that promise would not be mine. I could sing for hours, maybe a whole day" she said, having reasoned this out one day while listening to a song sparrow trilling for its mate. She had tried to imitate the sound, which was really not singing.

"You're such a *Doof Mädchen*, Gypsy. Wanting to be a bird. What other crazy things do you want?"

"To ride in a post coach, like that one that brings the mail to the *Gasthaus*. Her big brown eyes were focused on the road that led to Saarburg. "Then to sail on a barge on the Saar River and sail all the way to Trier. Maybe go on from there over the border to where the French people live. I'd talk to everybody. I'd ask them their names and what it's like to live in their village and whether they have some *Kinder* I could play with."

"You don't know one word in French. How would you talk to them? And anyway, women never get to do such. They got to stay home, slop the pigs, milk the cow, carry the water, and make food for the men." Theiss ran his fingers through his wind-tousled curls, laughing at her. You and Lis got to have the babies while us men have the adventures."

That made Leni mad. She cupped her hands, plunged them into the stream, and brought them up quick as lightening, aiming for Theiss' smug face. He yelped and wiped the water from his forehead and cheeks. As Leni was going back for more water, he jumped up and pulled her from her perch on the bank into the stream. "Soak you good, I will," he said. A flock of starlings flew out of the trees, startled by the laughter and squeals below them.

There were four rooms on the second floor of the Rauls' house. The big one at the top of the stairs was empty. Because the chimney ran through it, it was a good place for drying herbs and for a clothesline during the winter. Across the hall, kept warm by the animals in the stable below, were the sleeping rooms for the Rauls children. Pitt, Mathes and Theiss slept in one large bed in the back room that faced toward their fruit trees. The other room, the one that faced the road, had two beds, one of which Lis and Leni had occupied since Anna Maria left.

Eva slept alone in the other bed and wished that it were otherwise. There was still no hint from Johann Rauls that he wished to marry again. He lived each day as if it was a load he had to carry, one that he put down at night and took up again in the morning. His rare smiles were most often directed at Leni or Theiss, almost never at Eva.

So the first year went by followed by the spring and then the summer of the second. There was still no offer of marriage. But that was not what bothered her most. Eva, in her 35th year of life, had fallen in love for the first time. This new condition, this quickening of the pulse when Johann was near, the desire to take his tight cap of graying curls into her fists while she pressed her body against his complicated everything. She had started to desire this more than the security of marriage vows, and it made her timid when she should be bold and reckless when discretion was needed.

Each evening after her prayers, Eva lay quiet under her quilt; planning how she might bring the man she wanted to marry out of his self-imposed prison. Then she would ponder why, in spite of all her efforts, she continued to fail.

By the time of the church's harvest festival, the *Kirmes*, Eva had given up hope that Johann would ever speak of marriage to her. She sat alone on the stone wall beside the church while the festival swirled around her. She was like a stone embedded in a river bottom, somberly keeping its place while the current glided by. She felt like an outcast, gossiped about and disliked. There must be a way to change this, she thought as she sat there in the warmth of the mid-October sun, drinking from her mug of *Viez* and listening to songs that were beginning to sound a little off key from the effects of the alcoholic beverages. The sun was disappearing behind the forested hills to the west.

Late that night, when the festival was over and almost everyone else in the village was asleep, Eva still wore her best blouse and overdress. She sat on her bed, listening to the quiet, regular breathing of Lis and Leni who slept soundly after a day of fun and fresh air. She was thinking about a daring plan that frightened her with its potential for failure and heartbreak. As she pondered it, she heard a noise from downstairs. Johann was still up. She took it as a sign

In her stocking feet, she came down the steps, trying not to make any noise. But the boards creaked under her weight. The door to the *Stube* stood open and she could smell pipe smoke. She moved into the room and stood for a moment, looking into the shadowy room illuminated only by a single candle. Johann sat in his usual chair, as still as one of the stone statues in the church.

"Who is there?" Johann asked, sensing her presence.

She came to face him. "Cousin Johann, something makes me troubled. So I must talk to you."

He looked up at her. "What is it?" he asked, his face showing surprise that she stood there still dressed in her festival clothes at this late hour.

"The people in the village gossip about us more and more. They think we live in sin together. You must hear the whispers, the conversations that stop when you or I approach."

"Don't let it be troublesome to you. Let them *Klatsch*. You and I have sinless souls."

She hesitated before speaking again. This was a gamble, a roll of the dice, and she did not know what she would do if she lost. "I want no longer to be your housekeeper."

His look of dismay encouraged her.

"I want instead to be your wife, sleeping each night in your bed."

He looked at her, his face unreadable. His eyes moved from her face to her breasts, which pushed against the cloth of her low-necked blouse. His expression went back to its usual sadness. Eva counted her heartbeats and waited.

Finally he spoke. "For sure my bed is lonely since Maria died. I remember how good it was when she was in it with me, just the comfort of her body, so warm against me." His voice broke and he put up his hand to cover eyes that had begun to glisten with the tears he could not quite hold back. "Cousin Eva, I cannot marry you. I no longer could do what a husband does with a wife. You understand what I mean?"

It was not what she expected. She had been ready to bargain her way to a marriage proposal, planned what she would say if he responded to her with anger or indifference. She had not foreseen that he would tell her she could not arouse him. Humiliated and angry, she snapped, "So, I am not woman enough to be your wife? I can cook your meals, mend your clothes, and take care of your children but you cannot bear for me to be in your bed?"

He walked away from her toward the door of the *Stube* but after only a few steps he came back and took her hand in his. A little shiver ran through her; it was the first time he had ever deliberately touched her. "Understand me," he said. "I do not insult you when I say I will not marry you. You are a fine woman for a man's bed. But my Maria was the only wife I ever wanted. Since she died, I cannot do what a man does with a woman. I have tried. And I won't marry and hear all the congratulations, the joking, because it would be a pretense only, a mockery of the ceremony."

Eva stared at him, her mouth open a little. A trickle of sweat was moving slowly from under her right armpit down the side of her body. She wondered what woman in the village had not aroused him. Perhaps more than one could not. She whispered to him, "It's not yet so long since Maria died, maybe in time..."

He shook his head and dropped her hand. "I have learned that I have nothing to give; there never will be such a moment of pleasure again." He took her by the shoulders and brought her close to him. She could smell the pipe smoke on his breath. "When a man cannot do it even in his bed alone, he knows. Why do you make me tell you this to my shame." He gave her a little shake as he let go of her and walked toward the door.

Her common sense prompted her to leave him, to feel righteous anger, to walk past this man and his dark, lonely eyes, to retreat with dignity. From what seemed like a great distance, she watched an Eva she did not know. That Eva kissed his cheek and walked to the door of his sleeping room. Johann did nothing to stop her. The other Eva closed the door quietly, took off her blouse and overdress and hung them from an empty peg on the wall, sat on the bed and removed her stockings. She slipped under the quilt, still in her shift, waiting. Half an hour later, when Johann at last came into the room, she ignored the voice in her head that told her how foolish she was in loving this man who had nothing to give her. She held out her arms to him as he lay down beside her. She comforted him like a mother with a frightened child, holding tight to what was left of her dreams while he cried bitter tears and then drifted off to sleep.

Lis awoke shivering and reached out to retrieve her share of the quilt from Leni. The moon was full and the window not shuttered. *Fräulein* Eva's bed, closest to the window, lay in the path of the moonlight. Lis saw it was empty, the covers not even pulled back. The empty bed gave rise to her suspicions. She had seen and feared Eva's longing looks whenever their Papp was near. She got out of bed and tiptoed across the room to the doorway. She could hear little snores and the deep breaths of sleep coming from the boys' room. There was no other sound.

Using her hands and her bare feet to feel her way along the hall to the stairs, she crept downward into the kitchen. It was deserted. Embers still burned in the banked fireplace so she could light the candle that stood on its mantelpiece and go back into the hall with it. She pulled the stable door open and stepped inside. It was peaceful with the smell of hay, manure and animal breath. The *Stube* was dark and empty. The sleeping room was the only room in which Lis did not look. She put the lighted candle on the table and made her way back to the stairs where she sat down on the bottom step, head in hands. She thought of other reasons that the Eva would be missing from her bed. She could have tired of them all and under the cover of darkness gone back to her brother in Greimerath as she had often threatened. Or, robbers might have crept into the house, stuffed a rag in her mouth to prevent her from crying out, tied her up and taken her away with them. But she knew both of those ideas were formed from her wishes, not really possible. As she sat looking at the sleeping room door, she acknowledged the reality of what she had most feared for months now, that one night Eva would begin to share Papp's bed, where Lis had been born and where her Mamm had died. As she pictured her father's male part going into Eva, the events that had changed life so profoundly and the feelings that she had repressed so long began to rise like the kneaded bread dough placed in a warm place. They doubled in size. She was suffocating. Her mouth opened.

The first scream held all the tears Lis had not shed for her mother; it was the cry of an animal in pain as it feels the first bite of its predator. She heard it and was startled that she could make such a sound. She felt a kind of release as more wailing screams came. They mourned the loss of Anna Maria, her father's indifference, the undeserved punishments at Cousin Eva's hands, all the unfair things that had happened to their family in the past three years. Her ears rang with the sounds that came from her.

Eva had been lying awake in the bed when she heard the first creak of the stairs. She had thought it might be one of the boys going out to relieve himself, probably Theiss, judging by the light footsteps. She was glad of it; she and Lis had had to wash his mattress cover a time or two because he usually slept so soundly. She had waited for the scrape of the door against the sill, but didn't hear it. She had not wanted to get up to look because whoever was in the hall would see her emerging from this sleeping room. Johann should be the one to tell his children of the change.

The first scream did not completely wake Johann, sleeping with his back to her, and she began to shake his shoulders. At the second scream, his feet hit the floor and propelled him to the door, which he opened and quickly closed behind him as he went into the hall.

Eva left the bed, went to the door and eased it open a crack. It was Lis who made the hysterical sounds. Johann was shaking her but her shrieks continued. There were footsteps overhead and Mathes and Pitt came stumbling down the stairs. "Bring me a mug of water," Johann yelled and Mathes ran to the kitchen, returning almost immediately with the drinking cup that hung by its handle on the hook above the dry sink and water bucket. Johann took it and flung its contents into Lis' face. As if she had just awakened, Lis looked from her father to her brothers while she brushed water from her eyes and hair with the sleeve of her nightgown.

"What's the matter with you Lis? Why were you screaming?" Johann's hands were still on the girl's shoulders. When she didn't answer, he shook her again, but more gently. "Tell me what makes you scream so in the middle of the night?"

Lis lowered her head. "A terrible dream," she said. "I had a terrible dream."

Johann released her shoulders and stood up, bringing his hand to the back of his neck and rubbing it. "Go back to bed, girl," he said, "Try to go back to sleep."

Lis still seemed stunned. She made no move to get up. Pitt sat down on the step and put his arms around his sister, wrapping her in a bear hug. Eva could see Lis' expressionless face, eyes staring at the sleeping room door.

Leni slept soundly the night after the festival and woke with a smile on her lips. Yesterday she and her friend Katharina had eaten *Kuchen*, drunk apple cider, linked arms with the grownups to sing drinking songs, and danced with each other, spinning wildly until they were dizzy and bumped into anything or anybody in their path. When they saw the *Fräulein* Eva coming toward them, they had darted away together, running down the road laughing until their sides hurt and they tumbled to the ground to catch their breath. They had pushed away their white bonnets and let them hang at the center of their backs. Leni's thick dark curls and Katharina's fine brown tresses tumbled loose in the wind, brushing their temples and tickling their noses. "I wish it was *Kirmes* every day," Leni had said, the perfection of the moment already slipping away from her toward a tomorrow of chores and heartaches that hovered just outside her knowing.

Leni dressed and went to the stable to do her morning chores. The darkness had not yet been pierced by the sunrise when it was time for breakfast. As everyone ate the day's first meal of bread and *Haferbrei* porridge, Eva, Lis, and her father avoided looking at one another. Leni watched them, wondering why there was more than the usual amount of tension in the air. Pitt was uneasy too; his eyes moved from one face to another, the questions he wanted to ask wrinkling his forehead. When they had all finished eating, they gathered their baskets and potato forks and made for the fields where the potato vines waited patiently for the earth around them to be turned over and the golden tubers dislodged.

The leaves and stems of the potato plants were faded and brittle, no longer needing the sun that was slowly rising in the east. Pitt, Mathes, Theiss and Papp each chose a place in the field and began to dig their forks deep into the brown dirt under each potato hill, reaching down to grasp the stem and shake it until the clinging potatoes helplessly fell to the earth where Leni, Lis and Eva knelt to gather them into baskets. Leni always thought of digging for treasure when she saw the round, golden brown potatoes, some large, some small, and all emerging from the ground. She would try to guess which hills would have the most treasure hidden beneath them. She brushed away most of the caked dirt from the potatoes and gently tossed them into the baskets she had brought with her. Her hands probed around the edges of the gutted potato hill, careful not to mistake a hidden potato for a lump of dirt or a rounded stone.

Usually Eva kept a sharp eye on the sun, shouting when it was time for Leni and Theiss to start for the school in Zerf. Today she didn't seem to hear the church's bell ringing the start of the school day. She was watching Lis and Mathes who had paused in their work and stood facing each other. Lis spoke softly to her brother, eyes wary. The expression on Mathes' face changed until it looked the way it had the day he had stretched up his arm to feel inside a sparrow's nest in the stable eaves and touched the decaying baby birds inside. He stabbed his shovel into the next potato hill with an intensity that suggested a long-standing blood feud with this crop.

Theiss dropped his shovel, gave Leni a brotherly shove and the two of them left the field behind to start the hike along the road to the school. Leni begged her brother to tell her what was wrong with everyone; but he was as puzzled as she, for he too had slept through the night without waking.

Johann did not want to admit his need for Eva. He did not love her, had no desire to make love to her even had that been possible. Yet she had given him a precious if fleeting thing when she came to his bed. The touch of her hands stroking him, her body pressing against his had brought him a comfort he had not known since Maria died. He had drunk it in like a shriveled plant given water and now with the third anniversary of Maria's death just passed, he longed to ease the pain of remembering by lying in Eva's comforting arms again.

Just before St. Martin's day, Johann and his sons applied a fresh coat of whitewash to the drying room at the top of the stairs. They moved *Fräulein* Eva' trunk and the bed into the front corner of the room and used a hastily made tall and wide wooden clothes cupboard to form a third half wall and curtained entrance to Eva's new sleeping space. It smelled of potatoes, onions, drying savory, thyme and other herbs that were stored in the larger part of the drying room. Johann also replaced the creaking wooden boards in the stairs.

The *Fräulein* Eva now had a sleeping room of her own. Leni gave a little whoop of pleasure when the last of Eva's belongings were carried across the hall. She waited for Lis to smile. But Lis only sat on the stool near the window, her lips set in a hard line. She said not a word. She was not the same since the night of her screaming. The anger that had been inside her for so long, once released, had left her empty.

She had become so hollow that she sometimes wondered if a sharp gust of wind could send her airborne over Oberzerf and into the deep forest, and whether she would cry out if it did. She didn't think so. Her eyes looked out of her head, observing things without any feeling at all. She was a stranger passing through her own life.

During the days that followed, her father and Eva went on as if nothing had changed, though clearly it had. The *Fräulein* Eva had her own sleeping room, a room which was almost as unused as it had been when it held nothing more than drying onions, herbs, and mushrooms gathered from the *Wald*. Lis lay awake each night until she heard the faint rustling of the curtain that covered the entrance to Eva's room, the quiet footsteps in the hall and the sound of the door to her father's sleeping room closing with the faintest of sounds. It was only then that she would allow herself to drift off to sleep. She did not know why she had to listen for these sounds every night. Leni was in deep slumber beside her in the bed they shared. But her own body lay stiff until she had suffered and survived once more the nighttime ritual of her father and cousin Eva in bed together.

It was a cold, sunny day in late October. Hanni Rauls was walking along the Oberzerf road on his way to the Gouveneur gristmill when he saw Lis coming from the direction of the *Schurpenberg Wald*. On her back she carried a woven basket that was filled with dried branches gathered from the floor of the forest for use in the fireplace during the upcoming winter. Their paths had not crossed since the church's harvest festival, and Hanni was struck by the change in Lis. There were dark circles under her eyes, eyes that had lost their old imperious flash. She looked like she was sleepwalking.

"How goes it with the Lis today? How many hearts have you broken this week?" Hanni made his voice overly cheerful to try to free Liz from the distant place where she was locked away.

Lis just looked at him, as if to say that anyone with a brain the size of a nail head could see that things were not as they should be. Hanni was not insulted. He was encouraged to see that the old Lis, the one who did not suffer fools gladly, was not entirely gone. He waited for her to speak, to tell him what had caused this change in her; but she just tried to walk past him, her shoulders hunched as if the basket on her back was filled with chunks of rock from the Greimerath quarry. The flash of feeling she had shown was gone and the apathy had returned.

Hanni reached out and grasped her arm to stop her. "What is wrong with you then, Lis? You feel bad about something, I think. Maybe you should go talk to Magda."

"Just let me go. No one can help. It is done, and I will live with it until I'm old enough to go away like Anna Maria."

A stranger glancing at Hanni would certainly call him a plain man, indistinguishable from hundreds like him. A head that was disproportionately large topped his short, slender body and the dark, thick curls made it look larger still. His mouth was crooked and his nose very long. But his eyes were what everyone saw. They were a deep soft brown, surrounded by thick lashes, and they could fix on someone with so much kindness and empathy that the people who knew him, including his wife, thought him very handsome

As Hanni's eyes searched her face, it seemed to Lis that he could see deep inside her, to where her despair lay. Since it was as if he already knew what she would say, she found the words to tell him. "Papp and the *Fräulein* Eva sleep together. She goes to his bed when she thinks everyone is asleep. But I hear it. I know that they are sinning together every night."

Lis began to pound her fists against Hanni's chest, as a few small tears, quickly followed by many others, trickled down her cheeks. Hanni stood shocked into stillness while Lis hit him. Was his father-in-law himself living in a state of sin after he had humiliated his daughter and son-in-law because they had conceived their first child on the wrong side of the blanket? He shook his head to clear it and then caught Lis' wrists and held them in his large hands until she stopped struggling. When she finally stood quiet and drained, he transferred the basket of twigs from her shoulders to his, put his arm around her waist and started toward his house where Magda and a warm fire waited.

"Your Papp don't deserve forgiveness," Hanni said to Magda after the door had closed behind Lis. Anger tinted his face to the color of the red clay fields. "Just think how he insulted you in front of our family and friends at Helena's baptism and now to take that woman to his bed. We did our sin only once without marriage vows; and he acted like he was the Lord God himself, damming us to hell for it. Well, I wonder what the Lord God thinks of Johann Rauls and his whore." He kicked at the small stool that had been meant for use by the child they had laid in the cemetery at the age of three months. It crashed into the wall.

Magda bit her lip. Hanni was such a gentle man. She had never seen him this angry. She went to him and put her arms around his waist. "We have only Lis' side of this story, Hanni. Perhaps there is more to this than we know."

Hanni scowled at her and pulled away from her embrace. "Don't make excuses for him, woman. You heard the whole dirty story from Lis. She may be stubborn, but she don't lie." He turned his back to her, took his jacket from the peg on the wall, jammed his long *Zipfel* cap down over his ears, and left the house, slamming the outer door behind him.

Magda walked to where the three-legged stool lay on its side and righted it, then rubbed at the scuffmark it had made on the whitewashed wall, as if she could fix it with the touch of her hand. It was difficult to believe what she had just heard. She sat down on the little stool, her knees nearly touching her chin, and thought about her father and Eva under the wedding quilt that had come to the house as part of her Mamm's dowry. Did Papp and the *Fräulein* Eva really lay under it and do what she and Hanni did when the long day of work was over and before they fell asleep in each other's arms. She shivered, in spite of the warm fire.

CHAPTER 11
King John's Trip – August 1838

King John of Luxembourg was also the king of Bohemia. He was not a monarch who was interested in his subjects; he preferred to be on the battlefield. In spite of his blindness, he joined with the French in their fight with the English at the Battle of Crecy, binding a knight on horseback to his horse's left and right sides and commanding them to charge. In spite of his 50 other knights protecting this odd three-span knight on horseback, the blind king was killed there on the battlefield on August 26, 1346. In 1833, Prince Fredrick Wilhelm IV of Prussia, who was enchanted by the Rhineland's romantic scenery, visited the Saarburg region and, at the suggestion of the District Governor, decreed that the bones of the blind king should be brought to a chapel mausoleum to be built on the hill near Kastel. Klaus Hammächer, <u>Serrig; Landschaft, Geschichte, & Geschichten</u>*.*

The flax harvest was beginning and almost every farm family in Oberzerf was working in golden fields, uprooting woody stems and tying them together into bundles. Movement was everywhere as men in gray or blue linen tunics and visor caps, women in *Tertig* blouses under cotton overdresses and sun bonnets or straw hats labored on the hilly strips of land around the village.

Johann Rauls and his children were hard at work in the high field called "*Uber dem Rodenhaus.*" The August sun overhead was hot on their heads as they labored. Johann, Mathes, and Pitt worked side by side, seizing bunches of flax and uprooting them, almost in rhythm with each other. They paused occasionally to wipe their faces on the rolled up sleeves of their tunics, which clung to their sweaty backs. The long narrow field of golden flax swayed ahead of them in the light breeze, the stalks bending under the weight of the brown seed heads

Lis and Leni came behind, tying the flax into bundles. There was much to do if they were to finish the field tomorrow. From time to time Johann and Mathes would take the tied bundles and lean them together, placing them upright until the seed heads touched at the top and the rooted ends angled wide at the ground, allowing the air to pass through.

Lis was almost her old self these days. Eva was not in Oberzerf. She was beside her sister-in-law in the flax fields at Greimerath while her brother Gerhard lay in his bed, his leg broken. He had tried to stop a fight between two hot-tempered combatants at the quarry when one of them aimed a gravel hammer at the other and Gerhard's leg had received the blow.

Magda, recovering from the difficult birth of her second child, was not strong enough for the fieldwork with Hanni. During the day she stayed in her father's house, helping out with the kitchen and light stable chores while Eva was away. Theiss worked in Hanni's fields, taking Magda's place. In the evening, both families ate together in the house where almost all of them had been born. Leni thanked the Holy Mother of God every night for giving these moments of happiness back to her family and tried not to pray that Gerhard's leg never healed, keeping Eva forever in Greimerath.

The church bells pealed. It was high noon, time to stop to say the prayers of the Angeles and for the mealtime rest. They recited three Hail Marys and with them the three statements that told how God became man.

"The angel of the Lord declared unto Mary, and she conceived by the Holy Ghost.

"I am the servant of the Lord, be it done unto me according to they word.

"And the word was made flesh and dwelt among us."

When they finished praying, Mathes went to fetch the two baskets from the edge of the flax field where they had been placed this morning when work began. This flax field was far from their Einhaus in the village, which meant that the noon meal had to be eaten where they worked. The two woven willow baskets were packed with *Weinkraut* and *Zwetschgenmus* jam to spread on the slices of buckwheat bread.

Leni's mouth was watering as she bent to get her first food since their early breakfast. Her stomach growled so loud that Mathes shouted, "Run everyone, I heard a wolf howl." Leni's face burned red as everyone laughed at her, but she reasoned that the hint of a smile on Papp's face was worth the humiliation.

Their field was one with a border of a few trees at one edge. Other family groups who had also been hard at work on their own strips of land were coming to sit in the shade provided by the oak and beech trees' leafy branches. Villagers greeted each other but each family group kept to itself. This was not the time for gossip. Eating had to be done quickly and the work begun again.

After his father had taken a piece of bread, heaping it with the soft mixture of sauerkraut and apple pieces stewed in wine, Mathes broke the silence. "Papp, almost everybody in the village is going to see the king's bones come down the river on Sunday." He was trying again to win his father's permission for such a trip. "Please say we can go with *Onkel* Nikolaus and *Tante* Mari. They are taking their wagon to Serrig and will have room for all of us. From there we could at least watch at a distance."

Lis and Leni listened intently, silently willing their father to give his permission. In two days it would be Sunday. They, too, wanted to watch as the coffin of King Johann of Luxembourg, was brought from the town of Mettlach to the just-completed *Klause*, the crypt built to hold those five-hundred-year-old royal bones.

Their father had finished the *Weinkraut* and bread and started on a second helping. With his free hand, he tugged at a weed as if he had the throat of the emperor in his grasp. "The Prussian *Kaiser* taxes us until we can hardly feed our families but builds a splendid tomb for a king who has been dead for 500 years. What has been spent would buy two good cows for every farmer in the villages from here to Saarburg. No one should go to honor such a waste of our money."

Mathes had rehearsed his argument in his head all morning and now he was ready to speak it. "You are right Papp. The *Klause* is a foolish thing. But it is already built. Nothing changes that. Why not at least take a small pleasure in what our *Thaler* have bought. We are entitled to that much, aren't we? "

Johann Rauls' dark eyebrows drew together. He said nothing. Mathes' refused to give up and let that subject drop. He went on. "There will be a splendid procession and speeches by all the dignitaries. Such a mausoleum as they have made at Kastel is the envy of all the *Rheinland*. The trip to see the *Klause* and watch the procession will cost us nothing but some time. Please, Papp, if we go, we will be able to tell our children and grandchildren about it. This chance will never come again."

Leni held her breath and watched her father's face carefully, wondering what he would answer. He has not yet said no, she thought, and with Papp that was almost like saying yes.

Johann frowned, wiping at the sweat on his forehead with the back of his tunic sleeve. He turned to the willow basket to get another slice of the dark bread, this time with jam. "You make a good point that I had not considered, Mathes, and even though I do not approve of the Emperor's son and this wasteful *Klause*, perhaps you are right." Johann Rauls said no more. He spread a thick layer of the plum jam on his bread and Mathes did the same; wise enough to stop talking when he had come this close to victory.

The next day they were back at work in the field. It was cloudy yet somehow hotter than working in yesterday's sun. Hidden behind the grayness of the clouds, the sun warmed the heavy air until it was almost like steam around them.

In spite of her discomfort, Leni's dark eyes sparkled. Papp had given his permission. The five of them; Mathes, Pitt, Lis, Theiss and Leni were to ride with *Onkel* Nikolaus and *Tante* Mari to observe the ceremonies at the *Klause* from across the river in Serrig. Tomorrow crowds of people would watch while the barge carrying the coffin with the royal bones of King John would make its stately way from Mettlach northward toward Kastel. And she, Leni Rauls, would see a part of that journey. She wanted to whirl and twirl until she was dizzy with the delight of it. Instead she tied another flax bundle.

"Lis, " she asked, "Why do you think the Crown Prince would want such a big tomb for some king's ancient bones?"

"Because they are the bones of a long-ago ancestor of the *Kaiser* they say." Lowering her voice so her father would not hear, Lis leaned over and whispered, "*Onkel* Nikolaus says that this ancient King Johann is our ancestor too. That is why he wants to see the king's bones taken to the *Klause*."

"How could he be our ancestor?" Leni stopped working at the bundles and stared at her sister.

"Because we have a little bit of his royal blood."

"I don't believe that." Leni's small, callused hands pulled more flax stalks toward her. If she was royalty, why was she tying flax in the middle of a farm field?

"There's a lot you don't know about our family," Lis snapped, with the thundercloud expression that usually came when she saw Papp and Eva talking together.

After a short silence, Leni dared to ask, "Do you believe it?"

"Believe what," Lis said, her face still troubled, her mind obviously in some distant place that Leni didn't understand.

"That we have royal blood."

"I don't know. *Onkel* talked about it one time when he and Papp were drinking *Viez* in the *Stube*. Papp told *Onkel* Nikolaus to mind his tongue in front of me and sent me away. But Mathes got to stay. I went out but I left the door open a bit, and I listened while *Onkel* told the story to Mathes. Papp got mad and told *Onkel* not to fill Mathes' head with claptrap."

Leni wiped the sweat from her face and moved closer to Lis, the flax bundle she had just tied cradled in her arms. "Tell me the story, Lis, please?"

"No. You're only 10, too young for it." Lis spoke as one who has reached her 17th year and now knows everything in the world that can be known.

"I'll be eleven in just a few months. I can keep up with the work here in the field, just like you. And I can keep my mouth shut. Tell me, Lis, tell me," Leni badgered.

Lis saw their father coming closer and hissed, "Hold your tongue about this, Leni. If Papp hears a word about the story, he might forbid our holiday with *Onkel* Nikolaus. It makes him angry."

Leni said no more but she thought about it often during the long afternoon and promised herself that she would find out what everyone else already knew.

The early Mass was over, a hasty breakfast had been eaten, and the cleanup was underway. Magda saw that both of her sisters were bursting with impatience as they brought the now empty oat porridge bowls to the kitchen, preparing to wash up. She pushed them back into the *Stube*. "Go on then, outside to meet *Onkel* and *Tante* when they come with the wagon. I will do the rest of the house chores." Magda shared her younger sisters' excitement. She wished she and Johann could go too; but they were staying close to home with their tiny Maria, not wanting to take any risk with this second baby daughter after losing the first.

"Wait, Leni, let me look at you," Magda called as Leni reached the door of the *Stube*, following on Lis' heels. Leni ran back to her. Magda untied the white muslin cap with its edging of lace framing Leni's brown little face. The hair that the cap was supposed to cover was escaping in several directions, hair so curly that it defied being held back unless it was tightly braided. Magda sighed. Leni hated braiding her hair and often made a poor job of it. There wasn't time now to do more than try to make the loose braids a bit more secure under the bonnet. The hair might stay in place for a little while, but probably no longer than it would take for the wagon to reach the outskirts of Oberzerf. It was the best that could be hoped for with Leni.

Leni was shifting from one foot to the other. The black buckled shoes must be uncomfortable especially after the chance to go barefoot in the summer weather arrived. "Stop wiggling, girl," Magda said as she bent down and unlaced and then retied the laces of Leni's fitted bodice, straightening the blouse worn under it. The blouse had belonged to Lis and was still too large for slender Leni. Its neckline hung lopsided unless the bodice was tightly pulled together so that the blouse stayed in place.

When she had finished with the bodice laces, Magda smoothed down the bent-up edge of the dark blue skirt where Leni's white shift peeked out. This skirt had been hers once. It had been more than 15 years since she had worn it. The feeling of the linen material under her fingers brought a longing for the time when everything had been fresh and new; for the excitement of being young and impatient to get on with life, whatever it held.

"I hear *Onkel's* wagon, Mag. I have to go."

"Well, be off then." Magda kissed her little sister's cheek. As Leni ran to the door, her oldest sister murmured to herself, "Your carefree days will be over so soon, so enjoy every happy minute that you can."

Outside Mathes and Theiss were standing beside the wagon that held rough sacks stuffed with rye straw to be used to cushion the worst of the bumps on the road they would travel. *Tante* Mari sat on the wagon bench, where two flat pillows, filled with the more pliant rye hulls, had been placed to make the trip more comfortable for her and *Onkel* Nikolaus. She wore a cap, dress and blouse that were similar to the style worn by Leni and Lis. The square-cut neck of her white blouse was modestly covered with a wide embroidered cotton collar held together with a small broach. In spite of the warm weather, her fringed, gold Sunday shawl was draped loosely over her shoulders. In contrast to the long trousers that his nephews wore, Nikolaus Rauls was dressed in the old-time style, with black knee britches held up with a wide leather belt. His long knit stockings covered legs that were still muscular and strong. *Onkel* Nikolaus reached down from the open back of the wagon, holding out his hand to help Lis up. Mathes and Theiss jumped up after her. Pitt stood back, looking around for their father.

"Come on Pitt; hurry Leni," Theiss called. "We don't want to be too late to see the barge come in."

Grabbing the side of the wagon, Leni climbed on to one of the wooden wheels and then boosted herself over into the wagon box, hitting the floor with a thump.

"For goodness sake, Leni," Lis scolded, "stop showing off." Leni just grinned at her and tugged her skirt back down over her shift. She settled herself on one of the straw sacks.

"Where is Papp?" Pitt asked. He made no move toward the wagon.

"Your Papp isn't coming with us today, Pitt," *Onkel* Nikolaus said. "He will stay here and see to the farm. Jump up here now so we can get started."

"I can't go without Papp," Pitt said, frowning. "If Papp won't go, I can't go."

Mathes and *Onkel* Nikolaus exchanged glances. It was getting late. They had to leave now. Mathes tried one more time. "Pitt, Papp is not going, but he wants you to come with us. You know he'll be right here when you get back."

"No!" Pitt shook his head. "I'll stay with Papp today. He likes for me to be here with him."

Nikolaus Rauls sighed; he knew that it did no good to argue with Pitt when he shook his head like that. He was not like the others. His mind worked slowly and he did not know how to read or write. When his mother died, Pitt had begun to shadow his father with a fierce determination, as if he could keep him alive and on this earth through constant vigilance; and his father, who was more strict and stern with his other children, used a gentle voice when he spoke to this son who was so devoted to him.

Nikolaus went back to the wagon seat, and took up the reins. He snapped them and clucked for the horses to start, still hoping that Pitt would run after them. But Pitt waved and smiled. He stood watching them as the wagon drew away.

The church bells chimed six as they turned on to the main road that had accumulated more than the usual amount of horse and oxen dung. Clearly others were already on their way. When they reached the edge of the village, they overtook the wagon carrying Josef and Maria Philippi with their sons and daughters. Katharina was one of Leni's best friends, and they waved at each other and shouted greetings while *Onkel* Nikolaus guided his wagon past the oxen team that pulled the Philippi's wagon. Before long all the waving arms and smiling Philippi faces disappeared from sight as the horses were given free reign.

The road was rough and the wagon's passengers often swayed and jostled each other as *Onkel* Nikolaus struggled to hold the horses under tight control to avoid losing any of his passengers. They moved south and then west along the rough hilly road that would bring them to Serrig. For a long time there were only fields and a few trees to see. The horses strained to pull the wagon up steep inclines in the road, which in some places was not much more than a narrow track. They met no one coming toward them. Everyone traveled to the Saar today. As they entered the *Kammerforst* with its tall trees, they began to encounter more travelers, especially those going on foot over the grassy forest trails.

When Leni asked, for the third time, whether they were now near to Serrig, Uncle Nikolaus pulled the wagon to the side of the road and told Mathes to take the reins. Nikolaus walked to the open back of the wagon and climbed a little stiffly into it. He sat beside Leni in the place Mathes had vacated.

"Are you tired, *Onkel*?" Leni asked, "Will you take a nap now?"

Onkel Nikolaus raised his heavy eyebrows and his brown eyes twinkled. "No, Leni. I thought it was time to tell all of you the strange story of this King Johann and his bones. Who knows anything about him?" They all shook their heads.

Onkel leaned forward toward a wooden box covered by burlap that sat in the wagon's front corner.

"Story telling is thirsty work. I'll have a sip of wine before I start." He pushed the burlap aside and pulled a round clay jug from the box, tilted his head back and drank two hearty swallows. "And a little drop won't hurt any of you, not even you, Lenchen."

Tante Mari turned her head to look back at them. "Nikolaus, I do not think her father would approve. There is some cider for Leni."

"Allow the *Mädchen* to have a taste of the wine, Mari. It is a special occasion declared by the Prussian *Kaiser* himself."

After the jug was passed from *Onkel*, Lis, and Theiss, it finally reached Leni. She took the clay jug firmly in her hands, brought it to her lips and drank, a trickle of the wine running down the side of her chin. The wine was sweet on her tongue but something in it made the inside of her mouth tingle and her stomach feel warm. Her eyes opened very wide, and her uncle laughed as he took the jug from her. Leni had never been allowed to have homemade wine when it was served at home. This was her first time to be treated as a grownup. What a glorious celebration, she thought.

"Enough, I think, my little Leni. "We can't have you stumbling drunk into the Saar. King Johann's body floating on the river is enough for today."

"*Onkel*, I am not drunk." Leni was indignant.

"I am teasing you, Lenchen. Don't be mad at me. Let me tell you about the blind king." *Onkel* Nikolaus drank once more, head tilted back, and Leni watched the muscles in his tanned neck move with each swallow from the earthen jug. She waited with anticipation. *Onkel* Nikolaus was a fine storyteller, often changing his voice and acting out the actions of the people in a tale. When he stopped drinking, he sighed in pleasure and returned the jug to the box.

"King Johann of Bohemia was a restless man," he began. "He took as his wife a daughter of the royal family in a place called Bohemia, which is even farther east than the Prussian capital. With this marriage he became King of Bohemia. But his only love was the clank of armor and the clash of spear and sword in battle. He cared little for his new subjects."

The morning sun filtering down through the trees cast shadows that moved in ever-changing shapes across their faces and bodies as the wagon went forward. Leni lay back on her sack of straw, her arm curved under her head. "Did you learn this story when you were in school, *Onkel*?"

"No, I heard it only a few weeks ago when the schoolmaster Trapp asked me to take him with my wagon to Saarburg to find a new table for the schoolroom. We talked about the new *Klause*. That is when he told me the history of the king whose bones will be on the barge today."

Leni was puzzled, "The king's bones have been in Mettlach. How did they get there from that country to the east?

"Ah," said Nikolaus Rauls with a wink, "I was hoping one of you would ask. King Johann's first wife died, you see. A short time later he found a French princess to marry. He went riding off to France for the wedding, and he liked his new wife and the country so much that he never went back to Bohemia." Nikolaus bounced on his straw sack, and raised his hands as if he rode in a saddle and held the reins of a lively horse. "This king had been born in Luxembourg, and he felt very much more at home among the French. The French were always fighting with the English; and King Johann loved to put on his armor, call for his knights and ride off to battle."

"Do you know the name of the princess? Was she beautiful?" Leni thought the story was interesting but *Onkel* Nikolaus was letting out some important details.

"Her name was Beatrice. As for beauty, I can only guess. But he already had a grown son when he married for the second time. He did not need heirs to carry on his family line; his first wife had provided them. So I think he must have married this princess for love. Sad it was that not too long after they wed, he began to lose his sight and by the time he fought in the battle where those English soldiers killed him, he was blind."

"How could he fight in a battle if he was blind? You are making up this story." Theiss was frowning, not willing to be tricked into believing what was not true.

"That was what I said to Herr Trapp when he told me the story. But he said that today is not just the day the blind king died, but also the date of a big battle between France and England. *Ja,* the blind king insisted that he would fight to save his beloved France from the Englanders. His knights must have tried to tell him it was a dangerous thing to do. When he refused to listen, they had no choice but to obey him. They helped him dress in his armor and mount his horse. Then two of his trusted knights mounted up too, one on each side of him, their steeds tied tight to his. This way, King Johann had two pairs of eyes to see for him and to tell him where to aim his lance. The rest of his knights, they tried to form themselves into a human shield, riding in such a way that no enemy could get through their ranks to kill their King. That is how they all rode into battle."

Uncle Nikolaus grinned, sat up straight and tall on his straw sack. "Can you imagine the blind King Johann as he fights?" he asked. "*Holterdiepolter* swings the royal sword." His voice changed and became gruff, and he stared into space with unfocused eyes as he swung the imaginary weapon, moving his arm from left to right and back again as a blind king might do. "Oh, so sorry, faithful knight. We did not mean to cut off your head. But it sounded as hollow as an Englishman's head and little mistakes happen from time to time."

Hearing their laughter encouraged Nikolaus to continue acting out King Johann's battle charge. He raised his arm high; fist clenched, and brought it down swiftly. "*Kroch,*" he cried. "*Ach,* my faithful knight! Was that your arm that my trusty mace separated from your shoulder? Do forgive me." Nikolaus leaned forward as though he crouched over a saddle. He made a lance-thrusting motion. "*Bauf,*" he yelled and jerked his body backward as if he had run into a wall. "*Mein Gott,* what a sturdy Englishman that was. Come someone and help me pull my lance from his body. We killed a tree you say? Well come and pull out my lance so I can do the same to an Englishman!'"

Leni could not stop giggling at the comic battle *Onkel* Nikolaus had created for them. *Tante* Mari was laughing too although she turned around on her seat at the front of the wagon, and said, "Enough husband. Be done with your foolishness."

Uncle Nikolaus leaned back against the side of the wagon again and said in his usual voice, "When the fighting ended, no surprise that King Johann and all his knights lay dead on the battlefield."

"He was brave but also very stupid," Theiss said. "I would know better than to try such a thing. I thought there would be more sense in the head of a king."

"Why did they take his bones to Mettlach?" Lis wondered. "It seems odd that he was not buried there in France, or taken back to Luxembourg."

"You really want to know the rest of the story; you are not tired of King Johann?" *Onkel* Nikolaus asked as he wiped his eyes after his own laughter.

"*Ja,*" Leni shouted. "Tell us more."

"Tell us, tell us," Theiss and Lis chorused.

"You will think I make this up," Uncle Nikolaus warned, "But I swear the teacher Trapp, who knows about such things, told me the rest of the story. It is a comical ending for the king's odd life."

Onkel brought out the wine bottle and took another drink. "The king's heart and guts were embalmed and kept in a Dominican Cloister in France. They are still there maybe. The body then went in a solemn procession to Luxembourg and was put in an open tomb in the Benedictine Abbey there. A couple of times, the monks from the abbey had to hide the king's royal bones because invaders were coming. But up until the time of Napoleon and the French, the Benedictines always managed to rescue the king's bones and put them back in a place of honor in their church. One time, though, a thief made off with the king's skull. An Earl who lived in the Eifel got his hands on it, and it wasn't easy to persuade him to give it back."

"Is that how the king came to be in Mettlach? Were his bones stolen again?" Leni asked.

"No, the idea was to protect them," her uncle answered. "You are all too young to remember what it was like when Napoleon's army came marching through the Rheinland and Luxembourg. Some of these so-called soldiers were nothing more than thugs. They broke into churches and abbeys, stole whatever had any value, and smashed the rest.

The monks in the Luxembourg Abbey knew the danger so they hid King Johann's bones at the house of a baker. But that baker was very afraid of what might happen if someone found out."

Uncle Nikolaus, his voice high and shrill, rang his hands, imitating the panicky baker as he worried about himself and his bakery. "'Oh, what shall I do if they find me with these royal bones.' So he took the box with King Johann's bones to the Luxembourg pottery factory's owner, Herr Boch, who said he would keep the king's bones safe, and he did. When his factory moved to Mettlach a few years later, the bones went along and were stored in the attic at the new place. That is why they are coming today from Mettlach."

The wagon was overtaking more and more people on foot who would move aside as they heard the wagon approach. A young man and woman were ahead of them now, and they turned to look at the approaching wagon.

"*Hallo* Nikla," Lis shouted. She had recognized the young man. It was Nikolaus Meyer from Oberzerf, walking with his older sister Elizabeth who was called Betta. Both brother and sister waved at Lis.

Mathes stopped the horses. "Would you like to ride the rest of the way with us?" he asked, his eyes on Betta. Lis and Leni giggled. They knew that Mathes thought Betta was the prettiest girl in the village. Betta smiled shyly but did not reply. Her pale, oval face was framed by soft red-brown hair that suited the large, gray-green eyes fixed on Mathes.

Her brother Nikolaus showed no hesitation, "With pleasure," he shouted. "We've worn the leather on our shoes so thin that we can feel the forest floor same as if we were barefoot."

"Get in then," laughed *Onkel* Nikolaus, "and save your father a trip to the shoemaker."

Nikla and Betta started to climb into the wagon when *Tante* Mari said, "I am a little tired, Mathes. Help me down so I can finish the trip in the back with your uncle." She winked at Mathes as he helped her to the ground. "Maybe you would like to take my place, Betta? The view will be very good and you are young. You won't mind sitting on the hard bench. Or maybe Mathes will give you his cushion."

Mathes came close to tripping over his feet in his haste to help Betta up on the wagon seat and hand her his cushion to sit on. The tips of his ears were very red. Then they both sat stiffly, not looking at each other, and waited for *Tante* Mari to climb into the wagon's box and settle herself next to *Onkel* Nikolaus.

Young Nikla Meyer showed no shyness at all as he chose a seat on the wagon floor next to the sack of straw where Lis was perched. Nikla was as good-looking as his sister was pretty. He had pale blue eyes that were deep set under thick, dark eyebrows. His hair was dark too, almost as dark as Mathes' but instead of curling, it grew straight and a shock of it fell across his forehead, slanting over one eye. Once seated, he stretched his legs out in front of him, and looked toward Lis. Her eyes were cast down, as if the embroidery on her apron had become quite fascinating. Leni saw that she glanced to the side without moving her head and that her cheeks were a bit redder than usual.

Leni moved so that *Tante* Mari could sit with *Onkel* Nikolaus. Her eyes widened in surprise when her uncle reached up, put his hands around her aunt's waist and pulled her down to rest against him. He kept his arm around her, his hand covering hers as it lay in her lap. She leaned back against him and turned her head to smile at him.

Mathes looked around and saw that Leni was still standing, one hand braced against a corner of the wagon, the other clutching its rail as she gazed at *Tante* and *Onkel* in surprise.

"Sit down please, Leni," he said. "We need to get moving."

Leni looked at him in surprise. Usually he shouted, "Stop fooling around, *Schwachkopf,* or I'll make you sorry." She liked the effect Betta had on her brother's temper. She sat, and they started off again. She kept her hold on the wagon rail and turned her head toward the forest, hoping to see a wild pig or a deer, and she gave a whoop of pleasure as a *Haselhuhn,* the rust-brown grouse with its black and white head feathers, flew up at the sound of their approaching wagon. Lis was startled and shifted on her sack. Just then the road turned sharply, the wagon jolted, and she lost her balance. Nikla Meyer reached out to brace her on her sack, his hands at her waist.

"The road is rough the next few meters," *Onkel* Nikolaus remarked to his wife. He glanced at their new passenger. "Don't you want to sit on the straw next to Theiss over there, young Nikla? It would help protect you against the ruts in this stretch."

"This is fine for now, Herr Rauls." The young man stayed where he was. Nikolaus grinned; he had known what Nikla would answer.

They were coming along the strip of forest called "*Schwarzbruch.*" The air was fragrant with the odor of the tall fir trees that formed a dark green wall on each side of the road. Leni, bored with seeing only trees, untied her cap and took it off, letting it dangle over the edge of the wagon as she stood up and gripped the wagon rail, leaning her head forward and letting the breeze tousle her already untidy hair. She squinted and tried to see through the trees into the distance.

They came over a hill and around a bend. The forest thinned and the village of Serrig and the Saar River lay below them. This was the first time that Leni had seen a river of any kind. She turned her head first right and then left, but there was no beginning and no end to the glimmering band of blue green that flowed in graceful curves, shadowed in some places by hills covered with trees or green vineyards. Uncle Nikolaus pointed across the river where the land rose straight up from the ground of the riverbank.

"See that stony outcropping there. The new *Klause* stands at the very edge of those boulders."

Leni saw only the rocks of the steep precipice. The shape of any kind of building eluded her. Lis claimed to see it but Leni had her doubts because Lis always had to be superior. In another few minutes they came into the upper village of Serrig. A boy about Leni's age ran toward them, offering them a field of hay stubble where he would take care of their team. Uncle Nikolaus gave him a coin, and the boy led the horses to a spot near several other wagons. Most of them had been pulled by the now tethered oxen, which were contentedly chewing their cuds.

They all climbed down from the wagon box. *Tante* Mari held Leni back for a moment to smooth her tangled hair and push it back under the bonnet. *Onkel* Nikolaus and Mathes each retrieved a jug of wine from under the wagon seat and carried it with them. Theiss carried the basket with bread and cheese to be eaten after the barge landed and the formal procession to the *Klause* had disappeared along the road that wound up toward the *Klause*. The others carried the straw sacks from the wagon in the event that the barge appeared much later than expected and they wanted to sit. The village was nearly deserted except for the old ones who could no longer make the trip to the river's edge.

Everyone followed the main road down the hill toward the flat land at the edge of the Saar.

A great many spectators were already in place, eyes turned to the south, the direction from which the barge would come. They were still much too far away to see up to the *Klause* without squinting at the rocky cliff. It seemed, even when glimpsed, to be a part of the rocks.

Leni was disappointed. She had expected to see the mausoleum clearly but from this side of the river it appeared to be smaller than the tiny coin box at the back of the Oberzerf chapel.

"If we could go way up there to see the *Klause*, would it be as large as the cathedral in Trier?" she asked *Onkel* Nikolaus."

"*Ach nein*, it is small I think, compared to the Cathedral in Trier." It does not take much room to hold a small coffin with the bones of King Johann. But it is a very splendid building they say, and an honor for Kastel to have such a fine monument which people from all over Prussia will come to admire."

"Will we be able to see the barge from here?" Lis asked as they walked along the towpath. Everywhere there were other groups choosing their vantage points along the riverbank, most searching for trees or tall wild shrubbery to give them some shade during the wait. The sun was already warm, and it would be hot by the time the barge appeared and the ceremonies began.

"All of these folks seem to think this is a good place to get a look for the Boch barge." Uncle Nikolaus was thinking aloud. He motioned to a spot under some scrub oak trees on the hill above the towpath and tossed the straw sacks there, the lunch basket shaded by them. *Tante* Maria and *Onkel* Nikolaus took the biggest sack and sat down to wait, their backs braced against one of a tree's thin trunk. "Plenty of time to stand when the barge comes into sight," their uncle said.

Lis, Mathes, together with Betta and Nikla pushed their way to a spot close to the Saar River's edge, craning their necks forward to see if a barge was approaching and then looking back over their shoulders to watch the people coming down the hilly road from upper Serrig. Leni and Theiss tagged along after them, staring up at the distant *Klause*. There must be people up there, people who would see the dignified ceremony of the coffin with King John's bones being placed in that almost invisible mausoleum. Perhaps they lined the edges of the high outcropping across the river, invisible from this shore. The *Klause's* rocky surroundings glimmered in the sunlight.

"I wish we could be up there," Leni said, tipping her head back as she stared across the river at the high rocks. "Those people will see everything. Maybe they will even be able to go into the *Klause* to watch them put the king's coffin into his magnificent new tomb."

Theiss was looking up too. "Do you see any cannon?" he asked Leni. "I hope there are and that they fire them off when the ship comes."

Removed from the crowding people at the river's edge and part way up the hill, a man sat alone. He had long, curling hair, sideburns that grew down past the bottom of his ears, and a mustache under his long nose. A large, floppy straw hat shaded his face, and he sat crosslegged on a woven blanket the color of a hedge of golden broom flowers. A loose linen smock covered all but the cuffs of his shirt made of a material Leni had never seen before. It had a fine weave of fibers much softer than a village man's Sunday shirt, and it was gray with fine blue stripes. It was clear that he was not a villager from one of the neighboring towns. His gray trousers must have been loomed by a master weaver who used the finest wool. His boots were made of dark brown leather that had been highly polished but now had accumulated much of the dust of the road. Surely he was a well-to-do man from a large city. He had the largest pad of paper Leni had ever seen. He rested it against his knees and worked with a stick of charcoal that he moved over the pad with swift and sure strokes.

Theiss was walking on, but Leni worked her way back through the crowd, making her way up the hill path to a spot behind the man. She wanted a closer look at what he was doing without attracting his attention. When she was near enough, she saw that this stranger was working a kind of magic. Quickly and surely, the river appeared on his pad of paper, then the rows of people standing in wait, then the precipice with the tiny distant *Klause*. It was as if it had all lived inside the paper, waiting for the touch of this artist, for surely that was what he was. He could bring the scene around him to a black and white life. She stood without moving until Theiss started up the hill toward her, calling "Leni, is the view better from up there?" "No," Leni was forced to call out. Theiss turned and headed back to the river's edge.

The man turned his head and saw a girl of about eleven years, with curly hair escaping from the bonnet framing her face, standing close to him. He asked, "Do you think I have done justice to what is all around us?"

Even on her tanned face, the blush showed clearly. There was silence. Then Leni stammered, "How is it possible to make such a splendid drawing?"

"It took many years of study and much practice." The man turned away and began to draw more.

"It's wonderful," Leni said, moving a little closer. "What will you do with it when it is finished?"

Without looking back at her, he said "Probably I will not be satisfied with it, and I will tear it up. But if I am pleased with it, I will use it when I am in my studio in Koblenz. It will serve to keep my memory clear while I paint a watercolor from it. This is just a sketch, not meant to be displayed."

"You have a great gift from God. It is a beautiful picture," Leni said, her face so serious that the artist studied her.

"Would you like to see the other sketches I have made? From this side of the Saar you cannot see the beauty of the building that will hold the earthly remains of King Johann."

The stranger pulled pages from a pile of drawings that lay under the sketch he had been working on. "Yesterday I was up on the outcropping where the *Klause* shows off like the jewel it is."

Leni was awed by the way he talked. It was like the fine grammar that Herr Trapp used when he taught their classes, with no hint of the everyday dialect of the Oberzerf villagers. She moved close enough to see another page that was almost filled by a building so fine that she asked, "Is that really the *Klause*?" Leni had never seen a cathedral, but this drawing was what she imagined a fine house of God would look like.

"Oh indeed it is, *Mädchen*. This is the *Klause* built to the honor of King Johann of Bohemia. It is small compared even to the abbey church in Beurig. But although it is much smaller than churches in Trier and Koblenz, it has a splendid architecture. Do you see the fine windows? Herr Karl Friedrich Schinkel who built the *Klause* has created a work of art as a monument to the dead king. Even the window coverings are amazing; a thin iron piece instead of glass and into that he cut large 7-pointed stars and diamond shapes to let in the light. It is like the work of a magician."

"I thought there would be stained glass with pictures, " Leni said, "but this is better." The windows will make star and diamond shaped lights on the inside of the *Klause* when the sun shows through them."

"You have the soul of an artist, little *Mädchen*. Most people would have said, 'The windows are very plain. The Crown Prince will not be pleased that he spent so much money for something like this.' I tell you that those windows will shine more golden when the sun comes through them than any colored glass in the world. And when the sun is in the west, the stones on the outside of the *Klause* seem to be made of golden blocks that glow by themselves."

Quickly he showed her more drawings of the *Klause* that he had sketched when he stood on the pathway near the monument. He had also drawn pictures of the views to the north and south of the *Klause*. His drawing of the Saar far below showed a barge that was as small as a leaf on a small stream.

"Is that really how small the barges look when you are up there?"

The man nodded. To her disappointment, he put the drawings aside, and said, "Now that I have shown you my drawings, will you do me a favor?"

Leni stood silent, unsure what to say. She had been too forward. She didn't know this man and now he wanted something from her.

"Don't look so frightened," he said. "It is an easy thing I am asking of you. Just take two steps down the hill and turn to face me. Then talk to me about anything you want. You could tell me the name your father and mother gave to you or the names of your brothers and sister or the nickname of the boy down there who called to you and is now trying to climb that tree for a better view."

Leni did as he asked, her fear easing. There could be nothing wrong with complying with a task that was so easy and so public. When she had stepped away and turned to face him, she said, "My name is Magdalena, but everyone calls me Leni. My family comes from the village of Oberzerf back there to the east. The boy climbing the tree is my brother Mathias. Everyone calls him Theiss." She stopped because the man she had been talking to seemed to have no interest.

"Keep talking, little one. I am listening as I draw."

Leni started again. "I have another brother Mathias. We call him Mathes. "My oldest sister is named Magdalena, just like me; but she has been called Magda ever since I can remember. She is married and has a husband, our cousin Johann. My sister Anna Maria is away from home, just this year. I miss her. She was always full of funny stories and ideas. Then there is Lis, who is somewhere in the crowd down there. And my brother Pitt isn't here. He stayed at home with my Papp. He's afraid my Papp might die like Mamm did."

Still drawing, the artist frowned at the last sentence and to make sure the girl before him kept her enchanting smile, he commented, "So, there are two girls named Magdalena in your family and two boys named Mathias. May I ask why you were given the same names? There are many other names to choose from, like Adolf or Kunigunda."

Leni wondered why he didn't know that it would be an insult to name a babe something other than the name of the godmother or godfather. He must be teasing her. Kunigunda? Adolf? What silly names he had made up.

"Were you not named after your godfather?" she asked. Where do you come from?"

"I was born in Simmern, not so far away from Oberzerf. But my father came from Poland. He had to flee and eventually he met my mother who was from Koblenz. I was named Johann, because my father thought it a good, strong name; but I am called by my second name, Adolf."

Leni giggled before she could stop herself.

"So you think my name is amusing," the man named Johann Adolf said and laughed. "I like it because whenever I am in a large group and someone calls out Adolf, I know that they mean me." If my name was Michel or Peter, almost every other man in the room would look up from his conversation, wondering if there was a message for him or some problem at his home or at his shop."

All the while he talked to Leni, the man Johann Adolf was making those rapid strokes with his charcoal pencil on a new sheet of paper from his pad. She jumped back when he ripped it from the pad with a flourish.

"Come and look," Magda-Leni," he motioned. She walked to where he held the paper out to her. She took it and stared at it, motionless with amazement. A face very similar to the one she saw reflected in the windowpanes of their house had been captured with his strokes on the page. It was a picture of her, curly hair tumbling from her bonnet. Behind her were the Saar River and the high hill where the *Klause* stood.

"It is a picture of me and the river and the *Klause*! Oh it is very fine," Leni managed to say, her voice trembling. She handed the sheet back to him, and he wound it around a cylindrical pack of similar sheets.

"I'm pleased that you like it. Every pretty little *Fräulein* should have her portrait drawn in a sun-soaked setting such as this," he said, standing and brushing a collage of leafy meadow souvenirs from his trousers. As he bent to gather up his charcoal sticks, he paused in thought and then sat down again. He tore another sheet from his writing pad, tore if in half, and then into quarters. He took up the charcoal pencil again and drew faster than Leni had thought possible; first on one square, then another, another and another.

"These are a small souvenir to thank you for posing as my model today." He rose again, handing the four squares of paper to her. With long strides, he moved away quickly through the crowd before Leni could thank him. He did not look back but he raised his hand to his straw hat in a little salute.

A shout of excitement came from down river. People began to move closer to the very edge of the riverbank. "The barge is coming." "I think I see the barge." "Here it comes." The shouts were all around them. In confirmation, the cannons boomed a salute that echoed along the valley. As she watched and waited, Leni glanced at the papers she was holding. One raggedly torn square, in just a few strokes, showed the gathered crowd. The second was of the *Klause*, although in much less detail than the drawing she had seen earlier, the third looked exactly like the rock face of the stone outcropping where the *Klause* hid. The fourth square showed the same smiling face she had seen when the Herr artist had handed the large drawing to her. Johann Adolf Lasinsky was written on the side of each of the uneven squares.

What should she do with her treasure? She was not at all sure that the others, especially *Tante* Mari, would approve of her talking to a stranger, especially a man who was alone. Obviously everyone thought she was still with Theiss. She hurried back up the road toward Serrig until she came to a large boulder, probably used as a boundary marker. She dropped to her knees behind it and quickly lifted her skirt, reaching under it and pushing the drawings past the fitted waist of her overdress. The drawings should not show under her bodice and to make sure she would not lose them, she tied the sash of her skirt so tight that it was hard to breathe. Only Anna Maria's eyes would see these drawings when she had her next visit in Oberzerf. Leni knew how her sister's eyes would light up with appreciation of the adventure.

Less than a half an hour later, the barge, painted with the emblem of the Boch-Buschmann factory, was safely moored at the Kastel Staadt landing, and the sailors were helping several frock-coated or cassock-wearing dignitaries ashore. Eight young men who would carry the small coffin to the *Klause* met them. The polished wood box held all that remained of King Johann of Bohemia. Leni imagined that there was a fur-lined golden chest inside the polished wood of the coffin. That box held the royal skull with a jeweled crown and bones wrapped in a soft, red-velvet robe.

Someone in the crowd near Leni said that four of the young men were from Saarburg and four from Kastel, all chosen for their stamina. Leni did not understand how it could take eight men to carry that little royal coffin. They would hardly fit around its sides.

"Will they climb up there, Uncle?" she asked Nikolaus Rauls as she looked at the stark rock precipice across the river.

Nikolaus gave a loud, hearty laugh and several people turned to look at him. "They are not angels, Leni. They do not flap their wings and fly straight to the top. They will take their turns climbing the winding roads to the *Klause* until they are as high up the cliff we can see. It takes them maybe the rest of the day to reach it. But just think of it; when they reach the top they will have a view like no other, seeing the Saar flow along past the vineyards and villages."

Soon the royal coffin and its honor guard disappeared along the Kastel road. The church choirs of Saarburg and Beurig were singing a harmonious chant that drifted across the Saar with the west wind. Leni took off her bonnet, hoping to hear better and stood dumbstruck at the beauty of the sound. It was as if the notes were woven together into an intricate pattern like that of a delicate piece of lace. "This must be how the angels in heaven sing," she said to Theiss who stood beside her. He nodded without really hearing her or the singing; he was wishing that the cannons would fire again.

They were going back to Oberzerf as the sun lowered. Mathes had the reins again and Betta Meyer again sat beside him. They talked and even laughed with each other. In the silences, Mathes stole glances at her and then quickly moved his eyes back to the road. *Tante* Mari rested her head on *Onkel* Nikolaus' shoulder, and it nodded and bobbed as she dozed. Lis and Nikla Meyer shared one of the bags of straw. She had picked *Ganseblumchen* daisies and cornflowers and was braiding them into a crown, a task made difficult by the bouncing of the wagon. Nikla watched her, alternately handing her white daisies and then blue cornflowers from the pile beside him. Leni lay on the floor of the wagon, using the straw sack as her pillow. She was drifting off to sleep. But she came wide awake as Lis said, "*Onkel*, we told Betta and Nikla that we have the royal blood of King Johann. Nikla does not believe such a thing could be."

Onkel Nikolaus raised an eyebrow and drank the last of the wine in the wine jug. He regarded the empty container with a wistful expression before he set it down. Then he wiped his mouth with the back of his hand and grinned. "So, young fellow, you think we could not be cut from royal cloth. Well think again."

Tante Mari sat up, "That is only a tall tale Nikolaus, not proper for these young ones.

Leni laid very still, her eyes tightly closed, hoping they wouldn't know she was listening.

Nikolaus Rauls had spent the day enjoying the fruit of the grape. His cheeks were red and his tongue a little thick when he said, "Be quiet, wife. These children know about the bull and the cow and what they do. Why shouldn't I tell the story?"

He focused his attention on Nikla Meyer. "Had circumstances been different and the birth taken place on the right side of the blanket, I might have been standing in the *Klause* today, making a solemn face and pretending that I cared about my kinsman's bones." He laughed loud. "Graf Nikolaus of Oberzerf! But our ancestor had the bad luck to be born a French peasant. Her name was the French word for Magdalena. She was called Madeleine. They say she had dark, heavy hair. It fell in curls to her waist when it was not bound up and hidden under her white bonnet."

Leni thought to herself, "She had the same name as me and hair just like mine," so excited that her eyes flew open for a second before she pinched them closed again. All were focused on *Onkel* Nikolaus so no one saw.

"Madeleine was betrothed to a young man called Raoul, French for Rolf," Uncle Nikolaus was saying. "He was an apprentice weaver; and they were to be married as soon as she had served her time in the kitchen belonging to the French prince who owned the castle and the town around it. Madeleine was performing her service to the prince's household according to the law for peasants back then. It so happened that the daughter of that French Prince was to be married to Count Johann of Luxembourg, who was also the King of Bohemia. There was a great wedding celebration, and Madeleine helped to serve the guests. Afterward there was feasting and dancing in the courtyard for the house servants. Johann of Luxembourg and his bride came to watch those festivities for a while. The dances grew wild, as they do when there is no shortage of wine to drink. Madeleine's hair came loose from her cap and flowed down her back. That is why King Johann noticed her, even on his wedding night."

"Why would he want a sweaty peasant girl when he could have a princess with a crown?" Nikla Meyer took the chain of daisies and cornflowers that Lis had made, forming them into a circlet. "Your royal majesty," he said as he placed it on her head, making a small bow to her.

"Why does a village need only one good bull for all its cows?" *Onkel* Nikolaus hooted with laughter and slapped his knee. "Tell me hat, my fine young lad."

"Nikolaus, mind your tongue," *Tante* Maria said sharply.

Lis frowned at Nikla, taking the flower crown from her head. She gave Nikla a scowl. "Please keep on with the story, *Onkel*." *Onkel* Nikolaus was still chuckling. "Whatever my Lady Elizabetha wishes. A few nights after his wedding, a servant woke Madeleine as she slept on her pallet in a room off of the kitchen. He took her to a bedroom where King Johann was waiting for her. She spent the night in his bed; there was no choice. In those times, a pretty peasant girl knew her service in the kitchen of the estate was not the only service that might be demanded. Our Madeleine was given a length of fine cloth and a silver neck chain before she was sent back to her pallet. Over the months, the king's servant came to fetch her many nights. By the time she was released from the chateau kitchen to go back to her village, she was with child. She was quickly married to her betrothed, and as a wedding gift the couple received a cow and six chickens from the Princess."

"Why do you believe such a story, Herr Rauls?" Nikla Meyer asked, a cynical grin on his face. "Every family in Oberzerf thinks there is blue blood somewhere in the family. If all those stories were true, most of the kings and dukes would have died exhausted before they were 30."

Betta turned around and looked back into the wagon. "I apologize for my brother, Herr Rauls. I think you should stop the wagon right now and tell him to walk back to Oberzerf. He is so rude he doesn't deserve to ride."

"I don't mind him; I can prove what I say." *Onkel* Nikolaus grinned at the astonishment on their faces. Leni opened her eyes wide and sat up.

"Ah, little Leni, I thought you were listening," her uncle said and went on with the story as if he had never been interrupted.

"The child was a boy, strong and healthy. Madeleine called him Jean, the French spelling of Johann, after her son's true father. But he was recorded in the baptismal register of the village church as Jean, son of Raoul, or as we would say, Johann, son of Rolf. Each year on his birthday the King would come to visit the child and bring him a gift. By then King Johann had begun to lose his sight; first in one eye and then in the other. By the time the boy turned eight, the King could no longer see his son at all, but as usual he had a gift for him, three silver coins from the land of Bohemia. That was the last time young Jean saw his natural father. Before the boy's next birthday, King Johann was in his tomb. Many years later Jean the son of Raoul, married. Three of his sons, now known by the name Rauls, lived long lives and each received one of the

Bohemian silver coins before their father died. The coin that was given to our forebear still exists." *Onkel* Nikolaus reached into the pocket of his vest and brought out a coin. Holding it between the thumb and forefinger of his calloused farmer's hand, he admired it. "This is the Bohemian *Groschen* that King Johann gave to his son, Jean. By tradition it should go to the eldest son of the family. But our oldest brother Peter was like young Nikla. He thought the story was nonsense and planned to sell the coin as soon as our Papp died. Word of that plan reached our Papp's ears, and so he gave the coin to me instead. And I will give it to my Mathias when I die."

Lis, and Leni both begged to examine that royal coin, and Theiss was already reaching for it.

"Ladies go first," their uncle said as he handed the coin to Lis.

She ran her fingers over its surface, as if to see it by touch as well as with her eyes. Leni crawled over to look too. The coin was tarnished and worn. There was a crown on one side and some large letters that Leni could not read. When Lis turned the coin over, they saw a fierce creature with claws. It looked part animal, part bird.

As the coin was passed carefully from hand to hand, their wagon clattered along the narrow road. The setting sun hung low in the sky, and the tall fir trees cast blue shadows on the occupants of the wagon. As each tree's silhouette moved across Leni's body, she wondered if her blood might really flow with that same hue, and if the drawing of her that rested under the bodice of her dress resembled that first Madeleine.

CHAPTER 12
Changing Rules and Traditions – October 1838

On the wedding day, the bridal couple would leave for the civil ceremony at the registry office (probably in the town hall) and which was required by law and preceded the wedding at the church. Often some kind of obstacle would be placed in the way of the wedding procession, perhaps a chain, a pole, or a ladder. This obstruction could only be bypassed by the payment of a ransom. As a reward for the payment of this "Trinkgeld," (literally "drink money) the procession could go on. In earlier times, fiddlers accompanied the bridal couple on the way to the church. As they walked along, the bridal couple delighted the youngsters by throwing small coins. Anna Maria Rauls married Nikolaus Marx on January 23, 1839 in the Catholic Church at Heddert and then lived with her husband in the small nearby village of Paschel. <u>Catholic Church Marriage Register of Greimerath, Hentern, and Zerf.</u>

Young Nikolaus Marx kept his arms around Anna Maria's slender waist after the long kiss they had shared in the *Tante* Susanna's garden. It had taken Anna Maria's breath away. He had come up behind her with footsteps as light as a cat's and taken her by surprise. As she let out a little sigh of satisfaction, he said, "I have talked to my Papp, and he agrees that I have saved enough money to marry a wife and begin my family. He pulled her even closer to him, so that she could feel where his manhood stiffened against her. She bent backward a little so that she could see his face.

"And who will the lucky maiden be?" she teased. "Will you ask the proud Barbara whose father could make the shoes for all of your sons and daughters, or the giggling Margaretha who will find it a great honor to scrub your sweaty tunics by the side of the stream or..."

She got no further for he kissed her again and said, "You know it is you I am asking, Anna Maria Rauls. I have wanted you since the first day you came to Paschel and now I must know if you want me. Do you?"

Anna Maria's heart was pounding loud in her ears. This is what she dreamed of since she was old enough to know that there was a delightful difference between girls and boys. She wished for a handsome, strong man of her own, one who came from a good family, to give her babies and a home she could call her own. Now the question she had longed to hear had finally been asked of her. Did she want to marry the short, sturdy farmer's son who stood in front of her, a look of tenderness in his brown eyes?

"I do," she answered.

Claus tried to kiss her for the third time, but she broke free. She danced around the garden, "I do, I do, I do. I'm going to marry the Claus," she said to a cabbage plant, bending down to pat its round firm head, as a mother would pat the bald head of her child.

"Have you heard?" she asked the blue cornflowers blooming along the stonewall as she skipped toward the apple tree at the end of the garden, "Claus is going to be my husband."

She had always known that the man she would marry would be named Nikolaus. Each year, when she threw the apple peeling over her shoulder, she saw the "N" even if the others told her the peel looked more like an "O" or a question mark.

For the first year that she had spent in Paschel, she had thought many times of Oberzerf and how she had let Nikolaus Hendrichs steal kisses from her and run his hands down her back to her buttocks. Once away from Oberzerf, she longed for him, but less and less as time went on.

In the second year of her time with *Tante* Susanna, she had begun to notice the shy *Kerl* whose eyes followed her whenever she walked past his father's *Einhaus* or when she made her way to a pew at Sunday Mass with the *Tante* Susanna holding her arm for support. When he came to offer help with the repair of the garden wall that had many loose and shifted stones, she found that he had an unusual method of courtship. He did not tease her or try to lure her behind a stable so he could try to kiss her. He talked to her while he worked, telling her his dreams and asking about hers. She looked forward to the time she spent with him each day and was sorry when the stones in the fence were in perfect alignment once again.

Claus stood watching the beautiful girl who had just said she would be his wife. Anna Maria was not like anyone else he had known. He never guessed what she might do or say, and she made him happy inside whenever he was with her. When she came back to face him, he took her hand and squeezed it.

"When shall we tell your father and ask his blessing?"

"Anna Maria's eye's narrowed, and she frowned. "Why must you ask for his blessing? I am a grown woman of 23. If you want me to bring you a dowry, I cannot do it. I will never ask my father for anything. What I bring to you on my wedding day will be mine alone to give."

Claus went silent. Why should she be angry with him? Why did she have to ruin this joyful moment with her stubbornness? He knew of the trouble between Anna Maria, her father, and the woman, Eva, who lived in her father's house. His own anger flared. To go to a girl's father and talk to him man to man was the custom. His own father would expect it and assume that Anna Maria would have a dowry befitting a maiden of their class. How could he not follow this ritual? He wanted to tell this stubborn *Mädchen* he loved that it was a thing he must do; that she was being unreasonable. But as so often happened to him, the words he wanted to say disarranged themselves among all the conflicting thoughts in his head and dissolved into nothingness before they could reach his tongue.

Anna Maria sat down on the low stone fence that Claus had repaired so well, each stone precisely placed because that had given him more time with the girl who intrigued him.

"Well, why do you stand there frowning at me?" she said. "Perhaps I must tell the cabbage head, the cornflowers and the apple tree that I am not to marry you after all."

"Anna Maria, you know that the marriage announcement must be read in both of our churches and that you will be expected to marry in Oberzerf. I must at least tell your Papp of our engagement."

"Claus Marx, if I choose to marry you, it must be where I say; and I say it must be here, close to Paschel, in the Hentern church. I will not be led from my father's house to the church in Oberzerf. That would mean that I would have to stay under his roof for at least one night and have his hateful woman, his Eva, walk in the wedding procession to the church as if she belonged there. I will not do it. I have made a vow on this, and I never break my vows." Anna Maria's arms were folded tight across her chest, a sure sign that all was not well.

"You are unreasonable, Anna Maria." I don't care about a dowry as my father does but just think a moment. Your father may not give his permission for us to marry in Hentern and perhaps the Hentern Priest will not allow it either."

"The *Priester* will not refuse to marry us. Many girls whose fathers have contracted them out as serving maids have no money for a wedding party and marry quietly in the village where they work. The wedding banns announcing a marriage are read in both churches; you know that. That will satisfy the priest."

Claus wiped the sweat from his forehead with the back of his sleeve. He wanted Anna Maria more than anything he had ever wanted in all his life. But not going to her father before the marriage banns were read was a grave insult to a man who had done him no harm. This custom must be kept. He was determined.

"Where we marry is of no importance to me. If the priest says we can be made man and wife in Hentern, so it shall be. But I will not have your father believing that I am a man without principle who will marry his daughter without telling him, like a sneak thief who steals a goose. I will do the expected thing." He folded his arms and glared at Anna Maria who glared back at him.

"I am not a goose, Claus Marx; the property of my father to be carried away under your arm after you have reached an agreeable price for me."

The *Tante's* voice came from the kitchen doorway. "What's this? My Anna Maria has stopped her hoeing and the Claus does not work either? Whatever it is you talk of, it is not so important that it can't wait until after you come inside and have a bit of *Kuchen* with me."

As they sat around the long kitchen table, they told the Tante Susanna about their quarrel. The Frau Thielen had hands that shook and legs that barely supported her progress from the kitchen to her sleeping room. Her voice was sometimes hard to understand from the shaking that overtook her. But her spirit was young and spry. Since Anna Maria had come to help her, she had formed a bond with her. She recognized her own young, rebellious spirit when she listened to Anna Maria, and it made her feel young too. As she struggled to keep her hands calm enough to manage, she cut pieces of *Kuchen* for Anna Maria and young

Claus. Her mind was on the problem that had provoked the couple's quarrel.

They ate in silence for a time. The *Tante* Susanna said, "You two have become like a son and daughter to me. It would break my heart if I could not attend your wedding, but how could I go to Oberzerf, shaking and jerking on these good-for-nothing legs. Therefore, Anna Maria, tomorrow I will send Claus to deliver a message from me to your father. It will say that he must come here to Paschel to discuss an important matter concerning your stay with me."

Anna Maria and Clause stared at her. They had never seen her look so determined.

"When Herr Rauls comes, you both will be here. Claus will tell him his intentions and I will say to him, 'Claus is a fine choice of husband for Anna Maria. It makes me so happy that they have decided to marry, and to have the wedding here where I can easily attend will give me such pleasure. I do hope you will not refuse a tired and sick old woman that simple request!' and then I will pat his hand with these jerking fingers." She gave a pleading, innocent smile as if she was already talking to Johann Rauls. Then she winked wickedly and let out a whoop of laughter. It was so infectious that Claus and Anna Maria could not hold onto their scowls. In a fraction of a second, they were howling with laughter too. All three laughed until they were holding their sides and wiping their eyes.

At first, Johann Rauls remained reluctant to have his daughter marry without coming back to her home parish, but Magda mediated a fragile peace between her father and Anna Maria, and Johann and Claus' father came to a quick agreement in the matter of the dowry. In the end, Johann agreed to the marriage at Hentern. But one matter could not be resolved. Anna Maria did not want Eva to be part of her marriage procession to the Hentern church. She demanded that the woman she regarded as her enemy must stay away.

Johann was not used to demands. He held on to his pride. He would come to the wedding accompanied by her brothers and sisters. Eva, the cousin of their mother, would come too. If Anna Maria could not agree to this condition, he himself would not come either.

"If Anna Maria thinks so little of her father that she treats him like a servant, telling him who he may invite to accompany him, I will not be a part of the procession to the church or attend the wedding ceremony," he said to Magda. "Let her marry in Hentern as she wishes. I will stay in Oberzerf on that day and mend the oxen's harnesses."

Nothing Magda could say would change his mind. Anna Maria, as willful as her father was stubborn, would not give in on this point. If her father would not do as she wanted, she would marry without him among the guests.

In the fall and winter months before the wedding, Johann began to see Maria in his dreams. She chided him in the gentle way he remembered so well and told him that he had wronged Anna Maria, and that he must make things right. The dream came back again and again. Sometimes he begged her to tell him what to do. Other times he poured out his anger and hurt. Most often, he reached out and tried to hold her. Maria never answered, never came to his outstretched arms. He would wake in disappointment.

The dreams stopped when he took up his tools and began to construct a wedding chest for Anna Maria. As he cut and fitted, planed and polished, the chest became his act of contrition to his wife and to Anna Maria, his attempt to express in wood that which he could not say in words. When the chest was finished, he put a small bag with a delicate silver cross, strung on a black velvet band inside it. He had made a trip to Saarburg to buy it, somehow knowing exactly where to look, as if Maria's hand beckoned at the shopkeeper's door, urging him to come inside and make the purchase.

Two weeks before the wedding, he sent Mathes and Pitt to Hentern to deliver the chest, wishing that he could see Anna Maria's face when the boys carried it inside the house where she would live after the wedding.

Anna Maria was not the only one to push at the boundaries set down by custom. Lis was planning to do something unthinkable. She had decided to hire herself out as a serving maid in another village, not with a relative but with strangers. She was not sure just how she would do it, but her determination was as strong as her hatred for the relationship between Eva and her father. She would make it happen. The idea took root at the wedding meal in the inn at Hentern, and it was much on her mind as she and her brothers and sisters bumped along the road from Hentern to Oberzerf after the wedding celebration. All of the riders in Hanni's wagon were bundled in their heaviest wool outer garments and swaddled in quilts, for the January night was cold. The heated bricks at their feet had cooled before they had traveled for a quarter of an hour.

The moon was so bright and the sky so filled with stars that Leni could clearly see the faces of her two sisters and the blanket-covered lumps that were her brothers who had drunk a quantity of wine and were dozing on the floor of the wagon.

"Didn't Anna Maria look beautiful in her wedding crown?" Leni said to Magda and Lis.

"She did," Magda answered. "I think that Claus will be a good husband for her. He will not let her rule his roost."

Lis said, "I wonder how many arguments they will have each day and how many times Claus will be the winner. I would wager not too many."

Leni thought, "When Anna Maria covers his face with kisses, he will give her anything she wants." She didn't know why the thought of kissing made her face feel hot in spite of the frigid January night. She had exchanged appraising glances with one of the Marx cousins, a handsome boy with light brown hair, merry green eyes and dimples in each cheek that made her want to trace them with the tip of her finger. She wondered what it would be like to kiss him. Would his lips have been soft as his silky hair and would he have kissed her in return. She lay back on her straw sack and smiled up into the stars. Her sisters went on talking.

She was drifting off to sleep when she heard Magda's raised voice. "Lis, you cannot be serious. Papp would never allow it. Only the daughters of the poor farmers or the landless renters go off to work as serving maids in the homes of strangers."

Leni made no movement but she was listening so intently that her ears felt as if they were pushing away from her head and extending outward.

"You know how I feel about Papp and the whore." Lis said. "Why should I care about the family reputation? What is our reputation? The daughters of a man who keeps his whore in the same house as his family."

"Don't use such words, Lis," Magda scolded. "You sound like a trollop when you call *Fräulein* Eva such a thing."

"I just say what everyone in Oberzerf says behind their closed doors. Mag. I want to be away from that. I spend each day wanting to explode in rage. I thought I would get used to her, but my anger is only getting worse. I'm afraid I may kill her some day; just take one of the kitchen knives and cut her throat the way the butcher does a pig."

"Lis," Magda said, her voice a shocked whisper. "You know you would never do that. God in heaven, just the thought of it is a sin."

"That's why I must go soon, Mag. I have to get away from the temptation to sin; Father Guckeisen always tells us so."

"But even if you could convince him to let you go, Papp would have to make the contract between you and the farmer you would serve. He would get any money you earn. You would be lucky to get as much as a length of cloth at Christmas. How the Eva would like that."

"I don't care about the money. I just want to get away from our farm and from Oberzerf and go someplace where people do not stop talking when I walk by. I want to go far away where Papp won't find me."

"You must know that there is no way that Papp will consent to this or take you back if you do it without his permission."

"I know."

"I won't help you; I think this idea is a bad one. What if I tell Papp what you are thinking?"

"But I know you won't do that, Magda. That's why I can say this to you."

Their voices were very low now and Leni had to strain to hear as Lis went on talking. "Anna Maria understands. She will take me in until I'm sure I have work and can make my own way in life."

"But what if there is no job. Anna Maria and Claus are just starting out. They will have to work very hard just to live themselves and when the babies start coming, it will be even harder. You couldn't stay there very long. What will become of you if you do not find a place to work?"

"I will find a way to take care of myself. You can't talk me out of this, Magda."

"Have you thought about Leni? You will be leaving her alone with Eva, Papp, and the boys. She will have to take on your share of the work."

"She is Papp's favorite, always has been. He won't let the Eva work her to death."

Both Magda and Lis looked over to where Leni lay. She squeezed her eyes shut and commanded her body to stay as still as that of a cat watching its prey.

"Anyway," Lis went on, "Mathes will move a wife into the house one of these days." Her voice dripped with sarcasm as she added, "He almost stops breathing every time he sees Betta Meyer, and she turns red as a ripe *Kaiser* apple. It won't be long before Mathes starts courting her in a serious way."

"What about Nikla Meyer?" Magda asked. "I've seen the two of you with your heads together at the festivals."

"*Ja*, I like Nikla but he's just like me. He wants to get away from Oberzerf. He'll go the first chance he gets after he is free of military duty. Mag, he is thinking about leaving for good, going to *Amerika*. He says that a man alone has a better chance than one burdened down with wife and *Kinder*. He won't miss me much if I go away."

The wagon stopped. They were home. "Come on Leni, boys" Magda said. Leni, then Pitt, Mathes and Theiss sat up. The brothers rubbed the sleep from their eyes; Leni rubbed the tears from hers. They all got down from the wagon and made their way into the dark *Einhaus* where their father, still in his chair, smoked his pipe and waited for them.

Leni watched Lis closely for the next few months, but her sister made no effort to leave home. She was short tempered as ever. She did her work as always and whenever she disappeared for a few hours, Mathes was absent too. Leni stopped her vigilant spying by mid-summer and had forgotten about it by the time of the autumn harvest.

CHAPTER 13
A Teacher's Quandary – September 1839

In 1837, the school at Zerf was divided into an over- and under-level. The school population numbered over 100 children. Teachers also filled the position of Sexton, that is, a maintenance man responsible for the general upkeep of the building and sometimes for bell-ringing and supervising burials. Herr Nikolaus Trapp was the teacher of the Zerf upper school from 1837 to 1856. Christoffel, Edgar, <u>Der Hochwaldorf Zerf am Fusse des Hunsrücks</u>.

The schoolrooms on the Englestrasse in Niederzerf were always damp and dark, but Leni looked forward to each day she spent in this place. Last year Herr Goetten taught her class. He sat on his high stool instructing, his face serious. If you laughed out loud or were not able to recite the multiplication tables as quickly as he wanted, you were made to wear donkey ears and sit on a high round log called the "*Holzesel*." Leni had ridden that wooden donkey only once, but it was enough to make her wonder if a real donkey gave you such a sore bottom after an hour of riding it.

In spite of occasional punishment, Leni had been happy even in that schoolroom. She knew she did not do as well at her mathematics as she should. The school had no money for books to help explain the numbers. Herr Goetten taught them what he called "head reckoning," insisting that this kind of figuring would serve the boys well when it came time to figure out the ever increasing taxes due to the Prussian government. Leni understood by this that in the future she would have no need of mathematics since that was the duty of men.

Instead Leni focused her attention on reading and writing. When the marks and squiggles on the page of the beginning primer turned themselves into words, she could not get enough of them and turned the pages eagerly as Herr Goetten taught more. She hoped someday to read so many words that her head was filled to bursting. To recognize the words on the page and then to write them on her slate was a miracle, better than riding in a carriage all the way to Trier, which was one of her secret desires.

There was only the <u>ABC Namenbuch</u> to teach the alphabet and the <u>Elementar Buch</u> to practice reading. She hoped that someday she would have a book filled with words and bound in leather that would be her very own. In the meantime, she read these battered schoolbooks over and over, until she knew almost every page by heart.

Herr Goetten was not her teacher this year. Last year a young teacher with unruly brown hair, very blue eyes, and a dimple in his chin, Herr Trapp, had been hired when the school had been divided into two parts, an upper and a lower form. He was not so free with the strap as old Goetten and was well respected by the students he taught. Sometimes he brought his own books to read to them. This year she sat before him in his classroom and learned her lessons from a man who had been educated in Trier, which in Leni's imagination was a city filled with ladies and gentlemen who wore fine clothes and rode everywhere in carriages drawn by high-stepping horses.

Today was Friday, the time when Herr Trapp would read to them from the <u>Lives of the Saints.</u> His voice, low and mellow, was full of expression as he explained the difficult words to the students. Leni loved these reading times, and she had begun to skip along the well-trodden footpath that led to the school as she anticipated the upcoming pleasure. Then she remembered that she was almost 12 now, nearly grown up, and a student of the upper school. She stopped skipping and began to stride along as Herr Trapp did, head up and shoulders back. She was ready to take on anything that should come her way. When she saw her friends Katharina and Elizabetha, she ran to catch up with them. The three laughed and chattered and made guesses about when their good-looking teacher would take a wife and whom it would be.

Herr Trapp, as part of the religious study required by the School Board of Trier, had decided he could inspire his students with the exploits of God's heroes, those who had given their lives in some way to the service of their Catholic faith. On this November day he had chosen the story of St. Jeanne d'Arc; about how heavenly voices spoke to her, how she led soldiers in battle and gave advice to the French Dauphin before she was captured by the British, tried as a heretic and burned at the stake. As he glanced up now and then from his reading, he saw mostly passive, unconcerned faces looking back at him, except for some burning question alight in the Rauls girl's dark eyes. He wondered why she seemed so bemused by this story but gave it no more than a passing thought. He spent the end of the day reviewing the multiplication tables for those who seemed to have no idea that the human head was able to hold information longer than the time that it took to skip a stone across the creek that ran through the village.

After he had dismissed the classes for the day, he went back to his table and began to put away the books that covered it. He was surprised to hear a voice behind him.

"Please, Herr Trapp, I want to ask about something."

When he turned he saw it was young *Fräulein* Rauls who had spoken. Usually she was one of the first children to step over the scarred, narrow door sill, probably as anxious as he himself for the light and the freedom of the open countryside after a day in a classroom where the smell of the musty stone walls of the school room and of the more than 50 children whose bodies were rarely touched by soap and water hung thick in the air. It sometimes made him wish he had become a tradesman like his brother.

"*Ja, Fräulein* Rauls, what is it then? Have you a question about what we learned today?"

There was a moment of silence before the girl said, "Herr Professor Trapp, Jeanne d'Arc became a good soldier. Why is it that women now cannot be soldiers or shoemakers or sailors or schoolteachers or even priests? I have been wondering about this all afternoon. Is this a law of the Prussian Emperor?"

The young teacher was taken by surprise. No child had asked him this before. He had never asked this question of himself; just accepted its inevitability. Not one of the students or teachers at the seminary in Trier had discussed it. He already suspected that the answer he would give would not satisfy this young girl with the thoughtful brown eyes.

"No," he began, "It is not a written law of the Prussian government. But it is a thing of custom. Men are stronger than women, perhaps better able to do these things..."

His voice trailed off because he was unconvinced by his own words. Every day he saw the women of Zerf and Oberzerf carrying heavy loads in baskets strapped to their backs or bundles of heavy branches balanced on their heads. They wielded the sickle and scythe; they helped to dig the potato crop and carry heavy bags and baskets to the waiting wagons.

"It is only because the men are stronger?" Leni asked, frowning. "Many women are very strong though I suppose not quite so strong as men." She paused to think about what he had just told her, and Herr Trapp was about to turn away when she spoke again.

"But schoolteachers or priests do not need so much strength. Father Guckeisen says the prayers of the Mass, tends his garden and walks to visit the parishes at Oberzerf and Greimerath. Any woman could do that. I could do that. Why can't women be priests? They would be strong enough for such work."

"Church law forbids it," Herr Trapp used his most authoritative voice. He felt on safer ground here.

"But why is it forbidden? Does God not like women? I thought he loved all equally." The words were respectful but the voice that said them held a challenge in it.

Herr Trapp blinked and brushed the lock of unruly hair from his forehead. A woman priest, he thought. It's impossible; surely she can understand that. What had gotten into this girl who now questioned the Holy Catholic Church law.

His voice quiet, the teacher replied, "I think Fräulein Rauls that you must ask the good Father Guckeisen about matters of Church dogma. As for me, I think that if Our Lord had wanted women to be priests, he would have made some of them his apostles. That is my opinion."

He hoped that Leni would go now, perhaps to search out the priest to ask her perplexing questions.

Leni stood her ground. She frowned. "Girls are smarter than boys. It is the boys who stumble over the words in the book pages we read aloud or who cannot remember how to write their letters and yet there are no women teachers. Since a woman cannot be a soldier or a priest, why can she not be a teacher?"

"And do you think that a woman like you could keep order in a classroom such as this one, when the sturdy lads must be made to sit on the *Holzesel* and wear the donkey ears? Could you command them to do it and make them obey, Magdalena Rauls?"

Leni's chin came up. "I could and I would," she said.

Well, of course, that isn't all that is required to be a teacher," Herr Trapp said, again running his fingers through his unruly brown hair and rumpling it even more. "One must study at a special school for those who want to be teachers. I studied at the Seminary of St. Mathias in Trier, but it is only for men. I think that in a very large city like Köln there might be such a school for women, but I am not sure about this."

"Herr Goetten did not study at such a school. He learned to teach from his father before him." Leni's voice held a note of triumph.

"The law has changed since then. These days a special course of education is required of all teachers even though sometimes, a teacher is often not much more than a janitor, keeping the classrooms and the church clean and also in good repair. If a teacher wants to have a family, it is sometimes necessary that he have a skill such as tailoring or shoemaking, especially in the summer when there are no classes and no pay. Otherwise the teacher must be out in the fields with the herders, watching the pigs or the cows from morning 'til night. What woman could do all this and have a husband and family as well."

"I guess she could not," Leni said thoughtfully. "There wouldn't be time to do all the work that a wife does every day, teach lessons, and be a sexton or a herder too." For the first time, she seemed subdued.

Herr Trapp pressed on with his argument. "Indeed it would be very difficult even for an unmarried woman. As yet I have no wife and even I spend almost every cent of the small amount I earn to pay for the necessities. Now and then I can buy a book or a bit of pipe tobacco. I do not have to herd the pigs in the summertime since I can play the organ and train the church choir. That keeps me out of the cow pasture or herding pigs in the summer. But when I marry, I may have to do that other work as well."

Leni was astonished. "You are paid to play the organ when the choir sings? Paid for doing something so lovely? It is like the stars earning money whenever they shine."

Herr Trapp was again at a momentary loss for words. This girl saw things in such an unorthodox way. He sensed that if, given a free hand, she would turn the world he was so sure of into a place he hardly recognized.

"Of course it is wonderful to make music just for the beauty of it, but one must live too," he finally said. "If you, Fräulein Rauls, become a teacher and have to live without a husband, you will need to eat and have clothes. When the shoemaker gives you the shoes he has made for you, he will not be happy if you play him a song or two."

Leni scarcely heard her teacher's sarcasm. She asked, "How did you learn to play the organ, Herr Trapp? Was it part of the schooling to become a teacher?"

"No, it was not. From the time I was a young boy, I helped the organist, who was also my teacher, with his chores at the village church, and in return he taught me to play and allowed me to practice when the church was empty."

"I wish I had been able to do that when I was a child," the girl said thoughtfully. "I am too old now, I think, to learn to play the organ. I wouldn't like to be a pig herder. But if it is the only way to make enough money to live as a teacher…"

Her voice trailed off into silence but not for long. "I could do it," she said after her short pause.

Herr Trapp felt an amused smile come to his lips, and he covered his chin with his hand to disguise it. What supreme confidence the girl standing before him displayed. He said, "If you are going to be a teacher, Magdalena Rauls, you must do well at all the subjects. You are not a good student when it is arithmetic that I am explaining. I have seen you drawing on your slate instead of copying the sums or fractions that I am dictating."

Leni had to agree that she had not paid much attention when Herr Trapp explained the theory of fractions. It was so dull, and she had thought of it as a man's work. But now she saw she had been wrong about that. She said, "Perhaps I could do better."

"I would advise that you work very hard, then. Perhaps by the end of this year, we will see a student who can tell me all of the multiplication tables and who can divide numbers accurately. You must come to appreciate the importance of mathematics if you are so determined to teach.

"I won't change my mind about numbers, Herr Trapp. They never do anything interesting. Two plus three makes always five. Two times three always makes six. But they will never make a story."

Herr Trapp saw why the girl made no progress at her numbers. "Let me tell you a story about numbers," he said. "Maybe you will change your mind."

Leni gave him a sidelong glance, something he had noticed that she did when she had a strong doubt about what had been said to her. He motioned to her to sit at one of the benches and began, "Once there was a poor farmer named Holzkopf."

Leni giggled at the name "Wooden Head" which Herr Trapp has chosen for the hero of his story.

The teacher smiled but continued talking. "Herr Holzkopf wanted to improve his situation. He had a wife and many children to support. So he doubled his efforts, working for a rich farmer who paid him a small wage. Holzkopf and his wife also worked hard on their own small parcel of land. Soon he had enough money to buy an ox to help him with his labor. But at that same time, an excellent piece of land became available, and he had just enough money to rent it. He and his wife argued about what he should do. He wanted to snatch up the bargain of the land; she wanted him to buy the ox since it was she who often was needed to pull the plow. Holzkopf determined he should buy the land. His wife screamed at him that it was an ox that they needed. They were shouting so loud that the people of the village from one end to the other could hear them. Many similar arguments started as people disagreed about who was right, the wooden headed farmer or his weary wife.

Just then a charming young *Fräulein* named Magdalena came to their door and asked if she might be of any help. She was a very intelligent girl and suggested using arithmetic to aid them in deciding which course of action they should take.

Herr Trapp saw that Leni was thinking hard. "What do you think she proposed?" he asked her.

"The land," Leni said. "Buying the land."

Herr Trapp raised one eyebrow and gave her a questioning look. "Are you sure?"

It had seemed such a logical answer a moment ago but now she wasn't quite as sure. It was a difficult problem. It might make more sense to purchase the animal if its use could help one get more rye or wheat from land already owned. "The ox?" she questioned, waiting for her teacher to tell her the answer.

"If you knew more about multiplication, fractions, and sums, you could figure out the answer for yourself," Herr Trapp said. "Bring your slate here and let me show you."

He wiped the slate clean and drew a long line from its top to its bottom, dividing it into two sections. On one side he wrote "ox." On the other side he wrote "land."

"This is how we do it," he said as he began to write numbers.

When Leni finally left his classroom, smiling at the discovery that arithmetic had a purpose, Herr Trapp sat down in his chair to think. He was pleased that he had been able to teach this reluctant student that reckoning was of use to men and women alike. But her questions had unsettled him. Why was it that women were always consigned the role of wife and mother and allowed no latitude of thought? This girl, called Leni by her friends, was intelligent and able. But she would never serve on the village council, be a church warder, or for that matter, play the organ. He had seen how her eyes had sparkled at the thought of it. But he could not teach her. It would never be allowed. The village would be enraged at such a thing. Custom is a terrifying overlord, he thought as he began to prepare tomorrow's lesson. It defines us from the moment we draw our first breath and woe to the one who challenges it. Suddenly he put his books aside and went to seek out Father Guckeisen

The sun was setting, and a few dark clouds edged in gold were building on the horizon. Johann Rauls, sitting on the log bench just outside the *Einhaus* door, looked up in surprise as two men walking along the road approached his doorstep.

"Good day to you, Herr Rauls," Father Guckeisen said. "We have come to talk with you if you will spare us a minute."

The young schoolmaster stood respectfully at the priest's side, casting his eyes around the farmyard but saying nothing.

"Come in please," Johann said, rising from his bench and bowing his head in respect. He could not imagine why these two should be here.

"Seat yourself again, Johann," the priest said, placing a hand on Johann's shoulder. "We are warm from walking and the night is mild. Let us talk here on this pleasant evening. But I forget my manners. I believe you and our new teacher, Herr Trapp, have not met."

Herr Trapp reached out for Johann's hand and shook it heartily. "A pleasure, Herr Rauls," he said, "to meet the father of Mathias and Magdalena."

Johann was not used to hearing the formal names of his two youngest children and for a brief second he believed that Herr Trapp had his children confused with those of another family.

Father Guckeisen seated himself on the bench with Johann and Herr Trapp pulled up a stool that stood at the side of the door. "It is your Magdalena that we wish to talk about, Johann." Are you aware that she is the best student in Herr Trapp's classroom?"

Johann looked from one to the other. Leni was the smartest child in the upper school? His face registered confusion.

Herr Trapp spoke then. "Herr Rauls, Leni has the gift of a swift and curious mind. She learns quickly, with true understanding. With your permission, I would like to help her in the only way I know how, but your permission is essential. I myself am a lover of books about Germany's history, geography, and the lives of the great men of the past centuries. I have a little library of books that I have purchased for myself, and I would be honored if you would permit me to allow Leni to read some of them." He was wise enough not to mention Leni's hidden dream of becoming a teacher that he had inadvertently placed in her mind.

Johann frowned. His thick, dark eyebrows drew together, and Herr Trapp was glad he had begged their priest to come with him. His offer of a special privilege must not be misinterpreted. But Herr Rauls was obviously not pleased with this idea.

"My Leni reading your books? But why should she? This is a benefit for a young man, perhaps one who wants to become a priest or who has a well-to-do family that can afford to educate him to a profession. I love my Leni, but her future is to marry the man I approve for her and then to bear his children. If she is to learn more, it would be the household skills that she will need for her life with her *Mann* and their *Kinder*."

Father Guckeisen intervened. "Herr Rauls, the teacher Trapp offers your daughter a rare opportunity. And think how this will help her with the schooling of her sons when she bears them. She can be a second teacher to them. The world is changing, Johann. You know it."

He lowered his voice to a near whisper. "The more that the next generation, your grandsons, learn from more educated parents may help to bring us a democratic government."

Johann and Herr Trapp exchanged glances. What would the Archbishop in Koblenz say about a village priest who encouraged his parishioners to have such an unconventional attitude? The revolution that swept through France less than 50 years ago had not been kind to the Catholic Church and most of the clergy feared liberal thought.

"Father," Johann Rauls said, "you believe in more rights for the common people like us farmers and even the landless?"

"I do Johann, and I have no doubt that our dear Savior does too. He wanted all of us, both men and women, to be permitted to use the talent our Father in heaven gave us. That would make our land an upright place to live; where poverty and hunger are no longer the fate of people who work hard and deserve better."

Hearing Father Guckeisen's words of support for the rights of ordinary farmers and day workers, Johann was ashamed at his lack of belief in any of the words spoken by priests. Johann went to Sunday Mass, sitting, standing, and kneeling, to curb the gossip about Eva living in his house. He gave the words of each Sunday's sermon no more attention than the mooing of one of his three cows. What did they know of the hard lives of their flock, he thought. He had been unfair to this caring shepherd of his flock. He lowered his head in embarrassment.

"Father Guckeisen, Herr Trapp, I thank you for your attention to my child's education."

If only he could sleep in Maria's arms tonight. They always used their bed as a place to talk about the important or the trivial happenings of the day. It was a precious time. Sometimes Maria drifted off to sleep, a sentence half finished on her lips, and he would still be laughing softly as he himself left consciousness behind. Tonight they would have talked of their Leni, who was as smart a child as they had always believed.

Herr Trapp cleared his throat just then. Johann realized his mind had wandered. His callers were waiting for him to tell them his decision. His voice sounded weak to his ears as he said, "I am honored to accept your offer. When her chores are done, Leni may read books you have chosen, Herr Trapp. I thank you for your generosity." His voice shook slightly, and he turned his head away as if he had heard an unexpected sound behind him. He did not want the two men to see the tears that blurred his vision.

His two visitors seemed to understand. They thanked him for his decision, bid him a hearty *"Gute Nacht,* Herr Rauls," and quickly turned back toward Zerf.

When Leni came home from the school next day, she placed her book sack on the lower shelf of the scarred oak wall table, the place where she and Theiss kept their precious slates and chalk out of harm's way.

Cousin Eva walked into the *Stube* just as Leni stood up. "Your father is out at the *Bei Forsthofen* land working with Mathes. He told me to send you to him as soon as you came home from the school." Eva's expression showed an expectation that Leni was about to get her comeuppance and that it was about time.

The fields of *Bei Forsthofen* had forest strips of land that were divided among land owning farmers, and it was a long walk from the village to the fields in this part of Oberzerf's lottery-allocated *Gehoferschaft* parcels. The sun was already beginning to disappear behind the hills as Leni strode along wondering why Papp had summoned her to come such a long distance. He would be returning the five kilometers to their farm before darkness fell, a time that would not be too long in coming.

She was tired by the time she reached the place where her father and brother were working. They were cutting oak trees that had been stripped of their bark. That bark was in high demand by the tanners in Saarburg.

Leni always thought the trees looked naked when she saw them after the *Lohe* harvesting had taken their bark. It made her sad, even though she knew that these mature oaks had an important end coming to them. Most were cut into pieces that would heat their *Einhaus* all the winter long, even if it were a very cold year. And a few of the bare trees would serve a really special purpose. Her Papp would cut and shape them into the boards of the chest he had begun making for the time when Lis was ready for the announcement of the marriage banns. The chest would be carried to Lis' new home on the day she became a bride. After that, it would be Leni's turn to have one of Papp's beautifully made wedding chests fashioned from future stripped oaks that would be cut some year in the future. She shivered a little, fear and pleasure combined, at the thought of it.

"Come here, Lenchen," her Papp said, using the old pet name for her. It had been a long time since he had called her that endearment, and she cocked her head, looking at him in surprise as he came around the wagon and stood regarding her.

"I had a visit from Father Guckeisen and Herr Trapp last evening."

"I haven't done anything wrong, Papp," Leni murmured. Her hands were shaking a little, even though she knew that she had done very well in school these last few weeks, especially since Herr Trapp had explained the uses of arithmetic to her.

"I know you haven't done wrong," her father said. "They came with something else in mind. They told me that you are the best student in the school. I am proud of you, Leni."

Leni stared at her father, disbelief on her face. Her father, so sparing with any kind of praise, was proud of her. Herr Trapp and Father Guckeisen had honored them by visiting their *Einhaus*. She would not have been any more surprised if her father had told her that the Crown Prince of Prussia had appeared to offer her a pair of silk slippers.

"What do you say to all this, girl?" her father asked. "You are surprised? You didn't know?"

"No Papp," Leni shook her head emphatically. "Please don't tell anyone about it. The older boys, like the ones that were so mean to Pitt, also make life real hard for anyone they think is the teacher's favorite."

Johann shook his head. "So it is still the same as when I was a schoolboy. Well then, I will tell no one but Magda. She will be proud too."

Leni's smiled and breathed a sigh of relief although she was still puzzled about the reason the priest and the teacher had both come to tell this news to her father.

Johann read her expression and said, "As to why the good Father and your teacher both walked here to tell me that news – well, they asked my permission to let you borrow books from Herr Trapp's own library and to give you some time to read them."

Leni couldn't believe what she had just heard. She wanted to throw her arms around her Papp's neck; have him share her joy. But her father had not hugged or kissed her since before Mamm died. She silently waited to hear what he had decided, her heart beating so fast that she wanted to press her hands to her chest to quiet it.

"I told them 'yes', Leni. I know you will continue to do your chores and not misuse your time."

"Thank you, Papp," she said. "I will work as hard as I know how to do." The grave words came from a face alight with a wide smile.

"You go to Eva and get started on your work now," Johann said. "Tell her we may be late to our supper."

Leni nodded and ran back the way she had come. As he called for Mathes to start throwing the logs he had worked on into the wagon, Johann thought about the smile that his praise had brought to Leni. It lingered in his mind and a rare smile also came to his lips, so foreign during the years since Maria died. It felt unfamiliar but was a fine thing.

"Papp, would you like to see the book that I have borrowed from Herr Trapp?" Leni made her voice quiet, and almost tiptoed to the bench in the stable where her father sat, sharpening harvest-dulled scythes against his whetstone sharpener. Even though the lantern gave off a dim light, little sparks lit the workbench now and then as Johann brought one after another of the tools against the whetstone. He stopped to test the edge of the scythe he held and frowned, obviously not satisfied. Catching sight of the book in Leni's hands, he warned, "Be careful, girl. That book does not belong in the stable. You should keep it on the shelf in the *Stube*."

"I've wrapped it in one of our clean sack towels, Papp, so that my fingers won't soil it."

"Well, bring it here and let me look. Then take it back to the *Stube* where it will be safe."

Leni carried the book to her father, who did not touch it but bent his head to read the title on the cover, as if even his glance might soil the soft leather binding. "*Die Harzreise*," he said as Leni turned open the title page.

"Look Papp. It begins with a poem," Leni said. "Herr Trapp says this man will soon be considered one of Germany's best authors of poetry and stories." Her eyes were sparkling with the anticipation of reading this beautiful little book.

Another voice, impatient and loud, broke the mood as the door from the hall to the stable opened and Eva walked through it. "Leni, I've been looking all over for you. I want to spin and you must do more carding. Stop wasting time and get to work."

Leni turned to go. "Come back here, Leni," Johann called. You come too Cousin Eva. He always called her "Cousin Eva" when Leni or her brothers and sisters were present. Eva's face had its usual expression, the look of one who is ever expecting to hear unpleasant news.

"Leni, show cousin Eva the book."

Leni held it out, gripping the coarse linen cloth and worried that the book might fall, damaging the beautiful leather cover.

Eva squinted at it. "Why does she have that?" Her question was addressed to Johann; Leni might have been a piece of furniture whose only purpose was to provide a resting place for something much more valuable than she.

"Father Guckeisen and Herr Trapp have been kind enough to say that Leni, as one of the school's very best students, may read such books as Herr Trapp sees fit to share with her."

"To what purpose?" Eva was honestly confused. "A farm girl has no use for books bound in leather. She should spend her time learning what she will need when she has a husband and children to care for. Now come along and help me with the spinning, Leni."

"No!" Johann said. It was the voice of a patriarch rebuking one much more lowly and brooking no argument. He seemed to forget that he had said much the same thing to Father Guckeisen and Herr Trapp only a few days ago.

"Leni will read for a little time each evening after our meal. She is a bright girl and quick. When she finishes ten pages, she will begin her regular chores."

With that he picked up his scythe and held it against the whetstone again, concentrating on his own work.

Resenting the way she had been abruptly dismissed, Eva scowled but made no more complaints when Leni went back to the *Stube* and began to carefully turn the pages of the book, which glowed gold, almost like an ancient manuscript, in the light of the oil lamp on the table.

CHAPTER 14
A Change of Scenery – June 1840

Irsch, one of the villages near Oberzerf, has a raised plateau just outside the western edge of the village. Since the 1500s it has been called the Feuerstatt. That innocent-looking field was the place where four people accused of witchcraft and found guilty by the Catholic Church inquisition, were burned in the 1630s. One of the women was a midwife. She used herbs and potions to try to heal disease, making her a prime target for stories of sorcery. She was probably condemned to death for causing illness or death. Meyer, Ewald, <u>Irsch/Saar, Geschichte eines Dorfes</u>.

"I must ask you a favor, Johann," *Tante* Mari said.

She sat on the rough wooden bench, faded gray by time, which hugged the front wall of the *Einhaus*. The sky was darkening to a rich evening blue that many artists try to reproduce but none succeed. In the almost eight years since Maria Rauls' death, Johann's diminutive sister-in-law had aged; each year brought additions to the fine pattern of lines on her face. Her brown eyes, though, were alive with the sparkle of the enchanting maiden she had once been. At the age of 62 her skin was like a piece of fine linen that had been rolled and stored. The material was still strong but the creases from its many foldings grew deeper and more enduring as the years went by. She and Nikolaus still made a lively pair among the young ones at weddings and *Kirmes* dances. Everyone in the village knew her as *Tante* Mari, the skilled midwife who seemed like a part of their family. Most had known her since they were children. Her determined footsteps, still as rapid as in her younger years, were regularly heard as she covered the distance between her home and a cottage or *Einhaus* in need of her. There was sometimes the joy of a child's birth; sometimes the pain of a loved one lost. In happiness or sorrow, with gentleness and comfort, *Tante* Mari was there to do whatever needed doing.

"What is it?" Johann asked as he sat down beside her.

Tante Mari had never before asked him for anything, and he was taken aback. He had come to discuss the haying with his brother Nikolaus and was on his way home. Then *Tante* Mari had patted the seat beside her and invited him to sit as he came through the *Einhaus* door.

"You know that Lis has become interested in midwifery?" *Tante* Mari began. "She spends time with me almost every week, gathering herbs, making potions, and asking the most intelligent of questions. I have begun to take her with me to help if there is no danger of contagion. I must say that she learns fast, and I am coming to depend on her. She has a good head on her shoulders, and she does not flinch when there is care to be given, no matter how distasteful."

"I am glad that Lis has found an interest," Johann replied.

He knew that Lis was smart, strong-willed, and clever. However, ever since the night she had become hysterical when she discovered that Eva had shared his bed, she had kept her feelings locked as deep inside as he kept his own. That she allowed herself to be tender toward anyone in need of help surprised him, but he was glad of it. Soon it would be time for her to marry, and her instruction from *Tante* Mari would serve her well. In addition, it might ease the tension in his household. Lis spent much of her time with *Tante* Mari and his brother Nikolaus, and even though Eva complained that the girl was always gone when work needed doing, Johann did nothing to appease the woman he himself had begun to dislike.

Tante Mari considered carefully what to say next. She was setting out to extricate her troubled niece from her current situation because if Lis did not pull free of the dangerous and hostile passion that so often consumed her, it would surely eat her soul away. That Lis could not forgive her father did not surprise *Tante* Mari who knew its cause was Eva's sharing of her father's bed. The icy reserve Lis showed her family was also a dangerous thing. Gradually Lis had fewer friends. The more she kept to herself, the harsher her manner became. It was sad irony that she was becoming very like Eva, the woman she hated.

As *Tante* Mari had readied Johann's wife for burial, she had promised her dead sister-in-law, surely now in heaven, that she would watch over the bereaved children, especially the younger ones. She had gently coaxed Lis into this new role. Caring for the sick showed a side of Lis that was not easily recognized by her family and her friends. *Tante* Mari, watching her, saw a girl who was struggling to heal herself by healing others.

Johann stood up to leave. He thanked his sister-in-law for curing Lis of her ill humor. "It will make a nice change for all of us," he added.

"You think your Lis has truly recovered? My dear brother-in-law, you do not understand your daughter at all." *Tante* Mari's voice was sorrowful. "It is as if she does not really exist for you, and she is bitter and resentful. I think it would be best for her and perhaps for you, if you would let her have some time away from here. A chance to practice midwife skills would show her that you believe in her as much as you believe in young Leni."

Johann's face darkened to a scowl. "I treat all my children fair. I permit Lis to roam with you at will just as I allow Leni extra time for reading of the books Herr Trapp shares with her. Since you know so much about my daughter's needs, be so good as to explain to me what more I should do."

Tante Mari knew that in spite of what he had just said, Johann felt guilt at his lack of love for his stubborn and difficult Lis. This he would never admit, even to himself; he could not admit mistakes. Only his much-loved Maria had known how to calm his ruffled feathers when she found fault with him. *Tante* Mari started over.

"*Ja,* of course, Johann. You have been a good father." *Tante* Mari began again. "It is because of this that I ask you the favor I spoke of. Lis has, with me at her side, delivered a child, selected herbs for a potion as good as I can, and she stands with me at a deathbed, comforting and praying with the one soon to be taken. I am sure you would be so proud of her, but she hesitates to tell you of it. She has a special talent that should be encouraged. I ask you to allow her to travel to Heddert where they have just lost their midwife, an old woman, to a fever. It would only be for two or three weeks, and she would learn so much. Even more important, your permission would show her you take pride in her."

Johann stared at her. "Lis has said nothing to me of any of this."

A realization came to him and stung him like an unseen but poisonous wasp. Lis hardly ever spoke to him, her own father, nor did she seem to say much to Theiss or Leni. Mathes was the one she had trusted completely, but lately her brother's interests lay elsewhere. Mathes was distracted, shifting his awareness from his sister to young Betta Meyer who enjoyed his attention and encouraged it. Lis had withdrawn from the family, and he, her own father, had ignored her most of all.

Tante Mari went on, sensing that Johann was thinking about what she was saying. "Lis has the skills which I have taught her and which she has learned well. Let her try her wings. She will only remain there until another woman can be trained to take on the position of Heddert's midwife."

Johann rubbed his hand across the back of his neck. "Lis is young," he said. "I have grave doubts that she will be accepted by the villagers. She could be in a dangerous situation if she should make a mistake."

"Schillingen's midwife will travel to Heddert every few days to make sure Lis has help with difficult problems. The villagers understand that Lis is not experienced, but they will be glad to have some sort of help close at hand."

"A respectable young woman cannot live alone. I cannot say yes to this."

"I have a grand nephew with a wife and two young children who has a farm there. He came to me for help for the village. Lis can stay with him and his family until the new midwife comes."

"I do not want my child put in danger," Johann was pulling away again and his thick eyebrows drew even closer together.

Tante Mari reached over and touched his shoulder. "Surely you know that I would allow no harm to come to my niece. She will return back to Oberzerf healthy and also proud of having a skill she can pass on to another or use when she herself has a family."

"*Majusepeta!*" Johann exploded, jerking away from Tante Mari's touch, curling his hand into a fist and striking it into his other palm. Mari was hinting that he could not manage his children. This he could not accept. He had tried to raise his daughters to help others but only hurt came from that.

"Anna Maria went to help a relative, and it caused trouble that follows me to this day. She was never the same toward me after living away; I lost her. No, I will not risk sending another daughter off to help strangers. I refuse. Lis stays here, where she belongs."

Tante Mari had resolved to be tactful with Johann but this was too much. Red slashes of color rose to her cheeks.

"You sent Anna Maria away to solve your own problems, and you know that, brother-in-law. If you had let her stay and sent that woman Eva on her way, so many difficult times could have been avoided. You still have Lis and Leni. You are proud of Leni and her learning but what do you give Lis? She is the servant of the house, not the daughter, as long as Frau Eva is here. Your daughter must get ready to become a wife and her homemaking and nursing skills will make her a very desirable marriage partner. Now you tell me you are ready to be more pig-headed than the time you sent Anna Maria away. Only a fool makes the same mistake twice, Johann, and I do not believe you are a fool."

Johann stared at his brother's wife, always so calm and helpful. Now she looked like an angry mother goose, about to peck her enemy into pieces should it be necessary. He opened his mouth; then closed it again because the full force of her words had taken hold of him. What she had said was an undeniable truth. He covered his face with his hands. Then he turned his back on her and, like a man who has been dealt a heavy physical blow, he rose from the bench and walked down the road to his own *Einhaus*.

"Blessed Mother Mary, help me," *Tante* Mari said aloud, afraid that she had ruined the only chance for happiness that Lis would ever have.

Lis looked around, enjoying the landscape that was new to her, as the wagon traveled toward its destination, the village of Heddert near the larger village of Schillingen. She was not a girl described as pretty. Her lips were narrow and the bridge of her nose was slightly flattened because of a misadventure with a small rock thrown up from the wheels of a fast-moving wagon. Her hair had always suffered from a lack of brushing and the braids she wore did not shine; their brown color would be described as faded by most observers. But the face beneath the braids was strong and determined: and her rare smiles were delightful and promised that in a few years, when many pretty girls had lost their glow, Lis, now mature, would be a woman who was striking enough to outshine most others.

Lis had spent any free time during the last two years with Tante Mari just to escape the urge to strike out at Eva. That she liked the work of midwife almost as much as *Tante* did was a surprise to her. Now this;

a chance to do good for people instead of hating the woman she worked with every day.

Her father had not talked to her about the trip to Heddert. She had expected some words of advice from him, either harsh or kind, when it was time for her to leave Oberzerf. Praise from her father was something so rare that she had given up hoping for it. This time he had merely said that he had talked to *Tante* and given his permission for her to stay in Heddert for a few weeks. His expression was unreadable. She had expected a refusal and had been amazed when *Tante* told her that the chance would be given. But the tiny flame of hope that her father would show pride in her was dashed; and like the last flicker of a candle before it dies away for lack of air to maintain it, Lis let her own hope die and accepted her lot.

They were many miles away from the Rauls farm, getting close to the small *Einhaus* in Paschel where she would be a stranger, just as she was in her own home. She felt both hopeless and hopeful. How could such a combination exist together, she wondered. She was getting away from an uncaring father and the terrible Eva. There was sadness in her because she probably would not be missed. Yet her downcast heart was beating in a rhythm of excitement. As they drew closer and closer to their destination, that pounding heart grew so loud in her ears she was sure *Tante* Mari and *Onkel* Nikolaus could hear it.

Lis with the help of *Tante* Mari had worked to make potions from dry plant leaves and wild or garden herbs gathered in the previous autumn. All were pounded into powders to be mixed with boiled water when Lis was called out to help a villager in Paschel or Hentern. A makeshift linen bag held these treasures – her midwife kit. Each time she looked at it, she was proud that she finally had something of her own to care about.

Onkel Nikolaus was on the wagon seat with her, a *Zipfel* cap keeping his balding head with its curling fringe of gray hair warm. In the wagon box, *Tante* Mari lay on a mattress and pillow stuffed with straw, her cap shading her face from the sun and wind, a light quilt protecting her from sudden chills when the teasing sun slipped under the clouds to hide. *Onkel* Nikolaus sang a slightly bawdy song. Sometimes *Tante* scolded him for setting a bad example, but to try to change him would take away his earthy sense of humor, which his nieces and nephews loved and which had kept this aunt and uncle contentedly married for more than 40 years.

Nikolaus Rauls had a strong, loud voice. Carried along by the wind, it was likely that it reached into the little villages they passed along the way. Lis surprised herself by joining in now and then, the first time she had sung since the terrible day when Papp had forbidden song in their house.

Tante raised herself on one elbow and scolded her husband once more when she heard Lis voice some very unladylike words, but a little twitch at the corner of her mouth also appeared. Had the real Lis started to come out of hiding?

The weather was like Lis' mood, changing from one moment to the next. She alternated between thrilled or frightened. The June sun hid behind clouds, but came out now and then to shine on the green grass along the roadside. Wind gusts turned the hay meadows into a river of green waves that rose and fell, showing that the grass was growing toward its first cutting.

We are all subject to nature, Lis mused. For mankind, just as for nature, there is always change and sometimes it goes out of control. Like an apple, I was plucked too early from a nurturing tree, a sour green apple not much enjoyed by anyone. Can I still change and ripen; is there enough time to change my nature?

"Would you take the reins, Lis, when I stop the team. I think we all need a walk to the bushes. And maybe you would like to take a turn at handling the horses. Would you like to drive the team when we go on again?"

It was *Onkel* Nikolaus who had taught her the tricks of managing the reins.

"I would love to have the chance, *Onkel*. How many more miles to go?"

"Another hour and a bit more. Are you hungry? You should join your Aunt and have the comfort of a little something to eat," Nikolaus said. "We have the *Marmitchen* pots. I filled the bottom one with cold spring water this morning so that the *Quark* in the top pot would not get too warm."

"I am too excited to eat or rest," Lis said.

"Then you will not mind driving the team when we come back to the wagon? Mari and I can have a bite while we keep traveling, and she will have more time to spend with her nephew and his family before we have to head back to Oberzerf if we are there a bit sooner."

Nikolaus knew that Lis longed to handle the horses but, even though he had taught her how to do so, he rarely let her have the reins.

"Yes, of course *Onkel*." Lis answered his question calmly, but Nikolaus saw the gleam of delight in her eyes as he stopped the horse. They all took their stroll, and then he climbed into the wagon box; *Tante's* expression said, "Well done" when Nikolaus joined her in the wagon box.

Lis slapped the reins and make a clicking sound with her tongue to signal the horse that it was time to move on. She hoped that her uncle would let her keep the wagon seat as her own until they reached their destination. This was a sense of control that she seldom felt and in concentrating on the reins, her heart resumed a more normal beat.

An hour later, their wagon arrived at the edge of Heddert. This was a small village, hardly more than a few buildings, all of them quite small. Lis was grateful for a place that could not have that many sick people and overwhelm her.

Tante called out, "See, there is a Catholic chapel here as there is in Oberzerf, but most of Heddert's worship is held in the church in Schillingen. This little chapel is close to my nephew's home."

Just then a young man approached from the smallest *Einhaus*. It seemed that he had been waiting for them. Lis pulled back on the horse's reins, commanded "whoa," and with the roll of her tongue stopped the team.

Their greeter's hair was the color of ripe flax, and his eyes were the shade of a field of cornflowers. Those eyes, his long white lashes and crooked smile – her heart gave a little lurch. For a moment she stared at him and thought how much she liked his smile.

Then she was struck with wonder as a tiny girl with hair as white as her father's eyelashes came running through the door of the *Einhaus* where their wagon had stopped. The young man picked her up and said, "This is my little Kätti."

The child had the same smile as her father, and she immediately reached up her arms to Lis on the wagon seat, wanting to be held. Lis felt her expression soften to a gentle smile. She took the child from her father, holding her close. Don't be silly, she told herself as her eyes filled with tears. You are not a girl who fusses over every child and longs for one of her own. Take a breath and calm yourself.

The little girl reached out a hand and touched Lis' cheek. "You so pretty," she murmured, "You staying here to play with me?"

She threw her arms around Lis' neck and kissed her cheek. Lis buried her face in the child's hair to hide a new spill of tears.

The nephew Nikolaus helped *Tante* Mari down from the wagon box. Lis still sat with her arms around the child, her defenses demolished. Tears dampened her cheeks, but she tried to brush them away before anyone should see.

Tante asked her nephew dozens of questions about his wife Elizabeth, little Kätti, and the new little son, born only four months ago. She had seen the tears on Lis' face and wanted to give her a chance to compose herself.

At the same time, *Onkel* Nikolaus took the little girl from Lis and set her on the dirt path that led from the road to the *Einhaus*; then helped Lis from the wagon bench. He whispered, "Nothing wrong with affection for a little one. Don't be ashamed of a few honest tears."

As she wiped her eyes with the edge of her apron and took some deep breaths, Lis heard *Tante's* nephew say, 'My Elisabeth feels sick today and is sorry not to be out to greet you all. She still hasn't recovered well from the birth of our little Nikki. She is so happy to have the village's temporary midwife so close by!"

His wife and I have the same name. How lucky the other Elisabeth is, with a good-hearted husband and a beautiful little girl, Lis thought. She felt a pull on the side of her skirt. Little Kätti was reaching up to be carried. Lis bent, picked her up, and hugged the fragile little girl once more.

"And how are you, dear *Tante*; I hope the ride was not too uncomfortable," her nephew said after the torrent of Tante Mari's questions addressed to him finally stopped.

Then he turned to look at Lis, his smile even deeper and the corners of his eyes crinkling. "This must be Elizabeth Rauls, our much needed midwife in learning." He made a funny little bow. "We are pleased you will be living with us. *Tante* Mari did not tell us that our guest would be young and very easy on the eyes."

"Yes, you scamp, this is my Rauls niece. We all call her Lis," Tante said, a look of puzzlement on her face as she saw that Lis carried Kätti, cuddling her and playing a little finger-game verse as her mother had once done with her. This is not the same Lis who traveled with us this morning, *Tante* Mari thought. Lis never cries. Had the kiss from a little one brought about this burst of emotion and if so, why had she been so slow to realize how much her niece craved acceptance and affection? The second thought came immediately after. Will bringing her here be a good thing or have I begun something that I will be powerless to mend if it all goes wrong?

CHAPTER 15
Eva's Compromise – December 1840

In this story of the Rauls family, Cousin Eva and Igel Pitt are fictional characters. However, second marriages of men who were left widowers at the age of 50 or even older were common. They usually married younger women who could give them a second family and who also were strong enough to do hard work in the fields.

A love that is one-sided, not returned, is like a neglected cutting from a plant. It is meant to grow roots in water until the time it is planted in rich ground. A cutting kept forever in the water dies slowly, its leaves fading a little each day until they curl and shrivel. The stem rots because it has not been made one with nourishing soil. So it was with Eva Kautenberger and her love for Johann Rauls.

Eva sometimes still held Johann in her arms as he slept beside her, obviously unaware of her great desire for him. She was also holding onto the belief that someday there would be union between them, one that was legal in the eyes of the Church and carnal as well. Yet one year followed another and Johann gave her only the warmth of his body, his breath on her cheek as they lay beside each other. When yet another year with the Rauls family began, Eva knew in her heart, as much as she tried to deny it, that Johann Rauls would never be hers.

As her love withered, an angry despair filled its place until she began to dislike and then shrink from the sound of Johann's footsteps nearing her door at night. On the nights she came to his bed, she lay still with his head resting on her shoulder and cursed him for not noticing her rage and her hopelessness. The part of her that was sensible chided her for wasting seven years of her life on a man who wished to be with a wife who was nothing but buried bones in the cemetery ground. He has made use of me as he would a feather quilt or a wool cloak, she would think. I am no more to him than that. Each day she despised him a little more. But she had no other place to go. She was thought of as a loose woman, a wanton, and no other man, not even the most ugly of widowers, would have her. She resolved that the next time Johann approached her bed she would refuse him. But the flicker of hope in her heart betrayed her sensible self and her arms still reached out to him, though grudgingly.

Many times each day, she would think about leaving the farm, walking out of the door as Johann stared after her, perhaps cursing his foolishness in not offering her more than an occasional trip to his bed. But her leaving would be an admission that she could not hold a man, not even as his whore. The irony of it embittered her. She was an outcast in Oberzerf. How shocked those clacking tongues would be, she thought, if they knew that I am yet a virgin, a woman who has never, even by accident, seen the sexual parts of the man who comes to my bed.

In summertime, she did not mind her ostracism so much. Everyone was busy in the fields, one hand helping another in times of need. Even her hands were welcome. But in the long winter, she had no friends to join her in her work, telling stories of family and kin and sharing village gossip to make the spinning, weaving or sewing go faster.

After the early years when Eva had pinned her hopes on an eventual marriage to Johann and blamed his daughters for the failure of that dream, her animosity toward Leni had moderated.

Leni no longer flinched from each encounter with Eva. Lis, on the other hand, refused to fashion any kind of compromise with the woman she blamed for destroying love between father and daughters impossible. As the years went on, Lis turned almost as sharp-tongued and bitter as the woman she hated, defying Eva whenever she could and isolating herself from Leni who had chosen a different path in her dealings with Eva.

Leni did not pretend to enjoy Eva's company, but since she had no other woman to teach her the womanly skills she would need someday, she was willing to accept the gruff corrections. They were the only kind of instruction that Eva was capable of imparting to her. While Eva was still a woman with a tendency toward caustic criticism and lack of warmth, Leni learned whatever she could from her, even though Eva's lessons were like learning from a wasp that was easily provoked and had a painful sting.

Lis still turned to Mathes for whatever consolation she needed and pushed Leni and Theiss away. Leni found a second mother in Magda and a friend in Theiss who had a sympathetic nature hidden away under his blond curls, boyish pranks, and constant teasing. Pitt was the only member of the Rauls family who liked Eva. That was like balm for Eva's bruised ego, even though she knew that Pitt had a soft spot for every creature God created, no matter how it was regarded by the rest of mankind.

Unknown to Eva, there was a man in Oberzerf who envied Johann Rauls his good luck in having that Kautenberger woman.

Pitt Wiener was himself a widower. He was a "*Kleinbauer*," a man with only a little land. He worked at the Gouveneur gristmill to supplement his income. His hair, gray now but still very plentiful, had earned him the nickname "Igel Pitt." With his long broad nose, round ears, small black eyes, protruding belly, and short and coarse scrub-brush hair, the unfortunate man did bear a striking resemblance to a hedgehog.

Igel Pitt's only surviving child, a son, had been taken into the Prussian military to serve his three years of compulsory duty and had decided that he liked the life of a soldier better than the idea of spending his existence as a poor farmer who one day would inherit a small piece of land which would hardly feed him, much less a wife and children. He never saw his father again. With his son gone, Igel Pitt was left dependent on his own muscles and bones that could do a little less each year. His first wife had been a tall, sturdy woman with enough strength to chop wood into kindling all morning and to shock grain in the fields all afternoon. The cholera had taken her in three days. After that, the farm work fell to him alone, and he found it difficult without his powerful wife who had been able to do a man's work.

At first Igel Pitt refused to hire young village men looking for day labor. When at last he was forced to turn to them for help, he drove a hard bargain. Villagers laughed at the way Igel Pitt would reach into his money pouch, slowly caressing the coins before he gave them out, almost unable to bring his hand forth with any money in it. Work being hard to find, there was always some young man of the village willing to break his back for the pittance that Pitt Wiener reluctantly placed in his hand at the end of the day. The young men joked that if he had as much trouble getting his penis out of his pants as he did coins out of his purse, he was going to make his second wife a very bad husband indeed.

Igel Pitt wanted to remarry someone who could help him, a woman much younger than he and very strong. He needed someone like the Kautenberger woman who lived with Johann Rauls. Whenever he saw her, it angered him that Rauls should be so careless with this treasure. If he had such a woman, he would marry her within a month or two. This was not because he cared for her reputation or for his but because that would keep her always with him, bound by the strong marriage bond that the church considered unbreakable.

One day, as he was sharpening his scythe for the upcoming hay mowing, he wondered if this woman who slept in Johann Rauls' bed was happy with her lot. Most of the villagers avoided her; her usual expression did not invite easy conversation. He began to think of ways in which he might find out if she would have an interest in a more secure and married life here in Oberzerf.

Eva at first took no notice of the rather ugly, gnarled farmer who seemed always to be near her, no matter what the fieldwork of the day might be. Two of his small fields were next to the strips held by Johann Rauls and more often than not Pitt was hoeing or scything near her, working in a rhythm like hers, smiling at her with the obsequiousness one might give to the bishop or an official of their *Kreis*. When it was time to mow the first crop in the hay meadows, Pitt saw to it that his wagon came to the fields a little later than most of the others so that he could place it in a strategic spot which the fine Eva would be sure to pass when she left the field to begin the supper and the evening chores. One day, as she walked by on her way home, he gave her a little, knowing smile and winked. She stared at him and turned on her heel, but not before giving him an appraising glance.

So began Igel Pitt's courtship of Frau Eva, conducted with smiles, then with short furtive meetings on the paths to the fields, the forest or the Grossbach stream. It excited Eva. She had never been courted with such determination, never been courted at all except for the brief interest of the Greimerath widower who shortly after had stood at the altar with a much more comely maiden. What did it matter that this suitor looked like a hedgehog and had a gaping hole between his front teeth. He openly admired her, telling her over and over what a fine and handsome woman she was. Each time she left his company, she felt slightly giddy with a sense of her sexual appeal, at least to one man.

One hot day in early August he met her in the road, tipped his rumpled felt hat to her, and said in a hoarse whisper, "The deserted cottage behind the Gouveneur mill at four – please come. I will be there, and I have something special for you." So it happened that Eva slipped away from the Rauls' farm on a pretext of hunting mushrooms and became the lover of Pitt Wiener. As he penetrated her for the first time, she relished the pain. She closed her eyes and imagined it was Johann Rauls who took her. She had waited so long. Even as she cried out Johann's name, she pulled Igel Pitt deeper inside her.

As the days passed and *Martini* came, Leni noticed a change in Eva. She was pale, distracted and not as harsh. It seemed her mind was elsewhere. Sometimes she would stand staring out of the window as if she couldn't remember why she was there or what she was looking at. She jumped when spoken to and spent time in the outhouse several times each morning. One evening, as Johann Rauls came to his sleeping room, he was surprised to see Eva sitting fully clothed on the little wooden bench at the end of the bed. As he raised his eyebrows in question, she said, "There is something I must tell you."

"Have you heard the news?" Leni pulled Anna Maria aside at first chance when the Marx family came to Oberzerf for a visit on an unseasonably warm Sunday at the beginning of December. Now 26, Anna Maria was still pretty and as fun loving as ever, in spite of having given birth to the couple's first son Johann whom she adored but also managed with surprisingly skilled hands.

"What is it Leni? Your eyes sparkle like those of a Fräulein who has just found her true love. Who is he?"

"It's even better! Leni was ready to explode with the elation of being the first to tell her sister. "Eva is going to marry old Igel Pitt Wiener in just two weeks. They had to get a dispensation from the Bishop to marry in Advent." The look on her sister's face made Leni burst into laughter.

"A very short engagement, isn't it?" Anna Maria said, after she closed her mouth, which had dropped open a bit in astonishment. Then she started to laugh. "Why he's older than Papp. But I guess he's young enough. It looks like he's been spreading more than rye seed."

"Anna Maria," Leni laughed, "what a thing to say." But she shared the same thought. When had Igel Pitt and Eva been alone together? Not a one of them had thought that Eva could be tempted away from their father's house to spread her legs for the "Hedgehog", but almost certainly she had.

Just then Lis came into the *Stube* from the kitchen. Since she had returned after her time in Heddert, she was a new Lis, assured and much more patient than before. She sometimes sought out Leni, talking to her with a trust that never existed in the past.

The formerly reticent Lis, who rarely showed affection, kissed Anna Maria on both cheeks, causing Anna Maria to lose her grasp on her shawl, which fell to the floor. Anna Maria started to retrieve it, then stopped, stood up straight again and pulled Lis into a tight hug.

"I heard what you were talking about," Lis said with a wicked grin, when Anna Maria released her. "Eva is as prickly as a hedgehog, so Hedgehog Pitt should be her perfect mate."

"Lis, you've changed. You have learned to make sly comments almost as wicked as mine," Anna Maria laughed. "Come sisters, we must go, and you can tell me all about Eva and Igel Pitt while we eat the *Plätzchen* I brought."

Soft snow fell on the little church in Oberzerf on the December morning that Peter Wiener took Eva Kautenberger as his second wife. There were not many people to witness the vows or shout good wishes to them as they left the little church. The old widows who went to all the weddings and funerals looked knowingly at Eva's waist as she walked down the aisle, now a married woman. The Rauls family was notably absent from the church. Even at the moment that Father Guckeisen pronounced them man and wife, the bride's face showed nothing of her feelings nor did the groom's.

Outside a young man, Pitt Rauls, stood off to one side of the church, a few steps from the chapel. When the couple came through the door and drew even with him, he thrust a misshapen bouquet made up of dried lavender and fresh mistletoe branches full of white berries. His offering was tied together with a drooping bow of twine.

Eva's hand reached out and took the offering; then kissed the smiling young man on the cheek. The villagers talked of that and speculated for a few days before losing interest.

The bridal couple, Eva's brother and his wife, and a handful of relatives from Greimerath walked from the church to a wedding meal at the aging *Einhaus* that was now Eva's home. Eva had readied the food herself on the morning of the wedding and covered the table with a heavy piece of linen so the meal could be eaten when everyone returned from the church. Igel Pitt was too miserly to hire a "*Hochzeitsbitter,*" the wedding agent who would have arranged for someone else to do the wedding meal.

It was not the start to her married life that Eva had once imagined, and she knew her new life would be a hard one. After the wedding dinner all of the guests left, and Eva washed the chipped dishes that had been a part of the first wife's dowry.

Young Pitt Rauls' bouquet was the only token that Eva saved from her wedding day.

CHAPTER 16
A Courtship for Mathes – October 1841

Until the turn of the century, the rural suitor and the wedding agent were an essential part of the courtship process. When a country lad was ready to marry, he would take along with him a sort of godfather to help him in his courtship of a prospective bride. So when two men wearing white silk scarves appeared in a village on a Sunday, everyone knew why they had come. They would first unobtrusively scout the outside of the house and any outer buildings of the prospective bride's family. Only then would the talking get under way. If the suitor had good luck with his proposal, he and his "godfather", in accordance with custom would be invited to eat fried eggs and Schinkenspeck. However if bread and cheese with Schnapps were offered, then both men knew that this suitor had been rejected. Becker, Christiane, <u>Die Hunsrücker Kuche</u>.

The six balls of fluff in the hay-filled corner of the stable suckled at the mother cat's nipples and kneaded her belly, tumbling over each other with clumsy grace, funny in their determination to get any spot that at the moment they didn't have. They were impossible to watch without laughing. But the man sitting on an empty haywagon paid no attention. Just now his vision was focused inward - on his treatment of his family.

Johann Rauls lived in a state of black depression after Maria's death, and it had never completely gone away. The harsh words of *Tante* Mari about his near abandonment of Lis, and his remoteness toward his other children was forcing him to examine the scars which he had selfishly inflicted on the people who loved him. He must try to become the man his Maria would want him to be before all that love died. Anna Maria and Lis had already lost much if not all of their love and respect for him. He must regain it if he still could.

Lis had come back from Heddert seeming more the girl she had been before Eva tried to take Maria's place in their home, but she still avoided him. Although Anna Maria did come to Oberzerf with her husband and children for festivals, holidays or an occasional Sunday visit, her eyes showed she was still wary of him. Magda, having fought her own battle with loss and depression, understood his dark side better and gave him love in spite of the wounds he had inflicted on her. Leni had kept her trust in him, but he sensed her uneasiness.

His sons had fared better than his daughters and seemed to look up to him in spite of his dour ways and black moods. Working together to achieve a goal that was important to all of them, the care of the land that was their inheritance, bound them together. Pitt loved his father unreservedly, and Johann could return that love with something close to ease. If only he could open his heart to the others in the same way. He knew he must do better. But the knowing was not the doing.

He could take a first step, a small one surely, but one that would bring a little ease to his conscience. He would start a plan for Mathes' marriage.

Mathes had his heart set on the eldest daughter of the Meyer-Elsen clan. Theiss teased his older brother about it whenever he had a chance, and Betta Meyer seemed to look on Mathes with affection and even desire. The Meyer family was a sizeable one, which meant that this girl would not inherit as much land as one with fewer siblings. Because of that he foresaw no problem in arranging their marriage in spite of the interval that Eva had spent in his home. A husband with a fine piece of land usually spoke louder than gossip or morality. It would be a good match, and Mathes, with his generous nature, was the kind of son a man could trust in his old age when he needed the good will of his children to keep him from a dreary, freezing room where he was forgotten and half starved, as were many old men once their sons and daughters had received their land inheritance.

Tante Mari had been so right. He had walked in darkness of spirit far too long, had only thought of himself, and had been blind to his duty. He looked up and noticed the kittens for the first time. Their antics brought a hoot of laugher from him.

Pitt, never far from his father's side, came to sit beside him. "Why do you laugh then, Papp?" he asked. Have I done something funny?"

Johann smiled and reached out to touch his son's shoulder. "No Pitt, I don't laugh at you. I was thinking of my duty as a father, but the kittens distracted me and made me laugh."

Pitt picked up the gray kitten with white ears and paws, and it began to purr from his gentle strokes. He was puzzled by his father's words but also relieved. When Papp smiled, all was right with Pitt's world. He could carry on with his task, bagging up the potatoes that had been left to dry on the threshing floor and hauling the bags to the cellar storeroom.

Johann stood up with the intention of helping his son. He followed Pitt to the other side of the barn, bent down, and hoisted a heavy bag of potatoes to his shoulders only to set it down again. He realized he was putting off the resolution he had made only moments before. He must act now or his good resolution could fail him.

"Pitt, there is something important I must say to Mathes. I will be back to help you as soon as I can."

Mathes Rauls at age 24 was a serious young man with intense brown eyes framed by long eyelashes many a girl wished for. He was slender but well muscled from the abundance of work that fell on his shoulders as his father's main helper. Because he loved the land, part of which he would someday inherit from his father, he spent more time than most young men of his age thinking and planning, straight black eyebrows drawn together. This made many of the village girls think of ways to separate those brows and turn on his wide smile. That smile and handsome face made him an attractive catch for reasons other than the land his father owned.

Mathes, however, was immune to other maidens' ploys to attract his attention. He could see only Betta Meyer, and it was not her inheritance that brought his smile when she was nearby. When he looked at her, his knees felt weak, and he could feel his face flushing. Should she ask it, he would kiss the ground at her feet. He had not yet worked up the courage to talk to his father about an official courtship, but he hoped that Betta returned his feelings and would consider such a proposal with pleasure.

Mathes, lost in thoughts of the girl he loved, was startled when his father approached and sat down on the old, aged-wood bench where Mathes was cleaning the mud of the field from his boots.

"It is time to talk of your future, Mathias," Johann said. Mathes stood up and faced his father like the rabbit that has just caught the scent of the fox. The use of his baptismal name told him that the matter to be discussed was of the utmost importance and seriousness. His heart beat so hard that he was sure his father must see it moving his tunic. He couldn't seem to catch his breath. He told himself to remember that he was a man, not a boy, and that there was no reason for his panic; but still his hands shook so much he dropped the boot he had been working on. He had to put his hands in the pockets of the *Kittel*.

His Papp went on, "It is time you married and settled into the house here with a wife."

Mathes nodded because he was at a loss for words to respond.

"I think that you have begun to favor the daughter of Nikolaus Meyer-Elsen. Her name is Elisabeth. Is that right?"

"*Das stimmt*; that is true." Mathes replied. He kept his eyes down and wondered why he had made such a formal answer to his father's question. But how could he tell his father about his desire for Betta which drove him almost to distraction, especially when he was in his bed at night and the thoughts of her slim waist and high, firm breasts came to taunt him. He imagined lifting the skirt that covered her from waist to ankles and running his hands over everything that lay beneath.

Papp was still speaking. "She comes from a good family, *ja*? I can't say much for that rascal brother of hers who rattles on to all the villagers about how he will go to *Amerika* and become rich, but I respect her father and her deceased mother. I am thinking that, since it is high time you married, you and *Onkel* Mathias, your godfather, should pick a time to visit Herr Meyer to see if he will provide a dowry when you make your proposal. We will settle on the amount before you go to ask his permission. Do you have any objection to this plan?"

Mathes shook his head. He was too surprised to say anything. His father had not chosen one of the Wagner daughters or Merz distant cousins. Mathes had not believed in miracles since he was 12; today he had changed his mind. They did happen. He vowed to offer a prayer of gratitude each day until the end of his life to his own patron saint, Mathias, the apostle who had brought Christ's message to this part of Germany and who had a hand, Mathes now was sure, in the miracle which he had just been granted.

Mathes had been uneasy when he and Papp met with *Onkel* Mathias, his godfather to discuss with him the approximate amounts of land and goods the young couple must each bring to their union before it could go forward. He was afraid Betta's father would not agree. Had it been left up to him, the dress she was wearing was all that Mathes would expect Betta to bring with her on their wedding day.

His father and uncle assured him all would be well. It was the opportune time of year for a good outcome to the dowry discussion. The crops had been harvested and stored in the barns of all the farmers in the village and it had been a good year. The weather was not yet too cold for a stroll around the farm to discuss the possible match and propose what worldly goods each of the young ones would bring to the marriage.

Now the day of proposal had come. The two men, suitor and godfather, wound white scarves around their necks and walked to the Meyer *Einhaus*.

Herr Meyer came outside and strolled with them while the proposal was discussed. He was reluctant to have Betta marry, he said, unless he himself found a second wife. Betta's mother had died a year ago, and Betta had taken on the duties of rearing the young ones who were still in need of a grown woman's care.

Uncle Mathias was silent for a time. Mathes' fear grew greater the longer the quiet persisted. He glanced at his uncle who seemed to be thinking hard.

"Have you no immediate plans to take another wife?" *Onkel* Mathias finally said. He continued, "I know it is not a thing one should ask, but Mathes, my nephew, loves your daughter so I must put that question to you."

Another silence. It seemed to Mathes that this had become like a card game where suspense built as all waited for the next player to lay his card on the table.

"I am reluctant to answer such a question," Herr Meyer spoke quietly, as if he was afraid of being overheard. "I do understand why you have asked such a personal thing. I was once in the position of your nephew, blind with love for Betta's mother and fearful that my offer of marriage would be rejected. Yet my youngest child is only three years old and I still need Betta to take care of the young ones and to handle the duties her mother had until her untimely death."

Another silence fell and Mathes feared there would be no happy outcome to this day. He ached with the unfairness of life. Uncle Mathias should argue, should he not? He was the older and wiser one, the *Freiersmann*, and only he could offer some proposal that might make things right. But his uncle stood silent and made no response. Herr Meyer broke the silence just as Mathes' shoulders began to ache with the tension he felt. He glanced toward the *Einhaus* and saw a curtain move slightly. Betta must be watching.

"It is unfair to her, but to lose her now would make the life of our family almost impossible." Betta's father was changing the fate of both Betta and Mathes with that one sentence.

Then Uncle Mathias spoke. "Of course we understand," he said. "But do you really desire to keep Betta single for the rest of her life? My nephew is one of many young men who would gladly marry Betta now. I know you would not wish her to lose the chance of a husband and family that she has at this time. Betta is already 24, and it will be at least five or six years until she will be able to leave the management of your house for a home of her own. Her chance at married happiness may have passed by that time."

Herr Meyer's eyes narrowed slightly, and he gave uncle Mathias an angry look. Mathes knew that he did not like what had just been said to him.

"I am not such a wealthy farmer as your brother Johann. I will not hire someone to run my house and watch my children. I also will not be accused of living with a loose woman. You know that is what all here in Oberzerf called the Fräulein Eva. If I were to give my permission to your nephew, I would need Betta's dowry myself, to pay for household help. I am not a man who descended from Hansonis Rauls. He owned vast lands before the change of inheritance laws under the little Napoleon. Even now the land of Johann Rauls is plentiful compared with that of most other farmers. Why should I let his son have my daughter without getting something that his father can afford to give to the newly married couple as they begin life together." Herr Meyer's voice had risen and his face was red with anger.

The marriage proposal and dowry discussion had taken a very bad turn. Mathes, a mostly diffident young man, felt himself suddenly maturing, changing from a boy into a man, a very angry man at that. It was his beloved Betta they were talking about. He shouted down both men. "You are treating Betta as an item to be traded like a bag of rye seed or two fat geese. I am sickened by both of you. You talk this way about a maiden that I would give my life for?" His fists were clenched and his dark eyes blazed in anger. His godfather and potential father in law went silent - for a time that went on much longer than Mathes had ever expected.

Herr Meyer was the first to speak. "Calm down then, *Junge*. We are just talking. I see that you will certainly be a caring husband for Betta and that is important to me. We have not yet spoken of all that can be considered."

How much more can there be, Mathes wondered. What could Herr Meyer possibly want beyond what has already been proposed?

Herr Meyer spoke once again, "I must ask that both of you swear to keep my next words secret. Will you do it?"

Uncle Mathias nodded slightly at Mathes, eyebrows raised in surprise. Both said, "Of course. It is sworn."

"There is an unmarried woman who is farming her land in Irsch," Herr Meyer began. "She has one married sister, so their father's land was divided between them when that man died long ago. "

Both Uncle Mathias and Mathes were listening intently. Mathes, the tightness in his throat growing, wondered why they had been made to swear an oath. This was his proposal of marriage, not a gossip between the men at the *Gasthaus*.

"I have made an approach to her and to her family. She is not adverse to my proposal of marriage, and her sister's husband would be happy to buy this woman's share of the land. From the money for her share of the farm, she would come to me with a fine dowry. We may marry soon. Now that I see how the young one here cares for my daughter, we can talk further over a glass of apple *Schnapps*."

Leni stood still, interrupted from her work breaking the dry flax stems with the hackle comb. Mathes and *Onkel* Mathias were walking fast along the road. She dropped the hackle and went to meet them. When Mathes saw her coming, he ran to her and grabbed her, lifting her feet from the ground and twirling her around in a circle. "I have had fried eggs, little sister. They were the best fried eggs ever I ate, and I'll eat them again some day soon and forever." With her feet back on the ground once more, still feeling a little dizzy, Leni kissed her brother on the cheek. He was her serious brother, and she had never seen him so delighted or felt so pleased for him. She kissed him again on both cheeks. "I am so happy for you, Mathes. Thank God!"

But how would Lis, who depended on Mathes' brotherly support, react when he told her?

With the dowry and other settlements reached, it was time for the young couple to set their wedding date soon. It was already mid November and the ideal time for the marriage was between Christmas and the beginning of Lent. The outdoor work for the next growing season had not yet begun and there were no days of penance and sacrifice until Ash Wednesday. Today the Rauls family had been the guests of the Meyers for the traditional light meal at the home of the bride, with simple fare as tradition demanded. There was rye bread that Betta had baked herself and two kinds of cheese served on a porcelain platter painted with cornflowers, with wine and beer to drink. Both fathers had lost their wives and had not remarried, which meant that Betta served as both the woman of the house and the bride to be. Magda, as his oldest sister, accompanied her father and Mathes. The small group sat around the big oak table in the Meyer's *Stube*. The slight unease between the two families was mitigated when the *Schutzenengel* Peter, the youngest son of the Meyer family, was called to do his duty and accompany the betrothed couple when they drove to Zerf to meet with Father Guckeisen and set their wedding date. Peter was six, perhaps a little young to be the chaperone for a promised pair, but his eyes sparkled with mischief and intelligence, and he missed little of what occurred around him.

As they walked to the wagon for their ride to the *Pfarrhaus*, Peter teased, "Give Betta a *Schmatz*, a big *Schmatz*."

Since Peter's duty was to share the wagon seat with Mathes and Betta and guard her virtue, his instruction set the adults laughing. Mathes did not blush as he had long ago when Betta rode with him to see the transfer of King John's bones to the *Klause*. He grinned and gave Betta a resounding kiss on the cheek.

The guardian angel pretended he did not see that Mathes also managed to give his love's hand a squeeze, and that when he released it, he very slowly moved his own hand along her shapely backside as he helped her up to the wagon seat.

As Mathes took the reins and the three of them drove off, the still silent Peter grinned with pleasure. From his new brother-in-law Mathes, Peter would ask for a few coins to buy some honey candy when this ride was over. He was sure it would be forthcoming.

CHAPTER 17
The Gypsy's Words – Summer 1842

Continually moving westward, the gypsies reached Western Germany in about the year 1417. As the German peoples began to fear these intruding migrants and to suspect them of the occult arts, harsh measures were instituted against them and persisted for centuries. It was a misunderstood culture such as "a black bag, containing fragments of a bat worn round the neck by gypsy children, believed to ensure good luck..." Wadeck, H. E., <u>Dictionary of Gypsy Life and Lore.</u>

The drought! It was what everyone talked about. The men, women, and even the children longed for the skies to open and make the air fresh and the fields green again. Each Sunday the church congregation of Zerf and Oberzerf prayed for rain, but it was seldom seen during that July or August. By the end of the summer the meadows were mostly brown and the village well had given up its last trickles of water. So had the Oberzerf well on the Rauls' farm. Now everyone, even those with their own wells, had to follow the winding, dusty road to Zerf to get water from the deeper well in the larger village, but it was carefully rationed. The grandmothers of Zerf, too old to work in the fields, were its guardians. Two or three of them were always sitting on the rough bench nearby, taking note of who took more than the four buckets allowed to outsiders.

Leni and Lis made the trip each morning, carrying large buckets that, once filled, would provide their farm's only water supply for that day. Some water they would fill into a pitcher for drinking, some would be given to the mother sow with her piglets, as well as to their handful of geese. A small bit they would save in the big basin where everyone washed grime-covered hands before their evening meal, even though lately that served little purpose. What was left would be poured into the trough for their two horses and for their milk cows that the cow herder and his dog brought back from the shaded pastureland outside the village at dusk.

Even though a hazy sun was just rising, the air was heavy with moisture, foretelling a hot and humid day to come. Leni could already feel sweat on her upper lip and under her arms. She sighed to herself, thinking about carrying her heavy wooden buckets full of water back the way they had just come.

"I wish we lived in Zerf and had to get water from Oberzerf," she said to her sister as they reached the well and Lis started to lower one of the buckets. "Then the hardest part of the trip would be more downhill and our backs wouldn't be breaking by the time we get home."

"You can wish all you want," Lis answered as she yanked on the rope to bring up the first bucket of water, "It won't make the road slant downward when our buckets are full. Let's just get done with this before it gets really hot." She lowered her voice to a whisper. "Also we will be able to turn our backs on these sour faces before they start to scold us." And it was true that as the dry spell continued, the villagers in Zerf frowned more and more as their neighbors from other villages came to use the deep well Zerfers regarded as theirs alone.

When the buckets were full, the two girls started back toward Oberzerf, silent now with their breath coming harder as the road began to rise into a small hill. No one seeing them together would believe they were sisters. Lis was tall and strong-boned as was her brother Theiss, two years younger. Village women shook their heads and said that Maria Rauls must have made these two babies alone – they had nothing of their father about them. Both looked exactly like the Kautenbergers with their blue eyes, light brown hair and pink-cheeked faces. Leni, on the other hand, was made mostly in her father's image. It was plain to see she would never be tall; that her wiry, slender body would stay that way once she was fully grown. Her olive skin, oval face, and dark curly hair spoke of some ancestor's French origin.

The heavy wooden yoke on Leni's shoulders seemed to press down harder with every step she took. It was as if she was one of the oxen, laboring in the field with the wooden yoke rubbing and chaffing.

"Lis, if I was an ox, what would you name me?"

"I'd call you *Faul* because you'd be the lazy one that needed the switch to keep you going."

Leni's imagination was running on, and she didn't pay any attention to the jibe. That was just Lis' way. "I think I'd be called *"Neugier"* because I would be the nosy one, always looking this way and that, trying to see what was around me, not keeping my eyes on the row I was plowing."

"Right, Leni, the word curiosity would be the perfect name for you." Lis gave a little laugh and added, "That is your name from now on." She bent down and struggled with her heavy buckets so she could pick up a piece of broom hedge that had broken off and lay dry at the side of the road. She flicked Leni's bare arm with it and commanded, "*Hup, Neugier, hup*! Straight ahead, or you'll feel my switch!"

Leni laughed, jumped away, and ran a few meters until she was exhausted and had to catch her breath while Lis came along at her regular pace.

Lis had been so much nicer since she had come home from Heddert. She shared stories about her work as the temporary midwife there and about the little *Einhaus* where she stayed and helped with chores. She was sad to leave, Leni thought. She realized that Lis was enchanted with the two Birk children; and that by sharing stories about them with Leni, she could relive those happy times, perhaps the happiest moments in her life since Mamm died. The smile that lighted her face as she remembered gave Leni the daring to sometimes gently tease her. Before Heddert, such a thing would have been received with a deep frown and a sharp rejoinder. Now Lis showed an inclination to tease back. The two sisters began to draw closer.

Mathes was no longer the person Lis confided in. He was the husband of pretty, opinionated Betta now, and the young bride had wasted no time in establishing herself as the woman who made all decisions involving the running of the house. To everyone's surprise, Lis accepted her demotion without black anger. Her mind was on her midwifery and on her time in Heddert.

These trips to draw water would have been a painful time of silence before the change in Lis. Now it was a chance for two sisters who hardly knew each other even though they had slept together in the same bed since childhood, to draw closer every day. Both of Johann's daughters were experiencing a small escape from the loneliness that had permeated their days for so long.

When the two girls reached the poplar tree that marked the halfway point of the trip, they put down their yokes and buckets and sat at the roadside for a short rest. They pulled their skirts up, legs uncovered almost to the knees, to enjoy the dewy cool grass in the shade. Today they were quiet, each one thinking their own thoughts. Leni had pulled her bonnet from her head and was running her fingers through her curly hair, trying to bring what breeze there was down to her scalp and on to her overheated skin.

They heard its sound before it came around the curve in the road - a dilapidated gypsy wagon pulled by an unkempt horse whose bones nearly stuck out of its skin as it strained at its load. Leni's heart gave a little thump; she couldn't have said if it was from excitement or fear or a little of both.

"Don't look at them, Leni," her sister whispered. "Gypsies have the evil eye; they might put a curse on you."

But Leni was curious. She stared at the wagon. How could she not look? Her brothers and sisters teased her and said that she must have gypsy blood. Like a gypsy, she often wandered off, following a call that no one else heard. No matter how much she was scolded or even punished, she couldn't seem to resist the song of the birds in the trees or the fresh scent of the flowers in the meadows. Sometimes she just had to put down her scythe or her broom and go. She knew she would be scolded and punished, but she couldn't seem to stop. She wanted to go new places and see new things. In her heart, she felt like a gypsy.

The covered wagon was approaching them. A hide-like covering was attached to the sides of the box of the wagon and pulled over three bent pieces of pliable wood which reached from one side of the wagon to the other. The front and back of the wagon were open, allowing air to come through. A young man with long black hair and a sloping mustache held the horse's reins; a man of middle age rode on the bench beside him. Both men had pant legs pushed into worn leather boots and those legs dangled free from the wagon bench. Their shirts looked like the tunics worn by the men of Zerf, except for the bright, multi-colored scarves tied around their necks. Two women sat at the open back of the wagon, skirts almost touching the ground as the wagon slowly moved along. One was about the age of the elder of the two men; the other older still.

The wagon passed the two girls and then pulled to the side of the road, just beyond the roadside where they were sitting. Lis got up and pulled Leni to her feet. "Come on, Leni. Put the yoke back on and let's go. And for the love of our Blessed Mother, keep your eyes down as we walk by. They might let us alone if we just walk by them as fast as we can."

The two sisters put their yokes on their shoulders with the wooden pails balancing on each end. They walked keeping their eyes down, but for Leni the temptation to look was overpowering. "Don't look up, don't look up." She repeated the words in her head like a rhythmic little song. Then just as they passed by the wagon, her eyes stopped obeying her mind. Her head turned to the side as if some invisible hand was moving it. As she stared over her shoulder at the four occupants of the wagon, the oldest of the gypsy women pointed at her and said something in a language Leni had never heard before. The others stared and Leni quickly turned her eyes away. She felt her cheeks redden. The old woman called after her, "Don't be afraid, young one. Come, let me look at you, you pretty, dark-eyed child." Her words were spoken in German but with a pronunciation different from the dialect spoken by everyone in their village. The sound of it pleased Leni's ears and hinted of some sunny desert or distant shore far away.

Her head still down, Lis hissed, "Come on, Leni, we must get away from here." But it was no use. Leni's feet had grown roots so deep that she could not pull her feet up and away. She stayed where she was, looking back, while the wagon stopped, and the old gypsy woman stepped down from it, moving slowly and smoothing her rumpled skirt. Leni had never seen anything like it. Pieces of brightly colored cloth were layered over darker ones with no thought to pattern or color blend. It was as if it had been made in the dark with pieces only handled, never seen. Wound around her head, the old woman wore a shawl-like piece of linen cloth. It had lost its natural color, turned brown by the dust of the road and the sweat of many days travel. It was secured to her head by a bracelet-like chain that in some places dropped down to her forehead. It gleamed gold in the morning sunshine.

Now Leni's feet could move again, and they were walking toward the old gypsy, drawn by some invisible chain that pulled her along until she was close enough to see every wrinkle of the woman's worn, weathered face. The heavy lidded eyes had deep pouches under them, and their color matched Leni's own. Leni stopped, hesitating as the old woman reached out and took her hand, turning it over so that the palm faced up. Her bony brown forefinger with its dirty fingernail began to trace the line around Leni's thumb. "What is your name, my child?" she asked. Her voice was not wrinkled like her face; it was low and smooth like milk sweetened with honey.

Leni swallowed, her throat so dry it hurt when the sound came from it. "Leni," she murmured. "My name is Leni."

"What a pretty sound your name makes in my ears. Lay-nee, little Lay-nee," the old woman crooned, her tongue caressing each syllable, making Leni's name into a melody. "I will read your hand for you, Lay-nee, if you wish it. You are not one of us, but there is a bond with you. Do you feel it? I think somewhere in you there is a little of our blood. What will you give me to tell you your future?"

Lis stood at the side of the road, not knowing what to do, the wooden buckets with their wood carrier heavy on her shoulders. Her face was puckered with frustration. She should walk away and let Leni pay the penalty for being so foolish, but she couldn't leave her there alone with gypsies.

"I have no money," Leni said a little sadly for she wanted to hear what the gypsy woman would tell her about the rest of her life.

"If you will give me some of your water so that we can drink, we will seal our bargain." The old woman held out something that looked like the chalice used at Holy Mass. But this object was made of poorer stuff, probably some kind of rough metal. Yet it was beautifully formed, showing the artistry of a skilled metalworker. When the grownups talked about the gypsies and their wandering, they said that they were the ones who had willingly taken the money and made the nails that pierced the hands of Jesus. For that sin they had been condemned to wander the earth doing metalwork, despised aliens in any country they came to.

With a defiant look at Lis, Leni tilted her water bucket and filled the strange cup. The old woman took it and gave it to the older man. He drank in large gulps until the cup was empty. "Fill it again, pretty Lay-nee," the old woman said and Leni did – three more times as the others drank. Her heart was pounding in her ears, as if she had been running for miles.

"Now little one, let me see your hand again."

Leni placed her hand, palm up, in the outstretched hand of the old woman.

"I see a husband and children," the gypsy began, her fingertips moving from one line to another in Leni's palm. "You will deeply love this husband." She paused, frowning a little. "You will not have such a long life but much will happen in it."

She pointed to a spot in the line that circled Leni's thumb. "Here I see sorrow; you will lose people you love very much."

"Who," Leni asked, troubled.

"That I cannot tell you. But I see that you will live in more than one country in your lifetime, perhaps because there is some gypsy blood in you. You will live for a while among strangers but not alone. You will work hard all of your life and your children's children will be many."

"You are sinning, Leni. You are committing a terrible sin." Lis grabbed at Leni's arm and tried to pull her away. "Pick up your buckets; we have to go home."

"I do not need your palm to tell you your life, angry one," the old woman said. "I see it in the lines that crease your forehead. You will have two husbands and both of them will love you, but you will love only one of them. You will live to an old age but life will bring you little happiness."

Lis felt her legs go weak. She did not want to, but there was something about the old woman that made her believe every word she spoke. "Please, Leni," she whispered, "Come away from here."

Leni had never seen Lis so pale and so frightened. She had expected a tongue lashing, but her strong-willed sister was unexpectedly fearful and weak.

"Let me have the rest of the bucket of water, little one," said the old woman, ignoring Lis and looking deeply into Leni's eyes. "You can get more but they won't let us use a village well. A kindness to us will be rewarded."

Pulling away from Lis' grip on her arm, Leni bent, picked up the bucket that was still half full and gave it to the old woman, who handed it to the young man that drove the wagon. He emptied it somewhere inside and then bent down over the back edge of the wagon to give it back to Leni. As her hand grasped its hemp handle, she was careful not to reach too close to his slender brown fingers. But he took his other hand and covered hers, a small sly smile on his lips as his fingers touched her.

"Maybe you would like to come with us, pretty Leni." He squatted down, took her by the shoulders, and kissed first one side of her face, then the other.

Leni pulled away, frightened now.

"He won't hurt you, pretty one; don't turn away. Here, I have something for you." From the large pocket of her skirt, the old woman pulled out a little black pouch on a long leather string. There was also a round red-yellow fruit in her hand; one Leni had never seen before.

"What is that?" Leni asked now more curious than afraid. She ran a cautious finger over the fruit and touched its soft fuzz. It felt like the cheek of a baby. She smiled in delight.

"This is called *Pfirsich* in your language, and its flesh is so very sweet. Its nectar will run down your chin when you take a bite," the old gypsy woman answered. "It comes from trees that grow to the south where the winter snows stay only a few days and where the sun shines hot and bright. We picked many of these before we started our journey north. Some were green, and they ripened as we traveled. This is one of the last I have. I give it to you in thanks for the water you shared."

"Don't take that, Leni," Lis ordered, trying to take the peach away from her younger sister.

The old woman's eyes blazed and narrowed. "Be careful, young woman; I have many powers that you do not want to feel." Lis shivered and took a step back. She thought of the story of Eve, the serpent, and the apple.

Leni took the peach and said a soft "thank you." Then the old woman moved until she was behind Leni. Still fascinated by the soft, fuzzy skin of the fruit in her hand, Leni didn't move away. Before she realized what was happening, the old gypsy had tied the black bag around her neck, making a strong knot in the strings.

"What is this?" Leni ran her fingers along the leather strings until they reached the small black bag. Her fingers explored it; there were fragments of something unbendable inside. It felt like pieces of a hazelnut's outer shell, thin and sharp.

"It is *Kushto Bacht*. Those are our words for good luck. Because I think you are some way connected to us, I give it to you, little one." She took Leni's face in her bony, dry hands. "If you keep this always, its luck will follow you. It will protect you from many sorrows."

"Dunicha," the older man shouted and then said something in the gypsy language that was a near hiss. His anger was mirrored in the faces of the other man and woman.

The old woman raised one bony finger and her words had a dark and terrible sound, even though Leni couldn't understand them. The other three said nothing more. The two men helped the old woman climb back in the wagon and it moved away. As the sound of the horse's hooves faded into the distance, the two sisters stared at the red gold fruit in Leni's hand and the black bag around her neck.

"Throw it all away, Leni, throw it away right now. She wants to possess you so that the devil can bring some great misfortune to all of us." Lis had tears in her eyes as she pleaded with Leni. Leni pulled the black bag from her neck, and the two girls left it by the side of the road, crossing themselves and saying an Our Father and Hail Mary before walking on. But Leni couldn't throw the peach away. She had to taste it. Maybe then she would know the warmth of the sun of that land south of Oberzerf where the fruit had grown. For a moment before she ate it, she again stroked its fuzzy skin and rubbed it against her face. Its aroma was delicate yet powerful. She offered to share it with Lis, but her sister shuddered and crossed herself again, closing her eyes as Leni took the first delicious bite.

When she had eaten the peach, Leni kept the stone, putting it in her apron pocket to plant at the edge of the garden. As she transferred half of the water in the full bucket to the empty one, Lis did not wait but walked away quickly. Leni was not able to ask her if she too heard a little sound like the whimper of a baby. Was it from the abandoned leather pouch that Leni had meant to leave behind? Lis was already far ahead of her when Leni bent and picked it up, stuffing it in her pocket with the peach stone. Right or wrong, it made her feel safer.

Early though it was, the sun was almost as bright and the temperature almost as hot as high noon. Ten year old Michel, his father Mathias and his older brother Hannes were making their way along the rutted road that ran near the meadow where they planned to use the scythes they carried to cut the scant meadow grass of this drought-scorched field. What grass existed stood tall and ready to be cut, dried, and stored as feed for their animals in the coming winter. But because of the drought, this winter's food would be meager for animals and farm families alike.

The road the three Meyers walked led upward to the boundary marker that designated which fields belonged to farmers in Irsch and which land was the property of the farmers of Oberzerf. They had already walked close to an hour's distance away from their small *Einhaus* that stood near the church in the village of Irsch. They began this trek shortly after dawn and now, as they approached the Irsch meadowland, there was no escaping the knowledge that a sultry day of hard work for a scant hay harvest was to be the outcome.

Hannes carried not only his long-handled scythe but also a basket holding enough food for their lunch and a jar of their home-brewed wine. Mathias had a scythe too, and a jug of water to quench their thirst in between periods of cutting what crop there was.

Michel brought a short-handled sickle for cutting the short grass. His foot had been hurting ever since they began to walk although he had said nothing about it; he was dawdling along behind Papp and Hannes, wishing he could sit down. He looked at his right foot, the foot that had been throbbing more and more since he began the long trek up this steep hill to start the day's work. He saw that his shoe had blood staining it. He stumbled and gave a cry of fear.

Hannes and his father had been deep in a discussion about the group of Irsch farmers who were followers of the revolutionary nobleman Valdenaire. They along with this upper-class landowner had taken the dangerous step of petitioning the Prussian government for more rights for the peasant farmers. When they heard Michel's cry, they turned and saw he was no longer walking close behind them but had dropped back some time before.

As they watched, Michel fell to the ground, clutching his right foot and struggling to pull his shoe and sock off. Both of his hands were stained red as he tried to stop the bleeding from the bottom of his bare foot.

"What happened *Junge*" Mathias Meyer ran toward his son, untying the blue scarf around his neck to use as a bandage.

"I don't know, Papp." Michel's voice was shaky. "My foot hurt ever since we started out this morning. It got worse and worse while we walked, and when I bent over to rub at it, I saw the blood on my shoe and my fingers." Tears filled the boy's eyes. He took a deep breath and went on. "I thought I would see it was a sharp stone that got in my shoe. But there ain't a stone and the blood won't stop." Michel started to cry.

Hannes had reached them. He sat on the ground beside Michel and put his arm around his younger brother's shoulder. "We'll get you fixed up, *Michelchen*, don't worry. Papp and I know what to do." His words comforted Michel; Hannes could only hope that what he said was true.

"Move your hands away, *Junge*, and let me look." Mathias was on his knees too. He used the blue scarf to wipe at the blood until the ulcerated sore at the bottom of Michel's foot could be seen. Michel was bleeding as if he had stabbed his foot with a sharp awl. Mathias pressed the spot gently, "Does the sore hurt a lot when I touch it, Michel?" he asked as he tied his already bloody scarf around the foot.

"*Nein*, Papp. Only a little, Michel lied. He wiped at his tears, leaving streaks of red from the fingers that had held his foot. "Can you make the bleeding stop?"

"Hannes, give me your scarf," Mathias commanded.

Hannes Meyer sighed. He was wearing the scarf that the daughter of the innkeeper in Saarburg had given to him after he had teased and charmed her into her featherbed and climbed in after her. He had meant to wear it again tomorrow when he would be leading one of the teams of horses that pulled the delivery barges along the tow path to the villages like Serrig that lay near the Saar. The sailors would start the trip with a drink at the Saarburg sailors' inn and invite him to join them, since as one of the horse-handling *Halfen*, he was a part of the journey's crew. But the scarf around his neck would now not earn him a few more kisses from the innkeeper's daughter when her father was not looking. Still, his brother needed it, and Hannes had looked out for Michel since he was old enough to walk.

It wasn't long before both Hannes and his father knew that they had to get Michel back to Irsch immediately. Whenever he tried to stand, the blood began its heavy flow again. It meant that Hannes and Mathias would have to carry him back along the long way they had just come and find a midwife.

Absorbed in their problem, they did not hear the gypsy wagon drawing near along the meadow road until it was close to them.

"*Majusepeta*" Hannes muttered. "First Michel's trouble, now wandering gypsies to trample what is left of our crops!"

Mathias saw the old wagon with its patched cover in a different light as it passed them by. He let go of Michel's hand and although he was no longer as swift as he once was, Michel's bad state gave him enough determination to run after the slow-moving wagon before it was too far away.

"Run with me, Hannes," he cried over his shoulder for he already felt increasingly short of breath.

Comprehension dawned on Hannes. This wagon would be a way to get Michel home so much more quickly than carrying him. It was the answer to their prayers, even if it meant an encounter with the Romani heathens and their strange ways. Leaving Michel on the path, he ran after his father and overtook him, then raced past the sagging wagon. He stopped about a half meter ahead of it, turned, and waved his arms to get the attention of the driver, a dark-skinned man wearing a yellow print kerchief as a headband and a brown linen shirt that was open to his chest. He wore two long silver chains around his neck and had a profusion of black hair on his chest. He showed no inclination to slow the horse.

Two women, one old, the other of middle years were riding near the rear opening of the wagon. They began shouting for the driver to stop, first in German, then in their own language. At last the driver slowed the black horse with a yank at the reins and then made the rolling sound with his tongue that brought the horse to an immediate stop and fanned up a dust cloud from the road. The moment the wheels of the wagon quit turning, the two men on the driver's seat jumped to the ground, scowls on their faces, ready to take on the *Gadjo* whom they assumed did not want them in their town, on their roads, or near their fields. It angered them that these men were trying to deny them the right to travel peacefully. Well, they could give them any trouble they asked for.

The old woman stood at the back of the wagon, balancing herself with care as she tried to step down to the ground. An unexpected helping hand reached out to prevent her from stumbling. Mathias Meyer, although very worried about young Michel's bleeding, was the kind of man who always helped if he could. He eased Dunicha's step to the road and smiled when her feet were safely on the ground.

Dunicha studied Mathias' face, her dark eyes so keen it was as if Mathias could feel them touching his face. "A most dangerous problem has sent you to us," she commented softly so that young Michel, on his knees where his Papp and Hannes had dropped him, would not hear.

"We beg for your help" Mathias pleaded.

"And I want to help. You are an exceptionally kind *Gadjo*, a man who is not one of the *Romani* or gypsies as you call us, but who carries great love in his soul." She reached out and touched Mathias' lightly on his shirt near his heart.

The two gypsy men who had been watching moved quickly and stood in front of her, as if they were in control of what would happen now. But the old woman's next words, addressed to them in their own language, sounded harsh and caustic. Mathias saw them step apart and let her pass them.

Before Mathias could say anything more, Hannes joined them. The old woman's eyes gleamed as he came toward her. To his father's surprise, she took Hannes' right hand, turned it until she could see the lines of his palm and began to study them.

Mathias, so worried about Michel, wanted to intervene and beg the old woman for a wagon ride to Irsch for his son. The boy's foot had not stopped bleeding and each passing minute put his son in more danger. The old woman had said so herself, just a minute ago.

"Do not worry, father of Michel, he will be alright," Dunicha reassured him with a surprisingly soft voice. It was not the one with which she had been speaking to the two gypsy men. And she also reads minds, Mathias thought.

Turning back to Hannes, she traced her finger across the upper part of his palm and nodded to herself. When she looked up she said, "There is a young woman whom you must find. I was sure of it as soon as I saw you running after our wagon, and your hand shows it clearly: the hand does not lie. Without her, you will never have true love in your life."

Hannes, too, was anxious to go to Michel. He started to pull away, paying little attention to what this old woman was saying, but she held on to his hand with amazing strength.

"Just one moment more, handsome one," she murmured. She reached into her deep skirt pocket and brought out a small leather pouch that she pressed into Hannes' hand, folding his fingers over it. "The one you must marry to give you a happy life and strong, healthy children also has one of these. I gave it to her yesterday on a road not too far from here. Look for her and do all in your power to make her your wife and helpmate. I say it again. Without her you will never have true love."

Dunicha released the hand she had been holding, and Hannes felt a tingling, which did not go away. It was unlike any feeling he had experienced before, and he was unsure what to make of this old *Frau* or her prediction.

Turning to Mathias Dunicha said, "Bring your son. We will take him into the village." Father and son ran to Michel and linked their hands together to form a seat for him.

Meanwhile, Dunicha turned to the two gypsy men who both scowled at her. "Bring one of the sleeping rugs to the edge of the wagon. The boy can rest on it."

The younger woman cried out in shock, "No! That is not right."

"I forbid this Dunicha," the older man hissed in anger. "He defiles it! You will not do this."

Now the old woman narrowed her eyes. "You know I have the special power. You defy me at great risk. I do what needs to be done to make our future secure even when you do not see the need. Will you go against what I say? Do you remember when you obstructed my powers and went your own way?" The two men were silent as they brought her the rug she had requested.

Hannes and Mathias had reached the wagon. Michel was pale and his eyes were wide with fear as Dunicha led them to a spot beside the curtains that hung at the opening at the back of the wagon. A heavy wool blanket of red and orange, woven with what looked like the picture drawings that were carved on old boulders by the early tribes who had lived in the *Kammerforst* in Roman times, lay on the floor of the wagon. Dunicha pulled open the curtains and motioned for Mathias and Johann to lay the boy on it.

"Do not be afraid Michel," Dunicha crooned. "All will be well. This foot is not a danger to you. When you are grown, it will make it possible for you to travel far." Her wrinkled hands reached into the wagon. She pulled out a small brass bowl with a cover, a bit like the one the *Priester* used to hold the incense at a Benediction service.

Michel's eyes were dark with fear as the old woman began to sprinkle the gray, dust-like powder in the bowl on the bottom of his foot. As Mathias and Hannes watched in disbelief, the blood ceased its heavy flow. In a few moments Michel gave a little sigh, his eyes closed, and his tense young body relaxed. He was falling asleep.

Their priest said that believing in magic powers was a sin. But Mathias, so relieved that the evil time they had just gone through was over for Michel, thanked both God and the power of the old gypsy woman. He had no doubt that she had saved his son and that meeting this woman was a gift from God.

The two dark-skinned men who had been so defiant earlier showed no more objections. They turned and walked back to the seat of the wagon. They were ready to drive to Irsch as Dunicha had commanded.

As they started off, they drove slowly enough for Mathias and Hannes, who both walked behind the wagon, to keep up. In his tunic's pocket Hannes still carried the soft little bag Dunicha had put in his hand. The feel of it had been pleasant. He didn't believe in gypsy lore but there could be no harm in carrying it. His Mamm often sighed and said to his Papp, "No matter what kind of trouble Hannes gets into, our oldest son seems to lead a charmed life that brings him through."

CHAPTER 18
A Plan Set Awry – August 1842

A post coach driver was a very minor Prussian Government official. His coach had an official emblem painted on its door, identifying the vehicle as the possession of the Prussian Emperor. He wore a uniform, a hat with a plume, and a leather shoulder belt that held the horn used to announce that the mail coach had reached the edge of a village. In each town, he brought the postal coach with its two strong horses to a halt in front of the local inn where the innkeeper received a bag of letters and dispatches for the people of the town. He put any letters on their way to other places in a special pouch for outgoing mail. Sometimes, before going on to the next town, he led his team of horses to the village well for some water and acquired bits of gossip which he spread from one village to the next. Occasionally a passenger would pay for a ride to one of the villages along the postal route. Croon, Maria, <u>Die Dorfstrasse, Eine Bunte Heimatchronik.</u>

Lis had not attracted any young men from Zerf or Oberzerf although she had reached an age when it was almost past the time for her to marry. One or two young men made overtures which Lis herself discouraged. She continued her trips to the *Kammerforst* to gather herbs for her midwife kit and *Tante* Mari encouraged her to come along to help with her patients and further improve her midwife skills.

Each time Johann proposed a possible mate, Lis would frown, shake her head, and walk away from him. In spite of the promise he had made to himself to treat his children lovingly and try to understand their needs, too often Lis made his temper rise.

Lis was always the first one up in the morning. Just lately she had told Leni that she liked the feeling of being alone in the house, free to decide what she would do and how she would do it without anyone, especially Betta, looking over her shoulder. When she lit the fire or filled the kettle, it was as if she was in a kitchen that had been given to her to do with as she pleased. The family, even Betta, left her in peace and took it for granted that the early-morning kitchen duties were her domain, a part of Lis. Once a week she walked to the *Gasthaus* to meet the mail coach. Although the likelihood of a letter for the Rauls family was unlikely, her brothers and Leni were only too glad to be spared the time-consuming walk.

This morning the room was still as Lis quietly packed her sturdy travel basket. Everyone would be doing morning chores and would think that she was making breakfast before walking to Zerf to check the post. She had everything she needed, but she stood considering one last piece - the little wagon the *Christkind* brought to her one Christmas Eve. She cradled it in her hand for a moment before tossing it in a corner of the upstairs hall, where it landed upside down. When her father found where and how she had left it, she hoped it would hurt him in the same way he had so often hurt her.

Mathes had once had a wagon just like this one, also a gift from the *Christkind*. His had broken and been discarded long ago. But to her the wagon represented more than a thing to play with. As she grew older, she realized it was Papp's only gift to her at the time he still loved her just as much as the others.

What a silly little goose she had been. She had thought that since this wagon was a plaything for a boy, the *Christkind* knew she was a boy and that Mamm and Papp had it wrong. They insisted she was a girl no matter how often she tried to convince them she needed pants and a tunic just like the ones that Mathes and Pitt wore. Every night she prayed that they would let her change her name from Elizabetha to Peter, her godfather's name and let her sleep in the boys' room.

Then came a sultry afternoon when she and Mathes had run off together, taken off all their clothes, and stepped into the cool water of the *Grossbach*. To their surprise, they discovered that Mathes body had parts that were missing from Lis. Mathes had laughed and laughed at the flatness that went all the way to her legs. She pushed his head under the water, climbed up the bank of the stream, grabbed her shift and overdress, and ran home sobbing. She was a girl after all. Magda and Anna Maria didn't have Mathes' parts either. From that time on, when she was four, she kept wearing her shifts and overdresses. She never did learn to like them.

Time was passing, and she must keep moving or she would miss the mail coach that would take her to Nikolaus Birk, the man who had convinced her that being a female was not a bad thing at all.

Her basket bumped into Leni's empty bed as she hurried out of the room. Since Lis had come back from her midwifery in Hentern a few months ago, things had changed between her and her little sister. She and Leni might have been good friends if Eva had never come to stay, or if she stayed in Oberzerf and waited for Papp to find someone she considered a suitable match. She wished now that she could have told Leni about the letters from Nikolaus, and her plan to leave home and marry him if he asked her. Leni would have kept her secret. But it was too late for that. She was throwing away all connections with her family for a man with white eyelashes whose kisses made her knees buckle.

Out in the hall she looked into her brothers' room and saw that it was empty. That meant that morning chores were well underway. Mathes soon would slip away from the rest of the family and walk with her to the *Gasthaus* in Zerf where the postal coach stopped, and where she could board it and make the slow trip to Heddert. Mathes had always loved her no matter what she did, and he would be there to wave goodbye. She wiped at the tears in her eyes

She started for the stairs, stopped suddenly and turned around. Somehow she could not let that true display of Papp's love for her, small though it was, stay upside down in a corner. Grabbing the little wagon that fortunately had not broken in its fall, she placed it in the travel basket. Although her father had not shown her any tenderness since Mamm's death, she would keep this small reminder that when Mamm was alive, Papp had loved Lis too.

She made her way down the stairs, by habit avoiding the two steps that creaked, and hurried into the kitchen. There was one last thing she wanted to put in her basket, the wooden butter mold her mother had used for the days of Christmas. Only at *Weihnachtszeit* was its star design pressed into the freshly churned butter. For Lis that mold and press were examples of her mother's fond love for all of them – that extra special love she imprinted on her children all year round. She eased the star mold from its place on the lower cupboard shelf and hid it under the clothing, the linens, and the midwife kit she was taking away with her.

She gave herself one last look around the empty house. She thought she heard a noise from the upstairs room where her father slept but decided it was nothing more than the creaking any old house makes from time to time. She breathed again, opened and closed the outer door with hardly a sound and slipped around the side of the house where she waited for Mathes to come to her whenever he could.

Leni was as shocked as her father when their breakfast was not on the table after their morning chores were finished. She looked in all the rooms in the house and inside the barn, while her father went outside and called for Lis. There was no sign of her.

It was then that Leni remembered the long-ago conversation when Lis had threatened to run away from home and become a housemaid. Although she had seemed almost happy lately, it was always hard to know what Lis was thinking. Was there anything missing from her chest at the foot of her bed and the hooks on their sleeping room wall? Leni dashed up the stairs to check.

Lis had taken her good dress and shawl along with the modesty arrow that held her hair in place on Sundays and holidays. Her wooden clogs, a linen underdress, and her stockings were gone too. Leni was most surprised to see that the little wagon Papp had once carved for her was missing from the chest that held Lis' undergarments and linens. Taking the wagon with her could be her way of telling Papp that her connection to him and to the rest of the family was not irreparably severed.

Just then Betta shouted, "A loaf of bread and a pot of jam from the cupboard are missing and so is the strong basket that we use to bring in firewood."

Johann called for his sons to come from the barn and go with him to search for Lis and bring her back. Pitt and Theiss clattered through the stable door and into the hall. Mathes did not follow them.

"Where is the Mathes then?" Johann asked.

"I don't know, Papp. We thought maybe he was with you. We ain't seen him this morning," Theiss answered

"He and Lis must have gone off somewhere together," Johann snapped, forgetting for a minute that Mathes now had a wife. "Theiss, go and see if Mathes has taken his clothes away with him."

Betta, who had just come through the front door to join them, stared at her father-in-law in shock.

"Mathes would never leave me. His clothes are in our room, just where they should be." She was clearly offended.

Johann apologized; he had not meant to insult his daughter-in-law. "I'm sorry, Betta. Mathes and Lis have always gotten into trouble together. I forget they are not children any more."

Leni, about to report the missing clothes, saw a figure far away on the road that led from Zerf to Oberzerf as she passed the bedroom window. She dashed down the stairs and out of the back door. She was sure the mystery of Lis was about to be solved. As she had thought, the approaching figure turned into her brother, Mathes.

"Mathes," she cried, "have you found Lis?" His head was down, as if he did not want to look at his sister.

Though he had not replied, Leni continued with her questions. "Tell me, has she gone off to be a serving maid as she used to threaten? Is that why she has taken clothes and food with her?"

Mathes said nothing. He walked past her, his face so sad that Leni wanted to cry in sympathy for the hurt that showed in his eyes.

Johann, heading for the stable, saw Mathes coming toward him and demanded, "Where is she, Mathes?"

Mathes tried to walk past his father. Johannn grabbed his arm and hung on to prevent him from moving by. Mathes was forced to stop and face his father.

"I'm sorry, Papp. Lis made up her mind to go back to Heddert, and nothing I said had any influence. You know how she is."

"You should have told me about this crazy idea," Johann growled. "I know she got posts now and then. She said they were from folks who were grateful for what she did to help them."

Mathes flushed and looked away from his father. He choked out, "They were letters from *Tante* Mari's nephew; the husband in the family she lived with while she was the practice midwife in Paschel. She said that the husband Birk was begging her to come and take care of his wife and children who needed her. Two days ago, she learned from

Tante Mari that Birk's wife died. Lis told me the whole truth about that only yesterday. She said she was in love with the man, and he and his children wanted her more than we did."

Johann looked down at the ground. This absolute silence that followed Mathes last sentence was proof that Lis was right in her assessment of her place in the family.

Johann finally broke the hush that had fallen. "You let her go alone?"

"We walked to Zerf by the early light, and I gave her the money so she could ride on the seat of the mail coach. She took some food from the kitchen with her." Mathes, finished with his story, turned his back on all of them and strode away toward the house, Betta following close behind him.

Johann Rauls dropped down on the bench outside the house door. Leni and Theiss looked at each other, afraid of the expression on their father's face.

Pitt wiped his wet eyes with his shirtsleeve. "Papp," he pleaded, "let me go after her and bring her back to be with us again. She'll come if I ask her; she will. She made a mistake by leaving us; but like you always tell me, mistakes are a good way to learn."

"Let her go then," Johann muttered. "If she is so unhappy here with us, it is best that she goes. At least she is in a place where she is safe with a roof over her head. But from now on, all her links to our family are broken. She is no longer welcome here!" His voice was rough but Leni saw that his eyes were also filmed with tears as he turned away.

Was it to be as their Papp had just declared; that Lis was cast out from their family, and they would never see her here again? This was the place where she had spent her entire life. Leni felt sympathy for Mathes, Pitt and for her father, but she was suddenly angry with Lis. She had left without any goodbye at a time when their family was finally pulling together again.

There was a flash of lightening but no thunder. The storm was coming, but it was still a way off. The old gypsy woman had been something like that lightening bolt. She threatened Lis with a distant future that was bleak. Those words must have frightened Lis; they had been spoken with menace. They kept repeating themselves in Leni's mind as the thunder finally sounded. The squall that had darkened everyone's mood was coming closer. It was like the future that the gypsy foretold. Lis was taking her first step toward what was in store for her.

Warning drops of rain sounded a slow rhythm on the wooden planks of the hay wagon. The sun would come back after the storm, dry everything and life would go on as usual. If only the same could be said for the storm that Lis had begun.

Johann shook his head. "No," he said. His Maria sat at the edge of his bed. She took his clenched fist in her right hand and ran the fingers of her left hand lightly over his knuckles, coaxing his finger to open.

"You made a resolution, husband, to think first of your children, only then of yourself. Take my hand and listen to me. There can be no wounded pride or anger."

He tried to speak but no sound came. In spite of his outrage at the letter he had received from Lis announcing her wedding to Mathias Birk, his clenched hand slowly opened and then grasped Maria's. He felt the scar across her palm from the time she had grabbed the blade of the knife with which seven-year-old Pitt was trying to cut off Lis' sore finger. The ugly mark of the badly healed cut was a symbol of her love for her children, she always said. But there was something else he touched. It was the tiny toy wagon he had made for Lis when she was six.

"Do you remember this, my husband?" Maria removed her hand from his and left the toy in it. "You gave this to Lis on the day Leni was born. Do you know that Lis took this with her when she left home? She loves that man and his children and wants to take care of them, but she did not leave this symbol of your love behind."

As he fingered the toy in his hand it grew in size and weight until it was as big as one of his carved chests. He was nearly crushed by the weight of it.

"You can do it Hanse," Maria said. "Your pride is heavy but it will be lighter once you give her another symbol of your love, the wedding chest you will make for her."

As he continued to struggle with the bulk of the wagon, Maria kissed his forehead and left him. He awoke in a sweat, his breath coming in gasps.

Lis would not ask him to come to her wedding, but he would send the chest to her as he had done for Anna Maria. The spirit of his Maria was telling him that real love was sometimes a heavy thing to bear.

He began the wedding chest the next day.

Leni stared out of the window, listening to the chirp of crickets compelled to sing their notes as fast as the warm night decreed. She was alone in the room that had once been crowded with all of her sisters. Then she had often wished for more space in the bed or an equal portion of the quilt that she and Lis shared. At this moment it was hers alone, and she felt almost as abandoned as the day Mamm died. But this time there were no comforting arms of her sisters doing their best to sooth her while they cried with her.

"Stop moving" she whispered to the half moon that was drifting away toward the morning. "I'm not ready to grow another day older each time you glide your way from night to daytime to night again. Each day can bring new troubles." The moon paid no attention. Tomorrow there would be another rush toward evening, tomorrow night another moon. Her hand fingered the gypsy talisman. The old gypsy who read her palm told her that in her lifetime she would lose many people who were dear to her. Was Lis to be one of them?

This talisman was meant to bring Leni luck, and she held it as she asked God to protect the sister she hadn't realized she loved so much.

CHAPTER 19
Kirmes Celebration – October 1845

One of the nicest celebrations of the year was the Kirmes (Church fair). It was an opportunity to once again see friends and relatives, for feasting and for high-spirited dancing and celebrating. The wife of the house cleaned everything to a high luster: the walls of the kitchen were freshly whitewashed; windows and floors cleaned spotless; the copper polished and the furniture washed down. The husband thoroughly cleaned stalls, stables, and farmyard and moved the manure pile out of the area. The Kirmes guests arrived on foot or by wagon. They were all dressed in their Sunday finery. The table in the "Stube" was laden with good food, there was lively conversation and everyone felt refreshed and happy with life. Summarized from Morette, Jean, <u>Landleben im Jahreslauf.</u>

It was the day before the Oberzerf *Kirmes*, the church festival that marked the end of the harvest season, and from one side of the village to the other, each *Stube*, hall, and kitchen was being cleaned; farmyards freshened.

The *Kirmes* festivities for the Rauls families would be held at Magda's and Hanni's farm this year, and all were pitching in to help. While her father and brothers worked to give a cleaning to the stable and barnyard both inside and out, Leni and her sister-in-law Betta were whitewashing the kitchen and hallway walls that showed the effects of months of fireplace smoke. Magda was working in the *Stube* where it was obviously her intention to scrub and polish every surface until it gleamed. Eight-year-old Maria was with her mother in the *Stube*, but her brother, five-year-old Matte-*Schatz*, barefoot and dressed in a loose blue smock, was underfoot in the hall.

He was a *Schatz*, a treasure to his father and mother who had already lost two infants before this son was born. Just now the young treasure was splattering himself with whitewash from toe to top as he used his twig broom to spread the white lime mixture on a low part of the wall and on everything around him.

Leni wiped the sweat from her forehead. On this early October day the weather was sunny, and at midday it was as nearly as warm as high summer. It had been a mild autumn: the trees were still covered with green leaves, just a dot of orange or yellow showing here and there. Some of the flowers along the side of the house's plastered walls were still bright with color. She hoped the weather would stay like this for the *Kirmes* tomorrow. She glanced out the window and saw her father and brother-in-law filling the wheelbarrows full of manure, which they would take to one of their fields. The two would have the smelly pile cleaned away from the front of the house by the time darkness fell so that on Sunday, if the day was fine, the front yard space that bordered the street could be filled with benches for the many Rauls relatives from Paschel, Schillingen, and Greimerath who might stop by, villages that, like Oberzerf, lay scattered at the foot of the *Hunsrück* mountain range.

Her two brothers were emerging from the cellar, each carrying a barrel of *Viez*. They seemed to be joking with each other. That was a good sign. Lately they had not been the best of friends. Theiss resented taking orders from Mathes and Betta in addition to those from Papp.

The roadside door to the barn was open and inside Pitt was sweeping out the stalls and putting down fresh straw. He swayed and hummed as he always did. "He has such a sweet soul," Leni thought. He does whatever we tell him and never complains. It is as *Tante* Maria, *Onkel* Johann Bernardi's wife once said, "What God didn't put in Pitt's head, He put in his smile."

Thinking of her aunts made her sad. Both Aunt Maria and Aunt Magdalena had died four summers ago, just three months apart. There had been so many deaths these past few years. Uncle Johann was gone as well. "Stop those sad thoughts. Be glad that *Tante* Mari and *Onkel* Nikolaus and many of the others are still with us to celebrate this time," she commanded herself in an almost silent whisper. She went back to her whitewashing.

Betta, too, had paused for a moment. They were almost done; three of the four walls sparkled in their new white coating. By her expression, it was clear that Betta was estimating the time needed to do the rest of the job. Next would come the cleaning of the windows and scrubbing of the floors. There was much to be finished before the women of the house went to their beds this night.

They heard the giggles of Matte-*Schatz* followed by a loud howl of anger from Pittchen, who already knew that this was the best way for a three-year-old to get attention.

"Matte-*Schatz!*" Betta saw what had caused her son's beet red face and his rage. "Put down that broom this instant. You've put whitewash all over your cousin."

Matte-*Schatz* gave a wicked grin. He dropped his broom and wiped his hands on his smock but to no effect; the loose smock held more whitewash than his hands. His older sister Maria came with a bucket of water. She handed a piece of cloth to Betta and used another to wash off her squirming brother.

Betta scrubbed Pittchen's face and arms and dabbed at the whitewash in the curly hair on his head. Pittchen hiccupped and stopped crying when his mother gathered him up in her arms. She rocked him back and forth, soothing her angry child. When he smiled again, she put him in the cradle bed he would soon be too large for. Each time Betta looked at it, she was struck with admiration for the fine woodwork her father-in-law could do. She had been surprised when, during the final month of her pregnancy, Mathes' father had given her this cradle. As she had thanked him, he'd simply said. "I want every family that shares my blood to have a fine place for their newborn little ones."

Their first child, Pittchen, had slept in the cradle every night and claimed it as his own. But there would be a new baby in the cradle by this time next year; Betta was sure she carried a new son or daughter in her womb.

At the end of the day, the house was as clean as the three women knew how to make it. Leni was tired and her muscles ached. As she slid into her bed, she thought about tomorrow's festival, the games, the dancing, and the smiles of the young men. But she was asleep before she could let her imagination linger on the happy pictures in her head.

"Leni, wake up." Magda shook her sister. "It's time to get ready for the early Mass. Hurry up!" Magda was dressed and prepared to walk to the church.

Leni pushed her sister away and sat up with a confused expression. She tried to stop the pounding of her heart. "What a dream I was having, Mag."

"It was a bad dream?" Magda was pulling Leni's Sunday clothes from the cupboard.

"Not exactly bad, but all the same I feel frightened."

"Dreams mean nothing, Leni. Once I dreamed that I was dancing with *Onkel* Nikolaus, and he swung me so high that I got caught in a tree. I called for him to come back but he just kept dancing. I was up so high and then I slipped and fell – out of the bed."

Leni giggled and Magda added, "Like you, I'll never forget that dream, but only because it was so silly and my arm hurt for a week. After that I was afraid to climb a tree for awhile or to dance with *Onkel* even though I did both those things all the time before."

Leni thought about her own dream while she dressed in her *Kirmes* holiday clothes; the white soft blouse with its long sleeves and low, shirred neckline, the white petticoat, the dark blue cotton skirt printed with narrow yellow stripes. Tiny poppies lay next to the stripes as if she wore a neatly planted garden. Last came the red apron with yellow flowers along the edge. Leni was proud that she had embroidered the border. Magda was teaching Leni some of the skills which she excelled at.

Leni had been dressed in these very things when she and Theiss ran through the dream meadow, her black shoes with the silver buckles skimming through the field as if she had wings on her feet. Then she was not walking at all. They rode on the seat of an empty hay wagon. Although there were no horses, the wagon went forward, gliding along the Saar River. To her dream self, that hadn't seemed strange at all. By the time they reached the ladder in the river, Theiss had changed into a young man she didn't know. They were climbing the ladder's rungs. The wind blew her hair into her face, and she laughed without any fear that she might fall. When she looked down, she saw that the shore was crowded with people she knew. They waved to her, getting smaller and smaller as she climbed. Soon she was afraid and tried to go back, to climb down the ladder. The young man held her hand tight. As she struggled to pull away, Father Guckeisen appeared out of nowhere. He told her that her father was calling for her. Magda walked toward the ladder, hand in hand with their priest. They shook the ladder so hard that Leni slipped and fell toward the Saar.

Magda was right, that the dream meant nothing. She did not live close to the river. Then again, the dream could be a foretelling of what the old gypsy had meant when she read Leni's palm, "Something bad will take you far away from this village. You will live among strangers but not alone." Shivering a little in spite of herself, Leni hurried down the stairs where Magda and Betta waited for her to join them for the walk to church.

At the end of the early morning Mass, Father Guckeisen went back to the sacristy; and the women who would be preparing *Kirmes* meals genuflected to their God and Savior before leaving the church pews.

Tables and benches were already set out around the church. There would be games for children, card playing for the men, and music for dancing. The exuberant music along with the drinking of wine, *Viez*, and beer would combine with loud laughter, shouts of excitement, singing and linked arms as neighbors and strangers swayed back and forth to the music and sang along. Determination to win games of competition would redden the faces of the young men and bring cheers from watching spectators.

A rosy red glow was pushing the dark night sky away. Leni's companions pulled their shawls tight around their shoulders for it was still cold this morning. Leni couldn't feel it. She was filled with her own exuberance, the dream of the night forgotten. Her steps were effortless. It was like walking on the soap bubbles that floated up from the water on laundry day. I could walk right up the Hunsrück today, she thought. I could fly if I tried.

She smiled at the thought of Anna Maria and Nikolaus already on their way from Paschel with their little Helena prattling her non-stop questions. Papp said that Helena was the image of Anna Maria at that age and acted like her too. Soon they would laugh together and share stories. Lis had not come home since her wedding and, even had she wished to come home, could not be with them. Her second daughter, Maria, had been born only two months ago. Mathes had visited Lis and said the little girl was not strong. Leni said a quick prayer that the next year would bring them health and a chance to be together again.

Now Leni was almost eighteen; she had Papp's permission to join the *Kirmes* dancing. Theiss, after much begging on her part and teasing on his, had promised to be her partner until someone else asked to take his place.

"How will I be able to do any courting?" Theiss had moaned. "No one will want to dance with you! I'll be stuck with you for the whole *Kirmes*."

Distracted by her thoughts of a day filled with so much excitement, she followed along after Magda and Betta - through the door, down the hallway and into the kitchen.

"Leni, stop dreaming and take care that you don't cut off your fingers thinking about the *Kirmes*." Magda's words were sharp, but her smile was kind as she said them. She had been near 18 once, and the excitement of the *Kirmes* day when you wondered if you would see the one who would shyly or perhaps boldly court you some day soon, make you his wife and give you children.

The kitchen was full of activity. Leni was preparing the stuffing that would be roasted inside the goose. She peeled and cut apples, washed and chopped the giblets and mixed them both with currants and diced toasted bread. Magda, who had chopped the goose's head from its neck only this morning, was loosening and cleaning the neck skin to provide an extra place for large spoonfuls of the dressing.

When the neck skin was stuffed and the rest of the dressing packed in the bird's cavity, the trussed goose would be roasted brown and then gently cooked in meat broth mixed with wine. Leni's mouth watered at the thought of the slices that would be cut from it when they ate it for their festival meal.

Betta chopped and cried over the onions for the brown sauce that would cover the potatoes she had peeled and which waited for the proper time to start them cooking.

A little before 10 o'clock, relatives began to arrive. It was a fine warm day, with an overtone of fresh autumn air, and most of the relatives stayed in the farmyard outside the door, laughing and gossiping until it was time for the High Mass at the church in Zerf. Anna Maria came into the house and set Magda's table just as in the old days, telling tales about people she and Nikolaus had seen on the way and repeating the gossip from their village. Then a voice shouted that it was time to start walking to the church.

When everyone had gone off, it seemed very silent. Leni, Betta, and Magda went back to their cooking.

"All that work and over so fast." Magda said that every year when no one could eat another bite, and the women began to clear the table. The men patted their stomachs and went outside into the warm afternoon sun. Hanni, Mathes, Theiss and their brother-in-law Claus left for the church and the bowling competition. Leni's father and her uncles were in no hurry. They had seen many *Kirmes* celebrations. They took seats on the benches set up in the farmyard, smoking their pipes and enjoying a little *Wein* from the tapped barrel. They talked about the old days when they were young. More and more their stories included friends who were in the church graveyard.

The young Rauls and Marx *Kinder* raced, pushed each other, and made a tremendous din in the street at the front of the house, waiting for the time when their Mamm or Papp would walk with them to the church grounds.

It seemed to Leni that the clearing and washing of the dishes plus the tidying of the kitchen would go on forever. She could hardly hold still; the sound of the music in the distance teased her, called to her, promising her excitement. What seemed hours later, Magda, Anna Maria, Betta and she were finally shepherding the excited little *Mäuse* down the road toward the church where the *Kirmes* was well underway.

The churchyard was full of people, voices loud in order to be heard over the music and the cries of the young men who were competing in games, especially in the bowling contest. The beautiful weather had brought many of the villagers from Zerf and Frommersbach to the Oberzerf festival. Leni knew most of them. Here and there she saw familiar faces from the other villages as well.

Many of the older men were clustered around the long plank tables, drinking wine and talking about what they always talked about – the poor crops, the potato disease that was spreading, and the way the land that could provide them a living was getting ever more scarce, the high taxes that the Prussian Emperor was forcing on them. Some claimed it had been a much better time when the little Napoleon ruled them and made them a part of France. Others thought that within a year or so their fortunes would be much improved. They were putting their faith in the rumor that a railroad line would be built between Trier and Neunkirchen, coming right through Zerf.

Herr Zeimert, who operated the sawmill, longed for those future trains that would carry wood, oak bark and cattle to markets in Saarbrucken, Luxembourg and maybe even France. "Mark my words," he said, "Zerf and Oberzerf are going to grow and be more important than Saarburg. A steam locomotive will bring those Saar River bargemen to their knees." Eventually someone brought up the rumors of a revolution against the Kaiser that would be set off if the French revolted against their government again.

Meanwhile, the married women laughed and gossiped with each other as they kept a sharp eye on their little *Mäuse*, who ran and shouted and dodged in and out between the tables. There was much speculation about which couples would marry, where they would live, and which of the coming-year brides might have to bind their waists very tight on their wedding day. "But when the babe shows up five months after the vows are said," shouted red-cheeked Frau Zimmer, the shoemaker's wife, "the cat is out of the bag." She poured more wine from the pitcher, took a hearty gulp, and chortled at her wit. The other women laughed too, raised their glasses and one said, "Then let us drink to all the girls who will feel their sweetheart's hands in new territory tonight." Leni eye's widened and she moved away. Her cheeks felt hot as she imagined where those hands might be going.

As she walked past group after group, she saw that her father and uncles had left the relative quiet at the front of the *Einhaus* and had joined in the general cacophony of voices that came from the shady side of the church grounds. She sat down on the steps that led into their little church to listen. No one noticed her, not even Papp.

A man she didn't recognize spoke in a loud voice, "It's those damn inheritance laws that the little Napoleon gave us. What will you do, Johann? You have enough land now but so many children. And there are many others like you. What will this come to and how will the next generation live?"

Leni did not hear her father's answer but someone else shouted, "I say to hell with staying in this village where the taxes are as high as the ground is hard. One of these days, I'll pack up and leave for *Amerika*."

"I'll drink to that," shouted Nikolaus Annen, "I'm laying my plans right now so that my sons and daughters grow up in a place where there's enough land, and they have a good chance to leave more land for their children instead of seeing their holdings get smaller each year. I read my neighbor's letter from a cousin who scraped together enough money to get to someplace called "Mischigan." After two years he owned twice as much land there as he had here. 'No Prussian taxes to take my money,'" he said.

"I fixed the shoe of an agent selling passage on boats to *Amerika* from the Port at Antwerp," Jakob Schmieder, the shoemaker chimed in. "They got no emperor to tax them just for driving their carts on the road; no tollbooths at all in *Amerika*. He gave me a pamphlet about taking one of the sailing ships and settling where you get to keep the money you work for."

"They can vote for their government from among themselves. If we could do such, we would eat more than potatoes all the winter long." Johann Wagner, one of the farmers, muttered.

"We eat potatoes all winter if we're lucky." Peter Tomes banged his fist on the table. Many the years my *Frau* had to use the seed potatoes we had saved for planting to keep us from starving."

"They take our sons for their army. My sister in Schillingen's only son had to go to the Prussians. She and her girls do the farming. The neighbors try to help, but that *verdammt* Prussian conscription of her boy is killing her with overwork. So unless one of the girls finds a husband who can take over, my sister will probably be dead this time next year."

Joseph Hilgert's face was bright red with anger. "The French got the right idea - liberty, equality, fraternity - and cut off the Kaiser's head."

"You've had too much of that *Schnapps*," Nikolaus Annen said, looking around to see if any stranger was listening. "*Majusepeta*, keep your voice down, or you'll be on your way to the Kaiser's lockup."

Still sitting unnoticed on the church steps, Leni was listening to a kind of talk she had never heard before. Some of those men had very little land and big families to feed. They were the ones who sent their children knocking on the wealthier farmers' doors to ask for a warm meal on *Klöpfelnacht*; the ones who accepted the charity because they had no other choice. The Rauls family wasn't rich but they never had to eat the seed potatoes to stay alive until spring came. When she slipped away, part of her *Kirmes* excitement was left behind on the stony church steps.

Anna Maria held two-year-old Jacob in one arm while five-year-old Helena clutched her hand. Leni saw her sister and went to join her and the little ones. They were watching the bowling contest and both children were giggling. Leni remembered what fun Anna Maria could create. That had been such a blessing after Mamm died.

Anna Maria greeted her with a grin and asked, "Already mid-afternoon and still no sweetheart holding your hand? I thought I had taught you everything you needed to know, but I must have left out something important."

Leni laughed. "That must have been the day that Nikolaus Hendrichs walked by and you forgot all about me."

Anna Maria grinned. "I didn't forget. Because of staying to watch out for you, I didn't have to go to confess my sins to Father Guckeisen that day."

Quite a large crowd had gathered to cheer on the bowlers. Many men, young and old, were competing for a tempting prize – a fat goose given by the *Gasthaus* owner, Herr Seiler. Each man pitched the wooden ball down the packed cinder alley where nine bowling pins were set in a neat square.

Theiss was a part of the competition; he was about to take his turn. Leni knew he had been practicing in the stable all winter once his other chores were done. He was hoping to come home today carrying the goose. As she watched, he pitched the ball and all of the pins fell. A shout of approval went up from the crowd. As he came past her, he winked and walked to the end of the line while another bowler stepped up and took aim.

As the game went on, Leni kept her eye on her brother's most serious challenger. He was a good-looking fellow she had never seen before. Though shorter than her brother, he was slender and lithe with a slim waist and narrow hips. His light brown hair was cut very short and there was a deep dimple in his chin. She liked watching the way he moved as he came forward, took his place at the line, and with a graceful throw, started the ball toward the pins. He had tucked his shirt of homespun linen into the dark blue trousers he wore, and she could see his muscular shoulders strain the shirt a little. There were circles of sweat under the arms. Once again, all the pins fell when his ball hit them. The crowd muttered approval, but it was clear that they did not want an outsider to win the prize.

"I think he is **your** Nicholas Hendrichs," Anna Maria whispered into Leni's ear, "and he's got his eye on you too."

The stranger had turned and was coming back from his throw to resume his place in line, walking in Leni's direction. When he drew close to her, he paused for just a moment and turned his head so that they looked directly at each other. He had remarkable eyes; they slanted just a little and were a clear hazel color. They held mischief and arrogance and reminded her of fox eyes, bright and knowing. She met his gaze but her cheeks felt warm. His wide grin told her he had noticed and liked his effect on her. She raised her head higher and surveyed the church grounds, letting this fellow know that she gave him only a moment of her attention.

Anna Maria was laughing quietly as she squatted down next to Helena and retrieved the wooden shoes that she had kicked away so that she could rub her fat little feet in the soft grass.

Another bowler, Jakob Merz, stepped into position and rolled the ball. Leni smiled as he passed her on the way to the back of the line. Jakob, who everyone called Kobes, was only an average bowler and knew it.

"I should stop now," he moaned as he passed her. There would be no goose and no honor for him and his family.

Theiss was nearing her again as he moved with the line of young men waiting for their next chance to roll the ball at the pins.

"Do you know the name of that fellow who is nearly as good as you?" she asked when he was close enough.

"He's a friend of Father Guckeisen, I think," Theiss answered. "I saw them laughing together awhile ago before the bowling started. Maybe he's a relative from some other village."

He is from outside of our territory then, Leni thought. Why is he bowling at our Kirmes; it is not meant for outsiders. A player from our village or one of the villages around here should get the *Kirmes* goose. She wanted to put some distance between herself and the handsome bowler. She would walk away and put him out of her mind. Likely she would never see him again; why let him take up space in her head.

She walked toward the north end of the church grounds where two concertinas and a violin poured out lively tunes. Wooden planks had been laid across the grass to form a makeshift dance floor where there was some shade. A few couples standing on the sidelines joined the group on the dance floor; other perspiring, thirsty couples stepped off. It was a colorful moving mosaic of white, dark blue, and various shades of red.

From the long plank tables and benches nearby where card games had started here and there, men were shouting in pleasure and pounding the table when they made a good play. Even though the year had been a hard one for most of the families in Oberzerf, it was forgotten as the musicians played the rollicking old songs, and troubles were put aside for a few hours.

Her friend Greta and her brother Johann, who everyone called Hanschen, were dancing. Leni waved to them. Hans Mueller was partnered with his older sister. His sly, narrow face was wet with perspiration, and he stared back when he saw Leni waving. Did he think she greeted him? Did she want that? Leni had overheard Magda suggest to Papp that Johann Mueller might someday be a good match for her youngest sister. His father, with a large farm in Frommersbach, was regarded as an important man. In Oberzerf and in Frommersbach too, wealth meant a man had more than enough land to support his family. He could put meat on the table many times a year, not just Christmas and Easter. By those standards, Papp was also wealthy.

Leni's eyes sparkled as she thought about dancing with boys other than her brother, her skirt billowing out and her white stockings showing her neat ankles and small feet. It was hard to be patient. Would the bowling go on forever? It was already mid afternoon, and she and

Theiss had yet to put their shoes on the wooden planks of the dance floor. She pictured herself giving a warm smile to one or another of the young men who twirled their partners and danced by her. She would have Theiss as a partner when he got here, but as the dance patterns changed and intertwined, other hands would hold hers or touch her waist for that short time before she was turned back to her brother.

Cheering and loud clapping told her that the bowling was over, the scores counted, and the prize about to be awarded. She ran back to the bowling court, where a large crowd was gathering. She was just in time to see the wooden crate, squawking goose inside, handed to Theiss. She joined in the next cheer, clapping as hard as she could. Her eyes scanned the crowd searching for Anna Maria or for Betta and Mathes.

A voice behind her said, "Is that your brother who trounced me? I was late to my bed last night. Otherwise I would be carrying that prize." The voice yawned as the words were spoken.

She turned to see the fox-eyed stranger standing behind her, so cock sure of himself, so mocking. It angered her that he made light of her brother's victory. She decided not to reply to such a rude comment and started to walk away.

"Stay here and talk to me, pretty Leni Rauls," the stranger said and began to follow her.

"You are a rude *Kerl*," she said and glared at him.

"Yes I am." he grinned as he said it. "I'm also a very good dancer. I'll show you while you twirl your pretty skirt." He raised one eyebrow as if in challenge and then winked at her as he took her hand and began to pull her toward the dancing. His tunic shirt was open at the neck. The long rolled up sleeves showed muscular arms with a goodly amount of light brown hair on them.

"No, I won't dance with you," Leni said. Once more she tried to walk away but still he held on to her.

"Why not? Surely you must know how to do the dances. Every *Mädchen* can do these simple steps." He stopped walking then and looked at her insolently, or so it seemed to her. He wouldn't let go of her hand even when she tugged hard to loosen his grip.

"Yes of course I know the steps." Her voice was sharp with anger. "But I would rather dance with *Grossvater* Minzen napping over there than with you."

Her anger grew stronger still when he laughed and continued to hold her hand in his tight grasp as he replied, "He has not asked you and I have."

"I cannot dance with someone I don't know," she said, tossing her curls and raising her eyebrows. "My Papp does not allow it. And how do you know my name?

"I'm Johann," he said, "Johann Meyer from Irsch. My friends call me Hannes. I asked Father Guckeisen about you, and he told me that you come from a family with deep roots here in Oberzerf. He said you are intelligent and kind hearted. I've decided to take pity on you, even if you don't know how to dance."

Leni knew he was baiting her and did not reply, holding in rude words of her own. She was surprised that it was their priest who had given him her name. So he came from one of the Saar River villages. Irsch was not so very far from Oberzerf, but the grape growing villages close to the river and to Saarburg where the barges that floated up and down the river carrying cargo to and from places like Koblenz, Trier, and Saarbrucken gave them an air of excitement. It made the dwellers of those villages almost foreign. River village folk did come to Zerf, Oberzerf and the other villages that neighbored the hilly Hunsrück area, but not very often. In Oberzerf the rocky and harsh low mountain lands started. The meadows and the fields did not have a river or grape vines that embellished the other plainer strips of land where flax, potatoes, and grains were planted.

Leni had never been to Saarburg, the big city that governed their *Kreis*. It held a magical allure for her. How different it must be from Zerf and Oberzerf; a colorful, busy place full of people dressed in the kind of clothes only town people could have – walking sticks and striped silk vests for the men and layers of petticoats and dainty cotton gloves for the women.

Johann Meyer was still holding her hand when she brought her mind back to the *Kirmes* celebration. She tried again to free it, and this time he let her pull it away. She should have walked away but instead she brashly inquired, "Are you a sailor then; a very forward and conceited sailor?" He did not answer immediately, and she wished she had restrained her curiosity and gone off. But this young man, rudeness and all, had an odd appeal.

"Mostly I'm a farmer," he said after a pause, "But you are partly right. Whenever my father doesn't need my help on the farm, I go to the Saar and hire myself to the owners of the cargo barges. Usually I guide a horse along the towpath. Sometimes, when they are shorthanded, I work with the sailors on the barges themselves when they are sailing to Saarbrucken or even into France. There's good money to be made those times, and I like the sound of the river and the feel of it rolling beneath my feet when I spend some time working on the barge for a sailor who is missing for a day. I'd like to do something like that all my life, but I must take over all the farming soon; settle down. There is no one else to do it, and my Papp and Mamm are getting too old for the hard work." His serious and thoughtful words came as a surprise.

"I have only seen the river once," Leni said, forgetting that she did not like this *Kerl* and had resolved to walk away. "It was when we all watched the barge that carried blind King John's coffin to the *Klause*. I was only eleven then, but I have never forgotten how the sun reflected on the water. It looked like it was filled with sparkling jewels."

Why did I tell him that, she chided herself? Why did I have a desire to reveal myself to someone like him?

"You were at the *Klause* itself?"

"No, we watched from a place on the bank near Serrig."

He grinned at her. "What a shame you did not come to the other side. We might have stood together, holding hands like a courting couple, and listened to the singing."

"From my place on the other shore, I was quite satisfied with my view of the King's barge with all those high officials. Holding your hand - I think not!" The nerve of him, she fumed silently.

Just then an older man, slender and wiry, came and put an arm around her opponent's shoulders. His smile was infectious; and from the slant of his eyes and the shape of his head, Leni guessed that this was a close relative of her unwanted, mocking admirer.

"Better luck at the *Kegeln* next time, Hannes," he said. Then looking at Leni, he asked, "And where did you find this charming young woman?"

"Fräulein Rauls, I would like to present my father, Mathias Meyer. Papp, this is *Fräulein* Magdalena Rauls. It is her brother who has just won the ninepin prize." The introduction was polite and nicely done.

Leni wondered if her face showed her surprise at the change in Hannes Meyer. It seemed there was another side to his personality. His impudence was gone, and his manner was now mannerly and almost winsome.

"It is a pleasure to meet you," the older man said as he bowed his head slightly, acknowledging the introduction. "Your brother is an excellent bowler, *Fräulein*. My son here is usually the winner in any bowling contest so I admire the skill of your brother."

"I'm honored to meet you, sir," Leni smiled with pleasure. "You have come quite a long way to attend our *Kirmes*."

The gray-haired man smiled at her. "My son Hannes here, my younger son Michel, and I were invited to come to do a little singing. Your priest Father Guckeisen heard us at the Irsch *Kirmes* and asked if we would be agreeable to singing at the celebration here. I told him that if the day was fine and we were all, by God's grace, in good health, we would make the trip. He's a fine man, your Reverend Father."

"It is a long hard walk from Irsch to Oberzerf," Leni said. You are generous to make such a journey."

"I tell you, *Fräulein* Rauls," Mathias Meyer answered, "in our family we would rather sing than eat - especially if there is a chance that we might get a bit of applause.

A shadow darkened Johann Meyer's face, and he scowled at his father.

The older man seemed not to notice and want on talking, his tone of voice light and pleasant to the ears. "We don't mind a hike on a nice day. And when we walk home, it will be downhill. It's always wise to save the downhill trip for the end of the day, don't you think?" A smile played at the corners of Herr Meyer's mouth, but he said the words quite seriously. His eyes were not at all like his son's, she saw now. They had the same slant, but they were a deep, soft brown - kind eyes. She felt at ease with this funny, cheerful man.

"You are right, sir. I would always walk downhill if I had a choice," she said.

"Then you must walk downhill some day and visit our village. I'm sure my son would like that very much and so would the rest of my family."

Leni wished she could think of something clever and graceful to answer. But Johann Meyer's bold eyes and scowl distracted her, and her tongue seemed paralyzed. So she smiled and said nothing.

"Come, Hannes," Mathias Meyer said. "It's almost the time for us to sing. Michel is waiting for us at the front of the church."

Hannes Meyer said, "I think, *Fräulein* Leni, that our dance will have to wait until later." He bowed as he took her hand again and held it for a moment. When he let it go, she stepped away from him quickly, clasping her hands behind her back.

She watched them walk away. She felt suddenly lonely in spite of all the people around her. Her hand retained a pleasant little tingle. But no, she would not allow herself to be taken in by Johann Meyer's sudden burst of charm after his original rudeness to her.

Too soon the *Kirmes* was over for another year. Leni and Theiss had danced until the musicians stopped playing. Between dances, Theiss had spent his time talking to Maria Wagner who dimpled and seemed to like what she was hearing. Leni joined the group of young people who were resting on the benches that had been deserted, little by little, as the older people had gone back to their houses. She had smiled at Johann Mueller from Frommersbach, and he had smiled back. While she laughed and talked with the other village girls, she had felt the eyes of several young men appraising her, liking what they saw. There was something missing though; her excitement of the morning had not lasted through the day. Was it because of the dance she never danced with Hannes Meyer? No, that was ridiculous. He was such a self-satisfied *Kerl*. Leni was glad that he lived a far way off. She would probably never see him again.

After she had said her prayers and climbed into bed, she closed her eyes and her mind's eye saw the *Kirmes* grounds, and her ears heard the soprano voice of young Michel Meyer, the tenor voices of Hannes and of his father Mathias. They sang in lilting harmony, voices separating, converging, and then separating again in waves of soft melody. Leni had never heard a man of her father's age sing so wonderfully as Mathias Meyer. He brought forth a rich explosion of mellow, resonant notes from his slender, work-hardened body. Leni thought, "That is the way the Brandywine, escaping its old, dark barrels, would sing."

There had been funny songs, like the one about the twice-widowed woman who searched for a third husband because she had gotten used to being kissed. They taught the wine drinking songs of the Mosel and Saar, inviting everyone to link arms, sway from side to side in time with the music, and sing along. The *Schunkeln* of the rows of people, some moving left, some moving right did look like the waves of the river. Other songs had been pensive, telling of loneliness and loss, or tender, filled with words of love and desire. She knew many of these folksongs, but she had never heard them sung so well. The applause rang out over and over. Some of the songs had been sung again as the villagers stamped their feet, clapped their hands and called out the names of favorites like *Eine Seefahrt, die ist lustig, Die Lorelei* and the beautiful song about the butterfly. Johann Meyer's eyes had never left her face as he sang it, or so it seemed to her. Probably she would never see him again; he certainly was not a young man her father would approve. But it was fun to imagine the dance they never had. She drifted off to sleep with the words and melody echoing in her head - as if the *Schmetterling* had flown into her ears and fluttered there.

Reizender Schmetterling
Flüchtiges, kleines Ding
Willst du nicht einmal ruhn,
Mir es zu Liebe tun,
Daß ich gemütlich kann
Schauen dein Kleidchen an?
Flüchtiges, kleines Ding,
Reizender Schmetterling,
Schmetterling, setz' dich!

Charming butterfly,
Fluttering small thing,
Will you not rest awhile?
Do it for my love.
Show off your little dress,
And let me be friends with you?
Charming butterfly,

Fluttering small thing, Butterfly,
Butterfly sit!

EPILOGUE

Dunicha the old gypsy woman with second sight was sitting on the bank of a stream near a village in Lothringen. A vision was taking shape. It made a pretty picture. The charming dark-haired girl by whom she had been captivated during their travel near the village of Oberzerf, the young Leni, stood talking to Hannes, the handsome *Kerl* from Irsch. He was reaching out to her, forming the first link in a chain that would bring them closer to each other. She also saw shadowy obstacles lurking around them but not clearly defined.

As the night air grew cold, she wrapped herself in her blanket of red and orange wool and went to lie down on her simple cot, a look of thoughtful concern on her face.

GLOSSARY

Ach du lieber Gott – oh dear God
Ach nein – oh no
Alte Heimat – former homeland, old homeland
Banns of Marriage – announcement by the parish priest, three Sundays in a row, that a man and a woman planned to marry. If anyone knew of an impediment to the union, they were to tell the priest.
Bei Forsthofen – dialect name for a land area
Brotschiess – literally a bread shooter; long handled paddle to place bread at the back of a bake oven
Buben – boys, young men
Christkind – literally the Christ Child, represented by an angel with wings
Danke – thanks
Das stimmt – that is correct
Doof Mädchen – goofy girl
Du bist eine schöne Frau – you are a lovely woman
Einhaus – living quarters and barn together in one dwelling
Es ist ein Ros' ensprungen – a rose has sprung up
Esel – donkey
Feuerstatt – fire place (for a burning at the stake)
Fliege – fly
Frau – woman, wife
Fräulein – miss, young lady
Gadjo – Romani word for an outsider
Ganseblumchen – daisy
Gasthaus – inn, usually with a tavern
Gehoferschaft – uncommon type of land ownership where certain land is owned in common by all the farmers and divided by lot every three to five years.
Gut – estate
Haferbrei – oatmeal porridge
Halfen – dialect word for a man/men who handle/s the horse/s pulling a barge against the current of a river
Haselnuss – hazelnut
Hast du gut geschlafen – Have you slept well?
Hauptstrasse – Main Street
Heckenrose – dog rose, wild rose
Heiligabend – Christmas Eve
Holterdiepolter – helter-skelter

Hochzeitbitter – a person who invites people to a wedding, makes arrangements, and sometimes provides entertainment
Holz – wood, lumber
Holzesel – fat wooden log which was used to punish misbehavior by sending a student to sit on it wearing donkey ears
Hundrose – dog rose; also called a Heckenrose
Igel – hedgehog
Junge – boy, kid, guy
Kaiser – emperor
Kammerforst – heavy forest located between the villages of Beurig and Serrig and already inhabited by Celtic tribes some 700 years before Christ
Kaninchen - bunny
Kasten – a closet-like case or box
Kegeln – bowling
Kerl - fellow
Kind – child; *Kinder* – children
Kittel – smock
Klatsch – gossip
Klause – hermitage
Kleinbauer – small farmer
Kleine – little one
Kreis – circle, district similar to a U.S. county
Krippe – crib, crèche, manger
Kuchen – cake
Kuckuck – cuckoo
Kurbeln – round basket for shaping loaves of bread
Landrat – Prussian district administrator
Landwehr – army
Lenchen – nickname for a child; "chen" adds "little one" to a name
Lohe – oak bark for tanning leather
Los – go, move
Mädchen – girl, maiden
Mann – husband, man
Majusepeta – "Jesus, Joseph, Peter," a dialect exclamation of surprise
Marmitchen – round lunch pail with a section for warm or cold water
Mäuse – mouses. "Mäuse" means little mice; an affectionate way of saying "little ones"
Morgen – morning, area of land similar to U.S. acre
Neugier – curious, nosy
Nussmakronen – nut macaroons
Pfarrhaus – parish rectory
Pfirsich – peach

Plätsch – splash
Plätzchen – cookie
Priester – priest
Quark – similar to cottage cheese but smooth
Schatz – treasure
Schinkenspeck – bacon
Schmatz – kiss, smooch
Schneeglöckcchen – snowbell flower
Schunkeln – link arms and sway to the music while drinking
Schutzenengel – guardian angel
Schwachkopf – dimwit
Schweinerei – mess
Spitzkuchen – cookies with three corners; a triangle shaped cookie
Stube – livingroom, the main room for family indoor activities together
Takenplatte – iron plate inserted in wall between kitchen fireplace and Stube
Tal – valley
Tertig – cloth made from a mixture of linen and wool
Thaler – unit of money similar in value to the U.S. dollar
Verdammt Fliege – damn fly
Uber dem Rodenhaus – above a place called "Rodenhaus." Field sections were named by their proximiny to a well-known house or other landmark.
Viez – alchoholic apple wine fermented from small sour green apples
Wald – forest
Weihnachtzeit – Christmas, Christmas time
Wiedersehen – see you again, goodbye
Zipfel – pointed (as in a pointed cap)
Zurück – back

Acknowledgements

I will be ever grateful for the encouragement of all the people who supported me when I decided to write this novel, and I especially thank those who played a very special role in making HOUSE OF JOHANN a reality.

First and foremost I thank my sister Marilyn who found a multitude of ways to keep me writing when I was in danger of giving up. She always convinced me to go on just a little longer. She also read the manuscript and made great suggestions for improvement. In addition she took on the technical setup necessary to bring the book to life. I owe her so much!

Thanks also goes to Lynne Austin who listened to my dream of writing a novel based on my genealogical searches and pushed me into action, to Mary Palmer who kept me enthusiastic and shared genealogical sources with me, to Sue Vanderberg who never wavered in her belief that I was going to write a wonderful novel, and who, along with Karissa Vitale Adam and Dawn Vanderberg read the pre-publication proof and took the time to give me feedback about any lack of clarity or errors in typing and grammar, and to the innkeepers at the Stagecoach Inn in Cedarburg, Wisconsin, especially Liz Brown, who always renewed my enthusiasm when I came to the Inn to write in that historic 1860s setting.

I am also deeply indebted for the continuing encouragement and help of many special people who live in the Rhineland where HOUSE OF JOHANN takes place. My thanks to Ewald Meyer, the author of _Irsch/Saar: Geschichte eines Dorfes,_ and several other books; who took me anywhere I wanted to visit or do research, and who had the answer to almost every question I ever asked him about the history and customs of the people who lived along the Saar River; to Ewald's wife Helena who made each "after-trip" a _Kaffee und Kuchen_ lover's dream; to Hans Dieter Jung who gave me access to his collection of historic postcards of the city of Saarburg and surrounding villages in the late 19th and early 20th century, and to his wife Margret who was my wildflower identifier. Both were also great landlords when I made research trips to Germany as were Hans and Hedy Hoffmann. I'll always remember these people's kindness, as well as their warm hospitality, and I thank them very much.

Many thanks to Ernst Mettlach who shared his vast knowledge of the culture of _Kreis_ Saarburg in e-mail after e-mail; and Kurt Stenz, a talented researcher, who went out of his way to locate the original land

and tax records of the Rauls and Meyer families in the *Archive des Landes Rheinland-Pfalz* and sent copies to me.

Last, but certainly not least, my thanks to the Heiser family of Irsch. We found each other four generations after our German ancestors left the *Alte Heimat,* and who were a wonderful part of the search for my genealogical family connections, extending a warm welcome and their friendship to me.

ABOUT THE AUTHOR

Kathi Gosz, librarian and active genealogist, writes the previously untold story of the peasant families of the Rhineland of the 1800s, filled with the details of their daily lives. She draws from her genealogical research, from workshop notes, from German documents, from conversations and correspondence with researchers, but especially from local histories written in German that have been accumulated on repeated trips to the Rhineland. The YESTERDAY'S RHINELAND SERIES shares this cultural detail, with fictionalized elements that spring from the context of the research.

Kathi lives in Waukesha, Wisconsin, a little more than 100 miles from the place her immigrant ancestors settled in 1861.

Her blog is entitled, "Village Life in Kreis Saarburg, Germany."
http://19thcenturyrhinelandlive.blogspot.com

Made in the USA
Middletown, DE
03 April 2018